A TALE OF DECEPTION
AND ELECTIONS

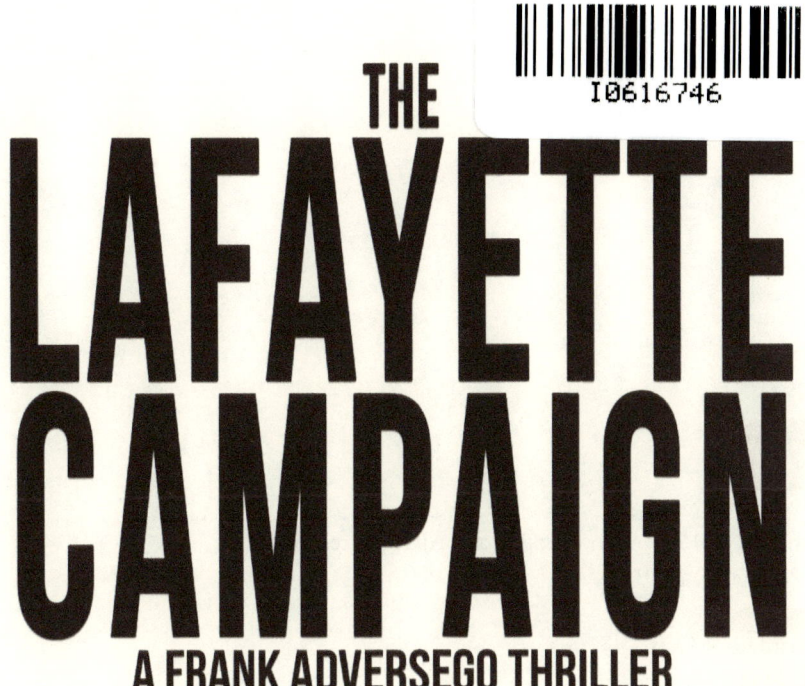

THE
LAFAYETTE
CAMPAIGN

A FRANK ADVERSEGO THRILLER

ANDREW UPDEGROVE

Starboard Rock Press
Marblehead, MA

Cover and Formatting: Streetlight Graphics

andrew.updegrove@gesmer.com
https://updegrove.wordpress.com/

ISBN: 978-0-9964919-0-7

To my mother
who was always
there for us

By the same author:

The Alexandria Project, a Tale of Treachery and Technology

The Doodlebug War, a Tale of Fanatics and Romantics

The Turing Test, a Tale of Artificial Intelligence and Malevolence

The Blockchain Revolution, a Tale of Insanity and Anarchy

Available as eBooks and in paperback at your favorite online book
site as well as at http://andrew-updegrove.com/books/
They can also be ordered in paperback through your favorite local book store

The Alexandria Project, The Lafayette Campaign and *The Doodlebug
War* are available as audiobooks published by Tantor Media.
You can find them wherever else audiobooks are sold.

Prelude

Tap, Tap, Tap

E NDLESS LINES OF code scrolling through the text editor...
        Here?

No. Farther down

Here? Check the cheat sheet to be sure

Yes

Type the new section of code in now

...Looks good

Now send it to the code compiler

Wait for the next signal to come back

Is that the right address?

Good again... and done

Hard to believe such a small piece of code is about to change the world

* * *

1

Hi Ho Adversego!

A BROAD, NEVADA VALLEY stretched before Frank Adversego – stretched as far as he could see. Something about the vista pricked at his memory. Something about the way the mountains converged in the hazy perspective of the far distance.

Ah – that was it. This was the stretch of road he'd traveled in ghostly moonlight a year ago, facing the uncertainties of the future and wrestling with the demons of his past. Against all odds, the events that followed had laid most of them to rest.

This time his attitude towards the unknowns that lay before him was positive, expectant even. Ahead lay Silverlode, Nevada, with a population of 600 – as isolated an oasis of wandered-off souls as you could find in the lower forty-eight states. It would be a good place to try and write a book. Perhaps it would even be a best-seller. Given his recent brush with fame, that wasn't impossible.

The music on the radio gave way to the news. He turned up the volume.

...brings the Republican field up to five candidates.

That's a lot this early in the game, isn't it?

Twelve years ago I would have said yes. But since then, campaign costs have skyrocketed – a candidate who waits too long to declare won't be able to raise enough cash to make it through the first primaries.

Sad but true. We've entered the age of the billion dollar campaign. And the costs keep rising.

He turned the radio off. Heaven help us all, the election cycle was gearing up again, and just like last time, a bunch of improbable candidates had come yammering out of the woodwork. Anyone would think the doors of some political Bedlam had been thrown open, letting a mob of raving lunatics loose onto the primary trail. Incredibly, one after another had risen in the polls, too.

He realized he was driving over 80 miles an hour again, and took his foot off the gas. It was hard not to daydream on endless, straight as arrow roads like this. Braking, he noticed someone standing beside the road up ahead with his thumb extended.

Damn. City boy that he was, Frank was conditioned to regard all hitchhikers as presumptive murderers, hell bent on luring hapless good Samaritans to their doom. But the guy must have seen that he was slowing down, and it might be hours before another car ventured down this deserted stretch of road. Damn again. He really ought to do the right thing and stop. He kept his foot on the brake and the slim young man bent over to pick up his bag. The camper rolled to a stop just beyond him.

Frank looked warily into his side view mirror. The hitchhiker had his back to Frank and was now picking up a bike with a front wheel that suggested a Mobius strip having a bad hair day: bent spokes bristled out at every angle.

Well, he didn't look too threatening, and it was clear why he was thumbing a ride. That was reassuring. But Frank was still annoyed at the prospect of straining to make small talk for the next few hours. He readily admitted to being a computer geek, and figured he must be at least fifteen years older than the hitchhiker. What the hell could they have in common?

He got out of the camper to help the cyclist strap his bike next to his own on the rack on the back of the camper.

"Here, let me show you how that works."

The hitchhiker turned around. "Thank you for stopping. It is my lucky day. I have been standing here only one hour."

Frank stopped in his tracks: he was staring at a short-haired, slim – and very attractive – young woman. And with a French accent to boot.

"Good. I mean, good I came along. Why don't you go settle in? I'll take care of your bike."

He took his time doing that while she climbed into the passenger seat, her bicycle pannier bags slung over one sun-tanned shoulder. Now what?

Once more behind the wheel, he eased the camper into gear. Wondering what to say, he settled for the obvious.

"Where you headed?"

"To Gerlach?"

"Where's that?"

"It is north of Reno. And you?"

"Silverlode."

"Ah! So perfect! I can fix much on my bike on my own, but I cannot straighten a wheel rim. And I have not enough extra spokes. But I can have a new wheel sent to me there, I think."

She gave him a bright smile, and then turned to look out the window.

They drove on in silence, Frank's hopes for a pleasant spell of daydreaming now dashed. Instead, he was painfully conscious of his young passenger as he drove on, eyes on the road but distracted by the image of her dark, long-lashed, glittering eyes. He also recalled short, black, wind-blown hair, warm, sun-tanned skin, and cheekbones that inspired him to wax metaphorical – cheekbones like... like the vaults of a gothic cathedral! He felt briefly pleased with that, and then foolish. He wondered how old she was.

He kept his now-gloomy eyes on the road. Long divorced and solitary by nature, it had been ages since he had found himself in close proximity to such an exotic creature. He wondered what her story could be, traveling alone in this empty part of the country. Eventually, his curiosity got the better of his awkwardness.

"What's in Gerlach?"

"The Burning Man festival. Perhaps you have heard of it?"

"Yes, I have."

Which was true. But he hadn't heard much. All he knew was that every year tens of thousands of latter-day hippies and countercultural types descended for some unimaginable reason on a sun-blasted salt flat in Nevada to build a temporary, psychedelic city dominated by an enormous, vaguely humanoid statue. A week later, they would torch the statue as the climax of the event, and the city would disappear as quickly as it had materialized out of the shimmering heat of the desert. Frank was even more uncomfortable around flamboyant people than he was around mainstream types. He was about as likely to attend a Burning Man festival as he was a debutante ball.

Silence again. It bothered Frank that he had found this young woman on a deserted road. He had a daughter back east who was only a little younger, and he'd be furious to find her hitchhiking anywhere, let alone in the middle of an almost uninhabited desert. To the extent anyone lived here, Frank was disposed to assume the worst. How strange would you have to be to live in a place like this, anyhow?

It was clearly none of his business, but finally he asked, "Don't you think it's dangerous for a young woman to be hitchhiking in such a deserted area?"

"Oh no," she said, still looking out the window.

No? Clearly, this young French woman didn't understand America and Americans. "Well, you're wrong, let me assure you!"

"I think not. But in any case, I do not worry," she said, fumbling for something in the pannier bags at her feet.

Surprised, Frank stumbled over how to explain something he thought was obvious to an attractive young woman he did not know who was not a native English speaker.

"Well, what would you do if someone picked you up and tried to, tried to, well… force his attentions on you?"

She laughed. "Shoot him!"

Frank turned to her in surprise. Arms crossed, she had a playful smile on her face and a small gun in her hand. The gun was pointed at his head. She waggled its barrel back and forth and silently mouthed the word "Bang!"

He jerked his head back to the road, eyes wide as saucers.

For a minute there was silence again. Then she giggled. "Probably I would not really have to shoot him. But one must be prepared to, no?" She slipped the gun into a pocket and returned to looking out the window.

Frank decided that he had exhausted his conversational skills as well as his need to know anything more. He wondered how much longer it would take to get to Silverlode.

A half hour later, his passenger abruptly became talkative.

"My name is Josette," she said. "And what is yours?"

"Frank," he offered after a pause.

"You are on vacation, yes?"

"Not really. I'm writing a book." Frank tried to sound nonchalant, the way he imagined a famous author might.

"A book! But that is so interesting." She looked around the inside of the camper. "This is a very impressive vehicle. If I may ask, what are all those controls?"

This was a topic he could handle. "Electronics mostly, all satellite based and with service available anywhere: telephone, GPS, Internet, seven bands of radio, you name it."

"I see. With so many instruments, I suppose you must have a generator, too?"

He shook his head, feeling a bit smug. "No. The top of the camper is covered with solar panels. I could run everything day and night, and never run the batteries all the way down. At least not in a place like this."

"Ah! Very good thinking." She pulled an ultra-light laptop out of her pannier bags. "So I may perhaps use my computer to check my email, yes?"

"Yes, with a password. Would you like it?"

"Would you mind?"

He paused; he wasn't used to sharing a password with anyone. But his router was set to prevent anyone but him from archiving a password, and good luck to her if she could remember his.

"Not at all. N!t2T3f$a5G ^m7T."

Once again they drove in silence, broken only by staccato bursts of typing and his passenger's occasional, musical laughter. For his part, he brooded unhappily over the fact that he was an out of shape, socially inept, middle-aged man sitting next to an attractive young woman who was as unmindful of his presence as he was acutely aware of hers.

With the sun going down, the road turned uphill, aiming for a pass in the ridge. After they passed through, a modest town appeared not half a mile ahead, snug in a fold of the mountain and illuminated by the brilliant rays of the setting sun.

"That will be Silverlode," he said.

His passenger looked up. "Ah! That is very good. You will please let me off here?"

Frank was surprised once again. But he obediently slowed the camper to a stop, scanning the roadside and wondering why his passenger wanted to disembark just there. They both got out.

"Thank you for the ride," she said as he unfastened her bike.

"Don't you want a lift into town? I think there's a motel there."

"No. I have everything I need to camp." She patted the heavy pannier bags slung over her slight shoulder. Then, half wheeling and half carrying the bike, she disappeared into the junipers that flanked the road.

He felt hollow and at loose ends as he motored slowly up Silverlode's main street, passing a gas station, a motel, a fire station, a few shops and cross streets, and finally a small supermarket. He pulled in and hunted for the shopping list he'd shoved into the glove box that morning.

It was dark by the time he'd stowed away everything he would need for the next few weeks. It was time to find a place outside of town to park for the night. Ghostly, back-lit clouds scudded across the sky, intermittently obscuring and exposing the moon as gusts of wind rocked the camper. The temperature had dropped dramatically with the setting of the sun; the readout on his dashboard told him it was 38 degrees.

He wondered how Josette was faring, alone in the blustery darkness.

*   *   *

2

Fancy Meeting you Here

FRANK WAS FRUSTRATED. He'd spent the last two days on his laptop and had nothing to show for it except make-work outlines and false starts. Lots of false starts. He ruefully admitted that he had not the slightest idea how to go about writing a book.

He stared at his latest lame attempt at an opening:

> *Never in the history of this great nation have we faced such a horde of vicious, invisible, insidious, and downright evil enemies. Each is more dangerous than the last, and the last cares as much for your welfare as Adolf Hitler. They must be stopped, and stopped now!*

He wished he had brought a printer along so he could crumple that up and toss it in the trash.

After eight straight hours of failure near Silverlode, he'd driven off to the same mountain pass where he had spent weeks of difficult but exhilarating cybersleuthing work the year before. He parked just where he had then – even set up his folding chair in the same place, where he could once again ignore the fantastic scenery that spread before him as he focused on the challenge at hand.

But no luck here, either. After another day's clumsy effort he still hadn't written anything worth saving. One sentence – couldn't he write even the first sentence better than a seventh grader?

He snapped his laptop shut and stomped from his chair to the camper. After exchanging his laptop for a beer, he stomped back.

Now what? He'd quit his job in the information technology department of the Library of Congress and ordered a MountainTamer expedition vehicle – the same kind of rig he'd rented the year before, but this time customized to his own requirements. It had cost a small fortune. He'd had this idyllic notion that he could just head back west and pick up where he had left off, substituting writing a book for solving the mystery that had taken over his life the last time around. After that he'd live off the royalties for a while and figure out what to do next.

But there was no urgency driving him this time. No CIA and FBI scouring the country for him, and no evil genius to ferret out and foil. Just this stupid book idea taunting him with his inadequacies. He threw the still-full can of beer at a Ponderosa pine twenty feet away and missed it by five.

Shit!

He started pacing back and forth, pulling up the mental list of past failures he kept at the ready for purposes of self-flagellation. Kicking pinecones out of his way, he luxuriated in the warm bath of self-loathing that best suited him in his blackest moods.

Ten minutes later he became dimly aware of a sound that had been building at the edge of his consciousness. Still only half aware, he stopped and turned to look out over the valley floor that lay thousands of feet below. To his astonishment, he saw a helicopter heading straight at him. It was only a quarter of a mile away, and closing fast.

He backed up and craned his neck upward as the roaring aircraft reached, hovered over, and then descended at the edge of his clearing, kicking up a cloud of dust and pine needles that nearly blinded him.

Eyes watering, he wondered what new strangeness was afoot, feeling like an awestruck earthling awaiting his first sight of whatever bizarre creatures might emerge from a UFO. Then one man, followed by another, jumped out of the helicopter and walked towards him, crouching under the still-spinning blades. To his relief, he recognized one of them.

"What the hell are you doing here?" he yelled over the descending register of the engine's whine, reaching out to shake hands with his former boss. Publicly, George Marchand was the Chief Technology Officer of the Library of Congress. But Frank had learned in the course of his recent adventures that this was the cover for one of the CIA's top cybersecurity strategists.

"I want to introduce you to someone," Marchand yelled back, gesturing to his companion. "This is Len Butcher."

Frank took his visitor in as he accepted his limp handshake. The man's profile ran in a nearly straight line from the tip of his long, bony nose to the margin of an almost white buzz cut. The overall effect was rather weasely. Frank decided the guy was probably some variety of creep, exact type yet to be determined.

He turned to George, "How did you know where to find me?"

"It's our business to know where people like you are," Butcher interjected. His adenoidal voice slipped neatly into the negative profile Frank was assembling for him.

"Oh, really? And who might 'we' be, not to mention, 'people like me?'"

George cut Butcher off before he could answer. "How about we go inside?"

Frank shrugged and led the way. Behind them, the helicopter pilot strolled around the clearing, checking out the view and looking with curiosity at the field of charred and twisted metal wreckage strewn below him. Flowers and grass were only just beginning to reclaim what must have been a pleasant mountain meadow before some unknown, violent event had burst upon the bucolic scene.

Once they were seated inside his camper, Frank leaned back and crossed his arms. "So what gives?"

"Frank, Len works with another government agency. They're aware of the essential role that you played in cracking the Alexandria Project, and they're hoping they can recruit you to help track down a new group that's also proving tough to find."

"Thanks for the vote of confidence, but that's not what I'm up to these days."

"That's what I told Len. But this is pretty important, so here I am. That, and the fact that the Director of the CIA promised the head of the other agency that we would do whatever we could to help persuade you."

"What's the other agency?"

"That's not important, Frank. As a matter of fact, you wouldn't recognize the name of the agency if I told you, which I'm not at liberty to do. As you know, things have changed a lot since 9/11. There are more than a hundred U.S. intelligence units now, within existing agencies as well as stand-alone outfits. None of the new independent units have been publicly disclosed, and this is one of them."

Frank turned to Butcher, "So what does it say on your identification?"

"When I'm working on this project, it says I'm an executive of a computerized voting machine service company," Butcher said, taking a plastic card out of his wallet and handing it to Frank.

"Anyway, Frank, that's why I'm along for the ride, to credential Len for you. Now how about we tell you what this is all about?"

"Okay, sure. I can at least listen."

Butcher leaned forward.

"So tell me, Frank. Been paying any attention to the upcoming presidential election?"

"Some. The President's going to run again, so no drama there. The Tea Party conservatives keep standing up one crazy whack job of a candidate after another. I can't believe any of them stands a chance of taking a primary, let alone the Oval Office – or at least I hope not. And the mainstream Republicans don't seem to have any candidates that people are very enthusiastic about." He hoped Butcher was a staunch conservative.

"It is an interesting cast of characters, isn't it? Have you heard any of the poll results, though? What people are saying about them?"

"No. Why bother? The primaries don't start until January."

"Because those 'whack jobs,' as you call them, are out-polling the credible candidates by double digits."

"So what? That's not unusual. It's mostly just name recognition at this point."

"Usually, yes. So how do you explain the fact that Julian Johnson and Roxanne Rollins are way out in front of Vance Cabot and Hollis Davenport?"

"Who?"

"Precisely. Makes you wonder, doesn't it?"

"Maybe they're just badly conducted polls. Or maybe they were taken in those candidates' home states."

"No and no. The polls were conducted in major cities across the country by top professionals."

"Then their data's flawed."

"Indeed. So what does that suggest to you?"

"Somebody's tampering with the poll numbers."

Butcher turned to Marchand. "Your boy's just as quick as you said he was, George."

Marchand gave him a dirty look and jumped in. "At this point, we don't have a clue who's behind this, but we do believe someone is altering the data on the pollsters' systems."

"Fine. But these are just pollsters – so why does Butcher's agency, whatever it is, care?"

"Well, as you may or may not know, the next election will be the first one where just about everyone will be voting on electronic rather than mechanical balloting equipment. In most states, they'll even be able to vote using their smart phones. People will fill in their ballots in advance, and then just download them at the voting booth. So that makes it pretty alarming that someone's tampering with poll data. For all we know, if they're hacking polling systems now, they may try to hack voting systems later."

"Okay, I'll buy that." Frank turned to Butcher. "But if you've got a hundred intelligence agencies plus the FBI to work on it, what do you need me for?"

"Here's the thing. We haven't figured out yet how they've penetrated the polling systems, let alone how they're changing the data. Until we do that, it's almost impossible to figure out who they are."

"Maybe no one has. Maybe it's employees with security privileges that are changing the data."

"It's not that, either. We had one of our own people input new data, and then read the results. Guess what? They don't match – what came out is different than what we put in."

"So? That just means someone got to the system before you used it. It's already programmed to change the results."

"Sorry. We used a brand new system, straight from the factory."

"Then they paid a guy that works for the vendor to change the polling software."

"No again. We've scanned the code against an earlier version – which does work fine – and they seem to match identically except for legitimate bug fixes."

"Then the malware feature was just lying dormant in the older copy, waiting to be triggered by something. Did you check that out? No? Doesn't your no-name agency have anybody working on this that knows what they're doing?"

"Of course they do," George said. "And so does the FBI. But so far, no luck. There are over two hundred thousand lines of code in the original software, and a lot of bug fixes and updates besides."

Sure, Frank thought. And there were also computer chips and firmware that could have been replaced in the servers the polling software ran on. Not to mention software modules that could be reprogrammed remotely, and an Internet connection that would allow the software to call on external databases for information not found in the system's memory. Any of those vulnerabilities could be the source of the problem. You'd have to check all of those meticulously, one by one. He began to think what tests he'd run in what order to find where the rat was hiding in the maze. It was an interesting problem.

"So what do you say, Frank?" Butcher said. "Want to show us how much smarter you are than our boys?"

Marchand watched the interplay between the two men. Butcher might not be a charmer, but he'd figured out mighty quickly which of Frank's buttons to push to get him to sign on. Or maybe he'd read the file the FBI had put together on Frank a year ago. Of course – that was the explanation.

Frank frowned. He had to admit he was intrigued by what he'd heard. It sounded like a pretty good hack. It would be interesting to devise a plan to get to the bottom of it, and then see whether it worked.

But that wasn't what he was here for. He'd been looking forward to getting away, making a clean break and getting a fresh start. After the revelation of his role in averting the crisis with North Korea, everyone at work thought he walked on water – at least for a while. But his old job was still painfully dull. Just a lot of ho-hum tasks, just like before. It wasn't long before he felt bored and ignored again.

The call from a publisher therefore came at exactly the right time. Would he be interested in writing a book about how he had cracked the Alexandria Project? He decided on the spot that he would. The next day he handed in his resignation and put in his order for the customized MountainTamer expedition vehicle – something he could live in off the road for a month at a time. Then he headed out to Nevada to spend some time with his father while he waited for its delivery.

Becoming a best-selling author wasn't looking so easy now. And he'd spent all of the publisher's advance and most of his savings on the MountainTamer and the equipment he'd loaded it up with. Maybe he should be taking this new cybersecurity opportunity seriously?

"Let's say I did. What happens next? I just paid a pile of money for this rig and was looking forward to doing some extended touring. And I've got this book I'm working on. I don't want to set that aside."

"No worries." Butcher said. "We know you've got this camper set up to let you do whatever you want wherever you want to do it. In fact, we'd like it to look like you're keeping to your original plans, so as not to attract attention. But we'll give you up to the minute, unrestricted access to whatever information and resources you need. We'll even give you a nice business card, just like mine."

Butcher slid another card across the table. At the top was the service company's name and logo, and below it were Frank's name, a hologram, and an ID number.

"Big deal. What am I going to do with that?"

"That's up to you. It may come in handy doing whatever you decide to do to get to the bottom of things. It's even programmable – you can be whoever you want, when you want, and your name on the website will automatically update at the same time."

"Do I get to wear a funny hat, too?"

Butcher frowned. "Whatever floats your boat."

Frank was pleased that he'd finally gotten under Butcher's skin. He stood up, took a beer out of the refrigerator and set it in front of Butcher.

"Have one on me. George, feel like taking the grand tour of my clearing?"

"Sure."

The two men stepped out and walked a dozen paces away from the camper.

Across the valley to the west, angry thunderclouds were building above the purple silhouette of the mountains.

"So what do you think, Frank?"

"I don't know. My last experience with the intelligence establishment wasn't what you'd call a love fest. And those were public agencies with Congressional oversight, not ones that most legislators don't even know exist. What would I be getting myself into?"

"I think everything would work out fine this time, Frank. You'd still have complete independence – no one expects you to become an integrated part of Butcher's team. Last time around showed that's how you work best. If you're successful, that's great. If you're not, that's the government's problem. Any time you felt like it, you could simply walk away. I don't know whether you're still making a killing in the online game space, but if not, the money would be really good. Consultants to non-existent agencies aren't tied to government pay grades or procurement rules, and that service company on the business card has a real office – even a receptionist. Not much else, but I can guarantee you their checks will clear."

As a matter of fact, Frank's second game idea had been a flop, and he hadn't yet had a third. With his book prospects in doubt, his economic future was looking murky at best.

"Would I have to report to this guy Butcher? He wouldn't be my pick for a detailer."

"Not a problem. He's a desk jockey, not a field manager. I can do a little interfering and be sure that you end up with someone you can work with. And you can contact me any time."

George waited while Frank brooded, hands in his pockets and staring out across the valley. Intermittent flashes of silent lightning were now illuminating the angry interiors of the thunderheads massing in the distance. Overhead, skittering silhouettes of bats sketched erratic paths across the fading sky as a freshening breeze enveloped him in the exotic smell of dust and sagebrush from the valley below. Wasn't just experiencing a place like this enough?

He kicked a pinecone. Well, no. He'd need something to focus on besides the scenery or he'd be climbing the camper's walls in two days. And it didn't look like writing a book was going to provide that focus – or an income.

He looked back at his camper, its windows aglow in the gathering darkness. In what way was this unexpected invitation not a gift? It seemed to be tailor-made to fill the inconvenient void created by his lack of writing success.

"Okay. I'll do it."

George clapped him on the back. "That's great. I'll go tell Len. Judging by those thunderheads, we'd better beat it back to home base unless you want company for the night."

Five minutes later, the whine of the helicopter's engine was receding in the distance. Frank felt his spirits lift as he watched the blinking navigation lights fade. To his surprise, he was happy to be back in the game.

*   *   *

3

Shelter from the Storm

NOT LONG AFTER the helicopter's departure, Frank was on the move, driving carefully down the jeep track through wind-whipped, driving rain, periodically blinded by vivid flashes of lightning. This wasn't the usual late summer southwestern thunderstorm, where only a few raindrops survive the long descent through dry desert air without evaporating. This was the product of a full monsoon front sweeping up and across from the Gulf of Mexico, the kind ranchers relied on to refill stock ponds and green up the grass again for their cattle.

Now that he had signed on with whoever it was Butcher worked for, Frank was anxious to get started, and he wanted a change of scenery to go along with his new objective. It hadn't taken long to pack up, but by then the storm was breaking over him.

The jeep track down the mountain was now a cascading sluice of storm runoff, forcing him to allow the heavy truck to ease itself down the steep grade in first gear. The going was different but no better when he reached level ground, where the deep, red clay dust of the jeep track had dissolved into a sludge the texture and color of borscht. He alternated gunning the engine to avoid getting stuck with hitting the brakes to avoid fishtailing off the track.

The racket of the rain hammering on the roof of the camper was still distracting as he pulled into Silverlode, mud-splattered up to the sills of his windows. The trip to town had kept him on the edge of his seat, and now he was hungry.

He opted for a saloon-themed restaurant next to the town's restored, late 19th century Opera House, which looked like the most hopeful option among Silverlode's meager epicurean offerings. Inside he found a dimly lit dining room and bar populated by a sprinkling of tourists and locals. He took a table and examined the menu he found standing between inverted bottles of ketchup, mustard and barbecue sauce.

He was trying to decide whether an emu burger was a local attraction not to be missed or a stupid premise to be actively avoided when someone appeared at his elbow. Expecting a waitress, he found a very wet and bedraggled Josette instead.

"Please, may I sit down?"

"Of course." He stood up, flustered.

"The wind blew my tent apart," she said. "It is in rags. So I came to town."

He took off his jacket and draped it over her shoulders. "That's terrible. You must be chilled to the bone."

She gave him a brave smile and nodded. "I thought this was the desert. So much wind – and rain! Who would have expected?"

Frank tried to catch the attention of a server.

"Let's get you something warm to drink."

The middle aged waitress that appeared promptly adopted Josette, returning almost immediately with a steaming mug of tea and a clean dish towel. Josette accepted both with gratitude and mopped her face and hair.

"I am so cold and hungry! I could not cook my dinner in all the wind and rain."

"Then we need to get you something to eat!" He handed her his menu, and she studied it intently.

"Tell me, please, what is 'pork barbeque?'"

"Shredded meat soaked in a spicy sauce. It's served on a hamburger roll."

She wrinkled her nose and opted for a grilled chicken salad served in a taco shell.

The waitress saw to it that their food arrived quickly, and Josette began to brighten. She smiled at Frank, and he smiled back.

They chatted about this and that while they ate, and gradually he became more comfortable. Then she asked, "How is your book?" and his smile faded.

"Oh, I'm still doing research. I'll have to do lots of research before I can start writing."

"Ah! You must be very patient."

He cleared his throat. "Were you able to get your bike fixed?"

"Yes, yes! My new wheel arrived at the post office this morning, thank goodness. Otherwise I would have had to walk to town in the rain."

"Will you be moving on to the festival now?"

"Oh!" She looked downcast. "It took so long for the wheel to arrive. I have lost much time. Today is Saturday, and the festival begins on Monday." Then she brightened. "But I can still, how you say, 'hitch a ride,' yes?"

Frank frowned. Hadn't this young woman seen any American movies? He was still convinced she would be picked up by some sort of crazy person before she made it halfway across the state.

Josette covered her mouth and laughed. "You are still worried for me! Don't be! It is not so dangerous as you suppose."

His ears burned. He was too out of practice to be having a conversation like this. Besides, she was young, attractive, and vibrant, and he was old, crotchety and self-conscious. It felt like his first date all over again, but without the excuse that it was a date. He waved to the waitress and made check-signing motions in the air.

She realized she had embarrassed him and changed the subject.

"So – do you stay in Silverlode for long?"

"No. I'm leaving tomorrow."

"Really? And where do you go now?"

"Why, I... I'm not exactly sure. You see, I don't have to be any one place at any particular time. I'm just touring – driving where my fancy takes me. I arrive somewhere, stay a few days, and then move on."

She put her hand on his. "Frank! I have an extra ticket – you must come and see the Burning Man! You will love it! They say there is nothing like it anywhere!"

Under cover of encountering a sudden desire to consume a French fry he retrieved his hand. "Oh, no, I mean, I can't do that! Really."

She gave him a sly look. "Ah! You are afraid of me! It is my gun, yes? Don't be!"

She reached into her bag, and pressed an almost weightless object in his hand.

He stared down at what was now obviously a toy plastic gun, and stammered, "No!" more loudly than he intended. Then, more quietly, "No, it isn't that at all. It's just that I've got work to do – I can't afford to be distracted – it's too hard to stop and start. I've got to maintain my concentration."

The waitress brought the check promptly and he paid it immediately. He stood up, and escorted Josette to the door, which he held for her. They stepped out onto a weathered wooden sidewalk sheltered by an old fashioned tin roof.

He was angry at his awkwardness and anxious to escape. But it was dark, and a boisterous rain was splattering noisily on the roof overhead and the street beyond, presenting him with a new problem. Now what?

"Let me drop you off at the motel."

She looked down, and then up into his eyes. "Every place in town is full. I have already checked. They say it has something to do with, how you say, a 'rodeo.'"

He opened his mouth half way, and then shut it again. Then where could she stay? He could scarcely offer to drop her back by the side of the road, in the rain, with her shredded tent. And it must be obvious that there were at least two beds in a camper as large as his. Damn!

Silence.

"I guess you could, I mean, I have two beds in my camper. Would you like to stay there tonight?"

Her shining eyes offered a "my hero!" look and his heart skipped a beat. "Oh, Frank, you are so kind!"

She looked down again before glancing up again, serious now. "I do not want to be a bother... but what else can I do?"

Frank found himself once again strapping Josette's bike on the back of his camper as Josette clambered up into the passenger seat, pannier bags slung over her shoulder. She chattered happily as they drove out of town, often placing her hand on his arm to emphasize a point. Behind them, the scattered lights of Silverlode glistened wetly in the night – the yellow and orange rectangle of the Shell sign, the upward-cast, white lights that illuminated the letters that spelled "Opera House," and in front of the motel, the small, red neon sign that read "Vacancy."

* * *

4

Frank's Long Day's Journey into Night

T HE SUN WAS baking the road ahead as Frank drove west, making its surface shimmer uncertainly. Just the day before, he had been sitting in his clearing swearing at his laptop, and now he was off on what could prove to be two wild goose chases – the first, to find someone a government agency that didn't exist claimed was hacking into pollster computer systems, and the second to chauffeur a young French woman to a countercultural festival for reasons he was trying hard to pretend he did not understand.

He yawned. Then he yawned again; it had been a long and sleepless night. While Josette was taking a hot shower, he'd gotten into bed as quickly as possible and turned off the light, lying on his side and facing the wall of the camper. He'd been divorced for twenty years now. With all too rare exceptions, those had been twenty very solitary years. Gazing appreciatively at an attractive young woman when she wasn't looking was one thing, but more than that was unthinkable. Still, he'd had a few beers at dinner, and he was determined not to give himself a chance to make a fool of himself.

The muffled click of the light switch in the camper's tiny bathroom came at last, followed by the sounds of a door quietly opening and closing. He all but held his breath until he heard the soft rustling sounds subside in the other bed, just three feet away. With a silent sigh that was equal parts relief and longing, he tried to empty his mind and get some sleep.

He had almost succeeded when he became aware that someone was slipping into bed beside him. His eyes snapped open, and most, but not all, of his body went rigid.

"Shhh." She settled her head against him, and began gently massaging his shoulders.

"So tense - you must relax."

He said nothing, and tried to focus on breathing slowly and evenly. It took many minutes, but at last the tension in his body began to seep away. Finally, his heart leapt as a wave of confidence began to rise within him. He turned toward Josette.

And then she whispered three short words in his ear - the three most unwelcome words a man can hear in the unshared heat of a not to be consummated moment.

"Just hold me."

In the blazing light of day, Frank decided they sounded even worse in a French accent.

He'd been afraid to move for the rest of the night for fear of waking his gently breathing companion. Wretched and sleepless, he had finally eased out of bed at dawn and started driving, leaving Josette to sleep peacefully on. He told himself that it was only because he had no other destination, anyway, that the direction he chose to drive was towards Burning Man.

A few hours later she joined him in the front of the camper, belting herself in and tucking her long, tanned legs beneath her. He was mildly shocked to see that she was wearing one of his T shirts, and not much else. "I hope you do not mind," she had explained, "Everything I have, you see, is still so wet!"

"Here," she said, "I have made us coffee." She handed him a cup.

"It smells different."

"It is French. So much better than what I found in your cupboard." She laughed.

Frank's spirits rose as he sipped his coffee and listened to Josette comment on the scenery rolling by. It had been so long since a woman had made him coffee, or passed the time of day with him as they traveled.

"Tell me Frank," Josette said, "this book of yours, what is it about?"

He was sorry for the change of topic. "Security – I mean, cybersecurity. Do you know the term?"

"Yes, we use the same words in France, except we say it like this: *la cyber-sécurité.*"

He nodded. "Yes, and it's a very big problem. There are criminals that steal your credit card information, foreign companies that make off with your product designs, spies that steal government information, terrorists that try to penetrate national defenses, and much more."

"Of course, of course. It is the same problem everywhere. But what exactly is it that you will write?"

He wondered how to make what he had in mind sound more heroic and less dorky than he expected it would. Then he had a thought.

"You recall the Maginot Line?"

"But of course. It was a great folly – and a great failure. We French spent many millions of francs building hundreds of miles of defenses facing east after the First World War. But the Germans built hundreds of tanks and then drove around it."

"Exactly. Well, that's something like what I believe is going on today on the Internet. We fool ourselves into thinking we're doing what needs to be done to protect ourselves from our enemies. But really we're just building another Maginot Line, only this time in cyberspace. Criminals and terrorists and spies are already getting around it as if we had no defenses at all."

She gave him a coquettish smile. "I am told that our French companies, they have not found it so very hard to get to your companies' information."

He laughed. "And you've been told right. The French and the Chinese are the worst of the lot when it comes to stealing corporate trade secrets. Your government even helps them! But there's much worse going on. Why, not long ago it came out that someone had hacked the controls of the Pentagon's Predator drones! We think the Taliban did it, but we don't really know. And shame on the Pentagon, because not long before that, someone hacked their way into the video feeds the drones were transmitting back to their targeting bases."

"Ah yes. But what is it that your book will say about this?"

That stopped him. He hadn't really taken the concept much beyond his general sense of outrage at the inability of people to appreciate the dire straits he was personally convinced the world was in.

"Well, I'll… give lots of examples of bad things that have already happened, and then examples of even worse things that are bound to happen if nothing is done. Then I'll describe what we need to do to prevent those things from happening."

"I see."

I see? That wasn't much of a response. She was looking out the window again, but after a few minutes suddenly turned around.

"Ah! It is ten o'clock. May we listen to the news?"

"Of course." He turned on his satellite radio. The announcer had just started to deliver the lead story.

"…announced his campaign yesterday at a press conference."

"Oh no," Frank groaned. "Now who?"

To his surprise, Josette reached forward and turned up the volume.

> *The Texas governor's decision was immediately acclaimed by the host of supporters that has been urging him for weeks to throw his hat into the ring. With the addition of Julian Johnson, the Republican field has now expanded to six.*

Frank snapped off the radio.

"I cannot believe the stupidity of the American people! How anyone could consider Julian Johnson for dog catcher, much less president of the United States, is completely beyond me. How does Texas keep coming up with these jugheads? It's like they've got a closet full of them down in Central Casting!"

Josette giggled. "This Mr. Johnson – he is not so good?"

"Not so good! He's appalling! He panders to every single bias and know-nothing creed in the ultra-conservative book of beliefs. He's signed the no-taxes pledge, claims global warming is a hoax, and says he'll wipe out the federal deficit without raising taxes. You tell him what he needs to say to get the nomination, and he'll be saying it before all the words are out of your mouth."

"So you think he does not believe in what he says?"

"Who knows? I can't decide which would be worse – that he's stupid enough to believe what he says, or corrupt enough to say what he doesn't believe. Either way, he better not get elected."

"If he is so bad, how can you worry that he could be elected?"

"D'you remember the last guy we elected who came from Texas?"

"Ah yes. You elected him *twice*, in fact. It did not turn out so well, did it?"

"No! No, it didn't."

"So tell me – these other candidates – do you think that they are any better?"

"Hah! I wish! Every species of loony ever hatched seems to be represented in the race this year. There's the Libertarian who thinks we should shut Washington down and hand the keys to the Capitol over to Wall Street. Then there's the former Dairy Queen of Wisconsin who wants the mothers of America to unite and throw every progressive out of government. And that just scratches the surface."

"Why is it that no one who is both conservative and capable runs for president?"

"They do. But it's the ultra-conservatives that come out to vote in the primaries, and those are the votes you need to get the nomination. Anyway, there is a guy in the Republican race who's sane, and intelligent besides – Hollis Davenport. But he doesn't stand a chance."

"Because?"

"Well, first off, he's a Unitarian Universalist. Most of them live in New

England, so not many evangelicals have ever met one. That makes them immediately suspicious. Plus, Unitarians are pretty skeptical about traditional Christian doctrine. Most don't believe in Hell and damnation, for example, so Unitarians must be some kind of pagan cult, right?"

She laughed, but Frank was still picking up speed.

"Then there's the fact that when he was a governor, he led the charge that resulted in his state becoming the first in the nation to pass a universal healthcare bill. The conservatives have never forgiven him for that."

"But why? Everyone in Europe gets healthcare. It makes so much sense!"

"And guess what? Going into the 2008 presidential election, *both* parties agreed that universal healthcare should be adopted nationwide."

"So? What changed?"

"Only one party won, and it wasn't the conservatives. So anything the winning Democrat wanted to accomplish immediately became nonsense or worse to some of the Republicans in the Senate, and a whole lot more in the House. If the President tried to make Mother's Day a federal holiday, the conservatives would call that Socialism."

"I do not think I will ever understand your politics."

"Why should you? I don't."

She stared out the window for a while before replying.

"You know, Frank, you Americans really should choose your presidents more carefully."

"No kidding. I couldn't agree with you more. Judging by the things they say, some people shouldn't be allowed to vote at all."

"But seriously, Frank. Your president wields so much power. What he wishes to do, he can do, whether other countries want him to or not. Look at Iraq and Afghanistan. Look at Vietnam. Look at so many other invasions – Panama, Grenada, Santo Domingo. The Bay of Pigs. All those military actions in just the last sixty years, not to mention all of the coups the U.S. supported! You Americans really should be more careful who you put in charge, because the rest of the world suffers the consequences, too."

He looked at her in surprise. Where had this come from?

"I suppose... I mean, of course, the President does have a lot of power."

"It's not the power that's wrong! If your President Roosevelt had not persuaded your country to enter World War II, Hitler would have won. It's when you elect a foolish president! You Americans insist on calling your president the 'Leader of the Free World.' If your voters want to elect a leader of the free world, then they should be sure they pick one who is up to the job!"

"Well sure..."

"Look who is running now! Roxanne Rollins! Roland Overby! Landa Goshen! And now your Mr. Johnson! What is the rest of the world supposed to do if you allow one of these fools to become president?" She stopped abruptly.

He drove on in silence, wondering how to respond to Josette. Because, of course, she had a point.

* * *

5

Got a Match?

I T WAS EARLY afternoon when Frank and Josette rolled slowly into Gerlach behind a 1960's era VW bug. Parked ahead, they saw a forty foot long something that resembled a cross between a Viking long ship and a Mississippi river boat.

"Ah! An Art Car!" Josette exclaimed.

"Excuse me?" Frank asked, craning his neck to examine the outlandish contraption as they passed.

"Burning Man is famous for Art Cars! We should see many more, and each one is unique!"

Unique was a necessary but hardly sufficient word to describe what he was looking at. Its gargantuan strangeness partially made up for the bleak insignificance of the hamlet itself. That much, at least, was not a surprise. Josette had looked Gerlach up online an hour before and read him what she found. A typical description read:

> Welcome to Gerlach, Nevada (pop. 450). In this thriving metropolis
> you will find one elementary school, one high school, one post office,
> one propane distributor, one gas station, one motel, 3 bars and that's
> it.

Temporarily there was more, though, because the Festival was about to begin. Spread along the roadside and in the parking lots of the few dusty buildings that together comprised downtown Gerlach was a line of brightly hued, open wall tents selling water, food, balloons, happy face condoms, mountain bicycles, and almost anything else that you might (or might not) expect a festival-goer to want or need. Colorful pennants fluttered in the breeze above a throng that would blend in well in Key West on New Year's Eve, only wearing even fewer clothes.

A few miles out of town, they reached the edge of a great salt playa that stretched for mile after heat-shimmering mile into the indeterminate distance. Towering over it on one side was Black Rock – the mountain that gave the local desert its name. Far out in the middle of the playa they saw a caravan of vehicles. Frank left the road and rolled off across the salt flat, eventually taking his place at the end of the long and slow-moving line of normal vehicles interspersed with the occasional hulking, impossible to categorize Art Car.

It was half an hour before they reached two small tents between which each vehicle was required to stop. A handmade sign proclaimed that it was the Festival Greeter Gate.

Frank rolled down his window and handed their tickets to a young man wearing khaki shorts, a broad-brimmed hat and sunglasses. A rather magnificent series of hair spikes stuck up through holes in his hat, giving the impression that he had permitted a small but dapper stegosaurus to pause for a rest on his head.

"Howdy. Welcome home."

"Uh, actually, I've never been here before."

The young man let out a whoop.

"We got us some virgins!"

Instantly the rest of the greeter gate crew surrounded the camper, opening the doors and dragging them out. Josette cooperated, laughing, while Frank acquiesced, grumbling. Mortified, he followed Josette as they were led to a wooden tower inside which hung a large bell. Hair Spike Man handed Josette a pole, instructing her to bang the bell while proclaiming that she no longer bore the burden of being a virgin.

Happy to oblige, she gave the bell an enthusiastic whack while confidently announcing her altered status, after which her forehead was anointed with a dab of white playa dust. Frank was not released until he had suffered a similar, though significantly less enthusiastic fate.

Josette watched Frank as they drove away, trying not to laugh.

"Frank, you must try to join in the fun."

"Fun? Where's the fun part? All I see is a bunch of weirdos baking in 100 degree heat a million miles from nowhere. And what's that?"

Ahead they could see what appeared to be a massive, openwork ziggurat, rising fifty feet into the air. Astride its apex stood an abstract, angular figure more than twice that tall, its legs slightly spread and arms outstretched high above its head.

"Why that is the Man, of course. What else would it be?"

But at this point, a sign directed them to the left, and they proceeded to trundle around the perimeter of the sprawling, semicircular city that was still erupting out of the alkaline lakebed. A week hence, it was destined to vanish like a mirage, as if spirited into the sky by the glittering waves of heat rippling upward from the desert floor.

Out of a dust swirl ahead, hundreds of bicycles began to emerge, each one propelled by a gaily painted rider, often topless, regardless of sex. A few moments later, the mobile mob engulfed them before leaving them just as quickly behind.

"Uh, can you tell me what exactly that was all about?" Frank asked.

Josette laughed. "Why must it be about anything?"

Frank was about to reply testily that everything was about something, but decided that at Black Rock Desert at this time of year he may have encountered an exception to that rule. The enormous triceratops made out of abandoned car parts that was trundling by them just then struck him as particularly relevant to that point.

It was almost dusk when at last they reached the area where vehicles were permitted to park. Only Art Cars and foot and bicycle traffic would be permitted into Black Rock City until the festival was over.

Frank was removing their bicycles from the rack when he heard Josette call out someone's name. Turning, he saw a group of young men and women on bicycles come to a stop. And Josette was running into the arms of a bronzed young man in shorts and sandals. A red bandanna was tied around his neck, and a wide grin was spreading across his handsome, stubbled face.

Frank stood dumbly by the camper. Josette had said she hoped to rejoin the group she had been touring with before diverting alone to Las Vegas to visit friends. But he had assumed it would take time to find them amid so much confusion.

Glancing his way, Josette saw him watching. She waved him towards her, but when he showed no sign of doing so, she took the young man's hand and led him over to the camper.

"Frank, this is Alexandre. Alexandre, Frank is the one who rescued me after I hit a pothole with my bike. My front wheel – it was such a mess! And then he drove me the rest of the way from Silverlode so I would not be late."

"It is good to meet you, Frank."

"Hi. You too."

Josette took both of the young man's hands in hers. "I will join you in just a minute Alexandre! Let me get my bike and bags." With a nod and a smile to Frank, he turned and walked off to rejoin his friends.

Frank took one of the bikes leaning against the camper and held it upright. "Well, here you go. Enjoy the festival."

"But of course you will stay, yes?" It had not escaped her notice that Frank had unloaded his bicycle as well as hers before she spied her friends.

He had already turned to reattach his bike to the rack. "No, no, my book, you know." When his bike was tied down, he turned around and shoved his hands in his pockets.

"Got to get back to work. Not likely I'd get anything done here."

She looked momentarily uncertain, but then she turned to look towards her friends. They were standing by their bicycles, waiting.

"Well, if you must. But I will miss you." She pulled his head down and gave him a quick kiss on each cheek. "You must promise to email me!" And then she was off, speeding away on her bike in a cloud of dust.

He walked slowly around to the other side of his camper where he could unobtrusively watch the young adventurers pedal towards the unworldly, ephemeral skyline of Black Rock City, above which the sacrificial Man's arms stretched upwards in a temporarily triumphant V. Before Frank, everything was young and frivolous and alive. Behind him was the empty desert.

"Enjoy it while you can, Big Guy," he said to the Man. "It doesn't last."

He climbed into the camper and turned the key in the ignition. Then he headed north.

*　*　*

6

Report of the Marvinites

F RANK GAZED OUT over the immeasurably vast canyon that stretched away for miles before him, bedazzled by the silent, bright sunlight of an early autumn morning. The enormity of the view was so overwhelming that the infinitely crenellated details of mesa, cliff and spire became dimensionless and unreal.

It was not like him to sit so placidly for so long. Usually an internal flaw of logic or syntax in a random thought would interrupt his musing, setting his brain to work analyzing the offending bit of idle mental processing. Only when the incongruity had been straightened out would his thoughts be free to wander once again. Or some inscrutable object or action would catch his eye, presenting a puzzle that demanded a solution before his musings could resume.

But not today. Barely a breath of wind stirred, and almost the only sound discernible was the distant twittering of swallows curveting in the void that yawned a few feet from where he sat in his trusty folding chair. Sometimes, their cheeps were joined by the wind-borne whisper of the river as it carved away at the base of the sheer wall thousands of feet below.

Normally, the motivation behind the actions of the birds would have piqued his interest. It would not have taken long for him to conclude they must be feasting on insects wafting upwards on air currents forming as the rising sun warmed the vaulting wall of the north rim of the Grand Canyon.

But the sensation of the sun on his face was wonderfully warm, providing the perfect, sensual counterpoint to the crisp morning air. Beneath the brilliant blue arc of the sky, the vista extending below and beyond was too varied and colorful, and the details too delightful and precise, to risk diminishment by pettifoggery. Better to submit to the near-narcotic sense of tranquility that view and sun so generously offered.

At some level Frank was aware that more than the perfection of the moment was urging his normally overactive mind to chill. Procrastination was also at play. He had not yet begun to delve seriously into the perplexing poll results he had agreed to investigate. If he was going to earn his keep on this project he would need to buckle down and get started. But he knew that once he did the riddle would torment him until he had an answer. Until then, there would be no more pleasant reveries like this. But I really should get to work, he mused.

He noticed a solitary little cloud on the horizon, drifting from west to east, and toyed with the thought of committing to get up and get to work if the cloud passed between him and the sun. It seemed like a safe bet. The sky was vast, the cloud was small, and the sun was also in motion. The courses of sun and cloud seemed just likely enough to intersect to make the promise not entirely bogus, but not so sure as to present a clear and present danger of imminent labor. Deciding that his virtue could be established at an acceptably low risk, he accepted his own bet and went back to basking in the warmth of the sun.

But it soon became clear that he might have wagered unwisely. Out of the entirety of the vast blue vault spread above him, the sun and the tiny cloud seemed intent on occupying the same spot at the same time. He felt his pleasant languor begin to evaporate. And then, far away, he saw it – the sinister shadow of the cloud itself, gliding slowly but inexorably up cliffs, across mesas, and down canyons. It was headed directly for him.

By the time his face turned cool in the sudden shade of the offending cumulus, he was resigned to the inevitable. The implacable spirits of the canyon had obviously determined that it was time for him to quit goofing off and get to work.

With a sigh he opened the computer that had been sitting idle in his lap and pressed the start button. Then he stared out across the canyon one last time, seeking inspiration in the erosional order that explained the seeming chaos that stretched before him. Winding somewhere amid the welter of electronic data he must now analyze there would be a slender stream of clues he would need to find and follow. Likely enough he would need to intuit what was afoot rather than see it, just as he could infer but not visually confirm the existence of the Colorado River weaving through the canyon below.

The analogy pleased more than helped him. He knew where he should begin looking for clues, but what sort of clues should he be looking for? He drummed the fingers of his right hand lightly on his thigh and pondered that question.

After the icons on his laptop screen flashed and settled down, he opened the investigation report he had received from the anonymous agency he had decided to call "Marvin." He spent an hour reading and rereading the report, searching for something the security experts at Marvin might have missed. But no luck. He closed the report. It was time to go to the source, or at least the next best thing, and perform his own investigation.

He logged onto his Wi-Fi network and called up the directory of one of the servers he had installed inside his camper. The hard drive of each server had been divided up into a number of "virtual machines," each one comprising an independent computer system. Some of these VMs were clean and ready to be configured however he wished. Others were exact clones of pollster systems already in use. Together, they would provide the lab bench on which he would perform his research and experiments.

He started by calling up a clone of a system that had already been compromised. Hopefully whatever had happened on the original computer would be reflected in the duplicate system he was now exploring.

His approach would necessarily be tentative at first. He'd need to make assumptions, and then test them to see whether he was on the right track. The first question requiring an assumption was this: had the polling data been altered before it entered the machine, or afterwards? The Marvin investigators had concluded that the data was still clean when it arrived. Frank wasn't prepared to believe anything from that source until he could confirm it himself, but for the time being he decided to adopt that assumption as well.

If they were right, the next step should be to determine what someone could do to a system to alter data without leaving any breadcrumbs. The Marvinites had explored this by entering data into both a compromised system from the field and a clean system straight from the supplier. When they input the same data into each system and then ran a report, both systems yielded the same inaccurate results.

He leaned back, hands laced behind his head. If he was the bad guy, how many different exploits could he design that could produce that outcome?

Well, most obviously, he could infiltrate the software provider and tamper with the code of the software before it was delivered. That could explain a lot, since all the major pollsters used the same program. Or, given how old some of the systems in use were, more likely he would corrupt an otherwise legitimate software update before the vendor sent it to its customers. He already knew from the report that each installed system had received software updates of all kinds – bug fixes, security patches and so on. All of this new input had been carefully tabulated, indexed and compared by Marvin's nameless minions.

The last way would be to hack into the installed units as well as any new ones awaiting delivery and infect all of them with some sort of malware. He reopened the report to see if the new units had been connected to the Internet for testing prior to delivery and couldn't find the answer to that question. If that was typical of Marvinite work, no wonder they hadn't made any progress yet.

By now, Frank had broken through his procrastination barrier and was beginning to warm to his quest. He set his laptop aside and began pacing back and forth on the edge of the canyon, his hands plunged into his pockets. Sun and view were now forgotten. So was lunch.

Had he looked upward, he would have seen a rare sight, one of the small number of California condors reintroduced to the Grand Canyon in an effort to reestablish a breeding population. Hideous to behold at close range but majestic in flight with its nine foot wingspan, the great vulture soared ever higher on a thermal, idly noting a small figure below that by turns paced, sat, and returned to pacing once again.

When the soaring bird sensed that its column of rising air was beginning to dissipate, it tilted its wings slightly and set a course for the opposite side of the canyon, miles distant. Partway across, it detected a tantalizing odor, and adjusted its course appropriately. When it reached the far side of the canyon, its hopes were rewarded: a freshly killed deer inadequately hidden by a mountain lion was located conveniently near the edge of a mesa.

Two hours later, the now bloated scavenger hopped awkwardly to the mesa's edge and launched itself into the air. Soon it was rising effortlessly on a new thermal, keeping its wings canted ever so slightly to one side so that it corkscrewed ever higher into the sky.

But as the bird rose, the sun sank. Soon the shadow of the canyon's rim began to cross the spires and plateaus below, and the upward rise of the thermal began to fail. Time to head back across the canyon, back to the limestone alcove in the canyon's wall where it made its nest.

Reaching the North Rim, the great bird lowered its right wing, and pivoted to the east. As it did, it noted that the small figure next to the camper was still pacing back and forth, back and forth as the shadows lengthened around him far below.

* * *

7

Me Client, You Server

FRANK WAS ONLY a couple hundred yards from his camper, but already he was gasping for breath. He wanted to blame the 8,500 foot elevation of the North Rim, but suspected he couldn't pin all of his distress on the thin air. After all, he hadn't engaged in anything more strenuous than a fast walk since high school.

He lurched to a halt and leaned forward, hands on his knees, gulping in the cold, clear air of the morning. Surely this was hopeless. What had he been thinking?

Well, that part was easy. The morning after dropping off Josette at Burning Man, he had taken stock of himself in front of the mirror in the camper. What he saw wasn't pretty. Why had he allowed himself to gain so much weight over the years? How had gravity taken such a grievous toll?

All the way across Nevada he had psyched himself up for the effort that would be required to repair the damage. He was only in his mid-forties – surely he could get back in shape. Alright, get in shape for the first time ever.

Anyway, all he'd have to do would be to start watching what he ate, lift some weights, do a little running, and stick with it till he reached his goal weight. It was just thermodynamics, after all. Burn more calories than you ingest, and the pounds must disappear. Piece of cake. Okay, bad word choice.

Before turning south in Utah to intersect the Grand Canyon, he had stopped to shop in the town of St. George. He bought a scale. New sneakers. A sweat suit with "Brigham Young" emblazoned across the chest. A set of weights. He had already spent hours on dieting websites, studying the mysteries of the weight loss game. Armed with his new knowledge, he crisscrossed the aisles of a supermarket for an hour, piling a shopping cart high with all of the food he figured he'd have to eat in order to lose weight. Nothing could stop him now.

Except, he gasped, that he might die trying. Maybe he'd have to build up to the running part a little bit at a time. Straightening up, he set off at a moderately brisk walk, chest still heaving.

A half hour later, he arrived back at his camper, tired, winded and hungry. He opened the refrigerator and stared at the plate of food he had prepared before setting out: four ounces of boiled chicken and six ounces of blanched broccoli. What joy.

He carried the plate outside, paused, and then reentered the camper. But after a second try on the scale, he still weighed exactly what he had before his "run." It began to dawn on him that it was possible the weight loss process might take some time.

He crunched his broccoli despondently and tried to remember where he had left off the night before. Okay. He'd decided to assume the bad guys hadn't tampered with the computer or the software before they were delivered to the pollsters, since many of their systems were evidently quite old. Next, he had taken it as a given that the pollsters would be no more security conscious than most small – to medium-size businesses – which was to say barely conscious at all. So it should be safe to assume that the bad guys could have slipped some malware into the systems of every major pollster without exception. But assumptions were one thing; before he could take this one as a given, he needed to know how hard it would be to hack the systems the pollsters were actually using.

He retrieved his satellite phone. A minute later he was connected to his detailer back at Marvin Gardens.

"Vickie, have they finished running the scan yet on the pollsters' systems?"

"Sure. Do you want the detailed reports?"

"Yes, but at the moment all I need is just the bottom line. Did any of them stand up?"

"Not even close. Surprised?"

"No, but one more question – did they use a Red Team, or just a commercial outfit to attack them?"

"Straight out of the phonebook."

Okay, that was useful to know. Running a scan meant that someone who knew what they were doing had tried to get past the firewalls of the pollsters' systems, the same way that a hacker would. A Red Team referred to one of the crack forensic squads of the National Security Agency. There was nobody better than an NSA Red Team, or at least so the government hoped. Since Marvin had achieved success using a commercial firm, Frank could safely assume that any self-respecting hacker would succeed as well.

All well and good. But if the hacker had gotten in, why hadn't Marvin been able to find the malware?

"So tell me about the server logs. Were they able to find the attack that got through?"

"Yes and no. As you'd expect, we did find some successful entries, but they were all pretty predictable, random 'bot attacks – nothing targeted at the polling data."

"'Bots" – short for robots – were networks of co-opted personal computers that hackers had already taken over. Office computers, home computers – any kind of computer – that a hacker had been able to access. Once inside, the hacker would install a program that allowed the owner to continue using her system the same as always, unaware that someone else was using it as well; at most, the computer might seem to run a bit more slowly than before. The malware would also integrate that computer into a network of thousands of other 'bots, all working together like a super computer to do the bidding of the Black Hat that had recruited them. Like submitting every conceivable password in a matter of seconds to get inside the firewall of a bank, a credit card processor – or even a pollster.

"Any evidence of spear phishing success?"

"Not that we've been able to tell."

"Okay, thanks. Appreciate it."

He went back to the edge of the canyon and stared out, arms folded. Spear phishing meant masquerading as someone an email recipient thought she could trust, like a coworker. A spear phishing email would contain a link to a website, or would include an attachment that the recipient was asked to open. In either case, the single click the recipient used to open the link or the attachment was all it would take to download the malware to her system. Now not only her computer, but her employer's entire system would be vulnerable. To be sure the hacker would continue to have access, the first thing the malware would do would be to create a "back door" that the hacker could later open at his leisure. When he did, he could prowl throughout the infiltrated network to his heart's content, wreaking whatever mischief he had in mind.

So where did that take him?

Since the server logs hadn't revealed any unusual attacks, that should mean spear phishing was still the most likely explanation for the multiple compromises, even if the scanning team hadn't been able to find a phony email. It wouldn't surprise him if at least one employee at each pollster fell for the gambit. Some of the best cybersecurity firms had been publicly humiliated when their own employees fell for such a stunt.

There was just one problem with that theory. Frank had duplicated Marvin's test with a pollster clone and a clean system. Just as the report predicted, Frank's test also yielded corrupted data from both systems. So much for the Moby Dick hypothesis – he hadn't opened any email on the new machine yet, so there was no opportunity for a spear phishing attack to succeed. Still, the bad guys had obviously gotten in somehow. He'd just have to keep running tests and hope to notice something the professional spooks had missed.

He turned on his laptop and logged back on to his pollster system clone. He opened up the polling program, picked a question template used for assessing the popularity of multiple individuals, and filled in the names of the current candidates. Then he input an arbitrary number of positive responses for each one, deciding that today would finally be Hollis Davenport's chance to lead the pack.

But when he called up a report, sure enough, it was Julian Johnson that came out on top instead. He had exactly the number of thumbs up Frank had assigned to Davenport, and Davenport had been given the favorable ratings Frank had awarded to Johnson.

He drummed his fingers on the arm of his folding chair and mused. There must be some kind of latent feature that had been lurking in the system or program all along, just waiting to be triggered. That would do it, right?

He called Victoria back.

"Vickie, did anyone try to figure out whether there was some sort of time bomb in the polling software? There doesn't seem to be any other possible explanation for what I'm seeing here."

"Of course."

"Well?"

"No time bomb. What do you think we are, stupid?"

In fact, he was still reserving judgment on that question. But his inability to get anywhere so far was making him feel more charitably inclined.

"Of course not. Just frustrated. Thanks."

Now what? Maybe if he added some new data and checked the server logs again he'd notice something.

But after five minutes of inputting random polling data, his server froze. Grumbling, he set it to reboot. Two minutes later he was still waiting, so he called up his laptop copy of the polling software and started entering information; he could always transfer the data back when the server came back online.

When he finished, the server was still cycling. And cycling. Annoyed, he ran a local report on his laptop, expecting to find that once again Johnson had tucked it to Davenport. But to his delight, he found that this time Davenport had held on to his lead.

At last he was getting somewhere.

* * *

8

That's Debatable

FRANK WAS SITTING inside his camper, a bowl of diet popcorn at one elbow and a small barbell at the other. The popcorn elbow was getting most of the exercise. On the opposite side of the camper hung a large flat screen TV, and on that set the latest, pre-primary season Republican debate was about to begin.

Like many Americans, he was curious to see how Randall Wellhead, the latest entrant to the Republican field, would fare in his first performance under the scrutiny of the public and the national media. Just like the earlier candidates, he had rocketed to the top of the polls almost immediately after announcing his candidacy.

The candidates were now walking on camera, taking their places at the semicircle of podiums arrayed across the stage. The crowd gave a rousing welcome, and Frank turned up the sound to better hear the pre-debate commentary.

Well, Chet, look at that – Randall Wellhead's heading straight for one of the two positions at center stage!

That's right, David. Courtesy of his sudden status as a top contender. You know, Texas is certainly being unusually generous with her native sons this year. Wellhead's not just another politico from the Lone Star State. He's the son and grandson of genuine Texas wildcatters. He's also senior minister of his own evangelical mega church, and a popular all-talk AM radio show host, to boot.

But he's not all tradition, Chet. Don't forget that a few years ago he confessed from the pulpit that he 'used to be' gay – said that one day he had, let's see, I've got his exact words in my notes here – yes – 'one day, I decided to give up the homosexual lifestyle. And with the help of the Lord, I put my secret sins behind me.' Ever since he's been preaching about how every homosexual can share in the same joys that heterosexuality has brought into his life.

Right, David. He wasn't in the political spotlight back then, though. Now that he's in the race, reporters are scrambling to learn whatever they can about his past. According to some of his high school girlfriends he put up a pretty good act for a closet gay.

Ha ha! Well, for those viewers that can't read those small signs on the podiums, that's Hollis Davenport standing to Wellhead's right – governor of a swing state and making his second run for the nomination. And what a resume he's got – Yale graduate, one prominent position after another in the private sector and now governor. Seems like everyone should agree he's one of the most capable contenders on the stage.

You'd think so, David, but the voters don't seem to agree – Davenport's always number two in the polls. He's always at least five points behind whoever's in the lead.

Right, Chet, but they never stay there long. Up until a week ago, the guy on the other side of Wellhead was the latest Great Right Hope – Julian Johnson, Governor of Texas. His turn at the top lasted maybe five days. I expect he'll be a lot more careful during this week's debate.

Well, if he isn't, at least he'll have company – Roxy's up there, too.

For our listeners benefit, Chet, let me note that you're referring to Senator Roxanne Rollins! How about a little respect for the Senate!

Well, David, she is also the former State of Wisconsin Dairy Queen.

And she wouldn't be Senator Rollins if she wasn't filling out the rest of her ex-husband's term.

Okay, I'll give you that. His tenure in office - and their marriage – didn't survive the headlines when he was caught in the act with the current Dairy Queen.

He must really love that Wisconsin cheese! Huh? Am I right?

The commentators were still having a good laugh over that one when Frank muted the sound. He'd been paying attention to the primaries lately and didn't need their snarky commentary to catch up. He guessed that next to Davenport must be Roland Overby, an unabashed Libertarian who was constant in his convictions and unimpeachable in his public and private life. Frank had to hand it to the guy – he'd dedicated his career to serving as a passionately independent voice in the partisan gutter of the House of Representatives.

He didn't have much to show for it, though – not a single piece of adopted legislation with his name on it. You almost felt sorry for him now - an elderly, scarecrow of a man with a shock of unruly white hair and a bleating voice. But he was still going strong, and still willing to speak truths that others were afraid to acknowledge. Too bad he also said things that no one with a robust relationship with reality said, either.

Anyway, he had a loyal following that didn't seem to mind it when he said the government should close the regulatory agencies, disband Congress, shut down the courts, and let Wall Street run the country. His ranking in the polls was rising, too.

Frank recognized Julian Johnson on Wellhead's left. And consigned to the boondocks at the ends of the stage Frank could just see Roxanne Rollins, Landa Goshen and Vance Cabot. Goshen was a City Councilwoman from Enid, Oklahoma. In an unfortunate display of bad timing, she had announced her candidacy just before the foreign policy debate. The problem was that a major part of her platform was based on having no foreign policy. She advocated killing three birds with one stone – or, more accurately, with approximately 432 billion large, quarried stones – which she would use to build a thirty foot wall surrounding the entire nation. All at the same time, she'd stop illegal immigrants and foreign invaders while calling the bluff of the climate fanatics on the left. All that nonsense about warming causing the sea level to rise! Once she had her seawall up, they could just shut up and stay that way. She continued to have a fanatical, but diminished following.

That left only Senator Vance Cabot, an elder statesman if ever there was one. He'd held and served honorably in almost every high level post a public servant on the national stage could hold – member of the House of Representatives, a senator and a cabinet member, not to mention serving on several important blue ribbon investigative commissions. As Chairman of the Senate Foreign Relations Committee, he was as highly regarded abroad as he was at home – a rare occurrence in recent years. A graduate of both Harvard College and Harvard Law School, he had argued several cases before the Supreme Court. Naturally, no one on the far right paid any attention to him.

The camera suddenly zoomed in on the logo that adorned each podium, and Frank saw that the debate was sponsored by conservative cable TV channel POX News, "The Network that tells you what you want to hear." He recalled that PN's parent company also owned KPOX, the radio station that hosted Randall Wellhead's talk show.

Sitting at a desk in the front of the stage was Russ Blovia, the debate moderator and host of one of POX News' most popular political commentary programs. The theme he had chosen for the debate was, "Is there Anything – Anything at all – that the Democrats Can do Right?" The crowd gave him a warm welcome as he walked across the stage, waving, to take his seat.

When the applause died down, Blovia welcomed the audience and introduced the candidates. Then he turned to the candidates to announce the rules of engagement for the evening.

"During our exchange of views tonight, I will enforce, and you will obey, the usual rules for a televised debate...." He squinted at the teleprompter and stopped to pick up a paper copy of his script. Then he laughed.

"Yes, that's what it actually says here! Well, why don't I go off script for a minute and get real.

"Tonight, I will ask each of you to stay strictly within the time limits, which are three minutes for answers to my questions, and one minute for rebuttals to the statements of other candidates, assuming you haven't already butted in. When you ignore the time limits, I will interrupt you politely, and you will ignore my existence."

"Interrupting the other candidates is forbidden, and when you do so anyway, I will jump in, and you will tell me, in so many words, to stuff it. Do I have that right?"

The candidates smiled and nodded in agreement.

"Good," Blovia smiled back. "So let's get started."

"Mr. Wellhead, you've made some pretty negative remarks about Democrats in the past. For example, just last Monday in Milwaukee you said that saying the typical Democrat is as dumb as a box of rocks would be insulting to the average box of rocks. Do you have any concerns that comments like that may make it difficult for you to win the election?"

Wellhead flashed his famously white teeth in a dazzling smile. "Not unless we let rocks vote!"

"Very good, Sir. Very good indeed! Just seeing if you were on your toes tonight, and clearly you are. Now what do you think the worst thing is that this Democrat President has done since he's been in office?"

"Wow – where do I begin? Well, let's see, how about I say when he sent our troops into Iraq?"

The crowd fell silent. After a moment, the moderator cleared his throat. "Ah! I get it. Now you're seeing if I'm on my toes! Good one! Of course, we all know that the President's predecessor, a Republican, took that action."

Wellhead looked at him blankly for a moment, and then panned the audience with his million dollar smile again as they laughed and clapped.

"Let's move on to another candidate. Mr. Davenport, when did you quit considering a Democrat as a running mate?"

Davenport scowled, and then forced a smile. "Ah, good one again, Russ. You almost caught me there."

"I'm not joking, Hollis. When did you?"

"I've never considered a Democrat as a running mate, Russ, and you know it."

Blovia gave a knowing smile and a big Vaudeville wink to the audience. "Of course not, of course not! Now Mr. Overby, a question for you." Overby smiled and blinked rapidly, his suit coat hunched up on his thin shoulders.

"What do you think of Democrat plans to tax the top 1% of Americans to bring down the deficit?"

"Oh my goodness, Russ, what a terrible idea! We should repeal all taxes! Why, if we just let businesses run things, everything would be fine! Just fine! The best way to let a free market economy be successful is just to leave it alone!"

Blovia nodded. "How about you, Governor Johnson? What do you say?"

"Well, I absolutely agree that the last thing we should do is tax the rich. Why, they're the engines of our economy! If we were to raise taxes, they might just decide to move out of this country entirely. Then what would we do? Who would buy the luxury cars Detroit doesn't make any more? And what about all those McMansions? If all those estates got dumped on the market at the same time, why, we'd have another real estate crash! No, I think the only smart thing to do is to cut taxes for the rich. Let's have a flat tax for everybody. It's incredible the Democrats can't see that."

"Does anyone disagree?" Blovia asked the candidates at large.

Most nodded "no;" only Cabot shook his head in the affirmative.

"Well, it's unanimous, then. We'll return to other policies the Democrats have all wrong after this commercial break." The screen flashed over to an ad for Bentley Motor Cars.

Frank shook his head in disbelief and got up to grab a beer and his laptop. How could it be that so many conservative candidates would think the best way to get elected was to defend the wealthiest 1% of the nation when unemployment and underemployment were over 15%, and the nation was running a half-trillion dollar annual deficit? And weren't Republican voters able to do elementary math problems? A flat tax would drop taxes for the rich while raising them for everybody else. It defied all logic.

He scanned his email, and perked up. He had just gotten his first email from Josette! He opened it.

>*Hi Frank! All is well here. Do you watch the debate?*

Not exactly what he had hoped for.

Yes, but I'm wondering why – they're all crazy.

She replied immediately.

>*I think so, too. But surely all the voters are not crazy?*
You have to wonder, given the polls.
> *I do wonder. The only two candidates that make sense are Davenport and Cabot. But no one pays attention to Cabot. And it seems that anyone new is always right away more popular than Davenport.*

Frank looked at his laptop. He wasn't sure where to go with this conversation, knowing what he did. Time to change the subject.

How was the Festival?
>*It was so wonderful! You would have loved it. I have taken many pictures. Perhaps I can show them to you some time?*
I'd like that. Where will you go now?
>*I will ride back east with my friends. When they return to France, I will stay here to study.*

As usual, she had taken him by surprise; he didn't recall her ever suggesting before that she might stay in the U.S. over the winter.

To study?
>*Yes. Last spring I applied for a fellowship at the Johns Hopkins Foreign Policy Institute, and they have told me that I am accepted! For the fall and spring, I will be studying your election and what happens afterwards. I must find somewhere to live now in Washington.*

He leaned back and stared at his laptop. Had he ever felt anything other than off-balance when conversing with Josette? Then he had another thought and phrased his next question carefully.

> *Just you? All of your friends will be returning to France?*
> >*Yes, just me. Oh – the debate is beginning again. Au revoir!*

He closed his laptop slowly and turned back to the TV screen. But he found it hard to concentrate.

* * *

9

Come into My Parlor, Please Do

LEN BUTCHER WAS sweating heavily. The cards had been with him at the blackjack table for most of the evening, but then his luck ran out. Across the table, a wiry rancher with thinning hair and weathered skin was making no effort to conceal his satisfaction that their roles were now reversed. Behind them, the cigarette smoke of elderly patrons rose from the maze of slot machines that provided the main attraction of the small casino.

Butcher never gambled in big cities anymore. But what the hell; every gambling floor was the same, and the stakes were lower here. He couldn't get hurt as badly when the cards ran against him, which seemed to be most of the time these days. Most importantly, nobody would recognize him in an out of the way, jerkwater casino like this, miles from anywhere anyone he knew would ever want to visit. If anyone back in Washington found out he was a hard-core gambler, he'd be out of a job.

He knew he'd been lucky to get his security clearance to begin with. But background checks had been perfunctory when his agency, and scores more like it, were created during the blowback from 9/11. After all, terrorists could be anywhere, so there was no time to lose; recruiters were scrambling for people with data mining and computer forensic skills, and there weren't a lot of people with that kind of training back then. And anyway, the people they were hiring wouldn't be doing field work; they'd be invisible, sitting behind computers in offices that didn't exist. There shouldn't be many opportunities for them to be turned or compromised.

Nor were these new agencies supervised in the traditional way. The hierarchy of their internal divisions had been established using a "cabinet" metaphor. Each department was analogous to a locked drawer, and no communication was allowed between any of those drawers. Each agency in turn was like a drawer in yet another, larger cabinet, and so on up to the top, each unit sealed off from the others.

It was all rather comical, really. First the administration created the Department of Homeland Security to unify the already vast and chaotic security apparatus that had evolved over the decades. That was supposed to prevent the data sharing failures that had made 9/11 possible from happening again. But that explanation was just for public consumption. Behind the scenes, the compartmentalization process was fractally repeating itself, guaranteeing that any progress made through common access to data would be cancelled out by ensuring that sharing analysis of the same data would be impossible.

To be sure, an enemy agent could never succeed in penetrating very far into this system through traditional means. But neither could any Cabinet officer, General or Admiral that was nominally in charge of any cabinet, let alone the whole, shadowy system.

All of which meant that no one was doing a very good job of keeping an eye on someone like Len Butcher, which suited him just fine.

The dealer was sweeping the last of his chips away as the rancher rubbed it in. "What's the problem, cowboy? Somebody rustle your herd?"

The other gamblers, all friends, laughed and waited to see how the tenderfoot would react. Butcher was about to say something he probably would have regretted, when someone appeared at his side.

It was a good-looking Native American in his mid-thirties, wearing jeans, hand-tooled boots, and a dark shirt with mother of pearl snaps. The laughter stopped immediately.

"I'll spot him $500," he said to the dealer. "That is, if you wish to play again, my friend."

Butcher paused. This wasn't how he wanted to get back on his feet, but he couldn't afford to let so much money go.

"Sure," he said, "I could play a few more hands."

The young man turned to the rancher. "How about you Bart – you in?"

"Yeah, Ohanzee, I'm in," he said, his expression turning sour. He glanced down at the large pile of chips in front of him with regret.

"Very good. Just the two of you then." He gave the dealer a look and a nod, and the dealer dropped a fresh deck of cards in the shoe before dealing the first hand. Butcher tilted up the edge of his face down card: an ace! And he had a ten showing.

"I'll stand."

Within a few minutes, the rancher's pile of chips was greatly reduced. He knew what was going on, but he was trapped, because the others at the table knew, too, and were enjoying the show. He'd never live it down if he turned tail now.

Butcher would have loved to wipe the rancher out, but when their piles of chips were about even, the young man put a hand on his shoulder.

"It looks like your luck has returned, my friend. Come to my office for a drink, and you can tell me your secret." He reached forward and slid a dozen of Butcher's chips over to the dealer.

Butcher followed him though the forest of slot machines, ignoring the retirees fixated on the spinning wheels that were gradually emptying their cups of tokens. At the other side of the floor, they passed through an inconspicuous door next to the bar, up a few stairs, and into a dimly lit room, empty except for an uncluttered desk, a leather couch, and a small but amply stocked wet bar in the corner. An expanse of tinted glass filled most of the wall they had entered through, providing a panoramic view of the casino floor. Viewed from the other side, it was the mirror above the bar.

"So, my friend. It is good to see you. How long has it been? Three weeks? Four?"

Butcher expected that Ohanzee White Crow, the manager of the Casino, knew exactly how long it had been. There wasn't much that escaped his attention. In any event, he hadn't played the tables anywhere but here since he'd begun making bi-weekly visits to his agency's new satellite office in San Francisco.

"Too long, Ohanzee. And too bad our election game is all over. Somebody at another agency, maybe the FBI, must have figured out what was going on. But hey, what a ride while it lasted, right? You must've made a bundle betting on the polls by now! Must be one of the best hustles you've ever pulled off, I'll bet."

White Crow wasn't about to share that information. As it happened, his guest had a drinking problem as well as gambling issues, not to mention a tendency to become arrogant and talkative when he was on a bender. It had been easy for the casino manager to learn more about him than Butcher should ever have shared.

"Your usual, my friend?"

"Ah, sure. Why not."

Butcher was watching him carefully for any hint of what his host might have in mind with his invitation. He'd been a fool not to be more careful in the past, worrying only about who might recognize him when he was gambling. The problem he hadn't considered was that he stood out like a snowman in a cactus patch when he showed up alone at the remote tribal casino at a time of year when tourists shouldn't be around. White Crow could smell a mark while he was still in the parking lot. It hadn't taken many drinks before Butcher let it be known that he was some kind of big shot back in Washington. And it hadn't taken many more before he was deeper in the hole at the tables than he could afford to be.

Too late, Butcher realized that White Crow had played him perfectly, extending him credit and making him feel like the kind of high-roller a casino treats like royalty, all the while discretely extracting more details on who he worked for and what he did. White Crow even presented him with a Sioux name – Teetonkah. But he didn't tell Butcher it meant "talks too much."

Butcher stared at White Crow's back as he poured his drink. He should never have taken White Crow's offer to let him run up his account, damn it. It always seemed that his evenings started well, but ended terribly. White Crow was always there to raise his credit a bit more, and what harm could a little more do?

Not much, it had seemed, until White Crow announced it was time for Butcher to pay up. By then, he was in the hole for more than $200,000, and with the housing crash, he owed more on his mortgage than his house was worth. With two kids getting close to college age, what the hell was he going to do?

White Crow was all too ready with the answer. Months before, Butcher had bragged that he could predict what the next presidential polls would show. When White Crow seemed indifferent, Butcher was annoyed, and bet him $100 he could prove it. The casino manager was happy to take the bet, and paid it gracefully when Butcher's prediction came true. By the end of a long night of drinks on the house, Butcher had once again told his host more than he should have.

The choice White Crow gave Butcher was simple: pay up, or feed secret data to him about the polling investigation. Given Butcher's financial situation, it wasn't really a choice at all.

For a while, he tried not to be too concerned. Surely the pollster hack would be discovered quickly, and he could report to White Crow that the game was over. But instead, he found himself sweating his way through the pre-primary season, supporting White Crow's bets with an ongoing flow of predictions based on the patterns Butchers' staff detected as one candidate after another entered the race and the polls continued to swing wildly. Butcher had no idea how heavily or openly White Crow might be betting. What if those who were looking for the hacker noticed, and busted him as well? He had no doubt that White Crow would turn him over in a heartbeat to protect himself.

By the time fall arrived, Butcher was desperate. That's when he thought to enlist Frank to figure out the hack. And now, thank God, the nightmare was about to end.

"Your drink, my friend."

Butcher accepted the glass with a confident smile. "I must have quite a credit with you by now. But, you know, I've decided to take a vacation from gambling for a while – quit while I'm ahead for once. Spend more time with the wife and kids – gambling kind of sits on your conscience after a while, you know? Anyway, I was pretty deep in the hole at one point and you let me run, so why don't we just call it even? Clear out my account and we'll just shake hands and call it quits."

White Crow gave a pleasant smile. "You have indeed done very well, my friend, and yes, it has been a good run."

Butcher raised his glass. "Great! Well, here's to the next president of the United States then!" He laughed, a wave of relief washing over him. "Say, don't you want to join me in a drink?"

"No my friend, you know I do not drink."

But Butcher was feeling a bit giddy. He walked over to the wet bar and spoke over one shoulder.

"Ah, c'mon. Make an exception just this once. Here – let me pour you a stiff one – it'll help you loosen up for a change."

When he turned around with the new drink, White Crow was no longer smiling. Butcher shrugged.

"Suit yourself," he said, and poured the rejected drink into his own glass.

"'Let me pour you a stiff one,'" White Crow repeated. "Where have I heard that before? It sounds so familiar. Tell me, Mr. Butcher, in all these times that you have gambled at Native American casinos, have you ever taken the time to drive around one?"

Butcher swirled the ice around in his drink. "Drive around one? Well, I don't know." He took an appreciative sip from the glass. "I mean, there's not usually a whole lot to see, is there? All of the little houses tend to look the same – I guess the government gives these pre-fab houses to you, right?"

"Is that all you've seen?"

"Oh, I dunno. I guess a school – store – couple gas stations. I mean, that's pretty much it, isn't it? It's mostly wide open country with some cows on it, right?"

"Actually, they're referred to as 'cattle.' You're correct, though, in observing that there isn't much to see on a reservation. No water, for example. And certainly no natural resources – your people kept all the land with value, didn't they? No jobs, for sure. Or hospitals. You didn't see a movie theatre, did you? Or a factory? Why do you suppose that is?"

Butcher had never thought about it, and didn't like the way the conversation had turned. "I guess maybe there just aren't a lot of people living on reservations, and they're all kind of spread out. Just like the old days, I guess."

"Ah, but you're wrong about that, Mr. Butcher. In the old days, we had much more land – much better land – land that gave us everything we needed. Before the white man came, we were self-sufficient. Healthy, too, and strong. Now we are weak, and we are sick. Today the average Indian only lives to his mid-40s. Did you know that, Mr. Butcher?"

Butcher began to tense up. "Gee, I'm sorry, I didn't know that. I know your people got a really raw deal a long time ago – everybody knows that. But it's better now, right? I mean, Washington gives you money, and you've got your own local government and, I guess, police and everything? I learned that, for sure, first time I came out here! Don't speed through the 'ole Rez in a car with out of state plates!" Butcher forced a laugh and raised his glass in a mock toast.

"As a matter of fact, no, it's not better now. In fact, it may be worse. Our unemployment is over 40%. The cattle are mostly owned by Anglo ranchers. The alfalfa you see is grown by them, too, on land they rent from us for a pittance, because what else can we do with it? The banks won't lend us money to buy equipment to farm it ourselves, or to buy cattle. Very many of our people have diabetes. More abuse alcohol. Do you recall where the alcohol originally came from, Mr. Butcher?

"Well, I guess your people must have made some, didn't they?"

"No, Mr. Butcher, we didn't. When an Indian came to town, it was great fun to get him drunk – watch him stagger, maybe even fall down. And it was very profitable to take all he owned in exchange for alcohol, once he became an alcoholic. You see, Mr. Butcher, Indians had never come in contact with alcohol before, and they become addicted to it far more easily than your people do. When you have no job, no money, no horse, no pride and no future, it is very tempting to drink."

White Crow stood up and walked to the wall of glass facing the casino floor. His arms folded and his back to Butcher, he said quietly, "Did I ever tell you that my father died an alcoholic, Mr. Butcher?"

Butcher said nothing, and the casino manager turned around. "No? He was 43, and I was just 14. The booze got my uncle Peter, too. Also my cousin Yiskah. He was only 33.

"Perhaps you have noticed that we do not sell alcohol anywhere on the reservation except here at the casino. But your people do, Mr. Butcher, just yards over the border between our land and yours. There isn't an Anglo town within 25 miles, but there is a liquor store right there by the side of the road. It is open

18 hours a day. Surely you have noticed it. No? Will you have another drink, Mr. Butcher?"

Butcher put his glass down carefully, wondering how he was going to salvage the situation. He tried to think clearly, and then spoke slowly.

"I'm sorry. It's obvious I've really touched a nerve here. But you've done well for yourself, and I thought you had left all that stuff behind you."

When he heard the words "all that stuff" leave his lips, he realized he'd stepped in it again. He continued more quickly, "But anyway, I know that the things white people have done to your people were shameful and terrible, and I guess I never knew that things were still so bad; I grew up back east, you know. I don't know what I can do, but if it helps to say I'm sorry, well, I really and truly am sorry."

He paused, and then continued. "Anyway, I'm glad that I helped you make a lot of money, so let's just clear out my account now, and I'll let you get back to running your business."

Butcher stopped and tried to look confident.

White Crow gave a wide smile this time. "Ah yes! Your account! Unfortunately, I'm afraid that we are not quite even yet. There were expenses, you see. Middle men – many, many Lakota middle men – brothers, cousins, nephews, second cousins – so many good people on this reservation and others placing small bets so that they would not stand out. Each must have their fair share, don't you agree?"

Butcher's face flushed. He wasn't used to being jerked around, and he wasn't going to take it from some tin pot casino manager, even if he was in hock to him.

"Don't try and pull that crap on me, Ohanzee! I know damn well you must have made a pile on this scam. We had a deal, and I'm not going to stand for you reneging on it. How stupid do you think I am?"

"How stupid, my friend? You mean, when I saw you drinking too much and losing in my casino over and over again – did I think you were as stupid as some drunken Indian?"

White Crow was speaking swiftly now, leaning forward until he was only inches from Butcher's face. "Stupid enough to sign a treaty with the white man, and then another treaty when the white man reneges on the first one, and then yet another one, each time leaving him with less and less land, until the stupid Indian has nothing left but a God-forsaken desert? Do you think the Indian was that stupid? Or did it ever occur to you that he had no choice?"

Butcher's mind was reeling, losing ground to the effects of the alcohol, the hour and White Crow's unexpected attack. It was a struggle to maintain his self-control. "I've said I'm sorry about that, but that's history. I had nothing to do with it. I've kept my word, now you keep yours!"

"Very well, then," White Crow said. "We'll do this the White Man's way."

He walked over to his desk and rapped twice. Immediately, a door in the rear of the room opened, and two burly men walked in. Butcher recognized two of the Native American bouncers that normally roamed the floor of the casino.

"Let me give you one final history lesson, Mr. Butcher. What I have learned as a Native American is that the only man who must keep his word is the one who has another man's foot on his throat. At the moment, Mr. Butcher, my foot is on yours."

White Crow was wearing his thin smile again. "Hopefully you have enjoyed our hospitality when you have stayed with us. I especially hope that you have found the up-to-date Internet and telephone services we provide to your liking. As the manager of this establishment, I personally monitor their performance. Quite closely, in fact, for special guests like yourself.

"Once again, it seems, you have not been very careful. I, on the other hand, have been quite diligent and thorough. For example, I know who you report to. And I also know how to reach him."

Butcher jerked backward, as if he had been slapped.

"So listen to me carefully. I will let you know when I am willing to raise my foot. Until then, you will do as I say. Now get out of my casino and await instructions."

Butcher started to speak, but the two bouncers were walking towards him. Instead, he backed up slowly towards the door that led to the bar, and was grateful when he reached it. As he was opening the door to complete his retreat, White Crow spoke one last time.

"A final word of advice, my friend. Don't make any travel plans until after November. You can expect to have a very busy election season."

*   *   *

10

The Doctor will Diagnose you Now

F RANK WAS PUFFING his way up the dirt road leading away from the canyon rim, focusing on his breathing. He'd managed to lose four pounds in the first week of his new regime, and another five pounds since then. He'd also progressed from walking fast to alternating walking with bursts of labored jogging. His new, more realistic goal was to reach the point where his jogging interludes were longer than his walking ones.

To his dismay, he'd been less successful on the technical front. Despite the revelation that whatever had been interfering with data on his server hadn't affected the same information on his laptop, he was still struggling to figure out why. Worse, when he tried the same exercise a second time, the data on his laptop did flip.

But what had changed? Had he done something different the first time without realizing it, or was there a vital clue he was missing?

Eventually, the answer came to him, or the first half of it, anyway: because his server had been restarting while he tried the test on his laptop the first time, the programs were disconnected from the Internet.

In the parlance of the trade, his laptop and software were temporarily "air gapped," and therefore immune from external tampering. That could explain why the data flipped when he ran the report the second time – by then, his server, his Wi-Fi and his Internet connection were all back in action, allowing whatever mischief the hackers had put into motion to travel from the host copy of the polling software to his laptop. Or perhaps the mischief had somehow been triggered via the Internet from afar.

But if that was true, he should be able to detect evidence that changes had been made to the program copy on his laptop between the first and the second test.

But no. He'd tried the same experiment on a brand new laptop he had with him, loading the polling software from an installation disk and running it thoroughly through its paces with poll after poll, all the while with his Wi-Fi card turned off. Sure enough, Davenport kicked Johnson's butt every time. But with the Wi-Fi back on, Davenport always went down to defeat. And yet Frank still could not detect the slightest change in his laptop software.

He mused on that quandary for several cycles of walking and jogging. How would he change something without changing it? He made himself break into a trot again. That wasn't quite the right question, was it? He should have asked how he would change something without the change being detectable.

That might be the right question, but it didn't seem to have an answer. Gasping for breath, he slowed once again to a walk.

He was still puzzling over that quandary as he showered and changed. And also while he stared across the canyon, eating the banana and cup of dismally uninspiring bran flakes that had become his daily breakfast.

What was left? Hadn't he already considered every conceivable possibility?

Maybe writing down all of the possible answers on a piece of paper for a change would help. He went into the camper for a notepad, and then started writing the possibilities down:

1. I just missed something.

2. Whatever is happening is happening somewhere else on the system.

He stared at the pad and couldn't think of another alternative – a dead end already. Then an old saying occurred to him: after you've eliminated all of the possible answers, all that's left are the impossible ones. At a loss for something more promising, he wrote:

3. It's quantum mechanics in action – it wasn't Johnson or Davenport that "won," it was Schrödinger's cat. Until I ran the report, neither and both had won.

Cute, but probably not too helpful. He didn't know enough about quantum mechanics to go anywhere with it anyway. So number three was out. He'd already done as much as he could on number 1, so if that statement was accurate, he didn't know what to do next. That left the possibility that he just hadn't been looking in the right place. But where else was there to look?

He began pacing.

Where to begin? Well, for starters he knew that the Marvinites had checked their own system and the pollsters', too, and had been unable to detect any changes. But maybe they had been looking in the wrong places as well, or the changes had been so subtle that they hadn't been able to detect them.

Maybe an analogy might help him see something. We already talk about viruses, and the analogy between biological and computer system infections really is very close. So maybe if he took the medical analogy further, that might lead somewhere. He liked that, and began walking faster.

If he thought of this as a disease, how would he go about diagnosing it? He'd look for symptoms. And he'd run a lot of tests.

He sat down in his chair again and picked up his pad of paper. So what were the symptoms?

All he could think of was the fact that the polling data was flipping. Was he still missing something? How about tests? Were there any he hadn't thought of yet?

No. He couldn't think of any. He'd run the server logs, and looked for anyone who had come and gone. He'd scanned everything there was to scan with every scanning tool he had. He'd run the object code of the polling software through an analyzer before and after the scans and the code looked the same. He'd even run tests that it made no sense to run at all. And finally, he was willing to swear on a stack of bibles that there wasn't a back door anywhere in his system.

So if he had already checked the pulse, temperature and blood pressure of the system and found everything normal, didn't that mean the patient must be well?

Well, no. After all, a thermometer could only tell you about a patient's temperature, right? And a wristwatch, her pulse, and a pressure cuff, just her blood pressure! None of them would be any use at all in detecting a heart murmur, would it?

Maybe there was a test he hadn't thought to run because he wasn't thinking about the right disease – the equivalent, for purposes of his medical analogy, of an electrocardiogram to spot a heart condition.

The sun was beginning to set by the time he gave up on that line of attack. It had seemed promising, but he still couldn't think of any data or test he'd missed.

Could it be that the answer was staring him in the face and he just couldn't see it?

He tried to clear his mind and give it one last shot. Maybe he had tried all the right tests – even the equivalent of the electrocardiogram. And maybe he hadn't missed anything. After all, there was a way that even an electrocardiogram might not tell you anything, and that was if you were trying to catch an intermittent symptom, and you hadn't run the test at the right time. You wouldn't know the patient had a problem unless you ran the test at the precise moment it was happening, right? That's why they had patients wear a heart monitor for a whole day of ordinary activity – to be sure they captured just the right few moments of abnormal activity.

That sounded good, because so far he'd always run his tests before and after the data corruption had occurred, and not while he was inputting the data and running the reports. What an idiot! Now he'd have to start all over again.

It was getting dark, and he was getting hungry. But he was impatient. What could he check quickly?

The only thing that wouldn't require running tests all over again would be to check the server's access log for the time period when he was running one of his clean laptop tests – the ones that encountered no problems while he was offline, but then produced altered data ever after, whether or not he was online.

He called the log up and scrolled through until he found the right time period.

It was slow and tedious work parsing through the endless lines of data. Nothing seemed to be out of the ordinary. The only traffic recorded on the laptop's modem was between the server and laptop copies of the polling software.

And then he looked again. That wasn't exactly right, was it? There was another line that repeated endlessly through the log, identically, every few seconds, so endlessly and reliably that he had ignored it entirely. Almost, you might say, like a heartbeat.

Excited, he ran his finger down the margin of page after page of the report, looking for one of the repeating lines that looked just a little bit different than the others.

And then he saw it – a single line that was just a few bytes longer than all the rest – and then one more slightly longer one, just a hundred lines or so further down. A slow smile of satisfaction – and admiration – spread across his face.

* * *

11

Time Out!

"THAT'S RIGHT, VICKIE. Simple as that. So can you guys take it from here?"

"Sure thing, Frank. No problem, and great work!"

In fact, it hadn't been great work that had finally allowed him to crack the mystery of the flipping poll numbers. Just the kind of attention to detail he should have brought to bear from the start. Once he'd spotted the few extra bytes of code he knew he'd found the exploited chink in the system's armor. After that, it had been relatively easy to work out how the rest of the hack had been carried out.

Settling back in his chair, he stared out across the magnificent gulf of the Grand Canyon, and smiled wryly. Only the mega-patterns of mesa and river, shadow and light jumped out of the vast canvas spread out before him. It was difficult to appreciate, or even to truly see, the infinite variety of distant details that together comprised the overwhelming vista. Not quite a perfect metaphor for what had made the puzzle so difficult to solve, but it would do.

He should have felt relaxed, luxuriating in the early autumn sun, but he wasn't. He felt good about cracking the problem he had been tasked to solve, yes, but now what? Suddenly he was at loose ends again, with nothing to fill his time except the discredited goal of writing a book. What was he going to do about that?

As he stared out over the canyon, though, he kept returning to the mystery of who had pulled off the polling hack. He wasn't particularly curious about the intruder's motivation, and anyway, that was Marvin's responsibility to figure out. What he really wanted to know was who had crafted such a simple and minimalist strategy for achieving whatever those ends might be. It was as close to a perfect crime, in the information technology sense, as Frank ever expected to see.

What had made the hack so masterful was that the transformation of the data seemed to occur as if by magic, leaving not a clue – almost – to indicate how it had been performed. Most elegantly, the hacker had taken advantage of a port – that is, a point of entry to and from the wild world of the Internet – that every computer in existence obligingly opened over and over again every hour of every day.

The purpose of that particular gate in any firewall was to allow the computer's internal clock to sync up with one of the super-accurate Internet time servers that existed solely for that purpose. Absent the resulting nanosecond corrections that a system made, its own clock would gradually get farther and farther out of phase with the true time, resulting in all sorts of problems as the discrepancy widened.

The constant time checks also fulfilled another purpose: each time a computer connected to a remote time server, it also recorded the exact time in the stream of its own activities. These time stamps could later be used to determine what had occurred when, such as a hacking incident. The irony of using that same port and mechanism to mount an attack that had defied so much forensic analysis added to Frank's appreciation of the hacker's style.

But other aspects of the hack had earned Frank's respect as well. Since all computers used the same network protocol to manage the time check/time stamp process, the hacker had been able to use just one subtle trick to corrupt the results of every pollster, regardless of the particular system they owned. Better still, the time check operation was built into the most basic functions of the computer's operating system, and not the polling software at all – in other words, somewhere an investigator would never think to look.

It hadn't taken Frank long to conclude that once the hacker succeeded in intercepting a pollster's time check signal, he had been able to create and send back a response that the pollster system's firewall would allow to pass. After he was inside, the hacker had to make only one very minor change to the system's operating system: simply replace the Internet address the computer called on to receive a time stamp with the address of a server owned by the hacker. Now, instead of calling on one of the many official time servers, the pollster's system would call on one that the hacker controlled.

But what happened next? No one had been able to find any alteration of the polling software at all. That's where the hacker's second clever trick came in. Instead of changing the polling software to do everything the hacker wanted and leaving it that way, he had made a minute change to a single routine in the program. All that was necessary to put his plan into motion was to add a single byte of data to the time stamp request that the polling software sent out when it was asked to generate a report. That would alert the hacker's server that it was time to leap into action.

The first thing the hacker's server did was to upload a module of code to the pollster's system that would falsify the data included in the report. Once the report had been generated, the same module would uninstall itself, leaving not a trace of its existence for an investigator to discover. Brilliant.

Frank estimated it wouldn't take the hacker ten minutes to update the module each time a new candidate entered the field. Once more, he shook his head in silent admiration. Any decent programmer could come up with something complicated and easy to spot. It took a real master coder to devise such an ultra-stealthy and minimalist approach. Who could it possibly be?

His musings were interrupted by a rare sound: the ringing of his satellite phone. He debated ignoring it, but then thought better. Besides one or two Marvinites, only his daughter had that number. Better pick it up.

He regretted that decision when he heard the grating voice of Len Butcher. But the call ended better than expected.

"Hi Frank – it's Len. Just wanted to thank you on behalf of the agency for figuring out how the poll results were hacked."

"Yeah, well, it wasn't actually all that difficult, once I finally figured out the right place to look."

"That's what I told my boss, but she insisted I call you anyway."

You bastard, Frank thought. Then why didn't any of your people think of it?

"Anyway, I wanted to let you know we'd like to keep you on the payroll, at least through a good part of the primary season. That way, if it looks like the hackers are at it again you'll be available. Are you up for that?"

Of course, he thought. What's not to like about all pay and no work?

"Sure, I guess. Why not?"

"Glad to hear it. If anything comes up, we'll be in touch."

Frank replaced the phone in his camper, and went back to staring out over the canyon. The primary season would begin in just a few weeks. Would the unknown hacker rise to that challenge? And if so, would he come up with as elegant a ploy again? He'd have to wait a few weeks for the answer to that question.

He began tapping his fingers on the arm of his chair. It had been uncommonly warm for this time of year. Any day now, the temperature would surely plummet.

If he hung around at 8,500 feet much longer, he'd have to start working inside the camper – maybe he'd even get snowed in for a couple of weeks.

He was feeling restless. And he was ready to kill for a decent meal. It was time to move on.

* * *

12

Vive la Revolución!

F RANK SCRUTINIZED THE establishments on both sides of the main
drag of Cedar City, Utah with consummate attention. He'd lost nine pounds,
and it was payback time.

He'd left his campsite before sunrise, driving on dirt tracks for four hours
before reaching a paved road. Now it was almost noon, and he had waited long
enough. Impatient drivers swung around him as he rolled slowly up the street,
compiling a mental index of every restaurant, bakery, ice cream parlor and other
type of food emporium in town.

At the end of the street, he reshuffled his priorities and his order of attack while
making a U-turn. So far, the ice cream shop was hanging on to first place; his very
soul cried out to become one with the lush richness of one of their more complex
offerings. But he was intrigued by the possibility that denying himself that reward
until after dinner might amplify the intensity of the ingestive experience.

But what if his sense of taste was satiated by then? It seemed like too great a
risk to take. Perhaps he should have one cone now, and another later?

The swirling visions of ice cream, pizza, and cheeseburgers that commanded
his attention provided a welcome diversion from his latest obsession. Since early

that morning, he had been feeling like Paul Newman in the movie Butch Cassidy and the Sundance Kid, constantly wondering, *who are these guys?* Now he was trying to devise a plan to answer that question. He told himself it was because it would be fun to show up Butcher's boys one more time rather than that he was simply avoiding his book issue.

So far, he'd had no luck, in part because the hackers had withdrawn from the field. Nothing suspicious was probing his virtual system now. And the poll results he read in the news seemed like they might be tracking the reality of public opinion. So where to begin, with the trail now cold? Maybe a change of scenery would loosen up his thinking.

It was time to head back east, he decided. Not all the way, necessarily, but at least close enough to score the occasional creature comfort when the spirit moved him. That's where he would drive next. But not until after lunch.

*   *   *

An hour and a half later, a painfully bloated and remorseful Frank Adversego wheeled his camper back onto Interstate 15, heading north. He thought he might be sick at any moment, and was beginning to think it might be a good thing if he was. Thank goodness the town's main street wasn't any longer.

Maybe thinking about his destination would distract him from his abdominal distress. His first highway option to head east would be Route 70, and the interchange linking the two highways was not far ahead. Route 70 would take him into Colorado. What was in Colorado? The Rocky Mountains? No sense stopping there. Too much snow.

Where did the highway go from there? He glanced at the road atlas on the passenger seat. Hmmm. Kansas. Was there anything in Kansas besides cornfields? What other options did he have?

There was a Route 76 heading northeast from Denver. That led to Route 80 in Nebraska. More cornfields.

He was about to flip the page back to Utah to see what lay farther north when he noticed where Route 80 went after it left Nebraska – Iowa.

Immediately, he was transfixed. That was where the first real test of the primary season would be held – the Iowa caucuses! If the hackers that had attacked the pollsters' systems were still up to no good, wouldn't that be where they'd strike next? He keyed Des Moines, Iowa into his dashboard GPS and glanced at the readout. Just over 1200 miles. He could be there in a couple of days.

*   *   *

Judd Powell was sitting alone in his car, parked for privacy behind a fast food restaurant a few blocks away from the motel where the rest of the Wellhead entourage was settling in.

"Yes, I was right beside him. I'm always right beside him. But what do you want me to do? Throw a bag over his head every time it looks like he might say something stupid?"

The voice at the other end of the line was characteristically icy. "I don't care what you do. The reason I pay your unreasonable rates is so I don't have to orchestrate your every move. Your job is to keep Wellhead from getting cornered by journalists to begin with."

"How do you expect me to do that? He's a candidate, for Pete's sake! And if he doesn't end up on the evening news every night, then you're calling me out for underexposing him!"

"That's your problem, and I suggest that you solve it immediately. There are plenty of handlers that would jump at the chance to replace you."

Powell gave an involuntary shiver, but not from the cold. This guy simply gave him the creeps. Getting screamed at by high strung clients was a given in his business. But yelling was easy to ignore. You just set the phone down until the guy was done blowing off steam.

But this guy never yelled. In fact, his voice never betrayed any emotion at all. When you were in the same room with him, his eyes never quit boring into your own. Lately, Powell had begun referring to his client as "the Cobra."

He picked at the remainder of his cold fries. Oh well. To be fair, the reporter from the local network affiliate had caught Wellhead being even more asinine than usual, which was saying a great deal. Instead of letting the press lampoon the other candidates over their own ridiculous comments, Wellhead had tried to get in on the fun, with predictably disastrous results.

Powell turned his car on, and the radio picked up the evening news. He cringed as he listened to Wellhead's unmistakable, folksy drawl utter the statement that had so delighted the liberal pundits – and infuriated his boss:

> *Well, I can assure you that if I'm successful in my quest for the Oval Office, I won't just offer my opinion on whether Fidel Castro will end up in heaven or the other place. Nope, I'll just send a few secret agents down to Cuba and force the Almighty's decision on that matter...*

That was as far as Wellhead got before Powell hustled him away from the reporter's microphone. But it had been enough to guarantee him airtime on every radio and TV news show for the rest of the day. Powell braced himself for whatever commentary on his candidate's remarks would follow. But instead, he heard this:

Former Cuban dictator Fidel Castro later published an editorial in which he wrote: "The selection of a Republican candidate for the presidency of this globalized and expansive empire is – and I mean this seriously – the greatest competition of idiocy and ignorance that has ever been."

Powell couldn't help smiling as the knot in his stomach began to loosen. Maybe that crazy old bastard of a revolutionary wasn't such a lunatic after all.

* * *

A few blocks away, Randall Wellhead's most trusted advisor put down the phone in his motel room. If his plan was to bear fruit, it was clear that he'd need to surround his candidate with additional layers of defense. Luckily, those defenses didn't need to be perfect. A previous candidate from Texas had proven that you could be quoted making less than cogent statements on a consistent basis and still be elected president – not once, but twice. That was a reassuring bit of recent history.

No, all he needed was to keep Wellhead from going so far off the deep end that no one could believe it when the primaries started to turn in his favor, ultimately giving him enough delegates to sew up the nomination. Or later, when the election went his way as well.

He poured himself a scotch and settled in to watch the rest of the broadcast on POX News. Happily, Wellhead's quote of the day wasn't noticeably more off message than those of several of his rivals.

It would be an annoying challenge to keep his candidate in check until the election, but really, it didn't matter all that much. He had already made sure that Randall Wellhead would be the next president of the United States.

* * *

White Crow sat at his desk, staring thoughtfully through the one-way glass at the sparsely attended casino floor on the other side. It was mid-afternoon on a weekday, and just a few early arrivals from the casino motel were sitting at the quarter slots. The only staffer present was the bartender, and he was leaning against the bar, watching one of the big TV screens on the wall.

The news he had received from Butcher – that the means by which the pollsters were being hacked had been discovered and blocked – was disappointing, but not in the way that Butcher had supposed. In fact, White Crow hadn't been using Butcher's polling data for betting purposes at all; that story had been for Butcher's consumption alone. With all the money available to him from other sources there was no need for poll wagering. But having advance access to the pollster data –

whether manipulated or not – had been very helpful to him in planning his own political moves. Now that Butcher's agency was closing down its investigation, data would no longer be accessible.

Or would it? If Butcher's agency had learned how to block the hack to the pollsters' systems, then they must know how to unblock it as well. And also how the hacker had managed to manipulate the data to begin with. Being able to alter the public's perception of who was the candidate most likely to win would open up possibilities he'd never dreamed of before.

He called Butcher.

"Hello?" Butcher was surprised to receive a call from Ohanzee so soon after his visit. He'd been hoping he could maintain a greater distance for at least a while, now that he no longer had access to any doctored polling information.

"I have some further questions. Tell me, have you informed the pollsters that they have been hacked?"

"Ohanzee, I can't —"

"Answer my question."

Butcher rose and closed his office door before returning to his desk and his private mobile phone. "No, and we don't intend to. Nobody wants the public to know the integrity of the election has been compromised in any way. You can bet the pollsters will be happier not knowing. And anyway, we wouldn't want to take the chance one of them would let the information slip out."

"Good. So what action have you taken in response?"

Butcher squirmed. He had just told White Crow what his agency would not do, and the thought of revealing what his agency would do filled him with dread. Surely that had to raise the ante if he was ever caught.

"C'mon, Ohanzee. You know I can't tell you anything like that. Please, you've got to cut me a break this time."

Ohanzee was not surprised. He had already guessed that forcing Butcher to take this next step might require a face-to-face meeting.

"Perhaps you are right. But since we're on the phone, I'm having a poker game Saturday night with a few close business associates. I'd like you to attend and I think it will be worth your while. Don't worry about the cost. I'll stake you and will send you the plane tickets."

"Me? Why? And I thought you never gambled?"

"In the casino, no. But privately, on occasion. I find it helps me understand my customers better. We'll start at 10:00 PM. I'll see you then."

* * *

13

Knock Knock (Who's There?)

F RANK SHOOK HIS head in disbelief as he turned the radio off. Who could have predicted that someday talking media heads would look to Fidel Castro for a cogent assessment of an American primary season? Frank might be having a hard time writing a non-fiction book, but thank goodness he wasn't trying to write a satire about U.S. elections. How would you parody a parody? All you could do would be to quote the actual candidates.

Anyway, that wasn't his problem. What he was wrestling with was what to do when he got to Iowa. Heading to where the political action was had seemed like a great idea the day before. It wasn't until he was well across Colorado that he remembered that Iowa was a caucus state, leaving almost no opportunities for a hacker to cause any mischief.

How could they? Votes would be hand-tallied in school cafeterias and community centers while the voters were still hanging around. Those tallies would be telephoned in to statewide party headquarters and added to a master list that would be reprinted in newspapers. Any attempt to tamper with the totals would be spotted immediately.

Maybe he should be heading for New Hampshire instead? They'd be using electronic voting machines there.

But the New Hampshire primary was still ten days away. That would be a long time to hang around with nothing to do. Better to chill in Iowa for a couple of days and hope to catch the scent of something that might prove interesting.

* * *

It was a busy Friday night at Max's Stockyard Steak House in Chicago. The popular restaurant was packed, and as always, Max Ginnople was standing at one of the vantage points he would frequent throughout the evening, taking in the carefully orchestrated bustle of the main dining room. He took pride in his establishment's reputation for excellent service, and there was no better way to maintain it than for each employee to feel his critical eyes incessantly surveying the room.

Overhead, orange lights flickered in ranch lanterns attached to wagon wheel chandeliers, bathing the diners in barnyard ambience. The walls on three sides were festooned with longhorn cattle horns and sepia tinted photographs of stiffly-posed cowboys. On the fourth, the cheerful hubbub of the bar crowd tumbled over the shoulder-high, recycled horse stall barriers that divided the bar from the dining room. Max glanced at his watch with satisfaction: every table was full, and it wasn't yet 6:30. It would be another good night.

He was paying particular attention just now to the hostess, and to the wait staff entering and exiting through the door that led to the private dining room. He wanted everything to come off without a hitch for the special party that had reserved it, so he crossed the dining room as soon as he noticed two men in dark suits appear in the vestibule.

"Good evening gentlemen. Are you with Mr. Barbash's party?"

"Yes. We want to make sure everything's in order before he arrives."

"Of course, of course. May I take your coats and bags?"

"We'll hang on to them, thanks."

He escorted them to the private dining room door and held it as they entered. When the waiters inside looked his way, he gave a slight jerk of his head towards the door. Obligingly, they disappeared.

He smiled at the men. "If you need anything, please don't hesitate to ask."

"We'll be fine. Can we lock that door from the inside?"

"Why yes, you can."

"Fine. We'll be finished by the time Mr. Barbash arrives."

He heard the click of the lock slide into place as soon as the door closed behind him.

* * *

Frank wheeled his camper into the parking lot of the first motel he found after leaving the highway. It was late, he was tired, and the appeal of standing under a shower with an unlimited supply of hot water had been growing on him ever since he'd left Arizona. But the parking lot was crammed with vehicles, some of which were vans supporting improbably long, telescoping booms at the ends of which video uplink dishes shuddered in the wind overhead. He parked under the portico and walked up to the desk.

"Hi. Have you got a room for one?"

"As a matter of fact, yes. May I have your credit card and a picture ID?"

Frank dug them out of his wallet.

"Is your timing always this good?" the desk clerk asked as he clattered away at his keyboard. "If you'd walked in any other time today, you'd have been out of luck. I just got a cancellation not two minutes ago."

"Then I guess it's my lucky day. Is it this busy all over Iowa?"

"Depends on where the candidates are. Tomorrow there's a debate at the community college, so every place in town is sold out for tonight."

Frank felt less lucky when he heard the opportunistically elevated room rate. But the next town was fifty miles down the road, and who knew whether he'd have any better luck there? Anyway, he was here to be in the thick of things, so why complain?

Soon, he was luxuriating in the steam of a shower blasting an environmentally inappropriate jet of soothing hot water in his direction. Ten minutes later, he was feeling reborn. And also ravenous. He strode off to the motel restaurant with renewed vigor. It was jammed.

"An hour wait at least," the hostess informed him. "Do you want to give me your name, or check out the lounge first? You might find something in there."

"Thanks, I'll give that a try."

The lounge was also packed, but there was one empty seat towards the far end of the bar. He squeezed himself in between two other patrons, wondering how long it would take the overtaxed kitchen to produce a meal.

The bartender, of course, was also busy. Frank didn't see a menu anywhere within reach, and he realized that he'd left his phone in the camper, leaving him with nothing at all to look at. He felt like a bump on a log sitting there alone.

He fixed his gaze on the soundless TV screen hanging above the rows of bottles behind the bar. The fact that he cared absolutely nothing about sports – and knew even less about any of them – made it a rather pointless and unsatisfying exercise.

Worse yet, the television was tuned to a hockey game. The players were milling around on the ice in what seemed to him to be aimless patterns as the puck moved around the ice.

Hockey! he snorted. Probably the dullest game ever invented, and the one with absolutely the ugliest trophy – the Stanley Cup – ever created in the history of the world. Not only did it look like a giant coffee urn, but the only way to tell which end was up was by reading the names of past winners on its side. And even then you had to wonder whether the inscriber had gotten it wrong.

He stared at the television pretending he understood what was going on. As far as he could tell, 99% of the time all the game was about was just a bunch of guys wearing helmets zooming around with sticks and occasionally ramming each other into the barrier that surrounded the rink.

He was relieved when the bartender handed him a menu at last, giving him something to focus on that he understood. He was still studying it when he heard a voice on his right. "So who you with?"

"I'm sorry?"

"Which team do you play for? Candidate? Paper? Cable?"

"Oh – Got it. I guess just 'voter.'"

"Then what are you doing hanging around here?"

His neighbor had clearly been sampling the bar's offerings for some time. Frank decided that a neutral answer would be prudent.

"Just passing through, but I hear there's a debate here tomorrow night. I've got some spare time, so I might stick around for that."

His neighbor grunted. "Well, it'll be a circus, I grant you that. If you haven't seen one before, in person and with your own eyes, it might be hard to believe it isn't all cooked up by the media. Me, I'll take covering a natural disaster every time. It's more authentic and there's usually less lasting damage. "

"So you're in the media?"

"Not as you're probably thinking about it. I'm just a lighting roadie for POX News. That's why I'm sitting here at the bar instead of ordering room service, like the guys with the microphones."

What should he ask this guy? He was more used to avoiding conversations in bars than encouraging them, but here was just the sort of person he should be trying to chat up for information. Maybe he could work his way in from the outside and figure things out as he went along.

"So what do you think about all the swings in the polls leading up to the primaries?"

"Well, there's only two possible explanations, right? Either the American people are crazy, or those polls were rigged."

Frank perked up. "So which do you think it is?"

His companion looked amused. "You serious?"

"Well, sure. And who would you think would be behind it?" He'd only been here an hour, and already he was making progress!

The man laughed out loud.

"Brother, if you'd spent as long as I have on this beat, you'd know only one answer makes sense. Each one of these candidates is more over the edge than the last, sure, but the good citizens that come out and vote for them are crazier than the whole bunch put together!"

The bartender put Frank's cheeseburger down in front of him, and he ate glumly in silence for a while. Then the man spoke up again.

"But I will tell you this. Something is going on. I just can't tell exactly what."

Frank's hopes rose again. "What do you mean, 'going on?' What is it you're noticing?"

"I don't really know. I mean I do, but it's hard to figure out what to make of it. Something just isn't right with the new front runner. I've covered three presidential campaigns, and nothing about this guy Wellhead's campaign makes sense."

"How do you mean?"

"Well, here's an example. You see those guys over there in the corner?"

Frank looked over his shoulder at a half dozen men and women sitting and standing around a table, laughing and joking.

"Yeah?"

"And those folks at the other end of the bar?"

Frank saw a similar group, obviously enjoying themselves.

"Yeah, okay?"

"Now look over there in the dining room. You see the people around that big table over there, the one next to the wall?"

He saw seven serious looking men, all wearing suits. They were speaking intently, leaning forward to hear each other over the din welling up from the tables crowding in around them.

"Looks like a fun bunch. Who are they? And who are the other ones?"

"The first group is Julian Johnson's posse, and the second is Roxy Rollins's. Now which candidate do you suppose that third bunch pledges allegiance to?"

"I guess it would have to be Davenport or Cabot, right? They look like pretty straitlaced Ivy League types."

"You'd think so, wouldn't you? Well, how 'bout if I told you they were Br'er Wellhead's handlers?"

Frank turned and looked again with surprise.

"Those guys? Have they ever listened to him? I would have expected his people to be wearing cowboy hats sooner than ties."

"Funny, isn't it? And you know what, everybody else he travels with looks the same way. Never seen so many politicos wearing dark glasses in my life."

* * *

14

Just a Friendly Game of Cards

B UTCHER WAS BECOMING increasingly anxious as he drove the long road from the airport to the casino. White Crow had made it clear the last time they'd met that Butcher would be kept on a short leash. But there were limits to how far he was willing to go. He might have been royally stupid in the past, but he was smart enough to know that if he didn't draw a line in the sand now, there would be no limit to what White Crow could force him to do in the future. Better to have it out now.

And he did have one ace in the hole, though he hated to use it: his wife's family had money. His in-laws had never been particularly fond of him, but if his wife said they were having a financial crisis, he couldn't believe they wouldn't help out. If he had no other choice, he was willing to ask them for whatever perhaps ridiculous sum White Crow might demand to let him escape. He tried to use that plan to bolster his courage.

Butcher was welcomed by the hostess as if he was the casino's most valued customer – that was a first! It made him even more suspicious regarding what this unexpected invitation was all about.

As he passed through the unobtrusive door next to the long bar, he saw three players already hard at work around a poker table in White Crow's office, cigar smoke rising above their heads like the steam in a sweat lodge. White Crow simply nodded towards the one empty seat without introducing him. Butcher slid in behind a large, neatly stacked pile of chips. He wondered how much each chip was worth, but decided not to ask.

The casino's most attractive server appeared at his elbow and set a large drink in front of him. "Your usual, Mr. Butcher," she murmured.

Butcher studied the other players without trying to be too obvious as he waited for the hand to end. That wasn't difficult, as the eyes of the players were focused on their cards and each other as the pile of chips in the center of the table continued to grow.

Two were Native American, one probably local, with a weathered face and a leather belt heavily decorated with hand-tooled silver. Around his neck he wore a bolo tie, the large, antique slide beautifully inlaid with turquoise and red coral. The other Native American was stylishly dressed in city clothes; either someone who had grown up on the Rez and made good, or maybe someone from another tribe. The last player was Anglo and dressed casually but expensively. Butcher bet the Rolex on his wrist was genuine.

Finally, the local Native American took the hand, and the deal passed to the Rolex wearer to his left.

"Five card draw," was all he said, and the cards started to snap down in front of Butcher and the others.

Butcher took a deep breath and tilted his face down cards back to see what he had. It had been a long day, and he was already well into his first drink. As usual, he tried to establish his balls right out of the gate, regardless of the hand he'd been dealt. With only an ace to work with, he matched and raised when his turn came around.

To keep them guessing, he drew two cards instead of three. To his delight, he now had a pair of aces. Two rounds of betting later, he took the hand, and another drink materialized at his elbow. As the game continued, he was astonished to see that the calm, analytical Casino manager was a terrible poker player. Not only was his technique inconsistent, but he took wild chances on incredibly weak hands, bidding the pot up recklessly and often.

When the game broke up at 1:00 AM, Butcher's head was swimming with success and alcohol. All of White Crow's guests had done well at their host's considerable expense, but Butcher had done best of all. The size of his pile of chips had tripled, and it had been impressive to begin with. When White Crow summoned the cashier to pay out his guests, Butcher was stunned to realize they must have been playing for $50 a point. Instead of counting out single banknotes, the cashier was handing out bundles of $100 bills. Butcher had never seen so much cash in his life.

But White Crow was unconcerned. As ever, he was pleasant and calm, though anyone else would be morose or downright belligerent. It suddenly struck Butcher that the real purpose of the game was to provide a cover for paying off business partners without having to account for the real reasons the cash was changing hands.

If that was the case, he couldn't take credit for his winnings at all. But why was White Crow throwing so much money his way? Butcher's elation collapsed as the answer came to him.

As feared, White Crow put his hand on Butcher's shoulder when the others rose to leave. "You have had an especially good evening, my friend. Perhaps you will stay a moment longer so that we may catch up." The distance between his pile of cash and the front door of the casino suddenly seemed impossibly great to Butcher.

There was of course no way to refuse. Butcher had noticed that two of the casino's bouncers were on duty at the front door when he had arrived. Doubtless they had been told not to let him leave until they'd received the appropriate signal from their boss.

"Sure, Ohanzee. Sounds good," he mumbled as the other men departed.

White Crow gestured to Butcher to sit down again, and walked to the bar in the corner. When White Crow returned to the poker table, he held a highball glass in one hand and a bottle of sparkling water in the other. An uncharacteristically warm smile ornamented his face.

"I am very happy for you, my friend. The cards seemed to be," he paused briefly for effect, "stacked in your favor tonight."

Butcher's responsive laugh was surprised but not forced; he'd never heard White Crow tell a joke before.

But there were more surprises to come. White Crow poured himself a glass of sparkling water, and then reached across the table to take two of the six bundles of $100 bills piled in front of Butcher. "We are now 'square,' as I believe you said before. You now owe me nothing."

Butcher was dumbfounded. He had tried to imagine every possible scenario that might transpire, and this was not one he had anticipated.

"Wow – that's great, Ohanzee. I mean, you don't know what a relief this is after our last meeting." He was about to ask what it was all about and then stopped. He had no need to hear anything more. Just a desire for once to get out of the casino while he was still ahead.

"Indeed, my friend. I felt badly about that," White Crow replied. "We have known each other for a long time, and it was not a good way for one friend to treat another."

The casino manager raised his glass, and Butcher guardedly raised his own in response. "Now that we are friends again," White Crow said, clicking his glass against Butcher's, "I know that you will be happy to do me a favor."

So now it – whatever "it" would be – was coming. Butcher began to sweat. "A favor, Ohanzee?"

White Crow leaned forward, his forearms on the table and his hands clasped.

"Yes, a favor. I'd like you to give me a bit more information about the subject we touched upon briefly the last time we met."

So they were back to that. And it wasn't a favor White Crow wanted, it was payback for the bribe he had just paid to Butcher. But why a bribe? The casino manager already had enough information about his drinking, betting and indiscretions to get him fired.

Then Butcher had another thought; he wondered where the camera and microphone were hidden. Trading secret information for money would put him away much longer than disclosing information to a blackmailer. He tried to choose his words carefully to avoid incriminating himself.

"Uh, Ohanzee, I'm sure you don't realize this, but if I were to answer the kind of questions you started to ask me before, we would both be breaking the law. You know I'd be happy to do any type of legal favor for you."

"Is that your final answer?"

Butcher felt more confident now. "It is."

"I see." White Crow unlocked a drawer in the table and took out a fresh pack of cards.

"I am disappointed, my friend," he murmured as he removed the band from around the pack of cards. "Very disappointed. I thought perhaps we might make a fresh start tonight."

Butcher said nothing, wondering what would happen next. He watched as White Crow set the deck of cards on the table, and then spread them in a neat fan, face down. Without looking up, he asked softly, "Are you certain you will not reconsider?"

What the hell was he up to? Butcher couldn't follow this at all.

"Yes," he finally said, his voice trembling.

White Crow looked up, smiling pleasantly. "Well then. Perhaps you will indulge me in one last hand of cards before you leave?"

Once again, Butcher said nothing.

"You wish to quit while you are ahead for a change? Is that it, my friend? No? Good!"

White Crow scooped a double handful of chips out of the table drawer.

"Here – I will stake you again – just like old times." He split the chips evenly between them and slid the fanned cards once more into a stack, setting the deck between them. "Care to cut the cards?"

Butcher shook his head no.

"Ah! We trust each other! A good start! The game is five card stud."

He snapped each card down smartly as he dealt, the small, sharp sounds echoing like pistol shots around the silent room.

Butcher looked across the table: White Crow had a king of spades up. Then he looked down at his own cards, and to his astonishment saw a card-sized picture of his house.

He looked up, eyes wide.

"Do you wish to bet my friend?"

Butcher was beginning to have difficulty breathing, and his mind was racing. He said nothing.

"No? Ah, but if you do not bet, our little game will be over too soon." White Crow reached across the table and slid several of Butchers' chips forward, and then matched them from his own pile. Then he dealt again.

Snap! Another card was added to Butcher's hand, but he was afraid to look.

Snap! The queen of spades now kept company with White Crow's king.

White Crow placed the deck on the table.

"A pretty card my friend. Worth a handsome bet, I should think." White Crow waited without success for Butcher to reply.

"No? Nothing ventured, nothing gained you know."

Butcher finally found his voice. "All the cards," he said hoarsely.

"What, my friend?"

"All the cards. Deal the rest of the hands now."

White Crow shrugged. "But that is not how the game is played, my friend!"

Then, as if having a sudden thought, he continued. "But of course! You are tired, and I am a terrible host for not noticing. We must finish up quickly, so that you can get your rest."

He laid the remaining cards out softly this time, dealing himself the jack and ten of spades, and Butcher two more card-sized photographs.

He set the deck down and leaned forward.

"It is your turn to wager, my friend."

But Butcher was silent, staring down at the new cards he had been dealt. The first was a photo of the puppy he had bought for his daughter's seventh birthday a week before, and the second was a picture of his little girl posing in front of a mirror, wearing a new birthday dress. The last was of his delighted, five year old son, reaching out to pet the new puppy.

White Crow cupped a hand to his ear. "Was it 'all' you said? Ah! You are very brash tonight – and you haven't even looked at your first card yet!"

He reached across and swept not only Butcher's chips, but his bundles of cash as well into the center of the table. Then he reached into the drawer and poured a double handful of red chips onto the pile.

"I have matched you, my friend. Do you wish to raise?"

Butcher's face was frozen, staring down at the cards.

"Ah, I see. You have already wagered everything you have in the world!"

With that, White Crow turned over his face down card, showing the ace of spades and completing a royal flush.

"And you my friend? I am entitled to see your last card, you know."

Butcher did not move. He already knew what it would show.

"Well then, I must turn it over myself." White Crow reached across and, very slowly, turned over Butcher's last card.

Of course, it was a picture of Butcher's wife. And not just any picture, but one taken on their wedding day. All three of the people he held most dear in the world stared trustingly back at him from where they lay defenseless on the table.

White Crow leaned back in his chair. "I believe the game is mine."

Then he swept the garish pile of cash and chips into the drawer and locked it. "I'm afraid that you will never learn to quit when you are ahead, my friend."

His bit of guerilla theater completed, White Crow leaned across the table once again. He was not smiling now.

"Now that we have seen each other's cards we will get back to business. When you return to your room, you will find a memory stick on your night table. Do not forget to take it with you when you leave. On it you will find the list of information and code I require. You will save those items to the memory stick, and then you will return it to me by overnight delivery so that it is in my hands on Tuesday. Then you will await further instructions."

White Crow rapped twice on the table and stood up. A hidden door Butcher had never noticed before opened to admit one of the casino's bouncers. He held the same door as White Crow left, closed it, and approached the poker table.

Too stricken too move or speak, Butcher looked up at the bouncer with unseeing eyes. With a surprisingly gentle touch, the big man placed a hand on Butcher's shoulder.

"It's time to go."

Butcher began to rise, but then sat down abruptly to scoop up his cards. Clutching them in front of him, he stood up again and followed his escort out of the room.

* * *

15

Introducing the Next President
of the United States!

I T WAS NOT late when Frank left the motel bar. After a month in the rumpled single berth of his camper he yearned for the crisp, clean sheets of the king-size bed in his motel room. But he also wanted to see what more he could find out about Randall Wellhead's staff before he went to sleep. Of course, with so many media people logging on, the motel Wi-Fi connection was crawling. So he made his way back to the rear parking lot where he could once again perch in front of the cramped desk in his camper.

But he couldn't find much on-line that was useful. And what search request should he use, anyway? "Randall Wellhead" AND "men in black?"

There was some chatter along the lines the man from POX News had shared. But it was all from early on in the campaign, when Wellhead was in "tease" mode. Those first impressions had all been nattered to death weeks ago, allowing whatever eyebrows the Wellhead team had raised to relax again

After a half hour, Frank was ready to call it a night. He shut down his computer and returned to his room. But halfway through brushing his teeth, he stopped. Damn. He hadn't checked his email, and he also hadn't heard from his daughter in days. That wasn't like her. He looked for his phone, and then his laptop. He must have left both in the camper.

Feeling abundantly sorry for himself, he trudged his way to the parking lot yet again. Entering the camper, he turned on the overhead light and the light bulb burned out with a pop. Damn again. He found a flashlight, turned on his laptop, and waited for his email to download.

Two minutes later, he was still waiting. What was going on?

He opened a browser, and that took forever to connect, too. Was some part of his system failing? He opened a diagnostic tool and saw to his surprise that his connection was transmitting data at a prodigious rate.

How could that be? None of his software should be automatically updating or backing up. He checked, and sure enough, nothing on his laptop or his server was processing anything at all, just his Wi-Fi router. What could his system be up to?

There was only one explanation he could think of, and that one didn't make any sense. Or at least he hoped it didn't. But there it was nonetheless: someone within fifty yards of his camper must have hacked into his very own, personally configured, super secure system.

* * *

He eased the back door of his camper closed and peered cautiously around the corner. The motel's main lot had been too full for a vehicle his size, so he was parked in an overflow area behind the pool area. Only a few cars and pickup trucks were there, one of which must hold the person helping himself to Frank's wireless connection.

But he couldn't see anyone in any of the vehicles nearby. It was hard to tell for sure, though, because the parking lot was unlit and the faint glow of a laptop might not be visible, especially from a distance. He'd have to walk around the lot to get a better view of each vehicle, one at a time to tell for sure. He wondered how many of those pickup trucks had gun racks. Maybe it wasn't so important to know who the hacker was after all.

And then he noticed it: an old VW camper with curtains drawn, parked in the very back of the lot in the shadow of some trees. Bingo. That must be it. He felt his courage returning. How threatening could someone be that drove a VW minibus?

He walked to the edge of the parking lot, keeping his camper in the line of sight of whoever was in the VW. Then, feeling foolish, he hunched over and scooted around the periphery of the lot, staying behind the ratty landscaping as much as possible. When he was in line with the minibus, he peeked through the trees, hoping to find a break in the curtains. But they were drawn tight.

Crouching once more, he crept out of the trees, edged along the side of the vehicle until he was in front, and slowly stood up until his eyes just cleared the bottom of the windshield.

Towards the back of the minibus, he saw the head and shoulders of someone silhouetted against the glow of a laptop screen. On the side of the camper, he could see a partially open cabinet. He couldn't see what was inside, but from time to time he saw the flickering of lights reflected on the back of the cabinet door.

He eased back down into a crouch. Now what?

He had no doubt that the person inside the camper must be the one that was piggy-backing on his Internet connection. But if they denied it, how could he prove otherwise? Maybe he should just sneak back to his motel room and forget about it. His haunches were starting to ache, so he sat down on the ground, once again feeling foolish.

Then the VW's engine growled into life and the headlights came on, bracketing his wide-eyed face between them. Involuntarily, he spread his arms and pasted his back as tightly as possible against the broad front of the minibus, trying not to be seen. Then, realizing he might be run over at any moment, he jumped to his feet just as automatically and spun around. Paralyzed like the proverbial deer in the headlights, he found himself staring face to face through the windshield at the person he had set out to find.

* * *

Otto Barbash was poised and posed at the end of Max's private dining room, dominating the room with his presence. Still at their tables, his guests were digesting an excellent dinner and enjoying their after dinner drinks. As always, Barbash was impeccably dressed, wearing a dark, bespoke suit and club tie. A silk handkerchief emerged from the breast pocket of his suit coat, folded to display three identical points and his personal monogram. A brandy snifter was cupped in the fingers of his right hand.

No longer young or athletic, Barbash still carried himself erectly and well. A luxuriantly thick and precisely trimmed white moustache provided an old-world touch to his dignified face. That feature, together with a lofty forehead and his military bearing, had led more than one acquaintance to erroneously recall Barbash wearing a monocle. Indeed, anyone noticing Barbash displayed against the rich paneling of the private dining room might easily think they were glimpsing an oil portrait of a 19th century diplomat attending an affair of state; only the red sash and star were lacking.

There would be no random glances into the private dining room this evening, of course, because the door to the room was closed and guarded by the two advance men. One of them was just now opening the door to admit the last of Mr. Barbash's guests.

All eyes turned to greet the two late arrivals, as the opportunity to meet – and pledge economic support to – Randall Wellhead was the reason for their own presence. Barbash remained apart at the end of the room, content to allow his wife Amelia a few moments in the spotlight. Elegantly coiffed and wearing a burgundy Empire gown, she rose to greet the candidate and introduce him to the guests. Barbash looked forward to using the interlude to exchange a few private words with Wellhead's companion, who was also shaking hands while discretely moving in his direction.

Barbash was always impressed by the fact that Richard Fetters was so much smaller in person than he appeared on television. In any setting, though, the thinness of the man's neck made his outsized head appear incongruous. Barbash wondered whether Fetters realized that the round lenses of his steel-rimmed glasses contributed to the impression that his face was a full, cratered moon rising from the collar of his shirt.

But no, that wasn't quite the right analogy, because it failed to take into account the man's extraordinary eyes. Barbash was always meticulous in his investigation of anyone upon whom he was considering placing his reliance, and he had made no exception with Fetters. Before consenting to a first meeting, he had studied him carefully on video as well as in text. From the first, he had been struck by the unnaturally large and piercing yellow-brown eyes that dominated the man's invariably immobile face.

Barbash observed that whenever Fetters spoke, he inclined his head slightly forward and peered over the top of his glasses, fixing those unblinking eyes on the object of his attention. The effect was unnerving. Once you were locked into Fetters's unwavering gaze, it seemed impossible to look away. It was not unknown for someone in a group, or even on stage, to simply stop speaking in mid-sentence, as if placed under his control as soon as they locked eyes. Yes, Barbash thought, as Fetters at last approached him. That was it. Not like a rising moon. Like a cobra, one with its hood fully extended and its eyes fixed on its intended prey. He extended his hand to Fetters.

"So good of you to come."

At the other end of the room, Wellhead was holding court, shaking hands and beaming his trademark smile with the casual ease of a natural politician. The cheerful twang of his voice was punctuated by the appreciative laughter of his listeners.

"The pleasure is mine." Fetters replied. "It's very good of you to host another fundraiser so soon."

"Of course, of course. One must go through the motions after all, mustn't one?"

"Indeed. Any other election year it would be most welcome. But in this campaign we mostly need to keep the money flowing in to keep up appearances."

"I'm not concerned. One expects high stakes at the most competitive tables. Our resources will be more than adequate."

A waiter materialized at Fetters's elbow, holding a silver tray. In the center stood a scotch in a cut crystal glass, served neat but for a few drops of water to bring out its bouquet. On either side of the glass lay a cigar, its end neatly trimmed.

"You prefer the Portlethen single malt, I believe?"

Fetters raised his glass in salute. "As always, you are an excellent host."

"That's because I always rely on my own refreshments and staff. I find that one can expect only so much when traveling, even from the best commercial establishments." He nodded, and a lighter materialized in the hand of his personal waiter. Leaning over, he drew gently on his cigar. Fetters followed suit.

Barbash looked with mild disapproval at Fetters as he raised his scotch to his lips. "I'm sure I don't know why you drink that peaty treacle when there are so many more sophisticated single malts available. I've always preferred subtlety over assertiveness. It's an approach that has served me well."

Fetters's offered back the off-kilter smirk his face adopted in lieu of a smile when the situation required a positive response. Subtlety had never been his style. The indirect approach of working through intermediaries and shaping events from a distance merely added complexity, and with complexity came the chance of mistakes. He preferred the sudden strike, backed by the kind of overwhelming political – or other – force that left nothing to chance. But he knew better than to fail to stroke the ego of one of his largest donors when his expectations had been so clearly signaled.

"Your reputation for finesse is of course well deserved. I expect the business world has taken pains to seek out the secrets behind your remarkable success."

"As a matter of fact, yes. There is a Harvard Business School case study. I could send you a copy."

"No need – I've already read and appreciated it. But would you not agree that the challenges of the current political environment demand more than nuanced actions? If we wish to restore sanity in Washington, I believe we'll need to be forceful before we can afford to be subtle again."

"Desperate times require desperate measures? Perhaps."

Barbash drew again on his cigar. "Thank goodness for private dining rooms, or I could never enjoy a decent after dinner cigar outside my own homes. And it does keep the others at bay."

He turned to watch the guest of honor work the crowd. Barbash gestured towards him, leaving a trail of smoke with his cigar. "How is it that this ridiculous caricature of a human being is the best foil you could find to execute your plan?"

"He is an oaf, I grant you. But he is also shamelessly tractable and in tune with our equally ridiculous times."

"Again – perhaps. But I wish it was otherwise."

"In any event, his role can be transitory."

Barbash turned to look at Fetters. "Transitory?"

"Yes, and hence my last minute decision to accompany Wellhead tonight. I've reflected on the plan I originally shared with you, and have a refinement to suggest.

"You'll recall that the last Republican we helped into office toed the line for quite some time, paying heed to the cabinet we suggested, and especially the vice president we so carefully selected to guide him. But eventually he became over confident and decided to make his own decisions. It was something we knew might happen, but regrettable nonetheless.

"Otherwise, our plan was shrewdly designed and well executed. I believe that with a small refinement, we can use the same approach and achieve complete success this time."

"And that 'small refinement' would be?"

"I believe that decisive action in the first instance is essential and will be well rewarded. Rather than rely on handlers to keep Wellhead in check, I've concluded that we need to replace him with the perfect presidential candidate a few days after the inauguration."

"Good God, man! Surely you are not suggesting an act of violence?"

"Not a violent act, no. In fact, quite the opposite. I would simply observe that it would not be difficult after a long evening of social imbibing to place a person with the rather substantial carnal appetites of Randall Wellhead in the way of irresistible temptation. Two irresistible temptations, in fact, and both shy of the age of consent. Needless to say, it would all look quite festive on videotape, even given the low quality of YouTube."

"But the scandal would destroy the administration!"

"Only if the video were to be made public, and I hardly think that will be necessary; at heart, the man's a shameless coward. Inviting him to a private screening shouldn't give someone his age an actual stroke, but it should be sufficient to convince him to play along when we suggest announcing that he has suffered one. And also to persuade him to go on to do the right thing shortly thereafter."

"Which would be?"

"Which would be to spare the nation another interlude like the second term of Woodrow Wilson, when the country limped along with an executive too incapacitated to govern effectively, and too stubborn to resign. After Wellhead does step down, he can enjoy a steady and miraculously complete recovery. Historians will always wonder what might have been had he not given up his elected office so precipitously."

Barbash exhaled and studied Wellhead through the slowly coiling patterns of dissipating smoke. The new plan had a certain merit, not least because he found the personality, if not the politics, of the candidate insufferable. Most importantly, there would be no need for Barbash to be personally associated with the execution of the plan in any way. Of course, Fetters had left out one extremely important detail. Barbash suspected he already knew how Fetters would propose to address that gap.

"I assume that you have already given thought to who Wellhead should select to be his Vice President?"

"Of course."

"And who do you propose for that honor?"

"I'm pleased to say that I enjoy Wellhead's complete trust. If called upon, I could hardly refuse to serve the Republic we both love so well."

* * *

16

Midnight in the Garden of Fast Food and Evil

F IRST THE ENGINE of the minibus died, and then the headlights. In the sudden darkness, Frank's bedazzled eyes could see nothing, leaving him frozen in place. He heard the door to the VW open and close, and then a quiet voice from a shadowy figure by his side.

"Hello, Frank. How have you been?"

"Fine. And you?"

And then, a familiar, musical laugh. "I think I have some explaining to do, yes?"

"Yes, Josette, I think you do."

As his eyes readjusted to the darkness, he tried to collect his thoughts. Should he be angry? Happy? Suspicious? All of the above? He needed a few moments to sort it all out.

"Let's go to my camper. I can make us something to drink, and you can tell me what's going on here."

"No, Frank, not there. Get in my bus, please. We will find somewhere to go and talk."

What? She'd been happy to climb into his camper when he found her by a desert road, but now that he'd caught her hacking into his server they had to talk on neutral ground? But she was already climbing into her car, so he followed her lead and climbed in.

He was about to vent his displeasure when she put a finger to her lips. He stopped, thought better of it, and was about to let loose anyway when she held her finger to his lips instead. Flustered by her touch, he turned and stared out the window, feeling simultaneously hurt, annoyed and helpless. It was not an emotional cocktail he was enjoying.

The unmistakable sound of a vintage VW's air-cooled engine spinning up into life filled the night for a second time. Josette let out the clutch pedal and eased the minibus into gear. She accelerated quickly through the silent motel grounds and onto the brightly lit strip of motels, fast food restaurants, and gas stations clustered around the highway interchange. A few hundred yards later, she turned into a deserted burger chain restaurant and got out of the car. By now, Frank was seething. He intercepted her before she could go inside.

"Alright, I want to know right now why you hacked into my system, and what you were uploading? And what's wrong with my camper, anyway? You were pretty grateful to hang out there before!"

Once again, she held her finger to his lips. With her other hand, she reached up and pulled his head down to hers, until their eyes were only a few inches apart.

"Your camper – it is bugged," she whispered. "Perhaps mine as well."

She took her hands away and he slowly straightened up. Slipping her arm through one of his, she led him obediently into the restaurant.

A few minutes later, they were sitting across from each other in a brightly colored, uncomfortable booth as far from the order counter as possible. Josette reached across the table and took one of his hands in both of hers, her face earnest and concerned.

"Frank, you must forgive me, please, for my rude behavior. I saw you in the bar last night and wanted to say hello, but it was so crowded. And then, when I tried to use the motel Wi-Fi, the connection was so slow. I thought you would not mind." Then she perked up, and gave him a coquettish smile. She traded his hand for her coffee cup. "But now you have caught me, so what can I do?" She gave her musical laugh and looked at him over its rim.

He tried not to melt, at least visibly. Was she manipulating him? Of course; but why? He'd be damned if he'd let her play him for a fool, especially since she must know by now how easily she could push his buttons.

"You can start by answering my questions. What are you up to? And how did you hack into my system without a password?"

"Why you gave it to me, of course."

He stared blankly, and then opened and shut his mouth several times without speaking. Of course he had. The day he picked her up by the roadside she had asked for it, and he had given it to her, imagining that he would never see her again.

"But how did you remember such a long password? My settings wouldn't allow you to save it."

"Ah, well, you see, I decided to type it first on my notepad so I could save it."

Damn it! Ever since he'd met this beguiling French scamp, five minutes couldn't pass without her managing to take him by surprise. How had she gotten so good at that?

She took his hand again. "But still, it was wrong, and I am sorry. Let me start at the beginning, Frank. I will tell you everything, and perhaps when I am finished, you will forgive me, yes?"

*   *   *

17

You Want Lies with That?

F RANK SAT STONY-FACED across the table from Josette at the fast food restaurant, an un-touched diet soda in front of him. Josette looked around as much to buy a little time as to be sure they were alone.

There was nothing to fear in that regard; the restaurant was empty but for the late-night skeleton shift, watching videos on their mobile phones somewhere behind the counter. Beyond the windows, the garish signs of motels and gas stations populated the black void of the sky like alien galaxies. Inside, they were awash in bright fluorescent light, as isolated as when they'd first met.

"So okay," Josette began, then hesitated, looking down at the cup of coffee she was holding between both hands.

She looked up, but he gave her no reassurance.

"Okay, so it is like this. You know, you Americans have not been so very good about picking your presidents lately, yes?"

"Who says?"

"Oh Frank, I know you agree — we had this conversation before, when we first met. And you make fun of your politicians all the time. So you shouldn't be surprised if we think the same in Europe."

"Of course I shouldn't – I think you'd be crazy if you didn't. But what does that have to do with anything?"

Now the words rushed out. "It has everything to do with everything! Don't you remember how your president treated us after 9/11? We had nothing to do with it, but he said if we weren't with America, he would treat us as if we were against you? He started a war we thought was unjustified, and then insisted we help!"

"Well, yes, of course. He wasn't very good at treating allies like allies, and that was wrong. But our current president doesn't think or act that way."

"That is true – and thank goodness. But what if he doesn't get re-elected?"

"Well, we'll all be in trouble. But that doesn't explain or justify your hacking into my server!"

"Um, perhaps it doesn't justify, but it will, I think explain."

Frank went silent again, determined not to help her out. After a moment she took a deep breath and began to speak in a more deliberate voice.

"You see, Frank, some of us in Europe are thinking that maybe you Americans can't be trusted to elect your own president. You are very fond of referring to him as 'the Leader of the Free World,' are you not? And in a way, you are right – what he does affects everyone else, whether we agree with him or not. Sometimes it is good for us, yes, but sometimes it is not so good. If you want to say your president is the Leader of the Free World, shouldn't the rest of us have some say in the matter?"

Hmm. He might have come up with that one himself, just to provoke an argument with someone for the fun of it.

"Alright, I'll grant the point, at least in theory. But where are you going with it?"

She shifted in her seat. Finally, clutching her coffee cup more tightly than ever, she blurted out, "So my friends and I decided we should do something about it."

It took a moment for the implications of her statement to sink in.

"*You!* It was you that hacked the pollsters!"

She looked up and nodded.

But he couldn't put it all together. "I don't get it – every new candidate jumped to the top of the polls, but none of them ever stayed there. So what were you trying to achieve?"

"All of them, Frank?"

Hadn't it been all of them? "Well, all of them except Hollis Davenport and Vance Cabot."

She nodded quickly.

Now he was even more confused. "But if you're worried about getting another bad president, why would you only inflate the numbers of idiots?"

She frowned. "We thought we had such a good plan, but it did not work.

You see, we did not want to pick a candidate for you – that would go too far. We thought if we made it look like one of the terrible candidates might get elected, it would make the smart voters work harder to support the good candidates. We did not plan to change any votes – just make you Americans think harder about who you want as your president. But it did not work."

"Well of course it didn't work! You were controlling the poll results!"

"No, Frank, it really didn't work. Your Mr. Davenport and Mr. Cabot never did well at all in the real poll numbers."

But he had stopped listening. If this was all true, then something he'd thought was a coincidence might not have been a coincidence at all.

"You didn't just happen to be stranded by the side of the road in Nevada, did you?"

Josette shrank back in her seat; she hadn't thought this far ahead when she decided to come clean. At last she shook her head from side to side.

Frank's mind was racing now. "Why did you want me to stop? What does your crazy project have to do with me, anyway?"

Her eyes darted around the room. They were still alone, but she lowered her voice anyway.

"Frank, you must never tell this to anyone – do you promise?"

He nodded.

"One of us works inside one of your very secret agencies. She works for one of the top managers, and he is not so careful always as he should be. Sometimes she is able to find things out. One of the things we learned was that you had been asked to find us. We wanted to be able to keep track of you so that we would know if you were getting close to doing that. Of course, we were very disappointed when you did."

Frank brightened a bit. "What's the agency's name?"

"Even the people who work there do not know. So we call it 'Voldemort.'"

"'Voldemort?'"

"You know, 'he who cannot be named.' What do you call it?"

Voldemort clearly trumped Marvin as a snarky nickname. "Oh, nothing. I just always wondered what it was called."

Frank felt his anger giving way to curiosity.

"What else were you able to learn about Voldemort?"

She leaned even closer. "That they have bugged your camper. That's why I would not go back there to speak."

That bastard Butcher! When and how had he done that? Had he used the bathroom while he was there? Maybe pressed something down between the seat cushions while they spoke?

Then Frank remembered – he'd left Butcher alone in the camper when he went outside to speak with George. How long had that taken? Ten minutes, at least? The microphone and transmitter could be anywhere, but he'd have time to think about that later. There must be more he should ask right now, but he was struggling.

"So does your group have a name?"

"Yes – we call ourselves the Daughters of Lafayette. You see, although we do not approve of all of your presidents, we still believe in America. And sometimes, we think, you still need some help. It is true, yes?"

"No men at all?"

She smiled at the look on his face. "Why do you look so surprised? Do you not think that women can be good hackers, too?"

Frank sat back and studied her amused face. There was so much information to absorb, and he suddenly noticed that he was exhausted. He looked at his watch and saw it was almost 2:00 AM. But there was one more question he needed to have answered.

"Who designed the hack of the pollsters' software?"

"Ah! It was such a simple thing. We could not believe it took so long for such a little trick to be discovered."

Her answer took him aback, but only for a moment.

"Yes, but who came up with it?"

With that, she gave her tinkling, musical laugh. "Why, it was me. Did you like it?"

* * *

Frank sat alone in the single chair in his motel room trying to make sense of everything he had heard. Most of what he thought he knew just a few hours before had been turned upside down, and he wasn't sure where he should go with the new information.

Assuming he could trust Josette (which was a quandary in itself), the Daughters of Lafayette had no further plans to influence the American elections. But if he shared that information with Butcher, Josette and her friends would surely end up in jail. He wondered if he could end up in jail if he didn't – especially if he continued to take a weekly check from Voldemort to watch out for someone he'd already found.

And then there was the biggest shock of all: that the nemesis he had been pursuing, the cracker he had come to grudgingly admire, should turn out to be not some sinister Romanian working for a puppet master yet to be discovered, or a cadre of black hats funded by the Chinese government, but, of all people in the world, Josette!

It was more than he could grapple with in the wee hours of the morning. Maybe in the clear light of day after a good night's sleep it would all make sense.

* * *

18

Breakfast at Epiphany's

F RANK STARED BLEAKLY at the bowl of dry oatmeal and fruit the waitress in the motel dining room placed in front of him. Could a life without bacon and eggs be properly called "life" at all?

Glancing up, he saw Josette standing by the hostess station. She had already noticed him, and gave him an awkward smile. With mixed feelings, he shrugged and motioned towards the second chair at his table.

When she had joined him, he waited for her to speak.

"I am happy you let me join you."

Was she, he wondered? One of the things that the light of day had made clear to him was how consistently she had toyed with him.

"Aren't you concerned about us being seen together?"

"I think not. No one is sitting close enough to hear us, and from the bug your Mr. Butcher planted, Voldemort is already aware that we know each other. If they are suspicious already, then they must be tracking me as well. And if they are not, why should we not meet for breakfast?"

For the first time in his life, Frank began to sense what it must feel like to be a person of interest living in a police state. At any time, you would need to assume you were being watched. And yet, what could you do, but continue to go about your normal life? It left him feeling more than a little unsettled.

He changed the subject. "So what will you and the DoLs do next?"

She made a face. "Please! If you must have a short name – we call ourselves the 'FdL'."

Frank felt he should be up to working out such a small byte of French, but his furrowed brows gave him away.

"Filles de Lafayette," she said primly.

"I just about had it – you should have given me another second."

She realized too late that she would have been smarter to have done just that. She began studying her menu.

"Well?" Frank said.

She looked up. "Well what, Frank?"

"What will you and the other 'fillies' do next?"

"Not 'fillies,' Frank, 'filles.'"

He gave her a smug smile. "You can look it up."

That sounded a bit too smarmy, so he returned to a question that had occurred to him earlier.

"How did you know where to pose by the side of the road in Nevada?" Then it hit him – Butcher had probably had a tracking device and a microphone planted in his camper even before it was delivered to him.

"Scratch that – I just got it. But if your friend at Voldemort knew so much about me already, what was the point in your scamming your way into my camper?"

"Because she did not know so much as you think. Voldemort has layers of security, even inside, as you might expect. And our colleague that works there is not so senior, you see. She works with someone named Len Butcher, and monitored your location for him, but did not have access to the information received from the microphone. So we would have no way to know if you discovered our secrets – if that happened, we worried that we might walk into a trap."

"So are you telling me you hacked my system way back then? What did you do – put in a back door so you could monitor what I was doing any time you wanted to?"

He was about to storm away from the table when he noticed that Josette was no longer looking meek and repentant. Instead, she looked determined, and also suddenly older.

"That's exactly right, Frank. This is not a game, you see. And we are not little 'fillies' – yes, I know that word. We are willing to take chances, yes, but we are not foolish. We have no wish to go to jail unnecessarily, or to fail in our mission. If that means hitching a ride in your camper and tapping into your system, yes, I was quite willing to do so."

Frank began drumming his fingers on his thigh. So now he knew how far Josette was willing to go to get information. Strangely, the realization left him feeling calmer.

For a time they sat in silence, staring at each other. Suddenly, Josette frowned.

"Frank, have you been sick?"

"Why do you ask?"

She looked at him more closely. "I don't know; there is something about you that looks different…"

Ah! He'd been wondering whether she would notice he'd lost weight – twelve pounds now!

"Well, I have been running and working out a bit."

"Oh! I see. Well, don't do too much." She reached across the table and turned his newspaper so she could see the headlines.

"Yeah, well as you may recall, I was up really late last night."

They went back to staring, this time at their silverware. At last, a waitress materialized at Josette's elbow.

"Sorry to take so long. What will you have, darl'n? Your dad's already ordered."

Frank's eyes grew wide; Josette tried not to smile.

"The fruit salad, please, and tea," she said, her accent clear.

"Oh! My mistake. Guess he's not your dad after all." She gave Frank a curious look and walked away.

Frank debated what to say next, and wondered whether he should simply get up and leave. He stared across the room and out the window. At last he said, "So what will you and your friends do next?"

"Ah!" she said, relieved. "Ah – yes, that is an interesting question. About that we are not so sure. It was never our intent to do more than try to motivate your sensible voters. But we failed so badly at that, did we not?"

"Yes, it does look that way, doesn't it? And if you hadn't been flipping the poll results, maybe Davenport or Cabot would be ahead right now! Did you ever think of that?"

"Yes, Frank. Indeed, we are wondering that."

"Really? Why?"

"Because towards the end we decided that this might be a problem, yes? So we did not do anything to the polls when Randall Wellhead entered the race. We were quite unhappy that he did so well, all on his own."

Frank's eyes looked a bit vacant as he tried to sort through the dates and events of the last month.

"So let me ask you this: did you and your friends ever instruct the pollsters' computers to start checking a legitimate time signal again?"

"No, no. We did not do that, because then we would have to hack the systems all over again if we changed our minds. We simply did nothing."

"You're sure about that? There's no chance that one of your friends might have decided to carry on anyway?"

"No Frank. Why do you ask?"

"Because when we checked the inputs to the pollsters' machines after Wellhead entered the race, the poll results were still being switched. So if you and your friends didn't do the switching, then who did?"

* * *

19

Treaty Time

THE PHONE ON White Crow's desk rang. When he saw the number in the window, he smiled.

"Hello, Dick. It is always such a pleasure to hear from you."

"I'm sure. What is it you want to talk about?"

"The debate tonight, of course. I want to be sure that our understanding is clear."

"Of course it's clear. I don't operate any other way."

"To be sure, and I apologize. I phrased that badly. I meant between you and Wellhead. He is not, to put it politely, very good at staying on message, is he?"

"He's been thoroughly coached."

"Has he had a chance to meet Henry yet?"

"No, but it's been made clear to him that Yazzie's off limits. I assume you can vouch for your candidate as well?"

White Crow liked the sound of that. There had never been a Native American presidential candidate before. "Yes. There are plenty of targets to shoot at besides yours, and anyway, that's not Henry's style."

"Good. And just to be sure there's no confusion – you understand that while we can promise to nominate Yazzie for Secretary of the Interior, we can't and won't guarantee that the Senate will confirm him. I don't want any repercussions if your man throws his support to Wellhead when he drops out of the race and then his appointment gets filibustered."

"I am quite familiar with how the process works. You can be assured that if you do your part, we will do ours."

Fetters began to respond, but White Crow cut him off.

"But hear me well when I say this: if it looks to us like your party isn't supporting his cabinet nomination strongly, you can be sure there will be consequences."

Fetters wasn't used to receiving threats, veiled or otherwise, and especially not from somebody like White Crow. But he needed to rely on the cooperation of the casino manager, at least for now.

"You needn't be concerned. We see Henry as a long-term asset to a Wellhead administration. He'll give us some cover with the environmentalists, and he'll add a non-Republican voice to the Cabinet without offending our right wing by taking a Democrat on board."

"Good. I'm glad that we understand each other." White Crow looked at his watch. "And now I see it's time to watch the debate."

* * *

Frank and Josette were sitting in the middle of a very full community college auditorium, waiting for the candidates to walk on stage. Frank had a tablet computer on his lap, tuned to the network that was hosting and streaming the debate. Sharing a set of ear buds, they strained to hear the two network commentators over the babble of the crowd surrounding them.

Of course the big news today was the entry of the newest candidate into the presidential race.

That's right, Roger. It's amazing how quickly this has all come together. Until his formal announcement today, just about nobody had ever heard of Henry Dodge Yazzie. But it turns out he was doing very well with his signature campaigns while the media was ignoring him. He's already qualified in eleven states to run as an Independent, and says he intends to make the deadline in all fifty.

That would really be extraordinary, Peter! It's amazing to see a Native American not only making a run for the Presidency, but gathering real support as well. Of course, we'll have to wait and see how well he does once the voting starts.

Frank took his ear bud out and turned to Josette. "A Native American in the race? How did that happen?"

"I have no idea." She typed in the address of a news site, and there, staring out at them, was the face of a fortyish, obviously Native American man speaking to a crowd of about fifty people. Behind him was a banner with big, bold letters that read: "Yazzie for President." In smaller text below it read: "It's Time for a *Real* Change in Washington."

"What does this mean for the election?"

"Probably not much for this guy. Unlike Europe, third-party candidates never stand a chance here. But sometimes they've taken enough votes away from another candidate to tip an election."

"Has no one here ever won as an Independent?"

"Not that I know of."

"But why?"

Frank strained to remember more about how his own country's political system worked. "Well, I think we've always had only two really successful political parties at a time, although I think the two we have today aren't the same as the original ones. Most voters have always been members of one party or another, although I guess that's not so true anymore – there are a lot of people today that don't identify with either party."

"So why then can an independent not win?"

"Ah, well, you see we've got this weird system left over from colonial days where the President isn't actually directly elected by the people. Instead, in all but one or two states it's a "winner take all" situation. Whichever candidate gets the most votes wins that state. Then, each state sends a certain number of representatives to participate in what they call the Electoral College – I guess they must be called "Electors." They're the ones that actually elect the president, although they're supposed to vote the same way the largest number of the citizens in their state voted. So even if a third-party candidate gets a lot of votes nationally, they never win a single electoral vote unless they get more votes than both of the main party candidates in at least one state."

"But still, that is possible, is it not?"

"Well, I guess it's possible, but it sure would be hard, with all of the money the main party candidates have to work with these days. And a third-party candidate would have to have a really clear, really popular platform – one that was different from what the other two candidates were running on or people wouldn't have much reason to vote for him."

Frank took the tablet back and started typing. "The only third-party candidate I can remember that did pretty well was a guy named H. Ross Perot."

He skimmed a page, "Yes – he ran twice, and the first time, even though he got almost 19% of the popular vote, he didn't get any electoral votes – not a single one. Almost 20 million people voted for him, and it was as if no one did. He had a fortune to spend on his election, too."

Frank read a bit further. "Wow – I'd forgotten this: a hundred years ago, Teddy Roosevelt ran as a third-party candidate four years after he stepped aside to let William Howard Taft, his Secretary of War, run for President. And Roosevelt lost terribly, too."

"And Mr. Taft? How did he do?"

"It looks like he was clobbered! Wilson – our president during World War I – got 435 electoral votes, Roosevelt got 88 – and Taft got only 8! And listen to this – even though Roosevelt got 11 times more electoral votes than Taft, he only had 4% more of the popular vote. Wow!"

"So a third-party candidate can take a lot of votes away, then, yes?"

"Sure. Back in 2000, George W. Bush probably wouldn't have won if a consumer advocate named Ralph Nader hadn't run for President, even though he knew he couldn't possibly win." Frank was typing again. "Looks like he only got 2.74% of the popular vote, and of course no electoral votes at all.

"Al Gore – the Democratic party candidate that year – actually ended up with 500,000 more votes than Bush. But that wasn't good enough, because Bush won in states with just a few more electoral votes than Gore. One of those states was Florida – he won that one by just 437 votes." Frank let out a low whistle. "And Nader got more than 98,000 votes in Florida!"

"I think I do not like your Mr. Nader very much."

"Yeah, a lot of Democrats felt the same."

Frank switched the tablet back to the debate coverage. "So I wonder which party this guy Yazzie would hurt the most?"

*　*　*

20

Hello – Is This the Person to Whom I am Speaking?

FRANK CHECKED OUT of the motel early the next morning. He had a lot on his mind as he motored slowly towards the highway.

He'd tentatively decided not to drive too far. The Iowa caucuses were only two days away, so why not stick around to see what would happen? The only question was where to hang out until then.

Then there was the question of what to do about his bugged vehicle, how to deal with his long-neglected publishing contract, and figuring who might have hacked the last poll – the one that Josette had claimed the Fillies hadn't influenced.

He tried to make headway on those issues but found he was too distracted. The problem was a certain guerrilla question that kept sneaking out of his subconscious to sabotage his concentration: what about Josette?

Neither had said anything much after the debate about where they would go next, other than to acknowledge that each would be monitoring the primaries as they hopscotched around the country – Frank, for Voldemort as well as to satisfy his own curiosity, and Josette, as part of her academic project, and to satisfy whatever other goals she had or hadn't shared with him.

At the moment, Frank was driving in a direction that would not preclude ending up in Des Moines, and he grudgingly admitted that his direction might possibly have been influenced by Josette mentioning that this might be her next stop as well. But where else should he go? And Des Moines was a big enough city that the chances had to be low that he would run into her anyway.

There seemed to be no purpose in dwelling further on that topic, so he tried to get back to something more practical. Like the fact that right now one of Len Butcher's staff might be listening to the same radio station he was, via a microphone hidden who knew where in his camper?

He wanted to find that microphone as a matter of principle. Well, more than principle. He didn't trust Butcher, and there were already things he'd found out that he hadn't shared with Butcher at all – such as who had hacked the pollsters. But if he found the microphone, then what? If he removed it, Butcher would know as soon as it went dead.

Maybe he could start by occasionally jiggling the battery wire a little bit, to introduce static. After a day or two, he could start disconnecting it occasionally, and then hook it up again a few minutes later. Butcher would think it was just a wire loosening up due to roadway vibrations.

No, that wouldn't work either. Butcher might have planted more than one bug. Frank would never know if that was the case unless he heard it through Josette. And what about his computer system? Maybe that had been compromised as well.

No, it was silly thinking about playing with wires. It was time to call in the cavalry.

He pulled off the highway at the next exit and parked at a gas station with a cafe. He pulled a small box out of a drawer in the camper, and walked into the cafe. Sitting down, he took a brand new phone out of its packaging – one of several cheap mobile phones, each loaded with twenty hours of prepaid time, that he'd purchased during his previous exploit and never got around to using. He pulled a napkin out of the dispenser on the table and copied the phone's number onto it two digits at a time: 21 52 53 86 41.

After the waitress delivered his coffee, he took his regular phone out of his pocket and called his father. But after letting it ring twice, he hung up, waited thirty seconds, and dialed the phone again. Good – his father didn't pick up.

When his father's "leave a message" recording was over, Frank pulled the napkin out and began speaking.

"Hi Dad – Frank. Hope all's well. Hey, there's a radio show that wants you and me to do that 'long-lost father-son team cracking the Alexandria Project' interview thing again. Would you let me know whether one of these dates would work for you? February 1, May 2, May 3 or August 6? Oops – one more – April 1? Get back to me, hey? Thanks."

He left a couple of dollars on the table and walked outside. Ideally, his father had been home when he called and had remembered the old signal about not picking up after a quick first hang up – kind of a sleazy way of avoiding paying long distance charges when you wanted to let someone know that you'd reached your destination safely, except this time he didn't hang up quickly the second time as well. Anyway, he'd get the recorded message eventually if he was out.

He was pretty sure his father would figure out that the message must have some kind of code in it, given the quick hang-up and the fact that the two of them had in fact never done a joint interview before. That should make him think to look for a message within the message, and the last part – "Get back to me, hey?" would clue him in to look for a hidden number. If he got that far, the rest would be easy: February 1 would obviously mean 21, May 5 would indicate 52, and so on.

Frank felt pretty cute coming up with that little gambit, but it was cold outside and the wind was sending a thousand fingers through the tiny holes in Frank's sweater. Maybe he'd been too cute and his father wouldn't think the message sounded odd. Or maybe his father was out of town and wouldn't get the message at all for days. He didn't want to have to wait outside forever before getting back into his bugged camper.

The prepaid phone began ringing.

"Hey Dad – nice work."

"Nice work? That wasn't exactly an Enigma class challenge, Frank. I hope you weren't too worried about somebody intercepting it?"

"At this point, no. But for what we're talking about now, yes, which is why I wanted to use a disposable phone. I assume you didn't call me back on your regular line?"

"Know more than that, do I," his father intoned in a solemn voice.

"Oh come on, Dad, can't we leave the Yoda bit behind with the last adventure?"

"A new adventure this is?"

"DAD!"

His father chuckled. "Okay, okay. So what's up?"

Where to begin? He hadn't been in touch with his father since his visit, and felt guilty for leaving him in the dark.

"Well, it's like this. Not long after I left your place, I was asked by an undercover type to help the government figure out whether someone has been monkeying with the presidential candidate polls. Turns out someone was, and I was able to figure out how they did it. They want me to stay available through the primaries, in case it looks like something funny starts happening again."

"Well, that's a relief. You mean people aren't really planning on voting for all the wing nuts the polls say they are?"

"That's hard to say. All we know is that sometimes they weren't saying they favored the particular wing nuts the polls said they did."

His father chuckled again. "Okay, so I assume you're working for my alma mater, the FBI this time?"

"Nope. This time it's Voldemort."

There was silence at the other end of the phone.

"Okay," Frank continued, "Not Voldemort. That's just what..." he paused before selecting a pronoun, "I call it, because it's some super-secret NSA type outfit that isn't supposed to exist, much less have a name."

"Interesting. So if you've already caught the hackers, to what do I owe the honor of this subterfugenous contact?"

How should he answer that? He hadn't exactly caught the hackers so much as been lucky enough to have one confess to him. And he didn't really want to start telling his father about Josette.

"Well, there's two things. First up, my job was to just figure out how the hack was carried out. It's up to Voldemort to catch the black hats. I think there may even be another group out there as well."

"And the second thing?"

"Right! That's the reason I'm calling. I think the guy from Voldemort bugged my camper when he came out to recruit me. Probably a geolocation unit, too, and who knows what else besides."

"Wouldn't surprise me a bit. They're just being thorough. And you did manage to give the FBI – the CIA, too – the slip last time, didn't you? Twice, as I recall."

Frank hadn't looked at it that way. But still, he had no desire to let Butcher know everything he said and did, much less have him find out about Josette and the FdL.

"Well, whatever. But I don't like the idea of someone I'm spying for spying on me, and I want to do something about it. Can you think of anyone from your FBI days that might be willing and able to scan my camper and find whatever's in there?"

"More than likely. We had annual meetings and I got to know guys from all over. Where are you, anyway?"

"Iowa."

"Give me a minute or two to dig around. Call you right back."

As promised, it wasn't long before the phone rang again.

"Okay. Got just the guy for you. Name's Howard – Howie – Schotz. I can give him a discrete call and let him know that you'll be stopping by. Take down this address...."

With a now-clear directional conscience, Frank drove back onto the highway and headed east. A sign informed him that it was 84 miles to Des Moines.

* * *

21

Every Picture Tells a Story (Don't it?)

I T WAS LATE, but Richard Fetters still sat before his computer screen. In less than twenty-four hours, the good citizens of Iowa would begin gathering in town halls and cafeterias to caucus, and the decisive phase of the primary season would begin. He was feeling uncertain, and uncertainty was not a state of mind he cared for. Indeed, he had labored long and successfully to wring every element of chance out of his political career.

Acquiring that ability had taken time, though, as evidenced by the row of pictures on the wall above his desk. The first one displayed a far younger version of himself, with arms upraised and a cockeyed smile, acknowledging the cheers of his campaign team as he claimed victory in his first Congressional race. Those had been heady days, with everything to gain and nothing to lose – a time when a roll of the dice meant opportunity rather than risk.

He had served three terms in the House, but the stress of defending a seat in a swing district every two years took its toll, as did the strain of feigning real interest in the welfare of the citizens whose hands he shook while stumping for their votes. When the senior senator of his predominantly blue state announced his retirement,

Fetters willingly accepted the invitation to run for the seat. As he expected, he was decisively defeated by the popular former governor he ran against.

But that was all according to plan. The party had needed a candidate to take the fall, and in politics, sacrificial lambs could be well rewarded if they were savvy enough to strike their bargain in advance. For Fetters, the payoff was trading the vicissitudes of elected office for the type of political power that could be built upon and consolidated without the need for constant glad-handing at coffee shops and county fairs.

That explained the next picture, in which he was accepting the party leadership of his state, and the one to the right of that, where he was being welcomed as the Chairman of the national party. In each picture his demeanor became more confident, the set of his brow more determined as he became more skilled at a game he was better suited to play. Back room politics were direct; either you had the clout or you didn't. When you looked another professional in the eye, each of you knew where the other stood in the political food chain. He had been determined to get to the top of that chain, and found that his dispassionate personality and calculating nature gave him the ability to realize his ambitions.

In the fourth picture the setting was more formal. This time, only his right hand was in the air. The other lay flat on a bible held by a Supreme Court Justice. He served four years as Secretary of Defense, a just reward for helping ensure the last Republican president's re-election. But his cabinet tenure ended when the Democrats took back the White House, and he had been on the political sidelines ever since. Still influential, yes. But without a top position to operate from he was no longer part of the inner circle that called the important shots behind the scenes.

That had been fine for a time, as his plan going into the cabinet had been to take an excessively well paid private sector job on his way out again, the kind that was always available to former Defense Department officials. That was how things worked in Washington, and he was not disappointed – in the fifth and final picture above his desk he was standing, arms crossed and legs spread, in front of the floor to ceiling windows of a lofty corner office.

Facing off Wall Street as the CEO of a multinational military contractor was not only obscenely remunerative, but also liberating in comparison to heading a public bureaucracy under the constant watch of Congress and the media. But it wasn't long before his new life became tame and uninteresting. He had no private sector experience to inform his decisions, and only generic managerial skills to work with. That made him dependent on subordinates who knew more than he did about the business he was supposed to be running. And he missed the behind the scenes intrigue of Washington, as well as sparring with a dozen other influential administration members for the ear of the president. Now he was the one at the top, and he found the similar machinations of his own management team to be tedious.

He found, too, that the techniques he'd refined in the political world weren't conducive to creating the type of cohesive, motivated management team that achieved results and drove up the value of his stock options. By the end of his second year in the private sector he was actively planning his return to the center of power.

But when he stepped down, he found that he'd underestimated the challenge of engineering his re-entry. Party politics abhorred a vacuum, and the hierarchy had reshuffled seamlessly as soon as he gave up his chairmanship. And none of the players that mattered were inclined to welcome him back.

Not that he had expected otherwise. While on the way up, he hadn't been shy about throwing a sharp elbow whenever and wherever necessary – indeed, he had cultivated a reputation as someone not to be trifled with. By the time he reached the top, his position was based as much on fear as respect, and fear leads to alliances of necessity rather than loyalty.

Better to pursue another approach, he had decided, and shortcut the laborious process of rebuilding a power base. This time, he would remain hidden in the shadows, aiming straight for the ultimate target and leaving nothing to chance. At his age, he only had room for one more picture on the wall, and he wasn't going to waste it.

Or at least that was the plan. Now, on the eve of the first primary, he was anxiously waiting to learn whether his careful planning would pay off. There was nothing further he could do to alter the outcome in Iowa, but still he pored through screen after screen of detailed field reports from the network of well-paid grassroots organizers he had hired. Each report estimated the number of voters that could be counted on to show up and commit to Wellhead, how many drivers had been arranged to shuttle elderly citizens to caucus locations, and whether local momentum seemed to be gaining or waning.

He shut his computer down at last. All the available data indicated that everything should proceed as planned. Except, of course, that this was politics, and politics was never totally predictable.

Still, Wellhead didn't need to rank even second so long as the percentage gap between him and the winner was not too great. All that was required was for him to survive the Iowa caucus as a credible candidate. A nice run of machine-voting primaries would follow, and everything would become easy. After clobbering his opponents in three or four states, the weaker candidates would start dropping out. Soon it wouldn't matter if he stumbled in one of the few other caucus states. It would simply be seen as a local problem, and any remaining candidates would be slinking off for the exits.

But still. He wasn't used to having this much riding on the actions of a few tens of thousands of caucus attendees.

He stood up and walked into the pantry to pour himself a drink. Enough of this. He was too much of an old hand to suffer from election eve jitters. But then he returned to his office anyway, and stared at the same field reports again until long after he had finished his scotch.

*　*　*

Frank was scanning the names over the dingy store fronts of a row of buildings in a tired looking section of Des Moines as he idled down the street. There it was – Great Plains Network Support, dark and closed for the day. He turned two corners as he'd been instructed to do and drove up the alley behind the building.

Halfway down the block he backed his camper up against a loading dock beneath a smaller version of the same sign and called the number he'd been given by his father, still using his disposable phone. A few minutes later, the metal door behind the camper shot up, and Frank stepped out the back door of his camper and into the building.

He found himself in a large room with bare brick walls and rows of old fashioned, four foot long fluorescent lights suspended from a high ceiling. Beneath were a half dozen 4' by 8' tables, strewn with tools, cables and the exposed insides of servers and other computer equipment. Banks of cluttered shelves lined the walls.

He was greeted by a late-middle age, stocky man with a double chin sparsely frosted with white whiskers vaguely approximating a beard. Frank could have predicted the plain white T shirt, baggy pants and old sneakers before he saw them.

"So you're Frank's son, are you? Your old man thinks a lot of you – used to talk about you all the time – what a computer whiz you were!" He held out his hand.

Frank was momentarily taken aback. At the time his father would have said those things Frank hadn't known whether his Dad was alive or dead, and couldn't have cared one way or the other.

"Thanks for helping me out on such short notice, Mr. Schotz – I really appreciate it."

"Call me Howie, and not to worry. Business isn't exactly coming out of the woodwork right now anyway. Let's go to my office and you can tell me what you need."

Frank followed him through a door in the back of the work room and found himself in a small store room rather than an office.

"Just another sec," Schotz said, pulling a ring of keys out of his pocket before unlocking another door and leading Frank down a flight of stairs.

The room they descended into was a far cry from the one directly above. The work bench here was uncluttered, the lighting was modern, and obviously sophisticated equipment was racked neatly along the walls.

"I'm a bit more organized than my staff," Schotz said as he led Frank through the work room and into a small office with a desk, a couch, and a wall covered with recognition plaques and other mementos from what Frank assumed were Schotz's years with the FBI.

"Everything done here I do myself. Have a seat." He gestured at the couch as he settled in behind his desk.

"So how's your old man doing? We only spoke for a couple of minutes. Is he still hanging out in the desert with the UFO crowd?"

"He's good, and yes, he's still out in Nevada most of the time. Guess he likes the peace and quiet. But we spent some time together last year, and since then he's been to Washington to visit me and my daughter."

"I read about what the two of you were up to. Sounds like you and he gave our old employer quite a merry chase. I'll bet he enjoyed that."

Frank laughed. "Yes he did. Luckily, the way things played out they couldn't just cut him off, so they still pay him to keep an eye out around Area 51. But he's not getting info out of the local office like he used to."

Frank pointed at the mementos. "It looks like you had quite a career with the FBI. Have you been out long?"

"'Bout ten years. Once I put in enough time to max out my pension, I figured it was a good time to move on. But most of what I call my 'downstairs' work I do for them, or to folks they send my way. The FBI has lots of local offices, but they're mostly staffed with field agents and administrative folks. Sometimes they send the specialist work to Washington or to a big regional office, but most of the time they send it out to a former staffer like me who's qualified and confidential."

Without missing a beat, Schotz changed the topic.

"So what can I do for you? Your Dad didn't really say, except that it was up my alley. And don't worry about the 'why' part of it. Just the 'what' will do. I don't need to know any more than that."

That suited Frank fine. He'd been wondering how to politely avoid answering that kind of question if Schotz pressed him.

"Well, there's an easy part – or at least I hope it's easy – and then there's a trickier part. The easy part is I'm pretty sure the camper I've got parked out back has at least one microphone and transmitter planted in it, and maybe more devices besides – like to track where I am. I need to have the whole vehicle scanned to find out where they are."

"Piece of cake. I can do that for you in no time. How about the tricky part?"

"Right. Well, my concern is that if we just pull out everything you find, the people that put them there will realize it, and then just plant new ones, and I'll be right back where I started. I've got a few ideas about what to do about that, but none that I'm very happy with. I'm guessing you'll have some better ones."

"No worries there, either. I've got a few tricks that will work just fine. But first I'll need to know how you want to handle it. Should the bad guys not hear or know where you are, or do you want to feed them some disinformation while you're at it?"

"That sounds interesting. What do you have in mind?"

"Well, a tracker is the easiest bug to mess with. I can give you a pretty cute little unit that you can use just like a GPS. Plug in whatever destination you want, and it will simulate you going there even though you're really going somewhere else."

"That's very cool."

"Yup. I can hook my device up in parallel with theirs without them ever realizing it. Any time you want to drop out of sight, you'll be able to flip the switch, program in a fake destination, and that's where they'll think you're going."

Frank felt a surge of elation. This was great! He felt like Sean Connery in an old James Bond movie listening to Q rolling out the new toys he'd get to play with.

"That sounds awesome – definitely, count me in for one of those. I don't know how or when I may use it, but the potential is amazing."

"It is pretty cool. If you plug in the date you want to be visible again, it'll also plot a course to arrive there the same time you do. Once your real location and the one it's transmitting converge, you just flip the switch again, and they'll never know that you've been somewhere else."

"I like that a lot. How about for the microphone? I guess I could just play loud music every time I don't want to be heard."

"We can do a lot better than that. And anyway, if whoever bugged your vehicle knew what they were doing, they planted several microphones so they'd be sure to hear you clearly wherever you were. Unless you put a radio in front of every one of them, they'll still hear you at least some of the time. And if you haven't been playing loud music up till now, they'll figure out that you're on to them."

"So how do you handle that?"

"I expect you know what a 'white noise' generator is?"

"Sure – something that generates masking sounds that cancel out real ones so you don't hear your noisy neighbors, or whatever. But with the room units, you hear the masking noise, so I assume you've got something better?"

"Oh heck yes. It'll set you back a bit, but as long as you don't mind the cost and only care about voices, I can install a unit that will white out any normal volume conversation you'll ever have in your camper."

"Great. So that just leaves data. If my on-board computer network has been hacked, can you install a parallel satellite receiver/transmitter while you're at it? That way when I don't want to be monitored, I can use the new system, but since I'll also keep using the old one for everyday stuff, they'll think that nothing has changed."

"Not a problem. Can you give me a couple of days?"

"That would be perfect. What do you expect it will set me back?"

Schotz had been taking notes while they talked. "Assuming I install everything we just talked about, it won't be cheap, but for your Dad's sake, I'll give you the equipment at my cost. You'd still be talking about at least $15,000, though. Are you in for that much?"

That was a lot of money, but less than Frank had estimated while Schotz was talking. And there was something satisfying about spending Butcher's own money to mislead him.

"I am, and thanks – really. I don't know where I would have gone to if my father hadn't introduced us."

"No worries. Just have your camper back where it is now by 8:00 AM tomorrow, and I'll get you back on your way by late afternoon the day after."

* * *

22

In Which Frank Sees a Ghost(writer)

WITH NOTHING TO do all day but wait for Schotz to work his magic, Frank holed up in a nearby motel, determined to finally make some headway on his book. But once again he found it impossible to write anything that didn't actively suck. Finally giving it up, he headed out for a run. The hell with Josette, he told himself. Whatever she might think, he was going to keep working on getting into shape.

As he huffed and puffed his way along, he reviewed the situation. His publisher was harassing his agent for a first draft delivery date. His advance was based on the understanding that the book would be brought to market quickly, before everyone lost interest in the crisis that it described. If he didn't deliver a manuscript soon, a penalty clause would kick in, and he'd have to return some of the advance instead. No matter how he looked at the facts, it seemed that he had run out of options.

After returning, he glumly emailed his agent to tell him he was willing to talk about working with a co-writer. Within ten minutes, his phone rang. Not surprisingly, his agent was delighted; earning his full commission had been looking less and less likely every time he checked in with Frank.

"Now you're talking! Matter of fact, just in case, I've been doing some looking around, checking out who was between jobs that you might like working with. I've found a guy who's been a technology journalist for fifteen years who I think would be just right."

"If he's so good, why's he available?"

"Stop and think about it. Remember all those technology magazines that used to have hundreds of pages of vendor ads? When was the last time you saw one of those?"

"Alright, a long time. But didn't they just go online, like everything else?"

"Sure, those that didn't go bankrupt first when the media world imploded. But all the technology advertisers went to the Internet, too. They can pick from billions of Web pages now at all kinds of sites instead of having to advertise in just a dozen magazines. A tech publisher is lucky if it can make a penny now for every dollar it used to make on print advertising. So they fired most of the tech writers long ago."

"I guess I kind of knew that, now that you mention it. Where did they all go?"

"A lot moved on to other ways to make a living, some – like this guy – are still trying to make ends meet by writing freelance. Folks like that are happy to grab a decent-sized project that pays real money instead of spending half their time hawking short articles instead of writing."

"But does he know anything about security?"

"Yup. Network security was one of the beats he covered when he was a staff writer. He's been selling cybersecurity articles regularly since then."

Well, at least he wouldn't have to explain basic vocabulary if he worked with the guy.

"How about writing a book, though? Has he ever done that before?"

"Yes and no. He hasn't co-written a book before, but he has authored a series of cyber-thrillers, and don't forget we're going for a popular audience here, not a technical one. We want someone who can put some excitement into the story instead of putting readers to sleep."

"What are some of his titles? I can duck into a book store later today and pick one up."

"You'll probably need to download an eBook instead; he hasn't been able to get a contract for any of his books, so he's self-published."

"Self-published? If he couldn't get a publisher, how do you know he's any good?"

"You really are out of touch, aren't you? Don't take this the wrong way, but if your name hadn't been all over the papers, you never would have gotten a publisher even if you had a dynamite book pre-edited and ready to deliver. And by the way, you may have a publisher for your book, but don't forget you'll still have to promote the hell out of it online. This guy knows how to do that, and can help you do what it takes."

"Like what?"

"You know – social media – tweeting, setting up Facebook pages, blogging. That's going to take hours a day leading up to your release date, and you'll have to keep it up for a quite a while after that."

"You never told me I'd have to do that! Isn't it the publisher's job to promote my book?"

"Come on, Frank. Didn't you look into the writing game at all before you decided to take a crack at it?"

Well, no, the publisher had called him. It sounded like a nifty idea, so he'd said yes and then hired Vose to help him negotiate the contract. Anyway, that sealed the co-writer deal. If there was anything Frank thought was more inane than Facebook, it was Twitter. The mere notion of having a Facebook page or a Twitter account, much less posting nonsense to it seven days a week, appalled him.

"Alright. You win. Have him get in touch with me. I'll see if we hit it off."

"Great decision, Frank. I'll be sure he calls you tomorrow. And if you say it's a go, I'll take care of all the paperwork."

Frank turned off his phone and tried to feel upbeat. What was there not to like about someone else doing all the hard work to put out a book with his own name on the cover? Famous people did it all the time. Why not him?

But he knew the answer well enough. What wasn't to like was that he'd have to work closely with someone for months on end that he didn't know, would probably have nothing in common with, and whose job would be to literally put words in his mouth. Ugh.

* * *

Across town, Henry Yazzie was also sitting in a hotel room. His phone had barely ceased ringing the day he made his announcement, and for twenty-four hours after that. But now he and his campaign manager rarely received calls from anyone. The media was focusing on the Iowa caucuses now, and so far as the press was aware, no one there had heard of him before his announcement.

Yazzie had heard the phrase "yesterday's news" before, but that hardly described this sensation of instant oblivion. It reminded him of a lapel button he'd seen once: over a picture of Andy Warhol were the words "Your 15 minutes are over."

And then the phone did ring.

"Hello – Yazzie here."

"Hello, Mr. Yazzie. Thanks for taking my call. My name is Baxter Maxwell, and I'm the Executive Director of the Centrist Coalition of America. You probably haven't heard much about us, as we're a recently launched umbrella organization.

Our mission is to support and coordinate the efforts of grassroots organizers that want to offset the impact of the Tea Party. Do you have a few minutes to talk?"

That was an understatement. He'd been doing a crossword puzzle.

"Sure, I've got a little time."

"Great – I appreciate that. As I was saying, we're trying to counteract the Tea Party, but that doesn't mean we're above watching how they've gone about energizing people. The big difference is that we're not trying to appeal to far right conservatives. We want to turn voter disgust with the 'politics as usual' approach of both parties in a positive direction. Our goal is to keep a Tea Party or a far left candidate, or a candidate willing to kowtow to one wing or the other, from winning."

Well, wasn't it about time someone did that, Yazzie thought. But why was this guy calling him?

"My reason for reaching out to you today is that we've been reading as much as we can about your platform. We're particularly impressed with your domestic policy positions, which are very much in line with our own leanings. We don't know much about your thoughts on foreign policy, but we're interested in hearing where you stand. If you're willing, we'd like to sit down with you and see whether there's enough alignment between your views and ours for us to consider endorsing your candidacy for president."

Maxwell was right. Yazzie had never heard of his organization, so his first instinct was to be cautious. On the other hand, he was hardly in a position to refuse a potential endorsement from just about anyone from a dog catcher on up.

"Well, thank you very much for your interest, Mr...."

"Maxwell. Baxter Maxwell."

"Thanks – sorry. I never catch a name the first time I hear it. Kind of a handicap for someone running for office."

Maxwell laughed. "I'm sure. Would you mind if I followed up by sending you an email with my contact information and a link to our web site? You can take a look to get a feel for what we're all about and then let me know if you'd like to meet."

"Thanks – that would be helpful. I'm afraid I'm not familiar with your group."

"No worries. So far we've been running something of a stealth campaign. That way when we do start asking for attention we'll have enough substance that the press and the pundits will have to pay attention."

Yazzie could scarcely fault that approach. He'd been following the same strategy himself. He pulled his laptop out and turned it on while they continued to speak, hoping that he'd be impressed by Maxwell's organization. It hadn't been too difficult gathering enough signatures to qualify as a candidate in western states with large Native American populations. Now he had to back up his claim that he would be on the ballot in all 50 states – including those without many Native American voters.

That was going to be tough – he and his team didn't really have a strategy they fully believed in to tackle any of the east coast or deep south states. Maybe this guy could help solve that problem for him, even if his organization was brand new.

"How many states is the Coalition active in so far?"

"That depends on how you define 'active.' We've only got boots on the ground in about a half dozen states right now. But that's okay, because our strategy is to help groups that already exist get traction, rather than engage in one-on-one recruiting or outreach ourselves. We believe that the only way we can force a change in Washington is to mobilize a big enough block of voters to prevent the extremists from getting nominated in the first place. In some states, we may have to settle for making far-right and far-left candidates moderate their positions in order to avoid losing, and then hold them to it."

Once again, Yazzie couldn't fault that line of reasoning – it paralleled his own plans, which were based on playing to the center.

"And I should also say that we're quite well funded. We don't like any of the candidates for President so far, but when we find one we do, we're willing to put serious money behind his or her candidacy."

Now you're talking, Yazzie thought. If they had more than what his own war chest held the last time he had checked – which was $12,432 – they could talk turkey right now. But he restrained himself; better to play it cool.

"Well, it certainly sounds like we have enough in common that it might make sense to meet. Let me take a look at your site and anything else you might want to send along and I'll get back to you."

"Excellent. I'll look forward to hearing from you when you've had time to digest it. Give me a call or shoot me an email when you're ready – either will be fine."

Tantalized as he was, Yazzie couldn't help feeling suspicious. Did this guy's organization really support his positions, or were they just hoping to get some support from Native Americans? Maybe it was all a bait and switch, and they didn't have any intention of endorsing him at all. Probably they'd just use a meeting as an opportunity to pitch their own policy positions to him.

Maxwell's email arrived within a few minutes as promised. Yazzie had already found the CCA web site and opened up their platform page. He paused and picked up his phone again.

"Hey Carson," he said. "Are you in the motel? Can you come over here? And bring your laptop."

Moments later his campaign manager arrived at their shared room. Carson

Bekin was also his chief domestic policy advisor (there was no foreign policy advisor), and wore many of the other hats usually shared by a full campaign team as well.

"What's up, Henry?"

"Just got a call from somebody claiming his organization is considering endorsing me for president. What do you think of that?"

"Prank call?"

"Thanks for the vote of confidence. But yeah, I'm trying to figure out whether he's real, and if so, what his game is. I just emailed you a link to his Web site. I'd like us both to check this out and then compare notes."

Yazzie went back to scanning the group's platform page; he had to admit that the alignment was tight between his own positions and those he was reading. On a first look, he didn't find anything he objected to strongly, and there was a lot he liked.

But how real was the support behind the CCA? The world was full of wanna-be organizations of all stripes, and anyone could throw up a web site these days that looked convincing.

He clicked on a tab that said "Coalition Partners" and began checking the links he found there. Every one led him to a site set up on a common template. Some were focused on an issue like global warming, while others seemed centered on concerns unique to individual states, or even single Congressional districts. The various state and local sites were cross-linked with the topical sites, so that users could connect with each other and act either locally or nationally, depending on their interests.

As he skipped around, he saw that the landing page of every site had an over-arching statement of purpose centered on breaking partisan gridlock in Washington. After that, each site included position statements relevant to its particular focus, backed up with supporting materials. Each site also offered online tools that interested people could use to organize meetings, set up mailing lists and the like.

He clicked on the "What You Can Do" tab, and saw that most of the sites had a meaningful number of people who had allowed their names to be listed as supporters, especially in the states holding the earliest caucuses and primaries. Almost all the sites also displayed event and meeting schedules indicating that activities were being held locally, with Iowa leading the list. Bar charts on every home page showed the pace of people signing up at that site as well as across all CCA affiliates, and the rate at which activities were launching locally and nationally.

Clearly someone had spent some significant money on the infrastructure supporting all these sites, and then fleshing them out with content. If the bar charts were to be believed, most sites were seeing good growth; some were taking off quite rapidly. But anybody could make up names and throw up bar charts.

He looked up from his screen. "So what do you think?"

"Give me just one more minute," Bekin said. He poked away at his keyboard a bit longer and then spoke again.

"I've never heard of these guys before, so I did a search on CCA to see what the buzz is. It looks like they've got some momentum building, mostly in local papers and at blogs. I checked the traffic rankings for some of the more active looking sites, and the numbers are credible – these aren't just shell sites."

"That matches this guy Maxwell's story. He said they weren't going to look for national press attention until they have some substance to point to. Still, I don't know – these are all cookie cutter sites. It's kind of a cute concept, but it's too much like social media for my taste – a mile wide and an inch deep. Just because somebody clicks on a link to add their name to a list doesn't tell me how they'll end up voting. And that's assuming there are real people behind those names."

Bekin nodded. "Well sure, I'd like to learn more about who they are and where the money's coming from, too. But at a first glance, they've got the traffic and the local news coverage. You can fake the former, but it would be pretty hard to pull off the latter. And sure, we don't want an endorsement from an organization that ends up being a liability."

He looked down at his screen again. "Still, I haven't seen anything to be embarrassed by in what they're supporting. And it looks like they've already got a pretty good following in some states we don't have a game plan for."

He snapped his laptop closed. "Face it, Henry. We're getting close to the end of the road here. We've spent all our time and money building up to the public announcement, and haven't had the resources to plan a real campaign from this point forward. Still don't. What do we have to lose by meeting with this guy?"

"I know. But I'm still suspicious."

"The Groucho Marx thing?"

Yazzie laughed. "Yeah, well, maybe. Anyone that would want to endorse us might be someone we wouldn't want to be endorsed by. Anyway, why do you suppose they'd be interested in us at all?"

Bekin shrugged. "Well, why not us? Can you think of a candidate from either party that isn't committed to such a fixed agenda that he can't have bipartisan appeal? And frankly, Henry, what possible suspicious motive could anyone have for backing us, anyway? No one takes us seriously enough to want to sabotage us."

All of which was true, Yazzie had to admit. So what *did* he have to lose by meeting with this guy?

* * *

23

Now You See Me, Now You...

"SO YOU'VE GOT two little switch panels here – one tucked under the dash to the left of the steering wheel, and one under the left side of your desk back in the camper. That way you can always flip a switch without attracting attention."

Frank reached under the dashboard with his left hand. "So I feel three switches."

Schotz stood outside the open door of the camper, pointing out his handiwork. "Right. The left one will turn on the white noise generators throughout the camper. The middle one will switch the GPS output from the tracer they installed to this new one on your dashboard. See if you can throw that switch."

"I can't."

"Good. That's because you haven't turned the dashboard GPS unit on yet. Before you can throw the switch under the dash, you'll need to turn that on, move this dial to the number two position, and program in a false destination. That way you can't screw up. For the same reason, you won't be able to turn the dial back to the number one position until your current location is the same as the one the tracer is reporting."

"That's pretty slick. So what's the third switch for?"

"That's a little bonus I threw in for your Dad's sake. I added an EPIRB unit in case you're ever really in trouble. It's the same kind of beacon that wilderness hikers and round the world sailors carry, because the signal can be detected no matter where you are. Just be sure you really want to be found before you throw that switch."

"Why's that?"

"Once you do, satellites will pick up the signal, calculate your location and report it back through a global alert system to the local authorities. It won't be long before you'll have to explain to someone why they tail-assed it to wherever you are to save your butt."

"Thanks. I hope I never need it, but that's great."

He climbed out as Schotz pulled something out of his pocket; it looked like a miniature LED flashlight.

"Last thing: hang this remote on your key chain so you can activate or deactivate any of the systems from outside the truck. The range is 100 feet, more or less." He handed it to Frank.

"It's got just one button on it, like you'd expect for a flashlight. Press it once and the flashlight will go on or off. But hold it down for five seconds and then press it once, and the white noise generators go on – press twice and they'll go off. Press and hold the same button for ten seconds and then press it once and the EPIRB will start signaling. Twice again is off. The button's raised and nice and big so you can find it in your pocket. That way you can use it without anyone noticing.

"And don't worry; I left a full sheet of instructions on your desk back there. You don't have to remember everything I just said."

"That's great, Howie. I can't thank you enough for getting all this done so quickly. What do I owe you?"

"My pleasure, and let's call it a flat $15,000."

"You're sure that's fair to you?"

"Don't worry, I'm still making a few bucks. And the EPIRB unit has just been lying around for years anyway."

He took the check Frank wrote out and stuck it in his wallet.

"You taking off right away?"

"I guess not; it's kind of late. Anyway, I'd like to catch the caucus returns on TV."

"Well, don't do it from your motel room. You're in Des Moines. After being worked over by the candidates and media for the past two years we can't wait to see the whole mob move on to harass New Hampshire. Still, Caucus Night here is kinda like Super Bowl Sunday. Except of course most of the players kind of suck."

Frank laughed. "Most of them do seem pretty clueless this year, don't they?"

"You're being too easy on them. Anyway, you might want to check out Maddie's – it's a neighborhood sports bar down the street. Big TV screens and the food's pretty good. Turn right at the end of the alley, and it'll be on corner of the second street you cross."

Why not? It would be less bleak than sitting in a motel room, and he wasn't in the mood for a half-cold pizza anyway.

* * *

Across town, Henry Yazzie was handing a delivery person a $20 bill for a half-cold pizza, biding his time till the caucuses ended. He glanced at his watch, and decided to give his campaign finance chairman a call for an update.

"Yo, Henry," a voice said after a few rings.

"Hi, Ohanzee. Thought I'd check in to see whether you've heard about a group I've just run into. It's called the Centrist Coalition of America – some kind of new grassroots umbrella group. I got a call from them today."

"Not ringing a bell. What did they want?"

"Seems like they're considering endorsing me for President."

"Huh! No offense, but you're not exactly a household word. Did they sound legit?"

"That's what I'm calling you about. Could you get one of the boys to see what they can find out?"

"Sure thing. I'll get back to you in a couple of days. Are you and Carson going to crash any parties tonight?"

Yazzie chuckled. "No, I think we'll just watch the returns from our motel room."

"Sounds like a wild time. Talk to you later."

White Crow hung up the phone and turned back to the man sitting next to him in the motel lobby.

"So what did Henry want?" his companion asked.

"He wants to know whether a group called the Centrist Coalition of America is legit. That's what you heard me say I'd get back to him about in a couple of days."

"What are you going to tell him?"

"After tonight's news broadcasts, I probably won't have to tell him too much."

"I expect not. He should be feeling pretty warm to the CCA a few hours from now, and shouldn't care whether it's legit or not. You got time to grab an early dinner before you head back to the Rez?"

White Crow glanced at his watch. "Yeah. A quick one. Let's do it."

It made sense. Although they'd spoken by phone almost every day for several months, it was rare that White Crow and Baxter Maxwell could meet face to face.

* * *

24

Why? Just be Caucus

F RANK SETTLED INTO a small table set against the long wall of the tavern Schotz had recommended. At the far end of the room, a serious looking quartet was playing eight ball. A fake-stained glass light, almost as large as the pool table itself, hung low overhead, making the men look like figures in a Hopper painting as they leaned, frowning, over the long, green surface to line up and take their shots.

Frank marveled at the large American flag on the wall next to his table. At least six feet tall and half again as long, it was made entirely out of red, white and blue beer bottle caps. The rest of the tavern's décor was largely made up of Iowa sports team paraphernalia, interspersed with the occasional deer head and beer brand mirror. As promised, there were three large TV screens dangling above the bar, giving every patron a ringside seat.

Usually there would have been three different sporting events adding to the cacophony of a busy night's crowd, but tonight each of the screens was tuned to caucus coverage: one to a local network affiliate, one to C&N, and the last to POX News. The talking heads were just getting ready to switch over to covering the first returns as Frank finished digesting the menu.

He scanned the room anxiously for someone to take his order; he'd skipped lunch and was now ravenous. The room was pretty full, with people standing as well as sitting at the bar, largely ignoring the TVs and talking. A middle aged waitress came over at last.

"You eating or just drinking tonight?"

"Both, thanks."

She plopped a glass of ice water and some flatware wrapped in a paper napkin in front of him.

"So what'll it be, hon?" she asked, a pencil hovering over her order pad.

"What's walleye like?"

"Walleye? You never had walleye before? Well, you better have that then, 'cause you never had fish that good. What else?"

"How about a Coors."

"Come'n right up."

The closest TV screen was running the C&N feed. Frank saw the network's lead anchor seated behind the main news desk, a sheaf of papers held in one hand. A dozen steps away stood another familiar figure, square-jawed and looking like everyone's image of an all-American college football player. He was dwarfed by a bewildering array of red, white and blue video screens that blanketed the entire back wall of the broadcast studio. Frank couldn't hear a word, but the closed caption function was turned on. He watched as the words scrolled across the screen.

> *Steven, as we wait for the caucus results, let's turn to an unexpected development. The biggest story today – so far, anyway - seems to be the surprise impact of Henry Dodge Yazzie on today's caucuses.*
>
> *That's right, Jon. No one was expecting anything of interest to happen at the Democratic caucuses, since there were no credible challengers to the President. But people showed up in more than half the Democratic caucus locations to support Henry Yazzie.*
>
> *Maybe you'd better remind our viewers who Yazzie is, Steven. He hasn't had much national exposure so far.*
>
> *Sure. Henry Yazzie is a Navajo businessman running as an independent. He announced his candidacy just a few days ago. He's on the primary ballot in eleven states so far, all out west.*
>
> *What makes him think he's got a chance?*
>
> *That's the really interesting part, Jon. It seems like a lot of people this*

year have been looking for a way to express their unhappiness with all the polarization in politics, but there aren't any moderate candidates to get behind. Yazzie's pitch is that government should try to serve all the people, all the time, instead of seesawing back and forth between extremes every time Congress or the White House changes hands.

If that's the case, why not show up at the Republican caucuses, too?

We're guessing they picked the Democrats over the Republicans because they'd get more media attention. There are so many Republican candidates it's tough for anyone to stand out.

When you say 'they,' Steven, who exactly are you talking about?

Apparently it's a group that calls itself Centrist Coalition of America. It's been around for less than a year, and until now hasn't attracted much attention. But it seems to be picking up steam now, with grassroots groups active in a lot of states already.

What else did they do that got so much attention today?

Well, Jon, they really changed the dialogue of the Democratic caucuses. The organizers thought they'd be done with their meetings in about an hour. Instead, the CCA folks stood up at the outset and challenged a lot of the President's policies and wouldn't sit down until they had their say. Of course, then the party faithful had to take their turn defending the President, so it ended up taking a lot longer than expected. The word got around, and it wasn't long before the camera crews started setting up outside the main caucus sites.

I expect that didn't go down well with the President's field staff.

What field staff? I expect they didn't see any need to be in Iowa at all, without a challenger to worry about. This really caught them flat-footed. I doubt they'll let that happen in New Hampshire.

What about the people who came to support the President?

From what we can tell, Jon, some of the arguments Yazzie's supporters made struck home with them. As you know, the President's approval ratings have been in the gutter, so a lot of the people that showed up were really supporting the party, not him. Most of them had probably never heard of Yazzie, much less read his platform. But now you and I are here talking about him on national television. Whoever is managing his campaign obviously knows what he's doing.

Suddenly, the screens behind him began flashing and pulsating like some massive slot machine getting ready to spit out a jackpot, and a shimmering, yellowish-green hologram of the anchor shimmered into existence next to his partner in front of the wall of screens. The virtual image of the anchor picked up right where his actual self had left off without missing a beat.

We'll have to wait and see what happens in New Hampshire next week. But right now, let's turn to the amazing, AMAZING display of technical wizardly behind us – after all, we're the world leader in technology-driven news reporting. The caucus results are starting to come in, and I know our viewers can't wait for you to explain how all these incredibly impressive displays work...

* * *

It was eleven o'clock that night when Fetters finally turned off the television, satisfied that the caucus numbers would change little as the last results trickled in. Everything had gone as planned, just as he had known it should. But he hadn't gotten to where he was in politics by taking anything for granted.

His phone rang.

"Good evening, Richard. You are to be congratulated," Barbash said.

"Thanks, Otto. Your money had a lot to do with it. The Centrist Coalition of America really came through – and they certainly are a lot better funded now than they were before."

"Not so much, I trust, that they'll have any real effect?"

"No, no, nothing like that much cash. Just enough to allow them to organize a good showing at about half the caucus sites today – quite a good return on investment, really. I'm expecting the Indians will provide very good value, too. Once we have Henry Yazzie formally on board we'll begin mobilizing the tribes across the country as well as the centrists and independents. Give me a few more primaries, and I guarantee we'll have the President sweating but good."

"Indeed, I will take great pleasure from that. But are you sure we needn't worry about things getting out of hand? As long as the President stays as liberal as he's been we'll have cover for Yazzie's increasing success. But if he starts to moderate his positions, that will become harder to explain."

"I don't think he can do that, Otto. He knows if he goes mushy the Latinos, the African Americans, the far left – they'll all just stay home. He's trapped."

"I expect so. But what of this Yazzie? What if he starts to take his chances seriously?"

"I'm confident we can keep him under control. He can't possibly think he can win, and if he doesn't throw in the towel and endorse Wellhead when we ask him to, there'll be no cabinet position for him."

"Still, he doesn't control his people. And he may refuse on principle. If so, there are enough Indians in some of the western states to affect the outcome in a close race."

"That'll never happen. The Indians haven't pulled together any kind of nationally coordinated movement since the Pine Ridge shootout in the '70s. I don't think it's possible for them to put a real campaign together in the short time available. If it looks like Yazzie is somehow getting a bandwagon rolling anyway, we can outspend him a hundred to one. It's amazing what money can buy during an election year, so long as you find the right people to give it to. And people like that can be found everywhere, I assure you. You just need to know how to look."

"Very good then. Are you feeling similarly confident going into New Hampshire?"

"Absolutely. Don't forget they'll be using voting machines there. It took a lot of time and effort getting out the vote today, but with a solid second place finish, no one will have any reason to doubt when Wellhead comes in first in New Hampshire next week."

"Excellent. In that case, it will be quite enjoyable watching the posturings of the other candidates in the week ahead. Well done."

Barbash felt an unfamiliar, heady recklessness after the call. He had directed his considerable wealth to bending the electorate to his view of the world for years. But whenever any of his resources were used in other than legitimate ways he had always taken care to maintain ample distance between himself and those carrying out the dirty work. This time he was being a bit more daring. The reward was that he could observe the chess pieces more clearly as they were moved about the board, secure in the knowledge that his opponents had no idea what they were up against. It was a good bet that they never would.

* * *

25

Call it: Your Book or Mine?

THE MORNING AFTER the Iowa caucuses, Frank was throwing a few articles of clothing and toiletries into the same beat-up suitcase he'd used since college when his mobile phone rang. He saw a Washington number he didn't recognize.

"Hello?"

"Frank?"

"Yes. Who's this?"

"Dan. Dan Grover."

Frank frowned. "Uh, should I know you?"

"Didn't Mr. Vose tell you I'd be calling?"

Oh – right he was referring to Perry Vose, his agent. "Sorry, yes, he did. But I don't think Perry mentioned your name. My mistake."

"Hey – no problem. Sometimes I can't remember my own name! You ever have days like that? Hey? Am I right? So where are you, anyway?"

Frank frowned again, holding the phone several inches from his ear to protect his hearing.

"Iowa."

"Iowa! No shit? Really? Who the hell goes to Iowa? Oh man – my bad! I mean, you're not from Iowa are you?"

"No – Brooklyn." He set his phone on the bed in speaker mode and took a seat a safe distance away.

"Whew! Hey, that was a close one, wasn't it? So hey – when're you coming back to D.C.? I hear we need to fire up the grill and get this burger out to the customer!"

The co-author his agent had recommended was comparing his book to a hamburger? Granted, he hadn't managed to write even a page of it on his own, but still, he'd been thinking of his book with a capital B. Something significant and respectable, to be toiled over and served up on a silver platter to a public that would consume it with respect – not like some fast food meal to be scarfed down with fries and followed with an indifferent belch.

"I don't know; I haven't really decided."

"Well hey – what's today – Wednesday, right? I bet you could be here Thursday night, if you push it. How's about we get together at 9:00 on Friday morning, and we can start storyboarding things out? What'a'ya say?"

"Storyboarding?"

"You know – nail the narrative down and anchor it with some really good action scenes – make sure we get a page turner people can't put down."

Frank stared at the phone in shock. "Dan, I think we need to go back a couple steps. I want to write a well-documented, serious argument that demonstrates why our society needs to wake up and address cybersecurity risks before it's too late."

"No! You're shitting, me, aren't you? With a million dollar story like you've got, you want to give them a cliff hanger! You'll never get a story like this again in your life! Man, I know a hundred writers that would give their left nut to run with a story line like this! Come on – you're yanking my chain, aren't you?"

That was it. "No I'm not. It sounds like this is all a big mistake. I don't know what Perry told you, but obviously what you and he talked about is different than what I have in mind. I'm sorry he wasted your time."

There was a long silence at the other end of the line before a very sober Grover spoke again.

"Okay, okay, hold on. I mean no problem. It's your book, right? So give it to me slow. What exactly is it you have in mind?"

Frank did as requested, elaborating on his plan to write a wake-up call that couldn't be ignored, using the well-publicized events he'd been involved in as an example. When he was done, there was silence again.

"Alright, I got it. Sorry. I guess your agent did kind of say that, but he also gave me some other details, too. Do you remember who your publisher is?"

Frank had to think a minute before he replied.

"Right! That's not exactly a literary house imprint, is it? We're not talking Farrar, Straus and Giroux here. These are mass market paperback guys. You know – they pump out thrillers and bodice-rippers for sale at Walmart. They gave you a big advance, too, right?"

"Well, yeah, they did."

"So what do you think they're expecting? Something from a professor, or a fast read that's going to open at number one on the Best Seller lists and stick there like glue?"

"Well, I don't care! It's my book, isn't it? Don't I get to tell the story the way I want to?"

"Sure, until you sign a contract. It's your story, but it's their advance! If you want to keep it, you better play ball or they'll reject the manuscript."

Now Frank was silent for a while. The guy had a point. He knew the publisher couldn't care less about wising the public up to cyber threats. What it probably wanted was a true-life thriller telling how a lonely nerd outsmarted the bad guys and saved the country – and the reader – from nuclear annihilation.

"Look," Dan added, "let's do this: we use the story as a vehicle to get your message across. Not all the time, but we keep putting it in there whenever there's an opportunity, and we make the read exciting enough that everyone will be sure to finish it. By the time they're done, they'll be terrified that something like this will happen again if we don't get serious.

"How about that? And don't forget, if you want to make a difference, you need to get a LOT of people to read your book. They're not going to do that unless you get them crapp'n in their pants."

Grover had been making some headway, but now Frank recoiled – not only did this guy want to write a literary burger, but it was supposed to get readers crapping in their pants?

Grover sensed he'd gone too far. "Okay, okay. So sometimes I get a little carried away. But you get the idea – if we hit the right balance point, the publisher gets what he wants, and you get what you want. What'a'ya say?"

If Frank could have looked through his phone, he would have seen that Grover was literally holding his breath. The journalist desperately wanted his name on this book, even if it was in smaller print than Frank's. And he wanted the book to be a hell of a page turner, so the five self-published and barely read thrillers he'd already written could ride the coattails of the new book's success.

Frank drummed his fingers on the fake wood of the table in his motel room. What the guy was saying made some sense. But it also made him uneasy. The last thing in the world he wanted was to thrust himself into the limelight. That was why he'd always refused to be interviewed.

"Well, okay. But you're going to have to let me drive the bus on this. If I'm getting uncomfortable with anything, you've got to promise me you'll yank it out."

Dan gave a silent thanks to the patron saint of bad literature. "You got it, buddy. So how about it? Your place or mine Friday morning?"

*   *   *

26

Vote Free or Die

"SO OHANZEE SAYS this guy Maxwell checks out?" Carson Bekin asked Yazzie.

"That's what he says."

"So what happens next?"

"I guess we call him back and say we're ready to get together."

Two hours later, Yazzie and Bekin were sitting at the Des Moines airport, feeling a bit stunned as they waited for the flight to Boston lined up by Maxwell. A car would meet them at Logan airport and drive them straight to Manchester, New Hampshire, where they would meet Maxwell for dinner.

"So how do we play this, Henry? It's great if we get this organization's support and all, but we don't want to lose control of our own campaign."

"I hear you, and I agree. I think we've got to just lay down the law and let him know that if he wants to endorse us, that's fine. But he's not going to run our messaging, or push us into doing or authorizing anything we're not comfortable with."

"Right. I sure hope we can have it both ways, though. All of a sudden this whole campaign is starting to feel real."

"What do you mean 'real?' If it hasn't been real all along, why have we been working night and day on this for the past year?"

"Well, you know. Up till now I've been thinking we're just trying to get some points up on the board – put Native American concerns on the national agenda – get some name recognition. Maybe most people forget all about us by Inauguration Day, but still, it puts a foundation in place we can build on for the next election.

"And let's be real – so far we haven't been able to sign up that many of even our own people to work on the campaign. Now all of a sudden we have all this publicity from Iowa, and we didn't get that on our own. Maxwell was showing us he can produce."

"Well, let's not get our hopes up. I can't believe we've seen all of this guy's cards yet. For all we know, this balloon pops at dinner tonight."

"Yeah, well, at least we got a free flight to New Hampshire. With our budget, that's a win right there."

*   *   *

It was a tired and apprehensive Frank Adversego that rode the escalator up from a Metro station in Dan Grover's neighborhood in Washington, D.C. He got out his phone to double check the address, and set off to learn what his hyperactive co-writer was like in the flesh.

Frank never looked forward to working with new people, and expected this project to be more uncomfortable than most. He knew he'd be dependent on this guy in every way, no matter what arrangement they came to.

Moreover, he'd spent some time checking Grover out online, and didn't like everything he'd found. To the good, the guy seemed to know technology, and that was a relief. But it looked like none of Grover's five thrillers had gotten any traction at all, despite the unremitting social media bombardment the author had unleashed on the reading public. Perry Vose might think Grover's familiarity with social media was a plus, but Frank's regard for social media was only marginally higher than his opinion of tooth decay.

Still, there was nothing to be done but try to keep calm as he carried on up the escalator until it disgorged him onto the sidewalk. A few minutes later he was standing in front of a three-story row house that he guessed had enjoyed at best a casual relationship with maintenance after it was carved up into apartments. He pressed Grover's doorbell and was promptly buzzed in. When he rounded the turn at the top of the third flight of stairs he saw a pony-tailed, fireplug-shaped individual wearing shorts, an untucked Hawaiian shirt, wool socks and sandals.

"Hey, Frank! Pleased to meet you. What time did'ja get in last night?"

"Real late. But here I am."

"Well, glad you could make it. Coffee?"

"Please."

"Great. Back in a jiff. Why don't you settle into my office here."

Frank walked into a room that could have been his own, with one pronounced exception: in addition to the collection of haphazard, worn furniture the room contained a large cat. Like Frank's living room, it had obviously not been subjected to a serious straightening up since the previous millennium. Teetering stacks of magazines occupied one window sill and a skeletal plant with two green leaves stood in the other.

One of the two chairs in the room stood in front of a cluttered desk with a laptop placed front and center, so Frank approached the over-stuffed chair occupied in an overtly proprietary fashion by the over-stuffed cat. It stared past him with a look that successfully conveyed the conviction that it had not the slightest interest in acknowledging his existence. Frank began to sit down nonetheless.

"Sorry, cat. It's the Law of the Bigger Butt."

Jumping down at the last possible moment, the cat retreated to the space beneath a bookshelf and glared at him with obvious ill intent, tail switching angrily from side to side as it considered its options for a counterattack.

"I see you've met my little Molly," Grover said, entering the room and handing Frank a cup of coffee. "She keeps me company most of the day."

Frank was even less of a cat fancier than a dog person, and figured Molly was not a topic to linger on.

"So how do we get started? I've never worked with a co-writer before."

"Well, that's pretty much up to you, but here are a few suggestions. At one end of the spectrum, you can do a first draft, and I'll edit it. At the other end, you can just talk at me and I'll do everything – figure out the narrative and pacing and write the book for you to read and comment on. Between those two endpoints there are lots of gradations of writing and control. Why don't we start by you telling me how much you want to do, and how much control you want to have?"

That made sense, but left Frank feeling a little taken aback. He hadn't really thought about how he wanted to work with Grover – only about how he didn't. He frowned and started drumming the fingers of one hand, then the other on the arms of the chair.

Grover tried again. "Well, how about this. We already talked a bit about what you want the book to say, so why don't we go over the narrative, and then we can work our way into the mechanics later? How does that sound?"

That, or anything else at the moment, sounded just fine.

"Okay, where do you want me to begin?"

"Well, how about where you first became aware someone was hacking the

Library of Congress? When was that? And what did you think was going on at the time?"

Frank started haltingly, but after a little while Grover no longer needed to prompt him with questions. Indeed, Frank soon picked up enough speed that Grover couldn't keep up by taking notes. With Frank barely noticing, he pulled a recorder out of his desk, and set up a microphone facing Frank.

It was fortunate Grover was a good listener, because Frank had never had an opportunity to tell his story before, start to finish. The only people he would have wanted to share it with had been personally involved, and his co-workers knew him well enough not to pepper him with unwanted questions.

As he reeled out the tale he found himself pausing sometimes to think about details that had passed him by in the heat of the moment, things that the FBI, CIA or the hackers themselves must have done, or been thinking of doing at the time.

At last, Grover looked at his watch. "Whoa – let's take a break here. It's ten to one, and if you don't need a bio break, I sure do. Give me a minute and I'll be right back."

Frank looked at his own watch with astonishment. Grover was right. He realized that his mouth was dry and his legs were stiff; he must have been holding them at the same angle for a long time. He stood up and stretched.

Grover reappeared and turned off the recorder. "So that was great, Frank. There's all kinds of dynamite stuff to work with there. We'll want to emphasize some of the more graphic stuff – like the predator missile taking out your camper. If that one doesn't get you a movie deal, Hollywood might as well close up shop. What do you say I try writing a couple of chapters for you to look at? That way you can get a handle on how I write, and see if you're comfortable with it? You're a busy guy, and if it turns out you like my style, we can just keep going that way, with you reviewing the text and telling me where I'm off base, or where there's something that needs to be added."

Frank felt like he should say no, but he was also feeling an enormous wave of relief. If Grover was really willing to write the book for him, why say no?

"Well, I have to admit, my schedule really is jammed up right now," he lied, "so while that's not what I had in mind, I guess there's no harm in giving it a try."

"Great – that sounds like a plan. Listen, I've got to get a couple of other projects tied up before I can work full time on your book, so why don't we call it a day? I'll get a draft done in, say, three or four days? Would that work for you?"

"Well, I guess that sounds fine. You can email it to me, and I can email back with my changes."

That was the last thing Grover wanted to do; he expected Frank's first reaction would be to explode when he saw the style Grover planned on using.

"Uh, we could, but let me make another suggestion. Obviously you've got to be really comfortable with the book, so why don't we agree to meet here on Wednesday at 9:00 in the morning, and I'll have the chapters waiting for you – maybe even get them to you in advance? Then we can talk about how they strike you, and we can figure out where to go from there?" He tried to not look concerned, but found himself leaning forward as he waited for Frank's reply.

Frank drummed his fingers for a moment. He was pretty sure he knew what was going on, and was determined not to be bulldozed. At the same time, he was becoming anxious to get the whole damn book project behind him as soon as possible.

"Okay. Alright, I guess that sounds like a good idea. So I'll see you on Wednesday."

They both stood up, and Grover clapped him on the back.

"Glad to be off and running, Frank. You've got a great book in the making here! I know you're going to be really happy with it."

Frank was much less sure, but there was no turning back now. At least ultimately all the decisions were his. He'd be tough with Grover if he had to.

The apartment door had barely closed behind Frank before Grover threw his fist in the air and mouthed a silent *YES!* Then he dove for his laptop to start tweeting:

> *Off to the races with the greatest cyberstory ever told! Stay tuned!!!*
> *#Bestseller #cybersecurity #thriller*

* * *

27

The Return of the Native

F RANK WALKED INTO his apartment and paused. Leaving aside his zombie-like return in the wee hours of the morning, it had been weeks since he last walked through his own front door. The time away, plus the morning he'd just spent in Grover's apartment, allowed him to see his own disheveled man-cave more objectively than usual.

The picture did not please him. It brought to mind a variety of adjectives, none of which was complimentary. At the head of the list were "cluttered," "worn-out," "messy" and "cheap."

He grunted and headed for the kitchen, and concluded that the same set of adjectives would apply there as well, abetted by "unsanitary" and "malodorous." Opening the refrigerator, he stared at the contents for longer than was necessary, given that all it contained was a half-full jar of pickles, the standard assemblage of ketchup, mustard and mayonnaise, three bottles of beer, and an ancient quart of milk. The sides of the milk container were so swollen it seemed likely the contents might reach critical mass at any moment.

Frowning, he removed a beer and set about opening and closing the few cabinets the tiny kitchen contained, peering blankly at their equally sparse contents: an unopened box of plastic knives, forks and spoons, six cans of soup (various), a box of crackers (stale), a blue silo full of salt. He should put together a shopping list. Maybe tomorrow.

Opening the beer, he moved on to the relative comfort of the one upholstered chair in his living room. Flopping down, he stared around the room, frowned again, and ruminated on what he was looking at. How long ago was it, exactly, since he and his wife had separated? Twenty years, close enough.

The furniture, some bought used and the rest inexpensively, looked shabby and sad, hard-used and poorly maintained. Almost nothing adorned the walls, but there were plenty of things on the desk, window sills and floor – stacks of CDs and books, cardboard boxes that had found their way behind chairs rather than into the recycling bin, old magazines, unopened mail. He began drumming his fingers, and then checked the time on his mobile phone: 3:10. What would he do for the rest of the day?

The mobile phone rang. Brightening up, he saw that it was his daughter, Marla, a grad student at Georgetown University.

"Hey kid! How are you?"

"Great, Dad. Where exactly are you now?"

He felt a pang of conscience; heading back to Washington so suddenly, he hadn't thought to call ahead to let her know he was on his way home.

"Ah, well, I'm actually back in town – yes, D.C. – got back real late last night. I hadn't been planning on it, but decided a couple days ago to drive back to meet my co-author."

"Co-author? Sounds like I've got some catching up to do. What else have you been up to?"

Where to begin? He'd rarely been in touch while he was sussing out the hijinks of hitchhikers and hackers.

"Oh, not a whole lot. Maybe we can get together when you're free? I'd love to see you."

"How about tonight? I'm desperate for an excuse not to study for an exam. Meet me at Sissy's at 7:00? It's on 18th Street in Adams Morgan."

Why not, Frank thought, staring at his dump of an apartment. What else did he have to do?

* * *

"So that's where things stand. This guy Grover is supposed to pitch me a few chapters by next Wednesday, and I'll see how I like them."

"Sounds like a good development, if you're not getting anywhere on your own.

But if you weren't writing while you were out west, what exactly were you up to all that time?"

"Oh, well, you know, there was a lot of driving, and I did try to write – did lots of research – you know how it is." He paused uncomfortably. He wasn't used to keeping anything from his daughter, and she had been his main confidante during the saga he was now trying to describe in print.

She looked at him sideways. "You just sat around in your camper all that time doing nothing but researching and not writing? Right. You would have been climbing the walls in two days. And don't think I didn't notice you've lost weight – have you been sick?"

"No! As a matter of fact, I'll have you know I've been getting myself back in shape. I'm running a few miles almost every morning, and watching what I eat, too."

"*You?* That's really great, but, I mean, *you?* What on earth brought that on? I don't recall you ever exercising or eating anything healthy in your life."

Marla paused and glanced up. Someone she didn't know had just appeared by their table and was looking at her with a quizzical and somewhat critical look on her face.

"Can I help you?" Marla asked.

Frank turned and stood up immediately. "Josette! Great to see you! I didn't realize you were coming back to Washington already."

Marla's face progressed rapidly from surprise to uncertainty, before settling decisively on mischief.

Her father was still standing by the table, now at a loss for words. Almost in unison, Josette and Marla said, "Aren't you going to introduce me?"

"Sure – of course! Josette, this is my daughter, Marla, and Marla, this is... Josette."

Josette frowned and crossed her arms; Marla crossed hers as well, but with evident delight. She was in no hurry to help her father escape from what was obviously an uncomfortable situation.

"Your daughter, Frank?"

"Yes, of course. Marla's a grad student here at Georgetown."

He turned to Marla with eyes pleading for help.

She relented, her curiosity getting the best of her. Who was this attractive, evidently French young woman? And more to the point, how did she know her father? Marla was also getting a twinge of realization that maybe there was a limit to how much she might want to know.

"Hi, I'm pleased to meet you. Why don't you sit down and join us."

"That's a great idea!" Frank said, immediately doubting that it was. "Why don't I get you something to drink?"

"Well, perhaps," Josette said. "I was expecting to meet friends, but they just texted to say that they will be very late. Frank, a pinot grigio would be very nice, thank you."

Frank started towards the bar. His first instinct had been to flee, since he hadn't yet mentioned Josette to Marla. With the two now alone at the table, though, he was regretting his offer.

It seemed like forever before the bartender acknowledged his existence. Frank tried to keep an eye on his table all the while, but the growing crowd made that difficult. When at last he returned to the table, Marla and Josette were laughing and chattering like jaybirds. Worse, they were doing so in French.

He set the glass of wine in front of Josette, who acknowledged it with the briefest of smiles. He knew barely a word of French, and was feeling completely lost until annoyance took over. How long were they going to ignore him? When he realized he was drumming his fingers on the table, he put his hands in his lap and leaned back, frowning. When he caught himself drumming the table again after taking a sip of his drink, he stuffed both hands in his pockets.

What could they be talking about? And worse yet, what could be making them laugh so much?

After a particularly explosive burst of laughter he finally interrupted. "'Allo! 'Allo! Pardon mois, or whatever – remember me?"

Josette, still giggling, put her hand on his arm.

"Oh! You are right! We have been very rude. But your daughter, she is so lovely, and we find that we have so much in common!"

"Sorry Dad," Marla added, giving him a knowing look. "But I'm hearing such *fascinating* things about your time out west. Who would have guessed from what you've just been telling me that you were having *adventures*?"

Josette put her hand to her mouth. "Oh! Perhaps I have been speaking too much! Frank – have I been telling Marla things I should not have?"

Frank had no way to tell, but fervently hoped that the answer was "no."

"Well, given that I don't speak French, how can I tell?"

"Perhaps I should leave you two alone for a few minutes so you can figure that out," Marla said, standing up. Once she was behind Josette, she gave her father an exaggerated wink before walking away.

Frank's ears were burning furiously. "Well, you two certainly seem to have hit it off."

"Hit it off?' I suppose that means we get along? Yes indeed – I like your daughter very much. But she is so very different from you!"

As usual, Josette had succeeded in knocking him off balance with the merest handful of words. For once she noticed.

"Oh! But of course you are very sweet, too."

Frank wasn't sure that "sweet" was what he was looking for and moved on.

"So what are these 'adventures' you've been telling Marla I've been having? Did you tell her about the hackers and everything?"

"Oh, no! I did not know whether I should or should not, so of course – no. But I did tell her how we met on the road, and how you helped me when my bicycle was damaged."

"I don't suppose you mentioned that you wrecked it yourself?"

"No! Of course not! How could I explain that without explaining everything?"

"What about Iowa? Did you mention that we ran into each other again?"

"No, not Iowa. Just Nevada. Up until you moved on and I stayed with my brother and his friends."

"Your brother? I thought that was your boyfriend?"

She laughed. "Oh no – of course not. But he is also my very dear friend, and we have always done much together."

"Then what else were you and Marla yakking about for so long? And what was so funny?"

"Oh, I do not know, just one thing and another – 'girl talk' I believe you call it?"

He would have pursued the question, but he saw Marla returning with a drink for each of them. The noise level around them had risen, and Frank saw that a band had arrived and was starting to do a sound check. They all leaned in closer to hear.

Marla settled her chin on her hand, elbow on the table. "So, are you two all caught up?"

"Just starting," Frank said, giving her a dirty look. "I expect that you and Josette are more in the know right now than I am."

"Oh Frank!" Josette hushed him. "Anyone would think you believe we'd been talking about you this whole time!"

Marla tried not to laugh, but not hard enough to prevent her father from seeing she knew this was exactly what he believed.

To his considerable relief, the band began playing in earnest, making it almost impossible to hold a conversation. As people began to move onto the dance floor, Josette leaned very close to Frank.

"It is so hard to hear; this is not so much a talking place later in the evening. Do you mind if I dance?"

"No, no – of course not. I'm afraid that I don't dance, though," he said, offering an understatement monumental in its proportions.

Josette just laughed, and then looked at Marla, inclining her head towards the band and raising her eyebrows.

Marla gave a thumbs up, and followed her onto the dance floor.

Frank watched with surprise as they blended into the gyrating scrum of bodies filling the space between his table and the band. He was even more surprised when he realized that everyone else on the dance floor was also female. Over the last hour, the varied, after-work group of patrons had gradually transitioned to a clubbing crowd. Only then did it dawn on him that for the first time in his life he was sitting in a lesbian bar.

Curiosity and discomfort competed for his attention until he also realized that he was almost the only male in the bar. Pure discomfort prevailed after that, as he wondered whether people would think he was some creep that wandered in off the street to stare. He found that his mobile phone suddenly become enormously absorbing. When at last the band finished its long, initial jam he tried to catch Marla's attention with a "save me!" look.

Almost immediately, the band swung back into action, and Frank watched as four young women, presumably the friends Josette had planned on meeting, merged into the crowd and greeted her. She turned to wave and mouth a goodbye to Frank as she returned to dancing.

Marla rejoined him and sipped her drink as she checked out the now-full barroom. The band had cranked it up several notches, and Josette was embracing the mood, her arms writhing above her head. When her eyes met those of one of her friends, it seemed to Frank that they gyrated closer until there was barely an inch between them.

"Shall we move on?" It was Marla, yelling into his ear. He nodded in agreement.

Soon they were outside in the brisk air, walking towards Dupont Circle as couples and groups, mostly of one gender or the other, pushed past them in the opposite direction. He drew a deep breath of fresh air and tried to make sense of what he had absorbed over the last hour. It had been almost no time from the moment he learned that Josette's "boyfriend" was in fact her brother until he began to conclude that the concept of a boyfriend might not be part of her makeup at all.

Marla's voice intruded once more into his thoughts.

"So, how'd you like the club?"

"It was okay, I guess. I know it will amaze you to learn this, but I don't get out all that much. I can't even remember the last time I was in this neighborhood at night."

"Yeah, well, neighborhoods change, don't they? I thought it was pretty cool, myself. I've been meaning to give it a try for weeks. I'll have to come back to dance there again."

"I thought you played on the other team?"

She laughed. "Oh, don't show your age so much. I've got lots of gay and lesbian friends. And anyway, their clubs are a lot more fun than the straight ones. Anyway, what do you think of Josette? She doesn't seem like your type."

"What do you mean, 'my type?' All I did was give her a lift when she needed one."

Marla gave him a wink. "Oh, you know, just asking."

"For Pete's sake! I'm old enough to be her father."

"Oh come on. She's 29."

"How do you know that?"

"Well, duh? How would I know that? She mentioned it while we were talking about what we were each doing in grad school. She worked for a while before going back for another degree. How old did you think she was?"

"I don't know – I'm not very good with ages. And anyway, I don't spend a lot of time around young people."

"Puh-leeze – you talk like you're in a rest home already. Anyway, I was just curious. She meets the half plus seven rule, and she seemed a little proprietary when we met."

"The what?"

"Half the guy's age plus seven. If the girl's that age or older, it's not creepy."

"So you're telling me there's a rule that defines the boundary between healthy interest and dirty old manhood?"

"Dad, there's a rule for everything. Anyway, why don't you level with me? What were you really doing out west for so long? I can't believe you were just pulling your hair out, despite the evidence to the contrary."

"What do you mean by that crack?"

"Well, you know, you are getting kind of thin up there."

Frank stopped, stunned, and searched for his reflection in the window of a store. Everything looked intact to him.

"I don't know what you're talking about, and I don't know why you'd want to say a thing like that, anyway."

"But Dad, you know, you are. Here – give me your hand." She held it up over the back of his head, and placed his fingers in the middle of what was undeniably a bald spot. He was speechless and visibly aghast.

Marla put a reassuring arm around his waist. "I just assumed you knew – your hair's been thinning back there for years. Look – there's a drugstore there on that corner. Let's pick you up some Minoxidil. It's supposed to work pretty well – they claim it can even make hair grow back."

Frank blindly followed her down the street and into the store. He found the proper aisle, and picked up a box of the store brand hair restorer. Part way to the checkout aisle he stopped, turned around, and roamed around until he found a hand-held mirror.

They spoke of one thing or another as Frank walked Marla home, but he was distracted by too many thoughts on too many topics to be much of a conversationalist. When they reached her door, she wished him luck with his book, gave him a big hug, and went inside.

He didn't need to look at his watch to know it must be late. Should he take the Metro or hail a cab? He thought of his cluttered apartment, his empty refrigerator, and his too-vacant life, and then started walking, his bagged box of hair-restorer bumping his leg with every stride.

* * *

28

Pulp Friction

DICK FETTERS SAT in his study, clicking through email and polling reports on his computer as he waited for the evening news to begin on the muted television across the room. He'd spent a ton of Barbash's money over the past two weeks on many fronts – publicists, social media flacks, advertising – the whole gamut of influence garnering techniques. This would be a make or break week in the primary campaign, and each of his efforts had to pay off or the whole strategy would be in jeopardy. Out of the corner of his eye he saw the network logo pop up on his TV. He reached for the remote to unmute the sound.

It had been quite an active day both domestically and internationally; the opening voiceover by the POX News anchor indicated that there would be no campaign news until the end of the broadcast. Well, that was okay. For now, it was what was going on in the trenches in New Hampshire that really mattered. He turned the sound lower and left the room to top off his drink.

Had he done everything possible? The answer had better be yes, with only two days to go until the second contest of the campaign season. He stared into the freezer, forgetting for the moment what he was looking for before dropping two ice cubes into his glass. What if Wellhead made such a fool of himself in New Hampshire that no one would believe when he won?

Back in his study, he stared out the window into the failing light of the fenced in courtyard behind his house in Georgetown. Before his wife had moved out, everything had been impeccably neat; shrubbery trimmed regularly, outdoor furniture arranged in perfect order. A blade of grass wouldn't have dared to show its head between the flagstones back then; now he could see withered crabgrass spidering forth everywhere.

Maybe the people who used to take care of things outside had stopped coming? What with being on the road so much over the past year he might easily have missed something from them in the mail. He swirled the scotch in his glass and took a meditative sip.

The words "New Hampshire" caught his attention. He turned to see a newscaster bundled up in a scarf and overcoat, the Greek temple portico and gold dome of the state capitol barely visible behind him as he leaned into the wind, one hand holding a microphone and the other pressing his headphone more tightly into his ear. Large flakes of snow turned from gray to bright white and then back to gray again as they blew through the brilliant circle of the camera lights. Fetters picked up the remote and turned the sound up as he sat down.

Good evening, Troy. As you can see, the weather's pretty awful up here. And the primary race is looking pretty chaotic, too, with candidates gaining and losing ground in the polls on a daily basis.

Thanks, Jeremy. Of course, that's not unusual this early in the season. With this many candidates still in the running, I wouldn't be surprised if the 'don't knows' still hold the biggest percentage.

That's exactly right, Troy. I don't think anyone's going to try and pick a winner on this one until the last votes are counted. The big surprise so far is that Henry Yazzie, the Independent candidate, is making a respectable showing up here in this Yankee stronghold. He's hardly in the lead, but he's not in the back of the pack, either.

That is something. Do you suppose that new video game everyone's been talking about has anything to do with it?

Who knows, Troy? It seems like suddenly a lot of people are using it as a proxy for their political position.

Let's take a quick look at that game, shall we? I'm sure all of our viewers haven't had a chance to check it out yet.

The camera cut to a shot of a split computer screen, with what looked like the same game displayed on each half.

We've got Donna Pinecliff, our digital media correspondent, here in the studio with us. Donna, tell us what we're looking at here.

Sure, Troy. This is the hottest new mobile game app these days, and it's still trending up.

Why two game shots, Donna? They look just the same to me.

I expect they do from where you're sitting, so let's pull the camera in for a close up of the left side of the screen.

As the image on the left enlarged, it became clear that a group of Native Americans was huddled around something. Sticking out above them was what looked like the head of a very startled cow. Suddenly, the animal was flying in an arc heading up and to the right, its limbs flailing wildly. The camera panned back just in time to see the hapless beast crash into the lookout tower of a log stockade with an American flag flying above it.

So what you see here is the "Angry Indians" game mode. Let's zoom in on the other side of the screen now.

The cameraman did as requested, and now viewers saw a group of blue-uniformed men, above which rose the head of an extremely unhappy bison. This time, when the catapult was sprung, it was the largest tent in a circle of tepees that was flattened.

And that, of course, is the Angry Cavalry game mode.

Looks like fun, Donna. Have you tried it yet?

I have — and I can tell you, it's really addictive. I guess it's not surprising that it's become sort of a sign of political allegiance to buy and play the game in one mode or another. Henry Yazzie couldn't hope for anything better than this to come along, and the Tea partyers seem just as happy to embrace the Cavalry version.

The news anchor chuckled.

Well, I guess you never know what's going to happen out on the campaign trail, do you? Thanks for the update, both of you, and hey, Jeremy! Stay warm up there!

Fetters clicked off the TV, grudgingly satisfied. So far, so good.

*   *   *

Frank was standing in a Metro car, one hand gripping the bar overhead, the other clutching a tablet computer displaying the first chapters he'd received from Grover. At the top of the page, it read "Working Title: 'The Alexandria Project,'" and below it began as follows:

> *LATE IN THE afternoon of a gray day in December, a panel truck pulled up to the gate of a warehouse complex in a run-down section of Richmond, Virginia. Rolling down his window, Jack Davis punched a code into the control box, and the gate clanked slowly out of the way. Once inside, he wheeled the truck around and backed it up against a loading dock as the gate closed behind him.*

Apparently this guy Davis was supposed to be going on duty at an underground, ultra-secure government data center. What the heck was that all about? He jumped ahead to see how the chapter ended:

> *If Davis had been able to electronically monitor what was happening on server A-VI/147 on Level Three, though, his confidence might have taken a hit. True, concrete and steel walls, surveillance cameras and Halon gas were more than adequate to protect the physical well-being of his facility against anything short of a direct hit by a "bunker busting" nuclear weapon. But the data on the facility's servers had to rely on virtual defenses — firewalls, security routines and intrusion scanners.*
>
> *And those defenses hadn't been enough. Someone had gotten inside.*

He grunted. Okay, Grover had obviously made this guy Davis up, but all the details otherwise were certainly realistic. And the dramatization did a good job of making the point Frank had been insisting on — that our existing cybersecurity defenses aren't adequate to protect us. Maybe this guy Grover would work out okay after all.

He clicked forward to the next chapter and continued reading:

> *THE NEXT MORNING, a morbidly obese Corgi named Lily was sniffing a tree on 16th Street, in the Columbia Heights neighborhood of Washington, D.C. A cold, insistent drizzle fell on her, but Lily*

didn't care, because Lily was sniffing at her favorite tree. Indeed, the meager processing power of Lily's brain was wholly consumed by sampling the mysterious scents wafting up from the damp earth, for this was also the favorite tree of every other dog in the neighborhood.

Where did that come from? Had Grover accidentally mixed in some text from something else he was working on? He continued reading:

Something was nagging at the edge of her senses, though. "C'mon, Lily! Hurry up!"

Lily turned her head. The annoying distraction was coming from the person at the other end of her leash, someone with sockless feet jammed into worn, black loafers. Above bare ankles, a pair of pajama-clad legs disappeared into a rumpled raincoat. She saw there was an arm holding an umbrella, too, and under the umbrella, a stubbly, forty – something face topped by thinning black hair. Lily decided that the face did not look happy.

"Ah!" she thought. "That would be Frank." Relieved that the distraction could be ignored, Lily returned to the important work at hand.

What the hell!?! He skipped ahead again:

A blue plastic bag inverted over his free hand, Frank scooped up Lily's grudging gift. He handed over the treat, jerking back with his fingers barely intact.

"Isn't that just the story of my life?" he thought bleakly as Lily happily consumed her treat. "Every day I give her a cookie, and every day she gives me a bag of shit."

Trudging home through the rain, Frank reflected that his day generally went downhill from there.

Okay, that last part was pretty accurate. But what in blazes was Grover up to here? None of this had anything to do with anything the book was supposed to be about.

Before he could read more, the doors of the Metro car opened and he realized he was at his stop.

Furious, he ran up the escalator, and not long after, he was charging up the stairs at Grover's place. He was about to start beating on the writer's apartment door when it opened, and he was face to face with Grover.

"Hey, Frank! Welcome back. How'd'ja like those first few chapters?"

Grover's smiling, expectant face took the bluster out of Frank just as he was about to let loose.

"Uh, well, I thought the first chapter – the Prologue, I guess you called it – worked pretty well. I read that on the way here. But I'd only just started in on the next chapter and I don't get what you're up to there at all."

"Oh, well, yeah, I guess maybe I should have laid that out in the email. C'mon in and have a seat. I'll join you in a minute and tell you what I have in mind there."

He entered Grover's study, and this time the cat vacated the easy chair immediately, giving Frank a dirty look. It ran under Grover's desk, where it could glower at Frank without its owner noticing.

"Deal with it, cat," Frank said in its general direction, and began looking around the room more carefully than the last time. There was a bookcase against one wall, and he saw that most of the shelves were stuffed with thrillers. Many had slips of paper sticking up out of them, and some were lying face down on the others, pages splayed to both sides. Grover was obviously a fan of the genre.

His co-writer walked in a moment later.

"So, I guess you would be wondering why I introduced you that way. See, what I thought was this – you've been portrayed in the news as this mystery man, right? You haven't given any interviews, and people don't really know you, so it's like you're this cypher or something."

"So? What's wrong with that? Can't we just keep it that way?"

"Well, I think that's kind of risky, sales-wise. People still remember what happened – or least as much as they really care about – that it all came out okay – so it's not like they think they really need to be told about that again.

"What makes for an interesting story is how you did it – what was going through your mind, what kind of sacrifices you had to make – you know, why it made a difference that it was you instead of some other geek - no offense - that happened to be in that place at that time."

"I can get that, but what does that have to do with me walking the damn dog in the rain?"

Grover thought for a moment. How could he explain what was admittedly just a quirky, intuitive guess on his part about what would make for a good read?

"Well, let's look at it like this. What do you think the popular impression is of people like you and me?"

"What exactly do you mean, 'like you and me?'"

"You know – geeks – nerds – wonks – people that sit behind keyboards tapping out code or stories about technology? How would a bus driver or an investment banker describe us?"

"Well," Frank paused. How would you describe a geek without using the word "geeky?"

"I guess they'd say we're kind of narrowly focused on technical stuff – not very social...." He stopped again.

"Right. In other words, someone that anyone that isn't a geek themselves would have a hard time relating to."

"Okay, granted. But let's get back to the dog and the bag of shit."

"Right, right. Well, here's the deal. Whether you like it or not, you're the hero of this book – no, don't stop me – if you don't like 'hero,' then let's go with 'main character' if that feels better.

"Anyway, people need to connect with you or they're not going to get grabbed by the book and stick with it. Think about it – if you pick up a book in a bookstore or 'look inside' online, how many pages do you skim before you decide whether to buy it or move on? One? Maybe two, max?"

"Okay, so I get that you have to flesh out the main character – okay – me – so that I'm something more than a pure stereotype. But isn't there a better way to introduce me than through the eyes of an over-fed, spoiled corgi?"

Grover sighed. How to say gently that an author has to work with what's been given to him?

"There are some rules that every author needs to follow – one of them is 'show, don't tell.' So if I start the book by saying that 'Frank Adversego is a middle-aged IT professional who lives alone and works for the Library of Congress,' would you like that any better? And would anyone read any farther than that?"

Frank frowned. That didn't sound so good, either.

"Alright, alright. But still, there's got to be another way to go about it."

Grover pressed his advantage. "Okay, sure. So help me out with some suggestions here. How would you go about doing it? Got some close friends you play poker or drink with? I could set up a scene with them to introduce you. Or a hobby – do you have any hobbies? I could use one of them to humanize you. Maybe there's a club you belong to – I could use that to frame your personality?"

Frank was silent. The answer to all those questions, of course, was no.

Grover had guessed that would be the case, and didn't want to rub the point in. "Look, I haven't had enough coffee yet. You want a cup? Yes? Okay. I'll go make a pot, and while I do, why don't you take your time, start at the beginning and read all of that chapter."

He held out a handful of paper, stapled together in the upper corner. Frank hesitated, and then took it.

Grover walked into the kitchen. He sure hoped this worked, as he didn't really have a Plan B. Sure, he could figure out a different opening, but if Frank dug in his heels on avoiding anything personal, it would be good-bye to the best seller list.

A few minutes later, Grover all but tiptoed up to his office door. What he saw encouraged him: Frank was leaning forward, elbows on his knees, both hands holding the sheaf of paper. He hadn't even noticed that Molly was now sitting on the back of his chair, twitching her tail just lightly enough against the back of his neck to annoy him without making him realize what was going on. Every few seconds he unconsciously scratched the back of his neck as he continued to read.

Grover walked in, mouthing "Bad Molly!" as he plucked her off the back of Frank's chair and sat in his own, holding the animal in his lap while he waited anxiously for Frank to finish.

Finally, Frank looked up. He was a bit startled to see Grover sitting there with the cat in his lap.

"Well?"

Frank gave himself a few moments to think before he gave his verdict. "Okay. You nailed it. I guess you nailed me, too."

This time Grover's sigh of relief was audible. "I'm glad you can see it that way, Frank – not everyone would. And I really think we're going to have a winner here."

Grover set Molly on the floor and picked up his laptop. "So shall we get down to work? I've put together an outline for the rest of the book I need to go over with you. And I've got a long list of questions I need to ask you in order to fill it out."

It was almost dinner time when Frank left Grover's place. The writer had been merciless in his interrogation, and Frank's head felt like it had been wrung out like a towel. Riding home on the Metro he mostly stared blankly at the advertisements and the people stepping on and off of his car.

Back at his own apartment, he opened his refrigerator, the contents of which were unchanged except for the addition of a twelve pack of beer. He decremented that count by one and carried the bottle into his living room, where he collapsed into his easy chair. After ordering a pizza delivery, he picked up his laptop and selected the most mindless movie he could think of.

Except to answer the door to hand a twenty to the delivery guy, he didn't stir for the rest of the evening, except to continue to reduce the rapidly waning number of brown bottles in his refrigerator.

*   *   *

29

One of Those Days When Morning Can't Come Late Enough

ARCOSS TOWN, JOSETTE was riveted to her laptop, waiting for the first of the networks and cable channels to predict the final percentages in the third primary of the season. At last C&N felt confident enough to make the call: Randall Wellhead had won again, and Yazzie had increased his share of the overall vote as well, just as the pollsters – again – had predicted he would.

With three primaries to rely on now, she was convinced that someone was manipulating the polling, and the voting as well. If so, the candidates that were benefiting most from that manipulation were Yazzie and Wellhead.

She set up a graph and plugged in the polling numbers and voting results for the top half dozen candidates for each of the primaries to date, and then looked for anything that might be suspicious. The one obvious pattern was that Wellhead always came out at the high end, and Yazzie at the low end, of the pollsters' predictions.

It was Yazzie's performance that had her most perplexed. Would anyone really believe it if this unknown Native American, running as an independent, started to look like he might actually win? Or could the person hacking the polls and voting have something else in mind? And what about this Centrist Coalition of America that had appeared out of nowhere? Were they really making a difference in recruiting voters for the Yazzie campaign, or was it just a cover to make his success more plausible? If so, then it might lead her to the hackers.

But not so far. She had spent hours searching online for information about the CCA, and had surprisingly little to show for it. In state after state, she found the same thing – a web site, and not a lot more. The sites themselves sometimes didn't have a lot of substance; on a casual inspection, there seemed to be a lot of structure, but when you looked at the actual pages, there wasn't really much "there" there – just a few, rather general paragraphs per page and lots of links to material at other sites.

How could there be so little substance, and so few news articles about the CCA, even in primary states like New Hampshire? Henry Yazzie had done no advertising and barely any campaigning at all there, but he had stunned the pundits by coming in third. Whether the voters seriously supported his candidacy or simply wanted to torch the traditional party system hardly mattered – someone still had to light the match.

She opened her secure texting account on the Tor network, and sent an email to the private address of her contact at Voldemort:

>*Do you hear anything about the CCA?*

She returned to combing through news articles. Whenever anyone was interviewed, it always seemed to be someone named Baxter Maxwell. A few local supporters could usually be seen behind him in video clips, but they only waved signs.

And then there were the polls to be explained. If the votes turned out to vary wildly from the polls, people would get suspicious about the credibility of one or the other. Did that confirm that the voting was actually legitimate, or did it confirm that both the voting and the polling had been hacked?

She heard a muted chime and saw that she had received a response:

<*The what?*

She responded immediately:

>*The Centrist Coalition of America. Does anyone at Voldemort find them suspicious?*
<*Haven't heard anyone mention them, why?*
>*Your department was investigating the pollsters; I thought they might find Yazzie's success in the primaries to be too good to be true*
<*We've been told the polling inquiry is closed*

That was a relief. But why would Voldemort abandon its investigation before it found the identity of the original culprit – the FdL?

Then she had another thought: why had Frank not been told that the inquiry was closed – or perhaps he had? She started typing again:

> *Yes? Who made the decision?*
> *<Len Butcher*
> *>Thanks. Let me know if anything changes*

Her thoughts returned to Frank. Did he know what was going on? Shouldn't he be in the loop, since he reported to Butcher's office? And if he did know, why had he not told her anything?

The answer to that was not too hard to guess. With a smile, she reminded herself that Frank was after all a pretty timid rabbit, and she had not seen him in a while. She'd have to do something about that, since all her other leads had gone cold.

*   *   *

Grover picked up his phone, surprised to hear it ringing so early. "Hello?"

"Hey – Dan. It's Perry. I'm about to hop on a plane but before I did I wanted to check in. How's it working out with you and Frank?"

"Good – real good, actually. Well, I mean it was a little touch and go in the beginning. Doing a mass-market approach wasn't what he had in mind. But I've convinced him it's the best way to reach the widest audience possible with his message."

"Good for you – I'm relieved. How about the story line, character development, that sort of stuff? Is he going to play ball with you on that, too?"

"I think so. I didn't pull any punches on a couple of sample chapters I gave him. I guess you could say he was a little horrified to start with, but eventually he started to feel a little better about how I was putting him out there."

"Why's that?"

"I don't know. He's a funny guy – on the one hand, he's pretty prickly about what he thinks he knows. But on the other hand, he's really hard on himself. As long as I stick to the facts, I think he'll leave the style and story line pretty much up to me. Even when it doesn't make him look real great. In fact, I think I'd have a harder time convincing him to let me make him look good."

"Well, whatever. As long as you get the first draft out on time and the publisher likes it, you'll make me a happy man."

"I'm on it."

"Great – and hey, before I forget it, how's the social media going?"

"Ah, I think we're doing okay there, too. We've got at least six weeks before the book is available even if the publisher pulls out all the stops, but I'm ramping up."

"You better! Normally we'd be hitting the gas three months before release. Anyway, if you've got Frank tweeting and everything, I'm even more impressed."

"That's not what I said. I'm doing the social media thing for him for now – a stealthy tease campaign that doesn't mention his name. No sense trying to push him through too many knotholes all at once."

"Probably a good call. Anyway, I'll leave that to you. See ya."

Grover was glad Perry hadn't pursued that topic any further. Grover had unleashed a storm of social media on every platform he could think of, trying to pull together a huge list of followers, all wanting to know what this big blockbuster, based on a true story, would be all about. Of course, that couldn't work if he was tweeting under Frank's name. And that was just fine, because it was Grover's own name that was on everything instead.

*   *   *

Frank lay flat on his back in bed, staring at the ceiling, his brain feeling as if it had mistakenly wandered into a wine press that was being cranked steadily tighter. His senses were also reporting that gravity was pressing down on his body more forcefully than usual, leading him to wonder whether the laws of physics had fundamentally changed overnight. No, he concluded, the more logical explanation was that these unpleasant sensations were somehow related to the volume of beer he'd drunk the night before.

He had already hit the snooze alarm four times. Still, he felt unable to face the prospect of trading his current horizontal orientation for the vertical. Anyhow, did he really have to get up? What would be the point? Grover was going to do all the heavy lifting on the book, and Voldemort hadn't given him anything new to do since his big discovery. There wasn't anywhere he needed to be today, or any day for that matter.

Eventually his bladder informed him that a trip to the bathroom was in order. When he could no longer resist, he cautiously levered the upper half of his body into a sitting position. Then he swung his legs out of the bed. Oof.

Feeling shaky, he leaned forward, elbows on knees and head in his hands, reconsidering his planned change in elevation. Maybe he could persuade his bladder to go back to sleep? He noticed that his bottle of aspirin was quite inconsiderately absent from his night table. Clearly all of the objects in his small world were conspiring against him. With a grunt, he stood up, shuffled into the bathroom, and unwisely looked in the mirror.

He wasn't happy with what he saw. For that matter, he didn't like the reflection of the messy bedroom behind him, either. He looked down, and noticed a paper bag sitting next to the sink. What could be in there?

He peered in. Right. The Minoxidil, and the hand mirror. He hadn't gotten around to reading the directions for the former, or been brave enough to make use of the latter. He leaned forward and looked more closely at his bleary eyes, bewhiskered face and disheveled hair in the mirror. Ugh. Another bad idea.

Okay, he thought, grasping the edges of the sink and staring at his binge-battered face in the mirror. Today I'm really going to get my act together.

He opened the medicine cabinet, took out a comb and the aspirin, and put his hair in some sort of order. Then, with new resolve and left-over trepidation, he picked up the hand mirror.

It took a bit of twisting and many ineffectual gyrations with his hand, because every movement came out backwards in the mirror. But at last he could see the right part of the back of his head. Sure enough, he was looking at a real, honest to goodness, not to be denied, almost completely bald patch of skin right where such an embarrassment usually hid out. Just where its owner couldn't see it, but everyone else could.

He pushed his face as close as he could to the bathroom mirror, but still couldn't see the bald spot as well as he wanted to in the hand mirror. Hmm. He fetched his phone from the bedroom and tried to position that just above the bald spot. Then he took a series of pictures while moving it around.

Flipping through the results, he tried to estimate how many follicles per inch were still refusing to surrender. The answer was not many, but perhaps enough to indicate that the battle was not yet totally lost.

While he showered, he wondered what else he should do to get his act together? As he washed his hair, he realized that while it might be close to non-existent in one place, it was pretty long everywhere else. There had been a time when he got his hair cut pretty regularly, back when he still used a paper calendar. He used to have a yellow sticky on it that said "haircut," and then every time he got one, he'd move the sticky a month ahead.

But one day the adhesive on the sticky had played out, and it started falling off the calendar. One day it disappeared entirely, and he hadn't gotten around to replacing it. That was ten years ago, and because he hated having to make small talk in the barber's chair, he had never gotten around to replacing it. After he was liberated from the tyranny of the implacable sticky, it was rare that he got around to having his hair cut more than every two – or three – months. Maybe he should invest in a new sticky?

Once out of the shower, he opened up the Minoxidil box and pulled out a small bottle, an eye dropper, and a piece of paper with instructions. He read the directions, filled the eyedropper, leaned his head forward, and then held the applicator above the back of his head.

Now what? Staring down at the sink, he started squeezing the eyedropper gently while making circles over where he thought the bald spot should be. Soon he felt small rivulets of liquid trickling down both sides of his face. Ugh.

He reflected that there was also the subject of clothes as he shuffled out of the bathroom. He hated buying clothes. Luckily, they lasted a long time. Marla, bless her soul, made a habit of buying them for him at Christmas, for his birthday, and for Father's day. But now that he'd lost weight, he'd need to get new ones. How was that supposed to happen?

At least he didn't think he needed to get shoes right now. He hated buying shoes even more than he hated buying clothes. Once, he'd been able to avoid buying a new pair of shoes for eight whole months after one got a hole in it, by buying padded insole inserts at the drug store. By the time winter slush finally put an end to that tactic he'd spent more on shoe inserts than he would have on a new pair of shoes.

He sat down on his bed, feeling overwhelmed. Was he really up for this? Maybe he should just go back to bed.

His phone was buzzing on his night table again, though. He picked it up to check the number. It was Josette! He swiped the screen.

"Hi, Josette. What's up?"

"Oh Frank, I am glad that I have reached you. What do you think of the latest primary results?"

"Nothing," or "I have no idea," would have been honest answers, since he hadn't bothered to listen to the results the night before. But he didn't like the sound of either of those options.

"Well, it's still early in the campaign, so it's hard to tell very much so far. What do you think?"

"I think the results are very surprising. Would you like to get together to discuss them? I could meet you for dinner?"

"Well, sure, or I guess I should say maybe. Let me check my calendar." He waited as long as he thought it should take to actually check a calendar, and then said, "Yes, I think I could, say after 6:30. Would that work for you?"

"Yes, yes, that would be fine. Where would you like to meet?"

Frank thought for a moment; he didn't particularly want to meet in a loud rock club again, but he didn't want to seem like he was totally out of the stream of real, living people, either.

"How about this – do you like jazz?"

"Oh yes – very much. What clubs do you like?"

He had no idea, as he hadn't been to hear live jazz in a dozen years.

"Let me check who's in town, and I'll email you with a suggestion."

"Perfect! I will look forward to seeing you!"

Frank hung up the phone. He'd need to go online and find out where people played jazz in town these days. But first he'd need to get a haircut and buy some new clothes.

*   *   *

30

What a Difference a Date Makes

F RANK GLANCED AT his watch for the third time in as many minutes, despite the fact that Josette was not yet late. With his other hand, he pulled the lapels of his new sport jacket a bit closer together against the wind that seemed to be waging a personal vendetta against him. It was definitely overcoat weather, but he didn't own one that could be worn over a sports jacket. There was a limit to how many clothing stores he could force himself to enter in a single day.

Then he felt a hand on his arm, and turned. Josette looked very different than he had ever seen her before; she wore a stylish, knee-length coat, complemented by a silk scarf, knotted just the way they were in foreign movies. He wondered whether she would try to kiss him on both cheeks, and was greatly relieved when she did not; he was sure he would make a mess of it.

"So good to see you. And I am so glad that you picked this club; I have always wanted to come here."

He held the door, and followed her inside, where they found two young women chatting at the hostess station. Eventually one turned and noticed them.

"Do you have a reservation?"

"Yes – for two. The name's Adversego."

"What an interesting name. Is it Irish?"

He stared at her blankly. "Uh, no, Italian actually. We're here for the music."

"Oh – then you'll want to go downstairs." She pointed to a doorway to her left and resumed her conversation.

Frank motioned Josette ahead, and followed her down a narrow set of stairs. At the bottom, they were greeted by another hostess. A grand piano and the usual welter of microphones, amps and instruments in stands crowded a low stage at the end of the room.

On the brick walls, the concentrated faces of Dizzie Gillespie, Willie "the Lion" Smith, Dave Brubeck and other jazz greats gazed out from black and white photos, each giving full, if silent, vent to their talents. Frank noticed that each was dated, and realized that the background of every photo matched the room they were in.

He helped Josette remove her coat.

"Ah, you are such a gentleman this evening! My mother would approve!"

Frank was grateful that the low light prevented her from noticing that he was blushing as he held her chair.

His discomfort was less the product of her comment than a reaction to her appearance as revealed when she removed her coat. She wore a casual but smart ensemble that complemented her lithe figure, and the opening at the top of her loose blouse was cut so wide that the material barely had enough purchase to stay on her shoulders. Indeed, from time to time it would slip off one shoulder or the other as they spoke. Sometimes a minute might pass before she unconsciously restored it to its proper position.

She was also wearing makeup for the first time. In the candlelight, her eyes seemed enormous and glittering, especially when she smiled. And she was smiling a lot tonight.

"Before we speak of boring things like politics – you must tell me how your book goes?"

He frowned as he considered how to answer that question.

"Ah, pretty well. That is, you see, the publisher has been getting very anxious to get the book out as soon as possible – while people still remember what happened. Because I got so diverted by the Voldemort thing, I no longer have enough time to finish the draft and then trade it back and forth with an editor. So we're sort of combining the two processes into one. Of course, to be fair, he'll appear on the cover of the book as a co-author."

"Indeed! That is very generous of you. Do you like him – oh! Or is it her?"

"A him, and yes, mostly." He caught himself starting to drum his fingers on the table and put his hands in his lap.

"Frankly, it's very strange seeing things in print that actually happened to me. I guess uncomfortable is a better word. So it helps to have someone else, uh, kind of keep the ball rolling. He nudges me to let things be said that I'd never actually write myself."

"Yes, I see. And your book – when does it come out?"

"I have a hard time believing it, but in less than two months. Then they'll want me to go on a promotional book tour."

"How exciting!"

"Huh! That's not the word that I'd use. I'll have to talk to local radio show hosts and do book signings while chugging around the country. I can't think of anything I'd rather do less – doing readings in front of the two people that show up, one of whom is confused and thinks I'm actually someone else."

Josette giggled. "Book readings? You?"

"Yes – 'book readings – me.' What's so funny about that?"

She put her napkin to her lips as she tried not to laugh again. "I'm sorry - it's just the picture I'm seeing. You, standing in a book store, reading about yourself to a few little old ladies. It's just…" She gave up and laughed.

Fair enough, he thought, and softened. "Alright, I grant you that. I'm not exactly Mr. Friendly. I hate socializing even with people I know. It's kind of my worst nightmare. Makes me think of the first Indiana Jones movie…"

"It had to be snakes!" She completed the thought for him, and this time they both laughed.

It wasn't until after they had finished eating that Josette finally got around to the primaries. She set her fork down, and leaned forward, resting her chin on her hand.

"So Frank, do tell me what you think about this Mr. Yazzie doing so well. He seems to have come out of nowhere, and now perhaps he is becoming a serious challenger?"

Frank started to analyze Yazzie's platform, but she interrupted him.

"I'm sorry, no. I do not mean his policies. I am asking, do you think that he is really doing so well?"

"You mean, do I think that someone's tampering with the actual votes?"

"Yes! Do you?"

Frank leaned back in his chair. "Why, I hadn't really thought about it; I've been pretty preoccupied with the book. But no, it doesn't seem all that odd to me that there could be a strong 'none of the above' kind of protest vote, especially this early in the campaign. After all, the President's popularity is in the toilet, and all of the Republican front runners seem to be unelectable. Why not?"

"Why not is not the same as 'why,' that's why!"

"Well, okay, but still, what is it that makes you suspicious? That guy Perot who we read about did really well for a while, too."

"It's like this, you see," she began, and then told him how little she had been able to find out about the CCA.

"Alright, so there doesn't seem to be a lot of information available about them. But still, why not just assume it's a protest vote?"

"Because it matches the polls so closely."

"But I fixed that!"

As the words were leaving his mouth, he saw a triumphant look spreading across her face. "Uh, didn't I?"

"That's what I thought, too. But today I checked with my friend at Voldemort, and she tells me that they are no longer trying to figure out who it was that had hacked the pollsters."

"That's good, isn't it? I mean, weren't you worried that eventually they'd figure out it was you and your friends?"

"Yes, of course. But still, why should they stop? Is it not a serious matter that someone had hacked those systems?"

"Sure, but so what? Why look a gift horse in the mouth?"

She looked puzzled at the metaphor. He tried again "I mean, why not just be grateful and let it go at that?"

"Because it matters! Don't you remember how much time and effort my colleagues and I invested in trying to help your voters realize the mistakes they were making? Why would we stop now, if it looks like someone is tampering with the election?"

"You mean, 'someone else.'"

"Shh! You are speaking too loud!"

Frank leaned in. "Sorry. But this still sounds unlikely – someone hacking both the polls and the ballot machines, too. Why do you think that?"

"Because I hacked one of the pollster systems again this afternoon, and the software has not been repaired!"

"Are you *crazy*? What if someone is still monitoring those systems?"

"Except that my friend says that they are not. Anyway, I was very careful. But don't you think it is quite a coincidence that the agency that discontinued the investigation did not remove the back doors? And that no one else – except us – knows that the pollster systems had been hacked?"

"So you think that Voldemort is trying to hack the election?"

"No. I think that Len Butcher is!"

"*Butcher?*"

"No, not Butcher only. I expect that he is part of some bigger picture."

Frank was still trying to process this when the band swung into its first number; he had been so engrossed in what Josette had been saying that he hadn't noticed as the musicians took the stage one by one and begin fiddling with their instruments. It was difficult now to discuss anything seriously, so they settled back into their seats to listen.

Or perhaps Josette did. As usual, Frank's mind was more engaged in abstract thought than in appreciating something as frivolous as music. Now what? Was Josette on to something, or was she simply reading patterns into events that weren't there at all?

And either way, did he want to have anything to do with it? Other than running into her once by accident in the bar, he hadn't heard or seen Josette since Iowa. And now, it seemed obvious, she had gotten in touch just to see how much information she could get out of him. He folded his arms and scowled at the stage.

When the band took a break, Josette tried to pick up the conversation where they had left off. But he was distant and uncommunicative, and she could not get him to concede that there might be something to investigate after only three primaries. Before the band came back from its break they left the club and went their separate ways.

* * *

Over the next weeks, two more primaries were held, and Fetters called a spreadsheet up on his computer to stare at the numbers he had been accumulating there. It was a very complicated piece of work, set up to incorporate both poll data as well as voting results across the nation. Now that he had the ability to influence the actual voting in almost every primary, the question was how to use that power aggressively enough to assure the desired outcome, but not so much so as to invoke suspicion.

The hard part had to do with the poll numbers. If he pushed the voting numbers too far too often, people would begin to wonder why his candidate always outperformed expectations, while the other candidates, at least as a group, underperformed. He only had a fixed number of votes to work with, since the votes cast could hardly exceed the number of voters that had checked in at the voting stations.

That meant that every time his candidate received an illegitimate vote, it had to come from someone else. Plus, the final results needed to be close enough to the pollsters' predictions to not raise suspicion.

That hadn't been too difficult to pull off in the first few primaries, because there were still so many candidates. The malware he'd paid to have developed only had to pull a small percentage of votes from each one.

But now he could see trouble ahead, because one candidate – Yazzie – was shooting up in the polls, and that meant that his voting totals needed to match the polls as well. Doing this had been part of the plan all along – he had wanted a credible candidate to siphon support away from the President – but he hadn't counted on Yazzie being this credible. To keep things believable, he had been forced to not only let Yazzie keep all his votes, but even shift some legitimate votes to him, instead of Wellhead. Luckily, the declining poll numbers for the other candidates were making that possible, but he worried that this trend might not continue. And as weaker candidates began to drop out, the situation would become even less flexible.

He switched the spreadsheet over to graphic mode and instructed the program to project the current poll trends out through the end of the primary season. Unless Wellhead's momentum picked up or Yazzie's slowed down, the independent candidate would be ahead of Wellhead by Election Day. Fetters adjusted the voting totals up and down for each candidate to see how many votes he would need to shift to avoid that result, and kept at it as the clock counted down to midnight. But no matter how hard he tried, he couldn't find a way to keep his candidate ahead of Henry Yazzie that wouldn't be significantly out of sync with the predictions.

* * *

White Crow called up the spreadsheet that one of Baxter Maxwell's boys had set up for him. The casino manager had been to business school, and he was impressed. It was a clever piece of work, set up to incorporate both poll data as well as voting results from all 50 states. Now that he had the ability to influence the poll numbers it was easy to use that power to indirectly affect voters.

Every other candidate was now suffering at his command. At the same time, the media was reporting that Yazzie was gaining greater credibility and momentum by the day. Voters that had never heard of him six weeks ago were now voting for him.

Better yet, since he had never revealed anything about Len Butcher and the poll hacking to Fetters, he didn't need to tamper with the actual voting at all. Simply by elevating Yazzie's poll numbers higher and higher, week by week, he could leave it to Fetters to do the high-risk tampering in order to avoid arousing suspicion.

Playing with the sliders on the software, White Crow felt like a kid in a game arcade again, only better. This time the game was Punch and Judy, and he was Fetters's puppet master, all without his rival knowing that someone was pulling his strings at all.

Within a minute he had all the poll numbers he needed to plant leading into this week's primaries. He looked at his watch: 8:45 PM. Time to take a stroll around the casino floor and make sure that all was as well there as it was with Henry Yazzie's inexorable march to the presidency.

Life was rarely this good, and he savored it as he greeted the regulars. He even tossed a few chips in the tip cups of his favorite pit bosses.

"Wonder what's with the boss tonight?" one whispered to a waitress. "He looks like he just pulled off another Little Big Horn."

* * *

Josette stared hard at the poll and voting spreadsheet she had so laboriously created. Now that she had five primary's worth of data, she thought that the trends were undeniable. True, the numbers for Wellhead and Yazzie didn't rise in precise lockstep, either with each other or with the polls. But if you were to draw a trend curve between their respective dots, there was no missing the fact that they rose in tandem, and much more smoothly than those of the other candidates, which jumped around considerably. Since this was true for both the polling and the primary results, someone had to be manipulating both.

The question was who? And how could she find out, all on her own?

* * *

"Dan, this is *it*! You've got to tone the text down or I'm going to back out of this deal!"

Grover looked up to find Frank shaking a thick sheaf of paper over his head. He looked rather like an old fashioned gospel preacher threatening his congregation with hell fire and damnation.

Grover adopted his most soothing, author-placating voice. "Right, right, Frank. Believe me, I understand how strongly you feel about the book not sounding like it's all about you."

"It's not just that! It's how you're portraying me – like, like I'm some kind of Marvel Comics character! Here – here's a good example! Listen to this:"

> *Looking neither right nor left, I careened at high speed – sometimes on two wheels – through the fleeing crowds that were desperately seeking to escape the Capital. I was just as desperate to reach my destination in the heart of the perhaps-doomed city, aware that I was the only man on earth that might still avert the impending nuclear apocalypse.*

"And anyway, my father was driving!"

"Yeah, yeah, I kind of see what you mean. Maybe I can dial that back just a bit." Then he continued, as he always did, in what had become their personal version of Kabuki theater.

"But you know, we've talked about this over and over. We've gotta sell a lotta books if you want to reach a lotta people with your message. And to do that, we gotta grab them by their, well, you know, with the story line and the action."

"That's what you always say. But there are lots of accurate books that become best sellers, and they don't have any of this crap! And here – how about this – the part where you talk about the President being taken to a tunnel so he can be whisked off to the underground War Room:"

> *Chaseman and Sanford followed silently down the hall of the West Wing, and then down the stairs that led to the White House kitchen. The Acting President tried a joke to mask his anxiety. "I suppose you'll be taking us through a secret door in the back of the meat freezer?"*
>
> *The General didn't laugh. "Hardly necessary, sir. Placing the entrance in the kitchen was a matter of necessity. The White House doesn't always lend itself well to modern modifications. Would you please press your right thumb on this pad, sir?"*

Grover nodded briskly. "Yeah! Pretty cool, don't you think? But I also considered having him drop through a hatch door under the four poster bed in the Lincoln Bedroom. You like that better? I can change it."

"That's not the point! How do you know what they did at all?"

"Well, you know, it's not like they're going to tell me, is it? But he had to get to the War Room somehow, right?"

Sticking with their script, Grover moved on to Act 2.

"Anyway, that's the type of book the publisher specified in the contract. So it's a little late to try and change the deal when we're two days away from the submission deadline and you've probably already spent your advance. And remember – you're not gonna get the big bucks unless people buy the book."

Grover had figured out early on that Frank had probably blown through his advance. Ever since, whenever Frank threw a tantrum, he would let him blow off steam for a while and then close off the discussion by bringing up the advance. As usual, it worked.

"Yeah, I know," Frank said with less energy, staring ahead. Grover waited for more, but nothing followed. Puzzled, he followed Frank's line of vision, and saw that Molly was holding Frank in a malevolent fixed stare. Grover wondered whether he should snap his fingers to bring him out of it.

Instead, he said gently, "So are we good to go, Frank?" His co-author broke free of the cat's gaze and turned to Grover with a surprised, "where was I?" look on his face.

Finally he said, "Well, can you at least tone down that first part?"

"Sure! No problem. So how shall we tie things up, Frank? Do you want one last pass at the draft before I submit it? Or can I turn it in and you can just read the first page proofs when they come back? I need to tell you, though, once it's in proof form, we need to be talking about typos and corrections, not rewriting, or the publisher will go ballistic."'

Frank stewed on that for a minute. On the one hand, he knew now that when Grover promised to tone something down "a little," he was using that word in the most diminutive sense possible. But on the other, the writer had worn him down. Frank had utterly failed at making line by line edits that resulted in text he would have allowed his own mother to read, much less the general public. And he couldn't bear the thought of reading the breathless tale of his own supposed derring-do one more time.

"I guess just go ahead and submit it." He knew when he was beaten.

* * *

31

The Salon of Mme. Falconet

S IMONE FALCONET STARED absently through the narrow window of her tiny, well organized kitchen. There was nothing particular to look at; only the windows of other apartments across the courtyard, some with their metal shutters already closed for the evening. Familiar sounds wafted up from below; a courtyard door closing as someone came home from shopping or a visit to the museum; the muffled sound of an annoyed child inside an apartment on another floor; the faint grumble of traffic rising from the Parisian street that lay beyond the opposite side of the building.

The sudden shrill note of the tea kettle behind her returned her thoughts to the moment. She turned off the gas and filled the china teapot on the tray she had prepared, and then carried it the few steps between the kitchen and her small, formally furnished sitting room. It was a seasonally damp, gray Sunday, but she left the lights off, content to let the shadows gather around her for a while.

She regretted the waning of the day, not because her weekend had been pleasant (although it had), but because its end would mean the commencement of a new work week. The arguments among the faculty had been particularly petty and annoying of late, and the data her dutiful research assistants had collected recently had been perversely contradictory. More unsettling was how quickly the new head of her department had consolidated the support of her colleagues since Henri Gaumont, his predecessor, had retired from that position. Gaumont had been her mentor ever since her student days at the university where she was now a professor, the Institut d'études politiques de Paris – quite a mouthful, and hence simply "Sciences Po" to anyone familiar with the prestigious institution.

The elevation of Richard Pissante to head the Political Economy department would have been regrettable enough, given his superior and abrasive manner. But his contempt for the theories she had spent her entire career developing was personal and professionally threatening. Whether he actually disagreed with her premises or only used them as a pretext for undermining a rival candidate to succeed Gaumont hardly mattered. The result was the same.

While her protector was in charge, there had been little that Pissante could do beyond sniping at her work in print and making disparaging comments behind her back in the faculty lounge. Now she could feel her position eroding, as one professor after another found it expedient to fall into line behind the new department head rather than risk becoming the target of his condescension.

She picked up a magazine, but it was growing too dark to read easily. Anyway, there was no use trying to avoid the question. Her departmental problem demanded a solution, because her theories were by their nature controversial. Some critics even called them fascistic, a contention she found simplistic as well as insulting.

Conventionally, the debate upon which she focused centered on whether the economic benefits of unbridled capitalism outweighed the positive social impacts of left-leaning policies. To Falconet, this was a question that was not even ripe for discussion. She held that the true enquiry should be into which political policies naturally default to economic success, and which to failure. Over a period of decades, she asked, would a democratic system be likely to achieve better results under policies favoring unrestricted capitalism, or ones which assigned a higher priority to achievement of social goals?

In her view, history amply demonstrated that regardless of political theory, the sheer inertia of human nature would inevitably lead to the same results. Ideology and revolutionary zeal might fuel a different outcome for a time, but ultimately people would return to acting in their own self-interest, regardless of what the rules and regulations might say. Those laws that were most consistent with self-interest would therefore be more likely to be observed, and those that were not would be avoided, thwarted, or periodically repealed, inevitably leading to a significant loss in economic efficiency.

She pointed to the almost universal failure of communist economies as examples. Even the few that remained, China, and even Cuba, were sliding inexorably towards capitalism.

Once one accepted this conclusion (as she argued one must), the question became how one could construct a political system that harnessed human nature to work naturally towards a better and more balanced result. Such a system would lead to greater social and economic stability, which in turn should lead to higher and more sustained productivity over time. This was where she believed lay the best opportunities for productive change.

It was easy to state such a theory, but hard to prove. She had therefore decided to investigate a single, more testable, dynamic in the relationship between governments and economic decisions. Specifically, she and her assistants had long sought to prove that democratic governments with short election cycles, regardless of whether they leaned left or right, would make poorer, and even disastrous, economic decisions, in comparison to those that had longer cycles. She reasoned that this should be true, because politicians would rarely change direction when economies seemed strong, but would usually alter course when economies were failing – whether it made real sense to do so in either case.

This should flow naturally from the fact that politicians facing imminent reelection contests would rarely be brave enough to change direction when all seemed well – even if policy makers believed that the good times were about to end. To do otherwise would risk being assigned the blame when the anticipated bad times indeed came about. On the other hand, a government that failed to act during bad times – even if a change in direction could only make things worse – could expect to fail miserably in the next election.

The solution, Falconet argued, was to move economic authority from officials in elected positions to those with long-term appointed ones, thereby rendering the policy makers as immune as possible to the temptation of making self-interested decisions. Her research therefore also focused on the relative success or failure over time of decision making by elected vs. appointed officials.

There was nothing particularly daring about Falconet's theories as such, so long as they were limited to drawing conclusions from verifiable data. Once one passed from the observation of the past to making recommendations for the future, however, the potential for invoking an immune response among those pledging allegiance to political correctness became clear. Her critics found her suggestion that vital decision making powers should be removed from regularly elected officials to be particularly problematic. Wasn't that a step towards fascism?

That was enough to invoke the scorn of Pissante, but she suspected there was another reason why he had subjected her to unusually aggressive attacks.

That reason was as clear as her own picture on the front of the magazine she had put down without reading. It was hardly the first interview that she had given, but the cover photo of herself was a first. A few years ago, she had, quite by accident, acquired a popular following outside of Sciences Po. She picked up the magazine to study its cover. Doubtless it did not help that she was tall and striking, while Pissante was professorially non-descript and fusty. He was unknown outside of academic circles, and it clearly rankled him that she should have the innate ability to present herself in both an authoritative as well as an engaging manner, using real-world terms that anyone could understand.

That should not have mattered. At Sciences Po, as at most other universities, a professor was (sadly) judged on the volume and placement of her journal articles rather than on her skills as a lecturer. But one day, as she had told the magazine's interviewer, a journalist from a leading newspaper seeking an intellectual French reaction to an upcoming American presidential election had been unable to connect with his usual academic source.

By happenstance, it was Falconet that he turned to next. He found her to be unusually quotable, and also she photographed very well. The article that resulted reached a wide and receptive audience, and it was not long before other journalists were seeking her out. Within a year, Falconet had become a popular commentator and a regular guest on a weekly television review of the news. That had not sat at all well with Pissante, who began referring to her as a mere talking head with questionable analytical abilities.

He also disapproved of the other ways in which she departed from the academic norm. Unlike most French professors, she was accessible to students and enjoyed debating with them both inside and outside of class. Soon, something of a salon developed around her, made up of her most talented students, mostly female. Unlike her professorial peers, they were open to new ideas, and also interested in having an impact on the world around them. These exchanges provided her with a refreshing opportunity to propose and debate hypothetical policies based upon her theories, something she would never do now in a professorial discussion. It also provided a pool of talented graduate students she could engage as research assistants. Many of these students remained part of her salon after they graduated, meeting to discuss the events of the day in brasseries or sitting on couches and chairs in front of the small marble fireplace in her apartment.

She poured herself another cup of tea, and picked up that day's *Le Monde* from the coffee table. As she leafed through it, she was confronted by the toothful smile of one of the American presidential candidates, a Texas governor who was taking a few days off from campaigning to engage in a "fact finding" trip abroad to burnish his non-existent foreign policy credentials.

She sniffed. Her students would certainly have something to say about that.

They had been particularly energized by the aggressive approach of the last American president, the one who had expected all American allies to simply fall in line behind U.S. policies, regardless of whether they agreed with them, or what the consequences to their own national interests might be.

When that president ran for reelection, Falconet asked her salon whether they thought her theories might be applicable to this problem. Was there a way that the democratic process could be restructured in order to guide the electorate to choose more enlightened decision makers than it would otherwise? Her question became a matter of earnest and ongoing discussion as the election approached, especially since the perennially testy relations between the U.S. and France was undergoing one of its periodic exacerbations. Politicians, pundits, and even comedians on both sides of the water found it expedient to take potshots at the other nation to shore up their own domestic popularity. The phrase "cheese-eating surrender monkeys" failed to elicit the same good-humored response in France as it did in the U.S.

One night, a member of her salon observed that Americans clearly were not to be trusted picking its own leaders. Why not do it for them, another offered, to general laughter? There was agreement that such intervention was not only justified, but that French tacticians could scarcely do worse than American voters.

The concept had immediate appeal, and also presented an enjoyable puzzle – how could such a scheme be put into action? Should the United Nations be enlisted, or should a covert operation be launched? A raucous debate ensued.

Falconet found the discussion unrealistic but also beguiling. What if her theories could be put to a real-world test? But the idea was of course absurd.

She realized that she had been musing for some time; the room had now become quite dark, dark enough that even her grandmother would at last have permitted her to turn on a light. Falconet picked up her phone to check the time – it was almost 6:00 PM. She also saw that she had email. Should she attend to it now, or leave it for the morning?

She had given up her land line years before, and had left the ringer on her mobile phone off since Friday, forcing herself for once to ignore her professional life for an entire weekend. But there must be a limit to such self-indulgence. She did have friends and family. She should check.

Scanning the list of unopened mail, she was surprised to see one from Pissante, evidently sent not long before. That was highly unusual, as he was famously computer illiterate. Falconet doubted he even knew how to type – sending letters and email was what assistants were for. The subject line read, "For your immediate attention." Curious, she opened it.

In fact, there was no message at all. Merely an attachment, which she tapped to open. When it did, she had to squint to read the brief text that lay between the date and the closing. It read:

My Dear Colleague,

It is of course with deep regret that I find that I must place you on paid leave, effective immediately. I am sure that you will appreciate that I am left with no alternative, given the gravity and delicacy of the current situation. An appropriate committee will decide, in due course, if and when it may be appropriate for you to resume your duties.

Instinctively, she made that small, explosive sound (*Puh!*) that only the French can properly execute.

Relieved of her duties! What nonsense! She had tenure, and this was, after all, France! The little man must be insane to even imagine that he could pull off such a stunt, regardless of the offense, whatever it might be, that he imagined to exist.

But what could that offence be? She looked again at her phone, and saw that she had received a long list of emails, some from journalists she knew, but others from reporters whose names she only recognized. She opened several, but each merely requested the opportunity to schedule an interview. What world event could have occurred that suddenly placed her opinions in such urgent and broad demand?

Puzzled, she reached for her television remote, and called up a news program dedicated to political news and analysis that her system had recorded earlier in the day. Almost immediately the image of the leader of the ultra-right wing party France First! appeared on a screen behind the two commentators. As usual, she was gesticulating vigorously in front of a highly responsive crowd.

Falconet gathered from the discussion that followed that the party, which had heretofore defined itself almost entirely by what it was emphatically against (immigrants, socialism, unions, gays, American cheese, and so on) had issued a manifesto. It described the new, anti-democratic policies that it intended to pursue at the local, regional and national level.

And then the commentator said this:

But is there anything that is so very new in this manifesto?

Ah, indeed, this time there is. It seems that the leaders of France First! are seeking to acquire greater legitimacy by claiming that their xenophobic positions are based upon a respectable theoretical base.

Such as?

As it happens, they have discovered the work of an author whose name has popular as well as academic familiarity – Simone Falconet.

The same Simone Falconet that we have had as a guest in the past?

The very same. According to France First! her research proves that the average citizen cannot be trusted to elect policy makers. Instead, the ruling party should be able to choose long-term appointees to make decisions that cannot be second-guessed by the legislature – or even the courts. They appear to have claimed her as their own Joan of Arc.

Horrified, she turned off the television. How could her research have been so grossly misrepresented? Once again, she sat in darkness. But her sudden invisibility was only a mocking illusion. She had spent enough time with the press to know that there would be no way, and nowhere, to hide.

*   *   *

32

Ma Chère Professeur

S IMONE FALCONET CONTINUED to receive (and ignore) calls from
reporters. She sent the same polite, written response to each journalist, stating
that while she was not providing interviews or commentary at this time, it should
be clearly understood that the France First! party was misrepresenting the results
of her research, as well as her own interpretation of the data.

Her email was harder to ignore. Although she had been placed on leave, she
still needed to keep in touch with her colleagues at Sciences Po and elsewhere
regarding papers she had submitted to journals for consideration as well as others
she had agreed to peer-review. Among the day's email she was pleased to find one
that read as follows:

> *Professor Falconet,*
>
> *I find that I need to make some decisions and would be very grateful
> if I could have your advice. Would it be possible for me to call you?
> Also, do you Skype?*
>
> *Regards,*
> *Josette*

Falconet was delighted. Josette had been one of her most intelligent students, and a much-valued research assistant as well. She responded yes to both questions, and suggested a time.

*   *   *

Falconet greeted Josette warmly when they connected. It had been more than two years since the younger woman had received her graduate degree, and the two had rarely been in touch since then. Josette asked many questions regarding her former professor's current research, listening attentively to her answers. Falconet welcomed the distraction from her current troubles, and warmed to the topic.

Still, she knew that this was not the reason that Josette had reached out to her. "But you cannot be so interested any more in my dry research. You are young and out in the world. Where now do you live? And what is it that I can help you with?"

Josette's face grew larger as she leaned closer to her laptop and her voice dropped. "Do you remember how distressed we were a few years ago with the American election?"

"Of course. I confess I was a bit amused. Yes, everything you and your friends said was true. But as you grow older, perhaps, you grow more resigned to the nonsense of politics. And we have elected our own share of imbeciles, to be sure."

Josette's eyebrows rose. "But Professor! What about your research and your theories? What use are they unless they are applied?"

"Well, of course I believe that my theories are valid. But academics are observers, not practitioners. We analyze the past, and hope that perhaps we help the world see itself more clearly. If our research can be applied to make a better future, then of course, we are happy. But that is for others to decide and do."

Josette said nothing, leaving Falconet at a loss. "But I am confused by your question. What exactly is it that I can help you with?"

"Professor, you do remember the very serious discussions we had, trying to figure out how the rest of the world could impress upon the Americans how much the decisions their presidents make affect us, and if that failed, how we might take action to lead the American voters to make more responsible decisions? Yes?"

"Yes, yes, I do recall. But what of it? Those were simply theoretical exercises."

Josette pressed her lips together. "Perhaps to you. But we have acted on those plans."

"What? You cannot be serious? Which plans? What have you done?"

Josette began speaking very rapidly, her face now almost filling the laptop screen. She did not go into all of the details, but she described how, with the help of some IT savvy friends, they had executed their plan; how she feared that the back door they had built into the pollsters' systems was now being exploited by someone else to affect the primaries; and how she believed that someone, presumably the same individual or group, had found a way to manipulate the voting returns as well.

"So, Professor, my question is this: do you know of anyone who could assist me in uncovering the person who has taken control of the pollsters' systems? Perhaps a French espionage agency? Do you know anyone who would be able to approach such a department?"

Early in Josette's monologue, Falconet had stood up and begun pacing back and forth in her small sitting room. When at last her former student quit speaking, she turned towards her own computer and spoke from a distance, her hands splayed open in disbelief.

"But how could you? How could you even devise such a scheme?"

"How can you say 'how could we?' We did it in your sitting room! You were there!"

"Yes, yes, of course I was. But that was just a discussion – we were playing little mind games – it is how we amuse ourselves in universities. But in the social sciences we never actually *do* anything – we just do research and write papers that nobody reads!"

Josette's face was flushed. She could barely see the face of her former professor in the shadows of her apartment. "Perhaps for you, but not for us! Have you forgotten? We were in Paris, and we are French! When a government runs amok, we do not sit back and cluck our tongues! We challenge whatever has become the new *ancien regime* when it begins to abuse the people. It was not so long before you went to university that students barricaded the streets of Paris and held off the government for days."

Falconet wondered why everyone was suddenly taking her theories seriously after ignoring them for so many years. What would happen if news of this exploit were to reach the press? She would lose her position forever. She sat down in front of her laptop again and tried to be calm.

"I am sorry, my dear. I did not mean to disrespect your ideals or your sincerity. It's just that this seems so, so dangerous? What if you were to be caught? I must assume you would be sent to jail! Have you considered this?"

"Of course we have. We do not intend to be caught, but if we are, then we will seek all of the publicity that we can get, and pursue our purpose that way instead. We will rally popular support to impress the Americans that they cannot simply take other countries for granted forever."

Falconet tried to collect her thoughts. She could not believe that she had in some way inspired – no, that must be too strong a word – that she had in some way been misunderstood to have advocated the taking of public, much less covert, action to influence the democratic political process of another country.

"I see. I do not approve, but I see. But you began by saying that you want my advice. I am afraid that I have no idea who might be an appropriate or safe person in France to seek out."

Despite her combative statements, Josette had expected Falconet to be surprised that her former students had moved from discussion to action. But she had assumed, perhaps foolishly, that Falconet would be more supportive than aghast. Perhaps she should simply thank the professor for her time and say goodbye.

Falconet began to soften as she watched the play of emotions pass across her former student's face. There must be something she could do to dissuade Josette from placing herself further at risk.

"Tell me what you want to do, my dear. Truly, I would like to help."

"It is this. I feel we have started something that we should finish. It was we that hacked into the polling systems, but we are not manipulating them now. And judging from the first primary results, things may turn out worse than if we had done nothing at all."

"Perhaps, but —"

"Wait – let me finish. We could go back, yes, and remove the software. But we thought that this had already happened, because a secret United States agency had already discovered the hack —"

"Josette!"

"– but not us, do not worry. However, I became suspicious when new polls and voting came out that did not seem possible, so I hacked into one of the polling systems again – and the tampered code was still in place. Only it redirects now to a different server that is not under our control."

"Can you not just remove it, then?"

"We could, but then they would know that they had been discovered, and also they could simply reinstall it. And the more times we play this game the more likely it becomes that we will be discovered."

"Could you not tell the authorities then?"

"I think it is the authorities themselves – this secret agency that no one has ever heard of – that is now controlling the systems."

"Why would you think that?"

"Because they have told the person who discovered the hack that there is now no reason for concern."

"Well, different authorities then?"

"But how would we explain how we got the knowledge? If they investigated us, they would surely be able to trace the original activities back to us."

"Anonymously, then."

"Why would anyone believe or take seriously such an anonymous statement? It is a very big country, and anyone we might think to approach, like the FBI, must receive mountains of nonsense every day that they simply ignore. They would assume that whoever wrote to them was simply another lunatic with a conspiracy theory."

Falconet could think of no more questions or suggestions. And she was sure that she had already heard more than it was good for her to know.

"It sounds as if you have no choice but to do nothing, my dear. I know this sounds cowardly, but you are swimming in very deep and treacherous waters indeed. As you say, if you go to other authorities in person, they will wonder how you could know such things, and your earlier activities may come to light. And if you try to interfere in any way, you will be in even greater risk of going to jail, now that the voting has begun. It may be that you will even find yourself in physical danger. No, however unsatisfactory my advice may sound, I think you must stand aside and let whatever may happen, happen."

She felt demeaned as she said the words, seeing the disdain they inspired in her former student's eyes. Whatever pedestal Josette had placed her on before had clearly toppled and shattered into a thousand pieces. But what other advice could she possibly give?

She watched as Josette's face diminished in size and clarity as she pushed her laptop away from her. "You have been very kind to speak with me on such short notice. It was very good to see you again." Then she signed off.

Falconet stared at her computer as the screen went blank, feeling greatly distressed. She had no doubt that Josette would ignore her advice. And also that if a group of her former students were to be apprehended, her own name and published writings would be dragged into the press as well. Was there anything within her power that she could do to prevent such a thing from happening?

At the other end of the closed Skype connection, Josette was feeling equally bleak. Although she had devised the concept behind the hack on the polling systems, her code level skills were not great. And given the dangerous course of recent events, she was reluctant to reconnect with her former conspirators.

Who could she turn to now?

There seemed to be only one alternative left. If she had had a greater command of American idiomatic expression, she might have concluded that all of her eggs seemed now to be in a single basket. And that the fussy, preoccupied chicken sitting on that basket was named Frank.

* * *

33

Another French Connection

S IMONE FALCONET WAS feeling frustrated, angry and helpless, and of those three, the last was most galling. She had worked so hard to achieve her success. Now she was struggling to devise a plan of attack to save it.

True, she had made some progress on the France First! front, but only in the sense that she now knew what had led the far-right party to discover and adopt a mangled version of her theories. According to a friend with ties to the organization, an unsigned white paper had been received by one of its strategists. The paper's author had briefly – and misleadingly – summarized her work and then applied it to support some of the most hateful xenophobic proposals of the France First! platform.

Given the immediate action taken by her department head, she had little doubt who the source of that document had been. But she had no proof. And the single interview she had finally given to a television journalist had proven to be a disaster. She had hoped that by presenting her work in person she could persuade any reasonable viewer that her research had been wildly misrepresented. Instead, she was allowed only to respond to ridiculous questions. What little opportunity she was given to correct the record was edited out of the final presentation.

She hoped to fare better with the detailed, written rebuttal she had prepared and submitted to the committee that would rule on whether she could return to her duties. But she feared that the truth of the matter would be outweighed by the public embarrassment the university had already suffered. A member of the committee whom she counted as a friend told her privately that she would be wise to keep a low profile and be patient. If she allowed the committee to sit on the decision for six months, perhaps things might die down sufficiently that she could be quietly reinstated. At present, that was quite impossible.

And then there was the question of Josette. The last thing Falconet's career could tolerate would be linkage to a vote-rigging scandal, and yet her former student seemed determined to continue on her mad adventure.

What more was there for her to do? She had no teaching duties, and there was little prospect that a journal would accept one of the papers she had in progress. Indeed, even traveling to her office was risky; a reporter writing a story about France First! might be waiting for her on the sidewalk outside her apartment building. With too much time and too few avenues to improve her situation, she found herself reading about the U.S. primary system and the progress of the current election season, hoping to find no evidence of what Josette believed was occurring.

Still, as she learned more about the candidates and their evolving fortunes, she could not help feeling a degree of admiration for her former students. Many of those running for president appeared to be caricatures of politicians rather than real candidates vying to lead the most powerful nation on earth. And yet people were voting for them (or not, if Josette was to be believed). She wondered whether de Tocqueville would be horrified or amused.

While scanning a news site, a vivid red and blue pop-up momentarily caught her eye. It was an ad for a book that was about to be released called *The Alexandria Project*. Why did that name seem familiar?

She clicked on the ad, but still could not make the connection, until she noticed the author's name. Now she had it. "Adversego" – so unusual – Josette had mentioned that name and book title, when they spoke. This was the person who had discovered the polling system hack, but agreed to keep secret the names of those behind it. She clicked through to the book site to read the short text about the author, and saw that he lived in Washington, D.C.

Perhaps that was fortuitous; she had been invited to present a paper at an academic conference in Washington in a week's time, and fortunately the invitation had not been withdrawn. Perhaps this Adversego person would agree to meet with her. Perhaps he might be open to persuading Josette not to endanger herself – and Falconet – any further.

* * *

Frank was puzzled by the email:

> *Dear Mr. Adversego,*
>
> *Next Tuesday through Thursday I will attend an academic conference in Washington. Although it is not my area of research, I am interested in the role played by information technology in the electoral process. I wonder whether you might have the time on one of those days to share your views with me on that subject, perhaps over lunch or at another time of your convenience? If so, I would be most grateful.*
>
> *With warmest regards,*
>
> *Simone Falconet*
> *Professeur d'Economie Politique*
> *Institut d'études politiques de Paris*

Perhaps this was what happened when you published and promoted a book. Why else would a person he'd never heard of suddenly contact him? If so, he had acquired yet another reason to wonder what inner demon had persuaded him that writing a book would be a good idea.

He read the email again. Why would this professor be contacting him? Nothing she would have read about him online would suggest he had any connection with the electoral process. Could it be just a coincidence? He doubted it, and began to see what he could find out about her online.

Immediately, he found a rash of mentions connecting Falconet with a far-right political party. That didn't look good. Further searching led him to a short biography at her university and a profile at a television station; he used an online translator to turn both into English. Despite the fractured syntax of the result, it seemed to tell a very different story. Although Falconet apparently did not feel constrained to follow in the footsteps of traditional theorists, her career seemed to otherwise have been completely conventional, leaving aside the fact that she was also a frequent commentator on the news.

He returned to the profile, and clicked on a link to one of the broadcasts in which she had participated. It took him to a view of a news broadcast stage, with a man and a woman sitting on opposite sides of a desk. They were of course speaking in French, but he was intrigued by the appearance and poise of the person sitting in the guest chair. She was likely about his age, and he found her appearance striking. Whatever she was saying, she was combining conviction with personality in an attractive and engaging way.

He mused for a moment. With the book almost finished and Grover doing all the work anyway, he had time on his hands.

He accepted her invitation.

*   *   *

Frank looked away self-consciously when he saw the hostess point out his table to the tall woman who had just walked in. It occurred to him that the brief glance she cast about the room before following the hostess to his table might have more to do with attracting attention then looking for him. And why not? She certainly had a commanding presence. Glancing around the room, he noticed that her survey of the room, followed by her studied indifference to those she was now striding past had the desired effect; several men were watching her progress to better appreciate the handsome, confident woman in the stylishly understated outfit. He caught himself drumming his fingers on the table, and placed his hands in his lap, where they reestablished their tempo on his thighs.

Falconet in turn was studying the person at the table she was approaching. He was conventionally dressed in a blue blazer and button-down oxford cloth shirt. When she drew closer, he stood up, revealing shoes that were in a rather deplorable condition, and pants in need of a good pressing. But that was fine; she found most French men to be effeminate and obsessed with their appearance. The relative indifference of this American to his apparel struck her as refreshing. He also looked fit, something that was rare among men his age in France, where exercise was generally considered unnecessary and even unfashionable.

"So very nice to meet you, Mr. Adversego," she said when she reached the table.

"My pleasure," he said, accepting and shaking the hand she extended to him. "But please call me Frank." He hoped that she would lead their conversation, as he didn't have a clue what to say next.

"You are too kind. And I am so pleased that you are willing to speak to me," she began as they sat down. "I have read of your role in the Korean crisis last year, and it occurred to me that you might also be knowledgeable about how computers are being used in connection with elections. Would that be so?"

He had rehearsed an answer that would reveal no more than he was willing to share.

"Well, yes and no. I've never worked in that area, but there's nothing particularly different about processing electoral data from any other type of information. To a computer, data is just data – the machine doesn't care what type of information it represents. And I am generally aware of the different ways computer technology is being used in this area, so depending on what you'd like to know, I hope I can be helpful."

"Excellent! Then with regard to the voting apps that I understand are now being used, do you believe these new technologies affect how people vote? Will they, for example, make people more likely to go to the polls?"

To his relief, Frank found Falconet to be gracious and interesting company. He did his best to respond to her questions as the lunch progressed, but had the odd feeling that while she was attentive to his responses, she didn't seem to care very much about what he was saying. To his discomfort, she seemed to be studying him more than the information he was conveying.

By the time the waiter was delivering coffee to him and tea to his guest, Falconet seemed to be running out of questions, and he had certainly run out of information he felt it was prudent to share. He tried to peek at his watch in such a way as to be noticeable but not rude, hoping that she would take the hint and allow him to escape.

"I'm sorry that I haven't been able to be more helpful. Perhaps I could connect you with someone with more knowledge in this area. Would you like me to do that?"

It seemed a simple question to Frank. But for some reason, the professor needed a moment to think before responding.

"You have been most kind, but no, I do not think that would be necessary." She paused again, and folded her napkin neatly before placing it on the table.

"But I do have one other favor to ask. I believe that you know a former student of mine – her name is Josette Fernald."

Frank hesitated. "Josette? Why yes. As a matter of fact I do."

So this meeting was anything but a coincidence. If this professor knew Josette and was asking him about voting technology, how much more did she know? He decided that it was his turn to listen and study his lunch companion rather than speak.

Falconet looked uncomfortable. "I fear that I owe you an apology, Frank. I am not really so interested in the matters we have been discussing; perhaps you could tell. But I was hoping very much that we could speak about Josette, and I did not know how to go about proposing that. Would you be comfortable doing so now?"

The honest answer to that question was an emphatic "no," but he decided that he wanted to know exactly what it was that Falconet wanted.

He glanced briefly to both sides to be sure that no one was paying attention to their conversation. "Well, I'm not sure. I mean, I don't really know her that well. What exactly is it about Josette that you want to discuss?"

Falconet leaned forward and spoke so softly that he was forced to lean forward as well.

"Frank, I do not wish to be so bold, but I must tell you that Josette has recently shared with me that she is engaging in certain… activities that strike me as being very – shall we say – very unwise. I have tried to advise her against this but she does not wish to hear."

Frank was feeling flustered as much by the large, dark eyes that were staring into his and the soft, urgent voice as by the words he was hearing.

"Josette mentioned your name when we spoke – please, do not be concerned – she mentioned it only in passing. That is why I asked to meet with you. I am hoping that perhaps you might be more successful than I in convincing her to come to her senses. If she does not, I fear that it will not end well for her."

Frank had heard as much as he wanted to hear. He leaned back and caught the eye of their waiter.

"It's rather warm in here," he said abruptly. "What do you think about taking a walk?" In truth, he did suddenly feel uncomfortably warm. But mostly he wanted to buy some time to think.

Falconet raised her eyebrows, but said nothing. Moments later they were walking along one of the Capital's broad avenues, weaving from time to time to avoid those traveling in the opposite direction. Falconet was not wearing the most sensible of shoes, and struggled to keep up with him. He said nothing for some time as he tried to work out how much to share with someone he knew almost nothing about.

After a half a block he realized how quickly he had been walking and slowed down.

"I'm sorry to be so rude – but you took me by surprise. And I'm afraid that before I can say anything more, I need you to tell me exactly what you believe Josette is about to do."

Simone gratefully resumed a normal walking pace. She drew closer so as not to be overheard.

"Josette is convinced that someone is manipulating your presidential polls and primary voting, and she is determined to find out who it is. Were you not aware of this?"

Frank ignored her question. "And did she say how she would go about doing so?"

"No. Only that she felt that she must do something. She contacted me to ask my advice on what to do."

"And what did you say?"

"That she must do nothing, of course! No, that it not quite true. At first, she asked whether I might help her contact authorities in France that might take an interest in the matter. But I have no way to do so, so I asked why she did not alert their American counterparts. She said that this was impossible. She suspects that it is the authorities that are behind the mischief."

Nothing new there. So what should he say? They were at the edge of a park, with the usual number of homeless people, strolling tourists and office-break idlers. He spied an empty park bench and steered them in that direction. When they reached it, they sat down at opposite ends.

At first, neither said anything. Falconet realized that reaching out had been a mistake, and looked at her watch. She really should be returning to her conference. She stood up, and once again held out her hand.

"I am very sorry to have taken so much of your time, Mr. Adversego. I will go now."

He stood up and ignored her outstretched hand, "No, I'm sorry. I've been very unhelpful; but I hope you can understand that there is very little I'm at liberty to speak about. But please, have a seat."

She gave a thin smile, and hesitated. But at last she sat down, and waited to see what he might say next.

Frank frowned and turned away for a moment before sitting down once again himself. A lone child, perhaps six years old, caught his eye, flying back and forth on a set of swings nearby. The little girl's face was intent and fearless as she pumped her legs harder and harder, determined to soar as high as the swing could take her, and perhaps a bit beyond. Already, she had climbed to the point where the chains of the swing were parallel to the ground, and still she pushed on. With a pang of remembrance, Frank recalled the sense of reckless weightlessness when the chains of your swing suddenly went slack. Then you plummeted straight down until they came taut again with a neck-snapping jerk.

It seemed as if the determined child must be tossed from her seat if she flew any higher, either on the upswing as she flew skyward, or in a random direction when the chains reasserted their authority. To Frank's relief, a woman materialized out of his peripheral vision, striding forward until she stood just in front of the swing's path. Stop! she ordered; No! the child screamed back.

Falconet was watching the contest now as well. Once more, the young girl flew upwards, but this time, during her precipitous descent, the woman leaped forward and seized the seat of the swing with both hands. Half running and half holding back, she slowed the swing down until the child's powerful momentum was absorbed by the woman's own backward-leaning weight, all the while attempting to avoid the child's rebelliously flailing legs.

Frank made up his mind, and sat back down next to Falconet.

"Okay, I'll speak with her. As I expect you know, Josette has quite a mind of her own. I will tell her that she is taking chances that are more hazardous than she realizes. I don't expect that she'll pay any more attention to me than she has to you. But I will try."

Simone gave him a real smile, and put a hand on his. "I cannot ask for more than that. You are very kind, Frank. Will you let me know if there is anything further I can do?"

He wished he could reclaim his hand, but it was still trapped beneath hers. "Yes," he answered without much conviction or intention to actually do so. "Yes, I will do that."

"Good!" she said, releasing his hand and standing up again. "And now I see that I must return to my conference." She looked around uncertainly for a moment. She laughed. "That is, if I can tell which way to go."

"Do you want a cab? It's easy to get one here."

"No, no. It is a pretty day, and you see so much more of a city on foot. Can you tell me, though, which way it is to the George Mason University campus?"

"Sure. I'm headed in that direction myself. I can get you started."

To his great relief, she changed the subject, asking him questions about the public buildings that were in view. The eyes of anyone passing the pair would have been immediately drawn to the tall, self-assured woman with the stylish scarf and a French accent. If they noticed her companion at all, it would have been to note how incongruous he looked in contrast. And yet the French woman seemed to be quite interested in what he had to say.

*   *   *

34

There's No Fool like a Middle-Aged Fool

F RANK WAS OUT on his morning run, sneakers flapping flat-footed on the pavement as he labored through his usual route. He'd decided early on that he'd train for distance rather than speed, since his body had gone to great pains, as it were, to inform him that speed was not on the menu. But that was okay. He was exercising to stay in shape rather than train for a race.

He was rather astonished that he was still running at all. He had always disliked exercise as a physically and socially awkward child, and particularly during gym class at school. The embarrassing gym outfit, the damp, malodorous locker rooms, and, of course, the more athletic, mocking classmates – all were seared forever into his memory.

He had particularly loathed running. Sports weren't part of his daily existence, and the gym program wasn't regular enough to get anyone into shape, even under duress. When he and his classmates were herded out in the spring to flog their symbolic mile around the school's soggy cinder track, he was usually the last puffing, aching, body to struggle across the finish line. The excruciating experience smacked of masochism, minus the payoff.

Now he found that the challenge of gradually building up his stamina had a strong appeal. And he had to admit that he did feel better for the rest of the day when he ran. Sometime during his second month of running his pain level had receded dramatically, and he now looked forward to the forty-five minutes each morning when he let his mind run as well, free from all distractions.

At least, he usually did. Today, as he ran in place waiting for a light to change, he wished he was one of those runners that blasted songs through earbuds into the defenseless inner sancta of their endorphin-stoked brains. Perhaps that might distract him from the tiresome loop his mind was insistently cycling through. Its focus was not his recent and predictable failure to dissuade Josette from pursuing her real or imaged hacker, but on her continuing pleas for assistance. And therein lay the rub.

It seemed as if some sort of phantom debate team coach had taken up residence in his cranium, refusing to leave him alone. Frank didn't like either of the positions available for him to argue.

The question, of course, was this:

> *Resolved: That Frank Adversego should render assistance to Josette Fernald in her quest to determine who is hacking the polls and voting in the U.S. primary election.*

He chugged across the street and turned west along the Mall. At first blush, the "con" point of view had strong appeal. For one thing, he was not yet convinced that either type of hacking was actually occurring. And then there was the abiding challenge of relating to Josette simply as a friend. Okay, he could cut himself a bit of slack on that issue, given her flirtatious ways. How was he supposed to react when she turned on the charm?

But that led immediately to the more pernicious part of the relationship – if he should even call it that. He was relieved to know that she was older than he had first assumed, but he was nonetheless sure that she had no interest in him. That would mean that when she flirted she was playing him for whatever her current purpose might be. The problem was that she was awfully good at it. That, and the fact that while it was sometimes humiliating in retrospect, it could sometimes be awfully pleasant in the moment.

No fool like an old fool, right? He was painfully aware that one didn't have to be that old to qualify for the part.

Reaching the Washington Monument, he made a wide, looping turn and began puffing his way back in the opposite direction. Then there was the "pro" side of the argument. Regardless of how he might feel about being manipulated from time to time by Josette, he couldn't help feeling paternally protective of her as well; it was as much of a "man thing" as was the old fool part, despite the apparent emotional contradiction. If Josette's assumptions were correct, whoever was hacking the election would scarcely hesitate to use violence if their scheme was in danger of being discovered. Who knew what they might do if they caught Josette sniffing around? Hell, his own government had tried to kill him the year before.

He swung back off the Mall and headed towards home. Time to play debate judge, and assess his own arguments. Should Frank Pro or Frank Con be declared the winner?

Both arguments had been persuasive. For a while his stride hammered out the refrain, Who should win? Who should win?

Two blocks later, there still seemed to be no decisive answer. Perhaps he needed to shed his judge's hat and take external information into account. He was, after all, still on the Voldemort payroll, so wasn't it his job to find out if Josette was right? And as an American, shouldn't he feel some responsibility to catch whoever it was that had the unmitigated gall to hack a presidential election? And finally, wouldn't he have to live with the consequences if he didn't?

Without realizing it, he'd picked up speed after leaving the Mall, leaving him totally spent by the time he arrived at the front door of his apartment building. His forehead resting on one arm pressed against the wall, he stretched out his hamstrings and gasped for air. It took more than a few minutes before his breathing returned to normal.

Grasping the front door handle, he gave it an irritated tug. Damn it, he decided. Frank Pro had won the debate.

*   *   *

It was one of those wonderful, spring-like days that defy expectations by sometimes dawning during a Washington winter. Josette and Frank were taking advantage of the good weather to hold a planning session outside.

Josette was surprised and pleased when Frank told her that he was on board. Even he was feeling better about the situation, because the day after his running debate with himself Vickie had contacted him with a new assignment: his instructions were to thoroughly check several voting stations during the primaries to see if he could detect any evidence of vote manipulation.

"But that is perfect!" she said. "How do they expect you to do so?"

He took out his wallet and began sorting through the various cards jammed inside. "Here. Take a look at this." He handed her the plastic card that Butcher had given him in Nevada months before and waited for her response.

At the top, she saw the words, "Lincoln IT Electoral Services." Below that it read:

FRANK J. ADVERSEGO, JR.

Field Service Representative

Josette puzzled over the card. "What does the 'J' stand for?" she said at last.

"That doesn't matter. The point is that I've got a way to check out voting machines to see if they've been tampered with."

"Ah! Yes, that is very good! Did you get this from Voldemort?"

"Yes I did. If you look for Lincoln online, you'll see that it has a very convincing website that says it sells and services all major lines of voting machines. I should be able to drop in just about anywhere and talk my way in."

"But what if they recognize your name?"

Frank looked very smug now. "Watch this."

He took what looked like a memory stick out of his pocket and plugged it into a port in his phone. Then he typed on his phone's keypad for a minute, and finally slid the plastic business card along a groove in the side of the memory stick. When he handed the card back to her, it now read:

MILLARD FILLMORE

Field Service Representative

"If you check the Lincoln website, you'll learn the surprising fact that the 13th President of the United States now works for Lincoln," he pronounced triumphantly.

Josette knit her brows, looking puzzled. "Was he really the 13th president?"

"That's not the point!" He'd be damned if he'd say it, but the point was that he had this really nifty gadget right out of a James Bond movie. How could she not be impressed?

"Okay, yes, I understand. This could be very useful to us."

Frank barely heard what she said after that. He was too busy mentally kicking Frank Pro down a flight of stairs.

*   *   *

Two days later, he was parking his camper across the street from the county courthouse in Promise, Kansas, population 1,257, founded in 1876, according to the sign at the edge of town. Flanked by enormous cottonwood trees, the terra cotta trimmed brick courthouse was an impressive example of 19th century civic architecture, intended to bear witness to the boundless future and inevitable prosperity of a fast-growing town on the Great Plains.

That was then, however, and this was now. The courthouse looked pretty well maintained, but the rest of the town was clearly a run-down shadow of its former self. Only the grain silos and agricultural businesses by the railroad tracks looked active. The store fronts on Main Street were largely empty – the newspaper gone out of business long ago; the bank locked up for good; a restaurant with a faded "Welcome!" sign hanging a-kilter inside a chained-shut door never to open again – all the commercial cornerstones of a once burgeoning local economy were fly-specked and dark. All that remained were a thrift store, a couple of bars displaying unlit beer-brand neon signs in their day-dark windows, and a pharmacy. There were more churches than businesses still hanging on.

Frank had read about places like this, but never seen one first hand. Like so many other towns in the depopulating Great Plains states, the economic viability of Promise had been sucked out of it by changing times. The process started with the interstate highway that was laid out twenty miles to the north instead of along the grade of the railway line that had turned Promise from a dusty crossroad into a bustling county seat a century before. The last nail in the town's coffin was driven home by Walmart, when it opened one of its superstores in a nearby town.

All of this had figured into Butcher's decision to pick Promise for Frank's first site visit after White Crow had ordered him to find out how the primaries might be being hacked. After all, how much of an IT budget could this hard luck town have? Frank should be able to get access to whatever he needed simply by flashing his card at the town office.

Or at least so it had seemed to Butcher. What he hadn't factored into the equation was that the person doing the flashing would be Frank Adversego, who was not only the antithesis of an undercover agent, but socially phobic as well. Ordering a cheeseburger in a bar was enough to raise his anxiety level, so the thought of penetrating the defenses of a voting district in person rather than remotely via an Internet connection was enough to strand him in his camper while he reviewed his plan of attack.

Fifteen minutes later, a policeman walked out of the front of the courthouse. He stared idly in Frank's direction before turning and getting into his squad car. Better get moving, Frank told himself. You don't want to attract suspicion before you even get started.

Still uncertain regarding what he would say, he climbed down from the camper and extended the handle of a wheeled tool case he'd picked up at the same Walmart Death Star that had targeted the shoppers of Promise. It didn't contain anything except his laptop, but he thought it added credibility as he towed it through the front door of the courthouse.

Inside, he looked for a directory, which turned out not to exist. Instead, there was a long, high-ceilinged hallway flooded with the morning light that streamed in through the large window at its eastern end. Its walls were lined with doors, each with a large frosted glass pane in the top half on which was painted the name of a department or official. He walked to one end, passing "Probate," "Clerk of Courts," and other unhelpful designations before backtracking and heading in the opposite direction, his footsteps echoing in the silence of what might as well be an abandoned building. Eventually he found a door that read "Electoral Commission." Taking a deep breath, he turned the handle. The door was locked. Now what?

He set off back towards the other end of the hallway, deciding that whatever lay behind the door marked Town Clerk might be his best bet. Sure enough, that door was unlocked. Inside, he found a small waiting room with a counter along one side, behind which was an open door. The soft, encouraging, sound of typing emanated from within.

He walked up to the counter, but whoever was typing was invisible, off to the side of the room on the other side of the door. On the counter was an old-fashioned bell, the type you sounded by striking downward with the palm of your hand.

He cleared his throat and waited hopefully for a minute. No luck. Taking another deep breath, he tapped the bell. The unexpectedly loud *ding!* made him jump, but a few moments later, he heard a chair scrape, and a gray-haired, 60-ish woman appeared in the doorway.

"Help you?" she said.

Frank had been prepared to confront the wife from the American Gothic painting, and was relieved to see that the woman looked pretty much like someone he might have met anywhere, assuming the time period was his childhood. She wore a gray wool skirt and an open, button-front sweater over a neat white collared blouse. Around her neck hung a pair of glasses on a beaded cord.

"Yes, thank you," he said, sliding his card across the counter. "We service your voting machines. I was doing a job up the road and my records show it's almost time for a warranty check of your units. I thought I'd drop by and see if I could knock that off while I'm in the area. Problem is, I see the Electoral Commission office is closed. I guess I should have called first, but is there anyone around that could show me to where you keep the machines?"

The woman picked up his card and settled her glasses on the end of nose. She peered at the card carefully, and then turned it over to see if there was anything else on the back.

"What kind of name is that?"

"You mean my name?"

She peered at him over the top of her glasses. "I think I can figure 'Lincoln' out on my own."

Frank began to sweat. "Sorry. It's a Scottish name."

She looked at the card again and then handed it back.

"Well, Mr. Turing, it wouldn't have helped to call anyway. The Electoral Commission only meets once a month when they need to, and that's not often. The voting machines are in the basement. If you'll have a seat, I'll see if I can rustle up the janitor. He can unlock the storage room for you."

Frank did as he was told while the woman dialed a number, failed to get the janitor, and left a message. She returned to her office, leaving Frank to study one of the agricultural magazine back issues that lay on the table between the two mismatched but equally uncomfortable wooden chairs in the waiting room. Lulled by the sound of typing from the office, he struggled to stay awake by updating himself on the latest developments in GPS-enabled farm machinery.

Fifteen minutes later the door to the hallway opened to admit an elderly man wearing faded bib overalls. Stoop shouldered and balding, his sad eyes struggled to hold up the large bags beneath them. Frank reflected that if he was an actor in a Western, he'd be cast as the guy who takes care of the horses and usually has a nickname like "Stumpy." It was always Stumpy who caught the first arrow when the Indians attacked.

He shuffled up to the counter. "Sally, you looking for me?"

The gray-haired woman who now had a name called back. "Gentleman here needs to check out the voting machines. Can you take him down there?"

Stumpy looked around, noticing Frank for the first time.

He studied on the situation for a moment. "Yup, I can do that."

He turned towards the door to the hallway and Frank trundled obediently behind him, trailing his mostly empty tool case.

After a few steps, his guide stopped and waited for Frank to pull alongside.

"Sorry to keep you waiting, son. Where you from?"

Frank tried to remember the address on the card. When he couldn't, he said "Philadelphia." His ears burned as he vowed to come up with a background profile before he tried this again. Shouldn't someone from Voldemort have provided him with something like that?

"Well, that's a bit of a drive, ain't it?" With that nugget of information secured, he shuffled along to a door marked "Stairs," down into a basement, past two restrooms, and at last to an unmarked wooden door. It took him some time to flip through the dozens of keys hanging from a ring hooked to his belt to find the right one.

"Everything you're looking for should be in here. You need anything else, you ask Sally to hunt me up."

Frank thanked him, and the sound of the old man's shuffling feet tapered away, leaving Frank alone in the silence of a half-dark room filled with large boxes. A bare light bulb hung on a wire from the ceiling, casting more shadows than light on the gray-painted stone foundation wall running along one side of the room.

Where to begin? He was used to sitting at a laptop looking at neat file names on pull-down menus serving familiar systems.

He wandered around the room looking for information on the outsides of the boxes, and finally noticed a clipboard hanging from a hook by the door. He was relieved to see that it held an inventory of everything in the room, with a number and the contents given for each box.

Twenty minutes later, he'd made good progress. He'd found a copy of the set up manual for the system, as well as a Wi-Fi router and a laptop preloaded with the system that the table top wireless voting units would communicate with. Figuring his odds were better than they should be, he turned the laptop on, and when it asked for a password, typed in "admin."

Sure enough, that worked. Whoever had delivered the system had never bothered to change the factory password before turning the system over to whoever it was who would be managing it, and that individual hadn't bothered to change it, either. So much for local security.

His next challenge was finding an Internet connection, as the air card on his own laptop couldn't find a signal to share. He found a courthouse Wi-Fi signal, but this time "admin" didn't work.

Making sure the door wouldn't lock behind him, he found his way back to the empty waiting room of the Town Clerk's office. Happily, he could still hear typing coming from the back room.

He walked up to the counter. "Uh, excuse me. Could I ask you for the Wi-Fi password?"

Sally came around the door and leaned across the counter.

"It's 'courthouse' – all lower case." She said quietly. "I didn't want to just call it out."

Frank thanked her and acknowledged her prudence.

Now that he had his super-secure password, he was able to set the system up in full operational mode. Then, sitting on an unopened box under the bare bulb, he got down to business.

* * *

"Sorry, son. Got to ask you to leave now. Closing up for the day." It was the elderly janitor, standing at the door.

Startled, Frank looked up. "What time is it?"

"Almost 5:00. Need to lock up. But you can come back tomorrow at 8:30, if you want."

Frank stood up. "Gee, can you give me another ten minutes? I just finished, but I need to put all this stuff back the way I found it."

The old man nodded and disappeared. Frank hurriedly packed up, trying to leave everything exactly as it had been before. He was just hanging up the clipboard when the sound of shuffling feet materialized down the hall.

As the old man locked the door, he said, "You heading back to Philly now?"

"No, down the road to the next stop. It's one of those jobs where you sleep in a different motel every night."

"I know what that's like. Used to be a salesman for a while after the Korean War. Then I wised up and came home to Promise. What more could you want out of life than what you can find right here?"

Frank was still musing on that koanic query as he drove past the last few neatly-kept homes of Promise and out onto the sea of growing soybeans that surrounded the town. For his part, he was simply happy for his first undercover mission to be over.

*   *   *

Twenty-four hours later, he was driving slowly around a loop of dirt road, checking out each of the half dozen empty campsites he passed along the way before he made a decision. When he did, he selected one where the usual picnic table and fire pit lay beside the chortling stream that gamboled in one end of the state park and out the other. He got out of the camper, and surveyed the scene, hands on his hips. The soft rustle of fluttering aspen leaves murmured above his head, and the late-afternoon sunlight energized the colors of the green grass and wildflowers surrounding the site, contrasting elegantly with the porcelain-white trunks of the aspens and the sparkling waters of the stream.

All of which was lost on Frank. He had just stumbled through his first radio interview, and was still smarting from the experience. His agent had suggested he try one out in the boonies before his formal book tour, which made sense to Frank. Somehow, though, he had expected an interviewer would be good at the job, or at least have prepared a few questions in advance. Instead, he had been ushered into a live radio booth while the show host read his book's promotional package for the first time. It hadn't been pretty.

He was looking forward to getting back to something that he was good at, which would be analyzing the data he'd collected the day before at the courthouse. It was an unseasonably warm spring day, and soon he was perched in his trusty folding chair, facing the stream. Once again, he was faced with the question of where to start.

He'd been able to capture a complete record of the recent voting process at the Promise courthouse, which he hoped would provide crucial information. Not only was the data still on the laptop that he had found there, but he'd been able to log on to the state electoral office to see what had been sent in from Promise, using the credentials he had received from Voldemort.

Combining what he had copied from those two sources, he had a complete end-to-end record of every vote from the moment it was cast to the point when it was included in the final state-wide tabulation of voting results. And he could confirm the path that each vote took as it was sent from the voting station to the laptop, and from the laptop via the Internet to the state data center, where it was entered into the appropriate cell of the database that yielded the final tally that was announced publicly.

The obvious first step for him now would be to compare the laptop totals with the state numbers. That took only a moment, and the two totals matched. So if there had been any tampering with the vote at this location, it couldn't have happened anywhere between the laptop and the state electoral center. This narrowed his investigation dramatically, and represented an important finding in itself.

It also meant that any mischief involving the Promise totals, short of paying people to vote as instructed, had to have occurred in one of only a few ways. The first was that malware might have been installed in the software of the tabletop voting station itself, where it could have converted a vote for candidate A into one for candidate B.

The second possibility was that someone sitting in the courthouse could have taken over the voting system's wireless network – or more likely planted a device there earlier to intercept the votes as they were sent from a voting station, and then alter them before forwarding them on to the laptop. But that didn't make sense – someone would have to plant a device at every single polling station in the country to rely on that technique – or at least in enough places in enough states to swing the election.

The third and final alternative was that malware programmed to convert votes had been installed on the laptop, either before it left the factory, or when it connected to the Internet. Or perhaps the malware had been set to simply ignore the real votes and assign a pre-determined percentage of the total votes to the candidate the hacker wanted to win. But which of the two realistic approaches might the hacker have taken?

Unfortunately, the voting stations didn't have any local memory storage. That was a shame, since it gave him nothing to compare to the totals stored on the laptop. So to explore that possibility, he'd have to look for malware on the software he'd copied from one of the voting stations. If he couldn't find any, that would leave only the voting stations under suspicion.

He was pretty confident he could find any malware loaded on either the voting station or the laptop. If he did, that would be a big win. It could then be removed from voting systems elsewhere, and he'd be a hero.

With his laptop now up and running, he got to work. When he wasn't tapping at the keyboard or staring at the screen and drumming the arms of his chair, he was pacing back and forth on the bank of the stream. Either way, it burbled and splashed away over honey-brown stones, blissfully indifferent to, but mirroring, the turmoil of his thoughts.

* * *

35

As a Matter of Fact, There IS an App for That

A DAY LATER, HE was behind the wheel again. As he pulled out of his campsite, he reported in to Voldemort on his mobile phone.

"That's right, Vickie. Everything was clean as a whistle. If there was malware anywhere on this system, I sure couldn't find it.

"Yeah, I'll dump all the data to the server so your folks can check it as well.

"No, that doesn't mean I'm sure nothing happened in Promise. One thing I'm thinking is that they might remotely de-install the malware after the voting is done, so a forensic investigator couldn't find it. So I'm on my way now to the next primary state.

"Right. This time, I'll do the same drill the day before the voting starts and see if I can find anything.

"Yeah, I'll send a report. Just wanted to give you a high level status sooner rather than later.

"Right. You too."

Frank had used his usual mobile phone to make that call. For the next one, he used one of his disposable models and switched on Howie's nifty white noise generator. The number he called belonged to a similar phone he'd given to Josette.

She didn't answer, and he didn't leave a message. But she called him back almost immediately.

"So sorry," she said. "I could hear the phone ringing, but could not remember where I had put it."

"No worries. Just wanted to let you know what I've found – or not – so far." He gave her a more detailed rundown than he'd provided to Vickie.

"So what do you do if you find nothing at the next polling place?"

"Well, maybe leave it at that. After all, we don't have any proof that anyone is doing anything at all. Every state has a different mix of people, and every time there's a debate it changes the minds of some people that had been undecided. And then, of course, you can rely on some of these buffoons to stick their foot in their mouths up to their knee pretty frequently as well. So how do you tell the difference between the effects of manipulation and random events?"

"That's exactly the point, Frank! If that's the case, why does Henry Yazzie do better every time, as well as Randall Wellhead? It can't just be random!"

"Is that still true?"

"Of course it's true! Haven't you been following the news?"

"Well, no, not really. In case you've forgotten, I'm doing the investigative bit of this project. Following the numbers is your job." After a bit of idle conversation, he promised to give her another update after his next investigation, and hung up.

Josette was annoyed and frustrated. She felt that Frank still didn't really believe that someone was hacking the voting as well as the polls. For that matter, she wasn't sure he was even convinced that anyone was still tampering with the polls.

*   *   *

Frank headed south and west to intercept his next primary, and the rising sun of the first morning after the voting found him sitting outside his camper, this time on public land many miles from the nearest town. It was a relief to be back in a state where he could simply pull off of a jeep track when he found a place he liked and set up camp. At campgrounds, anyone feeling bored could, and usually did, stroll by and ask what he was so busy doing on that laptop – didn't he know how to leave his work behind, huh?

He'd succeeded in getting all the information he wanted, from a large district this time instead of the tiny one he'd timidly targeted before. The experience had been more nerve-wracking – if the voting station supervisor had told him to talk to the IT director, they might have checked his business card against their records. No matter how good Voldemort was, he doubted it had planted a maintenance contract in the district's files with Lincoln's name at the top. What would happen if he ran into someone who was more thorough? Would the folks at Voldemort rescue him, or would they leave him languishing in some county lock-up till the Feds took him away for attempting to tamper with voting machines?

But that was a problem for another day. Right now, he was debating whether there was something he'd missed despite spending all day picking and poking at the data and analyzing it every way he could think of. But everything kept coming up clean.

Finally he shut down his laptop and sat, fists balled up on top of the computer, staring straight ahead, lost in thought, turning the same things over in his mind that he'd analyzed twice already.

The shadows of the trees were lengthening when some bored or rebellious patch of neurons in his brain registered the fact that something not far away was out of place. No, that wasn't it – not out of place – unusual. Grudgingly, his subconscious assigned a few additional ganglia to channel this new data, and then made the decision to alert his higher levels of awareness of its conclusion: deer.

Frank surfaced dumbly out of his reverie, and realized with surprise that three deer were staring at him, not thirty feet away: a young buck, its spike antlers still in velvet, accompanied by two does. Only their heads and necks were clearly visible; their bodies were hidden by the underbrush surrounding his campsite.

Fully aware now, he froze, fascinated, waiting to see what they would do. For two long minutes the answer was nothing but stare back. Finally, one doe, and then the other, briefly and nervously looked away and then turned back. Then the first one snorted, turned, and gracefully bounded away, as if bouncing on an invisible trampoline that was being towed off to the side. One after the other, the remaining doe, and then the buck, gave an identical snort, turned, and followed with equal dignity.

Raising himself slowly from his chair, he wondered if he would be able to still see them.

And indeed, there they were, only another fifty yards away, browsing peacefully, their heads disappearing to take another bite of vegetation and then rising again while they chewed, like a trio of ether filled dippy birds. From time to time, the buck turned to stare at Frank.

All the tension now drained from his body, Frank sat back down and contemplated the peaceful scene, suddenly aware of the sounds and smells that he'd been ignoring for hours. Overhead, he heard an indescribable sound, somewhere between a *beep!* and a *cheep!* But why did it sound so oddly familiar?

He looked up, searching for the source. Finally he spied the bird, and then a second, that seemed to be emitting the strange calls. They looked like too-large swallows, or perhaps small hawks, with long, pointed wings fluttering rapidly, each with a white bar on its underside. They made quick dips and jags as they flew, like bats. He guessed they must be catching insects.

Then he remembered. When he was in grade school, his parents would sit on the front stoop of their tenement in Brooklyn on hot summer nights. Like everyone else, they were waiting for some of the sun's heat to seep out of the walls of their apartments and for the cooling night air to seep in through wide open windows. As it got dark, he and the other kids would run around and scream in the street until even their crewcuts were soaked with sweat.

Eventually their parents would call them, and they'd join their families on the stoops, and everything would become peaceful and quiet. That's when he would hear those strange sounds from above, coming from the flitting shadows that appeared and disappeared in the faintly glowing patch of sky between the black silhouettes of the buildings. It was a mysterious sound that overlay the murmur of his parents and their neighbors, chatting and laughing quietly in the deepening darkness as the noise, commotion and anxieties of the day dissipated along with the heat.

His childhood had not, for the most part, been a happy one, but there had been something wonderful about those hot summer nights. Perhaps it was because he and the other children were still so young – too young to know that some of them would be jocks and others nerds, or that it would matter. Or maybe it was the anonymity and freedom of the darkness. He didn't know. But in his memory, something about those evenings had been magic.

His work forgotten, Frank listened to the nighthawks and watched the last colors of the sunset fade until there were no colors left in the sky at all.

*   *   *

The buzzing of a mobile phone woke him the next day. It was the one that only Josette would be using, and he decided to ignore it. For once, he'd had a blissfully peaceful night's sleep, and it was pleasantly cool in his camper. She must be anxious to know the results of his last poll station invasion. He peered out the window by his bunk and saw that it was gray and damp from an overnight rain shower. Well, let her wait.

But moments after that phone stopped, his other one started! Damn the woman! Not only was she badgering him, but she was using a phone that might be tapped as well. He ignored the ringing phone, grabbed the disposable one, and only just remembered to turn on the white noise generator before dialing.

"What?!" he barked as soon as she picked up.

"I have just sent you a link! You must look at it and call me right back!"

"Why? What is it?"

"No need to explain – you will understand as soon as you watch it! Call me back as soon as you're done." She hung up.

The hell if he would "call as soon as he was done," he grumbled. And he wouldn't be done for a while, either. *Not till I've brushed my teeth and made coffee and maybe gone for a nice long run.*

But half way through brushing his teeth he started to wonder what she had found. He assumed it might be just something from the day's news, but what if she had figured out something that he hadn't? He rinsed his mouth and turned on his laptop.

When he clicked on the link, he was surprised to see that he was watching a public service video about voting. A stereotypically bland, smiling actor was standing in a mock voting station, talking to the camera and pointing at things around her, explaining for first-time voters how they would check in and then vote on Election Day.

He turned the sound up as she began to explain how a voting unit worked.

> *When you enter the polling booth in your own community you'll find a machine that allows you to cast your vote. What model device you see will depend on where you live, and how recently your community bought its machines.*

> *At one time, voting machines were very large and mechanical...*

The camera cut to black and white archival footage, showing another bland, smiling woman, this time in a mid-calf dress, stepping into what looked like a double-wide phone booth, and then pulling a black curtain closed behind her. Impatient, Frank moved the slider on the video forward to take him back to the present.

> *Today, of course, everything is very different. As you can see, voting machines are much smaller. And although every manufacturer's device is different, every one sold in the last five years is now required to have a voter interface that meets new national standards.*

The camera zoomed in on the screen and keyboard of the voting machine, as the narrator's hand pointed out various features. At the moment, she was pointing at a round circle on the control panel that had an icon of a phone in it.

> *One of the reasons is so that, starting with this election, you can now use your mobile phone to help you vote!*

At that, Frank let out a whoop of joy. Of course! That's why he couldn't find anything on the voting systems – it was because the malware didn't have to be there at all – it could be loaded on the phones that a lot of people would use to vote! If he'd paid attention to the appearance of the physical voting machines at any of the locations instead of just focusing on their software he'd have realized that immediately.

His disposable mobile phone was buzzing again, and this time he grabbed it.

"So what do you think?" Josette said. "It must be the mobile phones that they are hacking, yes?"

"It's possible. I'll have to find out whether that's in fact the case."

"I've been thinking about that already. I think they would have used an app."

"Agreed. But which one? There are millions out there. You'd have to hack one that enough people would download to make a difference, especially since a lot of polling stations probably still use old machines."

"Yes, of course. But that's what should make it easy to narrow our search. It would have to be one of the most popular downloads, and of course free and available on every kind of phone as well."

Frank thought for a moment. "Probably one that could be remotely updated, too. Otherwise they'd have to preset the voting. They'd have to be pretty clever to figure out a way to do that in advance without the results sticking out too obviously."

"May we do this?" Josette said, "Each of us will look at the top downloads for this year and then we compare our best guesses for which apps to investigate?"

"I can do that. Talk tonight?"

"Yes! Until then."

He was prepared to believe that Josette might be right, but that didn't mean that they would solve the hack immediately if she was. He began to consider the possibilities as he laced up his sneakers for his morning run. Could a voting app have been hacked? He doubted that. Too obvious. However low his opinion of security precautions generally might be, he had to believe that a mobile phone voting app would have to have been secured and tested in every way imaginable.

On the other hand, by definition there would have to be a voting app on the phone, or the person couldn't vote. So somehow the hacked app would have to interfere with the voting one – maybe with how the vote was recorded on the phone or transmitted to the voting machine?

His thoughts continued to flow as he loped off. What kind of app should he look for? Better question: what kind of app would he choose to hack? Hmm. Well, he'd obviously want to target people that were likely to vote, so maybe the app he'd hack – or maybe even develop himself – would have some kind of political theme. If he was right, that would narrow the search a lot.

Then there was his earlier assumption that the app would need to be updated.

There were two ways that could be accomplished – it could log-in to the host server every time the phone connected to the Internet, or the app could provide the user with a built-in incentive to connect to the host site. Either would work, but people were sensitive about privacy these days. Tech-savvy users might disable an automatic function like that. So if he were the hacker, he'd give the user a reason to log on to the developer's site.

What else? Well, on days where primaries would be held in multiple states, and again on the big day in November, a sophisticated hacker would want to know what state you were voting in. That way the algorithm on the host program wouldn't have to alter more votes than necessary to get the desired result. So the app would also need to know your location.

That brought up privacy again, because phones were preset by the vendor these days to ask for permission before allowing the user's location to be disclosed. So again a smart hacker would need to provide an incentive for users to say "yes" when the request popped up.

So where did that take him? He mused on that for a while as he pounded along, oblivious to the fact that a cold fog had begun to rise from the wet landscape around him. Despite the fact that he'd made a lot of money out of an app not long before, he didn't use many and had never followed the app market closely. What besides games would get the most downloads? He didn't really know, but that would be easy to check.

He glanced at his watch. It wasn't quite time to turn around yet, but now that he had started to make some plausible guesses he was impatient to see where they might lead. He turned around and picked up his pace.

*   *   *

Josette pored over the results of an hour spent looking for app download data. There were more categories of apps to consider than she would have thought, but nowhere near enough data. For some categories she could find no rankings at all, and where she could, there was often no information about how many downloads each app had attracted. Nor was there any data about who was doing the downloading. Were they adults or children? Men or women? Midwestern farmers or Brooklyn hipsters? The detailed data seemed to only be available in expensive research reports.

She tapped the end of a pencil against her teeth and considered the options. It seemed that short of spending $1000 her best bet would be to look for high level data and then try and extrapolate from there. But even that kind of information did not seem to be sufficiently useful. Clearly there were a lot of downloads of games and the kind of software you'd want to make a mobile device more useful – map apps, contact managers and the like. But there were dozens, and even thousands of programs in these categories. If she was lucky, the hacker might have tampered with multiple apps in order to be sure that he captured enough phones to swing the election. But what if it was only a single app that had been hacked?

She returned to the best hard data she'd found, which listed the top ten downloads for the prior year. The numbers per app ranged from 29.5 to 86.1 million. Some were simply apps allowing you to access the top social media and financial sites. Two were map programs. Five were from just one mega high tech company. Was this where she should be looking? Those five apps together had probably reached over 100 million users, even if most users had downloaded several of them. But she guessed that these apps would also have the closest ongoing security supervision. Wouldn't the hacker worry that their malware would be discovered, or perhaps crippled by a software update, before the election?

Wouldn't it make more sense for the hacker to create his own app? Then they would always be in control of everything. If it were her, she would have launched dozens of apps, hoping that one would take off. Or, if she had enough money, she could buy an already successful one from its developer and then tamper with that.

She looked at her notes on game rankings. Much of the data she had found was global, rather than national, or reported just for a single platform rather than across all types of mobile devices. And since the app they were looking for would have needed to be released the year before so that enough copies would be on phones before the primaries began, the total number of downloads would be spread across two years, diluting its rank for each one.

She had to figure out a way to narrow the choices. She had learned that 59% of Americans supposedly played computer and video games, and that some of the most successful games had been downloaded tens of millions of times. That sounded like it could be enough. But how many users played only on consoles, and not on mobile devices? And what percentage of game players were old enough to vote? It was all such a mess.

She decided to download each of the top games for the last year and hope to stumble on a clue.

*   *   *

Frank was having a similar experience. After sifting through jumbles of unhelpful data he decided to shift gears, and go back to thinking how he would investigate an app if he did find one that seemed suspicious.

Leaning back to a precarious angle in his chair, he mulled the situation over. What would he do if they couldn't narrow the suspect app list to fewer than, say,

20 programs? It would take him forever to check that many apps for malware, and he might miss it even if the right app was on the list. There had to be a better way.

Antivirus software wouldn't help. Those programs only scanned for viruses that had already been identified. He'd have to either scan all of the code of every app using more sophisticated tools, or come up with his own test. And what would that be?

Well of course. Why did that take so long? Why not just buy a bunch of cheap phones, load one app on each phone, and then monitor its core functions while he used it at a voting station? Wouldn't that do it? He got up and stepped outside, walking rapidly and retracing his steps from his morning run.

It should work in theory, but it might be tricky. There were at least a half dozen different voting machine manufacturers, and even though the voter interface was supposed to be identical for all of them, a lot of the software deeper down would be proprietary, and the security of some machines might be better than others. And more than a handful of voter apps had been approved by the Federal Election Commission. What if the hacked app didn't work with every voting machine? And the apps were modified for each operating system, too – Apple and Android, and that was before you got to the smaller players, like Microsoft and BlackBerry.

He crammed his hands in his pockets and leaned forward into the wind, shoulders hunched. He'd have to have not just one phone for each app he tested, but multiple voting apps on each phone as well, to be sure he hit the right combination. And if he didn't luck out at the first voting station, he'd have to go to another electoral district, or even state, to try out their voting machines, unless he could download their software through Voldemort.

There had to be a better way than that. He bet the voting machine vendors, like most manufacturers, sold through distributors rather than direct to their customers. He'd received a mass of data from Voldemort back when he started on the project, but had never looked at it thoroughly. Maybe he'd be lucky and find a warehouse somewhere where a lot of different voting machines might be found.

* * *

Frank was feeling good when Josette called that evening. He'd confirmed that sure enough, voting machines were mostly sold through state government buying co-ops that pooled their purchasing power to get better deals. Those co-ops received their purchases through eight regional distribution centers that carried all sorts of goods, from paper towels to voting machines. There was one about 250 miles from where he was right now.

But before he could share his news, Josette spoke excitedly.

"I have it, Frank! I'm sure I do!"

"How can you tell?"

"I'm sure you'll agree. It's a game app – the fastest rising free mobile game since August of last year. More than 40 million copies have been downloaded so far, and it's still going up!"

"So that means it could be what we're looking for, but it certainly doesn't prove that it is. And what if it's just kids that are playing it?"

"You must look at it yourself. Then I think you will agree. I've sent you the link. Call me when you've had a chance to look at it." She hung up.

Frank sighed. He was too old to cope with youthful enthusiasms. There was no way he could be sure that any particular app was the right one until he visited that warehouse.

He opened his email and clicked on the link that Josette had sent. The app had a peculiar name: Angry Indians/Angry Cavalry. That wasn't very politically correct. He scrolled down, and saw that there were two sets of almost identical screen shots. Above one set, it said Angry Indians, and above the other, Angry Cavalry. Apparently, you could play the game in either of two modes.

He clicked on an arrow on a video clip of the Indian version, and watched as the animated Native Americans sent a terrified cow hurtling over the palisade wall of a fort. He hadn't been much of a history student, but he was pretty sure Native Americans never used catapults. Oh well, it was just a game.

He tried the Cavalry version, and this time it was a hapless bison that landed inside a circle of tepees.

Okay, so it was a best-selling game. Why would Josette be so sure that this was what they were looking for?

He did a search of the game name and was surprised to see that the top hits were all stories in the mainstream press instead of at gaming sites. It seemed that people who were politically engaged had piled on in masses. There was even an online gaming site where you could log on in one mode – say as an Indian – and play against people that had logged on as Cavalry.

He clicked through to that site, and saw that there could be as many as 83,124 cattle and bison in virtual flight at that very moment. There was a big scoreboard, too, showing which player was winning nationally, by state, even by city. Clearly, the electorate had found a healthy way to relieve their pre-election animosities while waiting for the big day. He checked another page and saw that, unlike some games, the only version available was for mobile devices. And it was free.

He had to hand it to Josette. The game checked off every block on the list of criteria he'd developed. But before he tried to inveigle his way into another establishment under an alias he wanted to be as sure as he could be that he was on the right trail. He called her back.

"So Frank! What do you think?"

"I agree, that looks pretty promising. But the only way we're going to know that this, or any other app, is the one we're looking for is by running it on a phone that we're using to vote on a real voting machine. Maybe several different voting machines, if it doesn't work on all of them. I don't want to have to do that more than once. Which other apps look promising?"

There was only silence at the other end of the phone. He waited, but still she said nothing.

"Josette?"

"Oh!" she exploded. "I cannot take it anymore! I have such a chicken to pluck with you!"

"Uh…"

"You can never believe that anyone else can come up with anything! And you insist on always making things so complicated!"

"Josette…"

"No 'Josette!' Unless you think of something yourself, it can never be right! You need to acknowledge that other people have brains, too!"

She paused for breath, giving him a chance to pose the question he desperately wanted to ask. "Uh, Josette…"

"What!"

"A chicken to pluck?"

"Is that not the phrase?"

"Do you maybe mean 'a bone to pick?'"

Silence. "Is that what I meant?"

"I think so."

"Oh." It sounded like she had calmed down. "Whatever. Still. I saw this and was so sure that this must be the one. Can't you just download a copy and test it?"

"Sure, sure. And I promise I will. But I might not find anything. And if I did, I'd still need to have the equipment on the other side of the transaction to be sure. And we haven't considered yet what we would do if we did find the right app, have we? I want to understand as much as possible before we double down on this one."

"Excuse me – 'double down?'"

"Sorry. Before we put all our eggs… Damn! Until we're sure we've got the right one."

Josette frowned. What he said made sense, but she had hoped that for once

Frank would agree with her immediately. It took some further nudging from him before she agreed to look for at least nine more credible possibilities while he started the long drive to the distribution center.

* * *

Let Me Give You My Card

F RANK HAD NOT enjoyed admitting to Josette that he was not up to date on the election. Politics didn't interest him, but he recognized that if he paid too little attention he might miss an important clue. Worse, Josette might pick up on it instead. So it was that when he arrived late in the afternoon at the town where the warehouse was located, he spent the evening catching up on what was happening in the electoral trenches.

The first impression he formed was that Henry Yazzie was riding an almost surreal wave of success. Everything seemed to be going his way. Why was that? He started skimming one news site after another.

The Centrist Coalition of America had officially endorsed Yazzie, and was bankrolling his campaign. It looked like they'd done quite a job organizing local activity, too, in every blue and swing state before the deadline. Most of the red states as well. And what do you know? They'd gotten Yazzie on the ballot in every single state! That took real organization and effort.

It wasn't going so well for the conservative candidates, though; they were still dragging each other's dirty laundry out for all to see. The President must be enjoying that....

Ah – too bad. Vance Cabot had dropped out. And he was the most experienced candidate by a mile. Not such a big surprise, though, after coming in last in Iowa and New Hampshire.

Thank goodness – Roxanne Rollins and Landa Goshen were gone, too. It had been fun for the late night comedians while it lasted, though.

Johnson was still hanging on, but probably not for long. It looked like his fundraising had fallen off a cliff.

Oh, and look here – crazy old Roland Overby was still waving the Libertarian flag. It looked like he hadn't broken into the double digits in a single primary yet, but here he was pledging that he'd keep yapping at the heels of the front runners all the way to the convention.

That left just who… right, Randall Wellhead and Hollis Davenport. So one of them would have to be the final nominee.

So much for the raw data. What were the pundits saying?

Frank hunted up a recording of one of the Sunday morning political news shows and settled in to listen as the host of the program quizzed his quests about the latest developments.

> *So let's start with Henry Yazzie. What do you have to say about him, Tom?*
>
> *What do I say? I say it looks like the whole world wants him to win!*
>
> *How so?*
>
> *Well, you got your unrest in the Middle East – of course. Then there's China getting more aggressive in Southeast Asia and Africa – that's where all the natural resources they want come from. Europe looks like it's going to drag our economy down with theirs – again – and ours had been stumbling to begin with. Finally, the President's numbers haven't stopped sliding since the beginning of the year.*
>
> *But why should that only help Yazzie? What about the Republican candidates?*
>
> *What about them? The conservative Super PACS are spending all their money running attack ads against each other's candidates. If you believed the commercials, you'd never want to vote for any of them.*
>
> *How about you, Margaret? Do you agree that when things go wrong it only helps Yazzie?*

Absolutely. The Republicans haven't passed a single piece of legislation yet that could boost the economy — and goosing the economy is what they ran on. And when the President proposed a big job creation bill, they shot it down. Then they accuse him of doing nothing. The voters are sick of it all.

Ray?

Of course the voters are. And why not? When the President issues an Executive Order to try and get anything done, the leaders of the House and Senate accuse him of exceeding his Constitutional powers. It makes everybody — except Yazzie — look like they're characters in a sitcom!

Shouldn't that help the President, though, Tom?

Not really. People just want to see something get done. Fair or not, they're always going to blame the man at the top if they can't make ends meet. And besides, there's this new rash of terrorist acts against U.S. interests abroad. The conservatives are having a field day attacking the President for not doing enough to safeguard Americans.

How about that, Margaret? Do you think that's fair? After all, Congress refused the President's request to improve overseas security just a few months ago this year.

Do you mean fair as in "fair," or "fair," as in Washington? [laughter]

Frank sighed and closed the video. Politics was certainly proceeding as usual in an election year.

Still, it seemed clear that more and more Americans were disgusted with the entire sorry, Beltway mess. He shouldn't be surprised that voters were attracted by what the good-looking young Native American candidate had to say. After all, everything he said sounded rational and mainstream. They weren't hearing that from anyone else. One commentator had even begun calling him the "Native American John Kennedy."

He tried another news show and fast forwarded a video until Yazzie's name was mentioned. This time the host was interviewing a former presidential campaign manager:

Well sure, he's had a pretty good ride. Of course, so far the President and the conservative candidates have avoided criticizing him directly.

Why's that?

Well, in the beginning I don't think they wanted to lend any credibility to his campaign by acknowledging that it even existed. The last thing any politician wants is a three-way race. There's too much uncertainty. And then I think they were also nervous about attacking a Native American.

Why? Native Americans are a pretty small demographic.

Right. But they might swing a few western states. And larger minority constituencies – like blacks and Hispanics – might read an attack against a Native American as indicating other biases on the part of a candidate. And anyway, Yazzie doesn't have a voting record, so they don't have much to work with.

Of course. But both the right and the left can criticize him for not supporting some of their main initiatives.

All well and good. But what does that leave them with? Calling him a "moderate?" That just further defines him as the only centrist candidate. And this just may be the year of the centrist.

Frank closed his laptop at the end of the interview and mulled over everything he'd heard. He was surprised how radically Yazzie's fortunes had changed. Even the press was being gentle, at least so far. Maybe that wasn't surprising; Yazzie's positive message must be more fun to write about than the incessant sniping and mudslinging of the main party candidates.

* * *

And then, of course, there were the polls. They continued to show Yazzie's popularity rising. If current trends continued, more of the Americans deemed most likely to vote would be casting their ballots for Yazzie on Election Day than would favor any other candidate. Publicly, party pundits pooh-poohed these polls. They said that when the time came to actually vote, the same people would cast their ballots for either a Republican or a Democrat candidate, just as they had for more than a hundred years.

In private, though, party leaders were panicking. It wasn't because they really believed that Yazzie could win. What did concern them was the fact that Yazzie couldn't be clearly categorized as either conservative or liberal. That made this election unique, leaving them with no way to tell for sure which party would lose the most votes to the increasingly popular interloper.

Although both would deny it, representatives of both the President and Hollis Davenport had contacted Yazzie's campaign manager to confidentially ask whether Yazzie would be interested in a discrete meeting between their respective handlers. The purpose was obvious – to determine whether he might consider discontinuing his campaign in return for a place in a post-election administration. Davenport's man implied that it was possible that his candidate might even consider Yazzie as a running mate.

Carson Bekin was sorely tempted by Davenport's suggestion. It seemed that Yazzie's rise in the polls couldn't continue forever. What leverage would they have after the election was lost? Now seemed to be the ideal time to capitalize on his unexpected surge of popularity. And if he became Vice President, he'd have to be taken seriously when the next election cycle came around.

But Yazzie would hear none of it. He tried to tell himself that it wasn't because his success had gone to his head, or that he had decided that he really could win. He assured Carson Bekin (as well as himself) that it was a matter of principle. Throwing his lot in with either Davenport or the President would mean betraying all of the policy positions he'd worked so hard to promote. Who would ever trust him in the future, even if he became Vice President?

So there was nothing for Bekin to do but convey Yazzie's polite, but negative, response to both sides. He wondered, though, why he hadn't heard from Randall Wellhead's people. Were they that convinced that Wellhead would win?

It was mid-August now, and the first national convention of the Centrist Coalition of America was set to get under way in Albuquerque, New Mexico. There was genuine curiosity over who Yazzie would pick as his running mate.

Would it be another Native American, a Caucasian, or someone of another minority ethnicity (and if so, which one)? Would it be a nobody, like Yazzie himself, or might someone with traditional political credibility roll the dice on Yazzie's surging fortunes? The media was paying close attention to Yazzie's travel plans, as well as to those of his closest aides for any clues that might suggest who he was considering.

* * *

Frank was fidgeting on the edge of a vinyl-covered chair in a small waiting room at the distribution center. The only other objects within view were a second chair, identical to his, a glass coffee table littered with old magazines, and a reception desk with no one behind it. The glass door leading to the interior of the building was locked, and all he could see on the other side were ceiling-high racks of boxes. He'd already pressed the button next to the sign that said, "For assistance, please ring."

He tapped his feet rapidly on the linoleum floor and waited. There had to be somebody inside – there were at least 65 loading docks on this side of the building alone, as well as a couple dozen cars in the parking lot. Maybe he should have figured out somebody to call first?

Then the glass door opened. A young man in coveralls came out.

"Can I help you?"

Frank stood up and smiled. "Yes, I'm here to check out the voting machines you're holding for shipment. There's a new software update we want to install before that gear gets shipped all over the place." He pulled one of his cards out of his wallet as he was speaking and handed it over.

The young man glanced at the card. "Okay. I'll need you to wait here a minute while I log your data into our system." He turned around and disappeared through the glass door.

Now what? What did "log-in the data" mean? What if his data got rejected? Would this guy call the police?

But the young man soon returned and led Frank into what looked like the world's largest "Big Box" discount store. Row after row of twenty-foot tall storage racks crammed with huge boxes ran off into the darkness of what seemed like infinity.

"Let's see...," his guide was swiping his index finger over and over across a tablet computer. "Okay – here we go: 'municipal polling equipment.' Figures, right? They couldn't just call them 'voting machines,' could they? Let's hop in this."

Frank sat next to him on a golf cart parked against the wall, and they drove for several hundred yards along the endless rows of racks, motion-controlled lights winking on ahead and off behind them as they hummed along. Finally, they turned down one of the aisles between the racks, and rolled to a stop. His guide pointed to the third shelf up on the left side and said "There you go. How many of them do you need to work on?"

After his experience in Promise, Frank had anticipated a question like this. "I'll have to check the numbers against my records. Maybe you could come back in fifteen minutes? After I figure out which ones I need to work on I'll need to take them down and power them up. Is there a place I could use for that?"

"Sure. We've got a room we use for breaking big boxes down and repackaging the contents for smaller deliveries. You can use that."

As the golf cart disappeared, Frank dragged a wheeled access ladder down the aisle and stared at the boxes, trying to figure out what each one might hold, and from which manufacturer.

By the time his guide reappeared, this time driving a forklift, Frank was ready to point out the boxes he wanted to work with. He'd arrived prepared this time, with complete lists of product numbers he'd pulled down from the vendors' web sites.

Ten minutes later, his selections were spread on tables in the packing room.

"When you're done, dial 100 on that phone on the wall, and someone will pick you up."

Frank nodded his thanks, and began cutting open the boxes and trying to figure out what exactly he was finding inside.

Far away, Len Butcher was deciding what to do about the information displaying on his computer screen. It seemed that one Alan Turing of Lincoln IT Electoral Services was engaged in an unauthorized visit to a very large warehouse in a state he had not been instructed to visit.

*   *   *

Six hours later, Frank was famished. He was almost finished testing systems from three manufacturers, using eleven identical new phones, each of which had three different voting apps loaded. Ten phones also had one of the apps on board that he and Josette had agreed upon. The eleventh would serve as his control unit. He'd used that one to provide baseline data that he could use to compare with the information he gathered from the phones loaded with the suspect apps.

After setting up the three voting systems, he programmed each to display three candidates for each of three offices: President, senator and congressman. Then he opened up the backs of his phones so he could attach a device that would monitor how much of the phone's processing power was being utilized on a constant basis.

He was rather pleased with the test plan he'd devised. The problem he'd been struggling with was how to detect malware when you didn't know how it operated, or which phone it might be on – if any. His solution was based on the assumption that the malware would consume at least some detectable amount of processing power when it went into action. Assuming he was right – and that the malware they were looking for actually was on one of the ten phones – the monitoring device should detect a spike in activity when the malware kicked in.

Or so he hoped, because he was also assuming that whoever had designed the voting malware would have pre-programmed its actions as much as possible, leaving nothing to pull down on Election Day except the command to change or not change a given vote. If he was right, that would mean that as soon as he turned on a voting app, or perhaps at some point in the voting process, the malware should turn on as well.

Getting down to business, he noted the usage rate when he turned the control phone on, opened one of the voting apps, used it to vote on one of the machines, closed the app, and then turned off the phone. Still using the same phone, he went through the same exercise using the next voting app, and then the next. Then he repeated the entire tedious sequence using each of the other two voting systems.

With his control record completed, he connected one of the other phones to the monitor. Perversely, he had decided to leave Josette's app for last. But after going through the same twelve-step process two more times, his patience was wearing thin and his hunger was growing annoying. He stared at the seven remaining phones, and then hooked the phone with the Angry Indians/Angry Cavalry program on it up to the monitor.

He watched the monitor intently when he loaded the first voting program, and with mixed emotions saw that the usage rate jumped to the same rate that it had on each of the other phones. So much for that, Josette. But his spirits fell as well, since in truth he had thought it was the best prospect as well. Maybe he would see results with one of the other voting programs or voting systems?

But the trial wasn't complete, so he touched the handset on the phone logo on the voting system and watched the monitor as the phone completed its wireless "handshake" with the voting machine and the two devices connected. And there it was! The processor of the phone had just kicked up a notch! A few seconds later, the processor sped up again – that must be the malware checking for updates! Then it dropped part way back and stayed there while he voted, after which it dropped back to the baseline rate and stayed there.

He raced through the rest of the steps for that phone, and got the same result using each voting program on each system. He didn't know how the malware worked yet, but now he knew that he had found it.

That was enough for today. He wouldn't need a variety of voting machines to take his next steps. Re-energized, he rushed through the process of repacking the systems into their boxes. While he waited to be picked up, he called Josette to give her the good news.

"Yes, that's right. Every voting app, and every system. Now I've got to figure out how they work. I'll get started on that tonight."

* * *

37

So Long, and Thanks for All the Cash

A S YAZZIE'S SUCCESS in the primaries grew, White Crow and Maxwell were pushing the envelope of their own plans. The CCA was no longer just another political action organization. It had announced itself as the country's newest party. Over the summer, its local chapters selected delegates, and in the middle of August, they began to converge on Albuquerque, New Mexico, for the first convention of the Centrist Coalition of America.

The event would last only two evenings and the intervening day, avoiding the seemingly endless minor goings-on of the major party conventions. It would also provide a more appealing platform for live media coverage. With Congress in summer recess and Wellhead the decisive winner of the Republican nomination, a public broadcast station was providing non-stop video from start to finish, and several of the cable news stations promised regular updates throughout the day, as well as an hour of live coverage each evening. Even the broadcast networks were airing highlights; one had announced that it would carry Yazzie's acceptance speech live.

Yazzie had remained coy regarding his choice of a running mate, playing the traditional game of waiting until the last minute in order to milk the media for all the anticipatory coverage he could. With both he and Wellhead running just ahead of the President in the polls, the announcement of his pick for Vice President would clearly be the story of the day.

The press was not disappointed when Yazzie's spokesperson announced at a press conference at 5:00 PM that the CCA nominee for Vice President would be none other than Vance Cabot – the candidate with the impeccable pedigree and almost infinite experience in government. The pundits immediately agreed that his choice was inspired. The straight-laced Cabot would never upstage Yazzie, but his experience would reassure voters. Moreover, his voting record and platform was the most moderate of all of the candidates that had vied for the Republican nomination. That would make him tolerable to centrists and less ideological members of both major parties.

Yazzie was therefore riding a wave of favorable media commentary when he and Cabot took the stage that evening following their formal nominations. The convention center's floor was packed, not only with CCA supporters, but with delegations from most of the Native American tribes across the country, many in traditional dress. They provided prime video opportunities for the film crews roaming the floor looking for delegates to interview.

Everyone seemed to want to be there that night. In a scene reminiscent of Barack Obama's nomination as the first African-American president, there was an enormous "feel good" effect among moderates and liberals: a major step was being taken towards redressing the wrongs of a shameful period in the country's history.

Maxwell had capitalized on that feeling by chartering fleets of buses to bring hordes of supporters to the hall. The mass of enthusiastic attendees testified to the now-genuine momentum that Yazzie's candidacy was demonstrating. As the network and cable video crews panned the enormous, boisterous audience, no one watching could doubt that however this unexpected phenomenon had come about, there was a true three-way race for the Oval Office.

*   *   *

That was certainly Fetters's conclusion, as he barked into the telephone with barely controlled fury. His anger had been growing exponentially over the past several weeks, not least because White Crow had been refusing his calls.

"What the hell do you think you're doing here? We never contemplated Yazzie being so successful."

White Crow had selected that evening to finally accept the call. He knew that at some point Fetters would begin to suspect he'd been double-crossed. But what could he do, really? He still needed a third-party candidate in the race for camouflage. White Crow savored the situation, sitting in a leather chair in a glass-walled, private office set into the wall high above the floor of the convention hall. He pressed the speakerphone button and winked at Maxwell, who was comfortably ensconced on a couch.

"Really? Are you quite sure? I don't recall there ever being any discussion about limiting my candidate's success. In fact, quite the opposite. I distinctly remember your concern over whether his candidacy would be credible. Wait a moment though – I have my notes here – let me check."

He picked up a newspaper and made rustling sounds while Maxwell stifled a guffaw. "Yes, I can confirm that. No discussions at all."

"You know damn well I wasn't bankrolling your boy to try and win. And you can be damn sure you're not getting another dime out of me!"

"Ah, well, I suppose I can't complain. You were most generous early on, before we were able to get our own fundraising machine in place. If you are finding you need to conserve resources now for your own candidate's use, I understand."

Fetters forced himself not to react. For all his anger, there was something he desperately wanted to know. Since Ohanzee knew that Fetters had been hacking the votes, he also knew that Fetters could ensure that Wellhead would ultimately win. So what was he up to? Was he planning on upping the ante, and demanding the Vice Presidency for Yazzie? If so, that would wreck all of Fetters' carefully laid plans.

But if it wasn't that, what was his game? Blackmail?

Meticulous planning and execution had allowed Fetters to pull off political gambles in the past that seemed audacious to others but which in fact were risk free. Now, on the threshold of his greatest play ever, this two-bit casino manager was threatening to reverse the odds.

"Very good then. So what is it?"

"Excuse me?" White Crow gave Maxwell another wink.

"You know exactly what I mean." Fetters' voice was icy. "What is it you want?"

"Want?" A thin smile played on White Crow's lips now. "Why the presidency, of course. Haven't you been watching our convention coverage tonight?"

"That's ridiculous, and you know it."

"Is it? Can you know the will of the American people so clearly?"

White Crow leaned back, imagining with grim enjoyment the thoughts that would be running through Fetters' mind right now.

And indeed, he was not far off. Fetters was just then asking himself if White Crow was taping the conversation. But damn it, if he wasn't, what *was* his game?

Fetters was determined to find out so he could devise a means to destroy this fool of an amateur.

His words came out in a slow hiss. "This is the last time I will ask you this question, so consider your response carefully. What is it you want?"

White Crow made him wait a full twenty seconds before he responded, softly and evenly. "My friend, everything I needed from you I have already received. Good luck to you and your Mr. Wellhead." He reached forward and disconnected the call.

*　*　*

Frank was bushed, slouched behind the wheel of the camper with only the green glow of the dashboard controls to keep him company. He had the air conditioning on high, with both dashboard vents directed at his face to help him stay awake as he drove on through the night.

He should have taken three days to make the drive instead of two. But after leaving the distribution center he had decided to make another marathon push back to Washington. He was tired of sleeping in the camper, tired of bad fast food and run-down laundromats, and tired of his own company. Okay, so he would still be stuck with his own company back in D.C., but at least the food would be better. And he could sit in his own apartment between wash loads at the run-down laundromat across the street.

He glanced at the clock in the dash. It would be two-thirty in the morning before he reached the beltway – another hour of driving. Could he stay awake that long?

Unexpectedly, he heard the sound of a duck quacking and sat up straighter. A *duck*? How had that gotten into his camper? Then he realized it must be the text signal from his phone. Marla knew he hated texting, and kidded him about being a troglodyte. She also enjoyed changing the text alert on his phone without being caught. Could this be her?

He fumbled in his jacket pocket for his phone and stared at the screen. It read, "Are you awake?" The sender was Josette. He could guess what she wanted – he'd told her two days ago he intended to start working out how the malware operated. But he'd started the long drive back instead, catching just a few hours of sleep along the way. Damn the woman anyway. Couldn't he set his own schedule?

He didn't feel like speaking with her, but maybe it would help him stay awake. He remembered to turn on the white noise generator, and then speed-dialed her.

She picked up immediately. "Frank! It is so late. Are you working on the hack?"

"No I am not! I'm driving."

"Driving?" She sounded disappointed.

"Yes, driving. I decided I'd rather work at home instead of in my camper in the rain by a dirt road in the God-forsaken prairie."

There was silence at the other end of the phone for a few seconds.

"I see. You sound so tired. We can talk when you get back. Drive safely." She rang off.

Wide awake now, he grumbled and bitched to himself about how demanding and focused Josette could be as he stared down the ghostly cones of his headlights into the empty night of the deserted highway. He told himself he wasn't really feeling lonely.

*   *   *

It was half past nine when Frank awoke – very late for him, but not late enough to catch up on his sleep. He swung his legs out of bed, rubbed his eyes, and shuffled into the kitchen to make coffee.

He looked morosely at his bleary-eyed face in the mirror as he brushed his teeth and tried to generate some enthusiasm for the task that lay ahead – figuring out how the malware installed on mobile phones managed to switch votes.

Then his toothbrush stopped in mid-stroke. Why not just toss the problem back in Butcher's lap? Say he'd discovered an app that was interfering with voting, and that the government should force the developer to recall or fix it. Problem solved!

Half an hour later he was showered and sitting at his tiny kitchen table, contentedly drinking coffee and reading the news until his reverie was interrupted by the sound of his doorbell. Who the hell could that be? He had to think for a moment what day it was – Tuesday – that meant it wouldn't be Marla; she'd be in class. Could a neighbor have forgotten their key?

He walked down his short hall to the intercom panel and held down the button. "Yes?"

"Frank, it is me. May I come up?"

Damn! Now she was even hounding him in his own home. Well, apartment. "Why?"

"To speak, of course." She left it at that, and waited.

Damn again! What was he supposed to do? He pressed the other button and heard the muffled sound of the downstairs buzzer over the intercom as the door unlocked. Then he raced back into the kitchen to tidy up as much as possible before Josette arrived.

He wasn't quite done when he heard her knock at the door. At the last minute he remembered to finish buttoning up and tucking in his shirt.

She smiled uncertainly when he opened the door. "May I come in?"

"Sure," he said, and led her into the kitchen.

"Coffee?"

Josette tried not to be too obvious as she glanced into the threadbare living room and then at the clutter of the out-of-date kitchen. She guessed – correctly – that the apartment hadn't been repainted since Frank had moved in some twenty years before.

"Please," she said. Still standing, he poured a cup and handed it to her. The hell if he was going to be hospitable.

"May we sit?"

"Sure," he said again. There was only one chair in the kitchen, so she walked into the living room. Glancing around, she tried to guess which chair wouldn't be the one Frank usually sat in and opted for a lonely straight-backed chair stuck in a corner. She held her coffee cup on her knee and sat uncomfortably erect.

Alright, he thought, this was overdoing it. "Here," he gestured to an overstuffed chair. "You'll be more comfortable over here." After a moment she moved to it while he sat down on the couch.

Normally Frank would have been embarrassed, painfully aware of the messy drabness of his apartment. But this morning he was in full "my home is my castle" mode and in no mood to make apologies. Arms crossed, he looked at Josette and waited.

"So, Frank, your trip back was no trouble?"

"Long. Just long."

"You will be able to work on the malware now, yes?"

"As a matter of fact, I think I will work on the malware now, no," he said smugly.

Josette looked alarmed. "But why?"

"Because there's no need to." Happy to be in control for once, he became more talkative.

"Now that I know what app they're using to hack the voting, I don't need to figure it out. All I have to do is tell Butcher, and he can tell the developer to pull the app off the market."

Now Josette was truly alarmed.

"But you can do no such thing!"

"Why not? Can you give me even one good reason why not?"

She struggled to translate her outrage into English.

"Because – your Mr. Butcher! He cannot be trusted! He may even be the person – the hacker – behind the app!"

"How do you figure that? He's been paying me to watch out for an attack."

"He's also the only one who knows how to hack the pollster systems! And that continues! If it's not him that is doing so, who is it?"

"How do you know anyone is still manipulating the polls?"

"Because they are! Remember that I had checked months ago?"

"Yes, but how about since then? Have you checked since then?"

In fact, she had. But the back door she had used was now closed. She wasn't about to share that with Frank, however, and in any event she was convinced that the hacker had simply opened another one.

"Have you followed the polls?"

"No, not particularly. But what if I had? How could I tell if they'd been altered?"

"The pattern is too clear. It's always Wellhead followed by Yazzie. Other candidates rise and fall, but they stay always the same."

"Really? Isn't that what you'd expect? It's called 'trending,' right?"

"Not in every state! That could not happen. In red states, in blue states – remember how the other candidates bounced up and down. They still do."

Frank had in fact been paying more attention to the polls than he was willing to admit, and he had noted with particular surprise how inexorably Henry Yazzie's popularity continued to grow.

"Okay, so let's say for a minute that you're right. I can just tell someone else instead."

"And then what do they do?"

"Well, like I said, they pull the app."

"You do not think the hacker could just do the same thing again, with another app?"

"Not this late in the election year, no. But why take a chance? They'd wait and pull the app at the last minute."

"How would they do that? It is already on so many phones."

"Well, they could say that there was a security hazard using it, and people would want to delete it. Or they could have the app vendor push out a patch that removed the malware."

"How could you know that whoever you talked to wasn't part of the same conspiracy?"

Frank was cynical enough about government for that shot to hit home, but he wasn't going to admit it.

"Leave that to me. There's someone I can contact that I'd trust with my life."

"But you must not! He may be trusted, but how do you know you can trust who he thinks he can trust, and so on?"

Of course he couldn't. But he'd also had enough of this conversation.

"Listen. I've been out of town for weeks now. My book will be out soon and I've got to take care of a few things. Let me think this over and I'll get back to you."

She looked at him uncertainly, and concluded that there was no more to be gained for now. She stood up and handed him her still-full coffee cup. Then she kissed him lightly on both cheeks and let herself out the front door.

Later that night, he received an email from her. Attached was a spreadsheet with the polling and voting numbers for each of the candidates, together with a statistical analysis of the likelihood of Wellhead's and Yazzie's numbers rising in parallel as consistently as they had throughout the primary season relative to the significant swings of the other candidates across red states and blue. The odds were 112,876,521 to one, and the methodology was unimpeachable. Josette was right again.

*   *   *

38

Just a Friendly Game of Chess

G EORGE MARCHAND WAS immersed in conversation with an old friend who by any measure had done well for himself, though his harried face and tired step suggested that his success was bringing little joy at present. To anyone that recognized him as Jim Harwood, the President's Chief of Staff, the reasons would be clear. With terrorists striking abroad, political enemies setting ambushes at home, and the President's approval rating in a continuing slump, the administration was more than usually beleaguered. What Marchand had just shared was an unwelcome addition to the burdens he already carried.

"So you're telling me that this Adversego guy thinks that not only the polling numbers, but the actual votes are being tampered with?"

"That's right."

"And you believe him?"

"Yes I do. He's not only technically very good, but he's smart and totally honest."

Harwood let that go. Everyone in Washington claimed to be honest. Sometimes they even were – when it coincided with their best interests.

They walked in silence while Harwood took in the implications of what Marchand had just told him. Perhaps a whole season of primaries had been hacked. The polls – unfortunately, only for the Republicans and Yazzie – couldn't be trusted. Marchand wanted the President to act, but he was already getting hammered unmercifully by the Republicans for taking Executive actions when Congress refused to act.

"So what specifically are you saying we should do?" Harwood asked.

"Well, you could make the game company shut down the app so at least the November election will be clean."

"What if it leaks out why we've done it?"

"Why would that happen?"

"Because everything in this town leaks if there's something in it for somebody."

"Well, you'd tell the truth – that the administration didn't find out about the hack until just then."

Harwood snorted. "You mean until the Republicans had nominated a clown that the President should be able to beat?"

"The Republicans don't think that."

"The smart ones do."

"Well, then the primaries can be run all over again!"

"Really? You think that would be a good idea? Think what the Republicans would say to that! They'd say the whole story had been fabricated to put off the election! They'd say that the President was staging some sort of camouflaged coup to stay in charge until his poll ratings recover. What could he have to lose, the way they are right now?"

"But you've got to do something! You can't just let an election go forward when you know it's going to be hacked!"

At the moment, Harwood was more than half inclined to do just that. If the President was defeated, disclosing that the voting had been hacked would be enough to nullify the election for certain. And eventually the President's poll numbers had to come back up. Perhaps there was a way to have it both ways. But he needed time to think.

"No, you're right, I can't. So here's what I think you should do. This Adversego guy is the same IT pro that pulled our chestnuts out of the fire last time, right? So who's a better choice to do the same thing again? Let's get him to hack the hack."

"What do you mean by that?"

"Well, if he's such a hot shot, why don't you get him to figure out a way to kill the malware without the bad guys, whoever they are, knowing it's happened? Then we have a clean election, and if word does ever leak out, no one can complain."

"What about the primaries? What are you going to say about those?"

"What am I going to say? I'm not going to say anything."

"How do you expect to justify that if word gets out?"

"I won't have to, because this conversation never happened."

Marchand stopped and stared at him. "Are you serious? You're really not going to do anything about this?"

"That's right. Things are pretty desperate – worse than even the Republicans know. The President can't afford anything more hitting the fan right now, and there are plenty of things going on overseas only the CIA is aware of. Any of them could go off any minute."

Incredulous, Marchand said nothing as the two men faced each other in the early fall sunshine. Finally his friend said, "Look, anything you need, just ask for it. You'll get it, no questions asked. But face to face only! Work through my aide, Bobby, and remember that those conversations won't be happening, either. Good luck."

The President's Chief of Staff turned and walked off, briskly now, his hands jammed in his pockets and his open raincoat flapping behind him. Thank God there was one disaster he could leave on someone else's plate for a change.

*   *   *

What would he have up his sleeve if their roles were reversed? That was the question Richard Fetters was asking himself as he stood in his study, swirling the ice in his scotch and staring out over his rain-soaked patio. Water dripped from the ivy growing on the trellises, and the early darkness of the advancing season seeped between the slats of the fence that surrounded the small, neglected oasis behind his townhouse.

What indeed? The easy part was this: if he were White Crow, he'd need to either block Fetter's ability to manipulate the voting, somehow force Wellhead out of the race, or make the Texan's victory so improbable that no one would believe the returns if he won. Conveniently, those were nearly identical to the choices that lay on Fetters's side of the table: he could outflank any attempt to block his vote manipulation, force Yazzie out of the race, or tar him so badly that no one would believe it if the voting tallies indicated he had won.

Very well, then, Geronimo. Fetters enjoyed a friendly game of chess as well as the next man. Indeed, his only passion in life besides politics was chess. Game on.

The third option he'd reviewed was easy to dispose of. If either candidate's victory was too improbable to be believed, both would be at risk: anyone investigating the November voting would surely look into the primaries as well, and each was vulnerable there. Under that strategy, a draw could be the same as a loss, so neither player should want to play that game.

What about forcing the other candidate out of the race? That was a time-honored political gambit, and the moves were well known. But that made it a difficult attack to pursue, because the other player would be watching for it, and would be on the attack as well.

So that game was possible, but tricky. To win, he'd have to have both the best defense and the best offense, thwarting White Crow's attempts to smear his candidate, while succeeding in smearing his.

That game worried him the most. Wellhead was manifestly vulnerable, and he'd scrubbed Yazzie a year ago before agreeing to the deal with White Crow. He'd failed to find a single blemish of any sort. But that could be fixed. Still, time was short. Finding something to work with took time, and setting up someone surrounded by handlers and the press might prove impossible.

Either way, he still had to rely on manipulating the vote. If White Crow figured out a way to block him, or how to manipulate the vote himself, Fetters's whole strategy would collapse. That would be the aggressive game he'd play if he were White Crow, and also the one where the moves would be least visible. It might be impossible for either opponent to know that he was moving into a trap until he was checkmated. How could Fetters counter moves he couldn't see?

That was worrisome. The people he'd hired to hack the voting hadn't found it to be particularly challenging, so why would White Crow? What if he slipped his own malware in at the last moment? That had to be the game he was playing.

Fetters was out of his league when it came to technology, and being out of direct control of a situation was not tolerable. He stood up and poured himself another scotch. The rain had stopped, and fog was now streaming through the chinks in the fence that defended his patio. Already, he could barely see its boundaries in the gathering gloom.

Well, screw it. There had to be a way to outflank his opponent, and he was determined to find it. He pulled a notepad out of his desk and started to make a list of the field operatives he'd need to enlist. If Yazzie so much as dropped a piece of litter, Fetters was going to know about it. And White Crow – well, that bastard wasn't going to take a shit without someone telling Fetters how many sheets of toilet paper he'd used.

He would also have to contact the hackers he'd hired many months ago and had hoped he would not need again.

* * *

Frank hadn't seen George Marchand since he had hopped out of a helicopter on Frank's wilderness doorstep. At 9:30 in the morning the commuter breakfast crowd had already passed through, leaving the sitting area of the sandwich shop deserted as planned.

"So let me get this straight. I can get support from the administration as long as they preserve deniability. That means if this blows up in my face, I'm all alone, right?"

"That's pretty much it."

"So why would I want to do this? Why don't you go to the FBI or your boss at the CIA instead?"

"After the President's Chief of Staff says the administration won't get involved?"

"Okay, but that still doesn't tell me why I should put *my* head on the block."

"Don't you think it already is?"

"What's that supposed to mean?"

"Well, you tell me that you've visited several voting places and a voting machine distribution center. If things blow up and there's an investigation, that might very well come to light."

"But I was working for the government!"

"I see. And what's the name of the agency you were working for?"

Frank opened his mouth and then shut it. George pressed his point.

"Do you have a pay stub from them?"

"You know I don't, George. It's from that voting machine front company they set up."

"I see. Ever been to Butcher's office?"

"No. I have no idea where it is."

"Uh huh. And who do you suppose would be conducting an investigation if there is one?"

Frank was getting angry.

"You know who."

"Yes I do. The FBI. Got any friends there?"

"Damn it, George, you know they'd love to hang me out to dry. But you got me into this mess – and the last time, too, for that matter – so how about getting me out of it for a change?"

"You're right. I did get you into this, and at the moment I'm extremely sorry I did."

"Wonderful. I feel better already."

"Hold on a minute – I'm not through. I can't go to my superiors to get approval for this, but I can start leaving my fingerprints on everything you do. And remember, it's already documented back at the agency that I came out to Nevada with Butcher. The orders for that came all the way from the top. I'll start checking in with Butcher from time to time in a way that won't attract attention, but in retrospect it will look like you must be working under both of our directions as well. And I'll stand by that story."

"I appreciate that, but how does that help me?"

"If things blow up, the CIA will have to step in to defend itself. And you can be sure they'll be happy to try and take the credit if things go well. Anyway, I'll be putting myself at equal risk to you. I'm afraid that that's the best I can do, at least for now."

Frank drummed his fingers for a while, and then picked up his coffee cup. "Refill?"

"Sure"

Marchand watched Frank take his time at the service counter. What would he do if Frank said no? He didn't have a fallback plan.

When he sat down again, Frank held his cup in both hands and stared at his old boss.

"Okay, right now I'm not saying yes or no. I'll get back to you when I've made up my mind."

Marchand frowned. Well, that was better than a no. He wondered what it would take to turn it into a yes.

"Thanks, Frank. I truly am sorry I got you involved in this."

Marchand expected Frank to stand up, but instead he continued to sit there, looking unhappy and uncertain. He had the sense that perhaps Frank was waiting for him to say something that might convince him to sign on. But what could that be? Yes – that might work. He leaned forward.

"Frank, for what it's worth, keep in mind that it looks like you're the only person right now who's in a position to stop someone from stealing a presidential election. That's a pretty big deal. Oh, and one other thing: what's the use of knowing you're the smartest guy in the room if you can't prove it now and then?"

* * *

39

Can I Borrow your Phone
to Make a Call?

"HEY – LOOK who's here!"

The pit boss poked the new blackjack dealer in the ribs and pointed at a tall, anxious Anglo entering the casino.

Len Butcher had been summoned by White Crowe to receive further instructions. As he walked past, the pit boss grabbed his arm.

"Yo, Len. Want to introduce you to one of our new people. Atsa, Len here is Ohanzee's new naalté'."

The other man guffawed. "Really?"

"Sure. And with Ohanzee, once you're a naalté', you're a naalté for good."

Butcher pulled away, their laughter echoing in his burning ears.

He knocked on the door to White Crow's office, and waited to be let in. Two minutes later, he was still waiting. Now the pit boss was chatting with a bartender, pointing Butcher's way and laughing.

Butcher finally heard the electronic lock release, and let himself in.

"Sorry to keep you waiting; things are busy. Let's get down to business."

White Crow was seated behind his desk, leaving Butcher standing and wondering whether he was expected to remain so. Well, the hell with that. He dragged a chair from across the room and sat down.

"So here's where things stand. I've got to know what this guy Adversego knows about how the voting is being manipulated. Tell."

"I don't know. I know he's hard at work at it, and I expect he's making progress. But I don't know for sure."

"Well, find out. Whatever it takes, I want to know by the end of the week how it's being done. Get that for me, and we'll call it even on what you owe me. If you don't, we'll be having a different conversation."

"You mean you called me all the way out here just for that? Why didn't you just call me?"

"Because I want something else. A way to monitor your behavior so I know that you remain loyal. Let me see your phone."

"My phone? Why?"

"I am not going to ask twice."

Butcher handed it over. White Crow tapped the keys and began swiping through screens.

"How did you know my password?"

"'Jim&Kate?' I'm sure I never could have guessed. But you log on often enough at the tables that anyone could see." He held the phone up.

"Can you tell me what this icon is for?"

"It's my email account."

"Exactly. No, no need to give me your password; I have that, too." He closed the phone and put it in his pocket.

"Now hear me. Don't even think about changing your password, switching to a different email account, or opening a new one. Before you're back in your car, I will have extracted the data on your last 10,000 emails – who to, who from, and how often. If I see any changes in these patterns, I will immediately let your superiors know that you have granted access to someone outside the agency."

"Please, Ohanzee...."

"That's all."

"But Ohanzee!"

"I said that's all!"

Butcher waited a moment more, and then made his way to the office door. With his hand on the knob, he paused and turned.

"What's a 'naalté?"

White Crow looked up. His face relaxed into his thin, trademark smile. "Ah, naalté! So funny you should ask. It's what our Navajo brothers call a slave. Tell me – was there anyone in particular you had in mind?"

As Butcher closed the door behind him, he heard a sound he had long doubted existed. White Crow was laughing.

* * *

Frank was deeply immersed in the code of Angry Indians. He'd never consciously decided to help Marchand out, and if his old boss had called to put the question to him right then he would have said that he didn't know. But the puzzle of how the malware operated had been tugging at him, and there seemed to be no harm in figuring that out.

The voting apps he had downloaded all worked pretty much as he would have expected: each displayed the candidates, provided blocks to be checked after each one, displayed the results of your voting and asked you to confirm your choices, and then sent the results to the voting machine when you touched your phone to the wireless voting logo.

He could see why they were so popular with town governments as well as voters. Not only did they display all kinds of information about each candidate, but they also allowed you to vote before you went to the polling station. That meant shorter lines, since those using apps could vote in a matter of seconds instead of puzzling over minor office candidate choices and reading ballot measures they weren't aware of until they were standing in the booth.

He expected that confirming how the vote got changed inside the phone wouldn't take him too much time, now that he knew which app to focus on. And he'd already seen it in action once at the distribution center, so he had an idea at what point in the voting process something suspicious happened. The more interesting question was to figure how whoever had hacked the app decided which votes should be redirected to which candidates. The simplest way would be to just change every vote to whichever candidate it was the unknown culprit wanted to win.

But that would be too obvious. Somehow they had to figure out how many votes needed to be switched, and in which states, in order to win but not arouse suspicion. If they were really good, they'd also factor in which way a given district usually voted, so that they could begin changing votes as soon as a voting station opened. And since the election would be won by electoral votes rather than by a national, popular majority, they'd have to calculate the number of votes they needed on a state-by-state basis.

Judging by the results of the primary voting and the spreadsheet Josette had prepared, he was quite sure that the voting adjustments were happening in real time, or close to it. Someone, somewhere, must not only have a very detailed and robust algorithm, but some pretty impressive processing power as well, and was using both to switch just enough votes from one candidate to another in real time to get the result they wanted.

But how would they know, from state to state, how many votes to alter? Most of the accumulating vote totals stayed out in the field until the polls closed. That meant that the hacker would have no access to the real voting totals as they were piling up, voting station by voting station.

Frank stewed on that for a while. How would he tackle that? And what did he have to work with? Well, for starters, so long as no one closed the back door to the polling systems, the hacker would gain a pretty good idea going into Election Day how people were likely to vote. That should allow them to start with a pretty good idea – say plus or minus five percent – how many votes needed to be switched.

But that wouldn't be good enough if the race was closer than the polls predicted, or if the polls themselves were off the mark. And that could happen, since you couldn't predict with certainty which people would actually get off their butts and vote.

Anyway, what the polls were saying now wouldn't tell him much about how the hacker had developed their algorithm to begin with, since they would have had to devise their plan at least a year ago. Back then, they would have had to take all possibilities into account, and they also couldn't know how many mobile phones they could infect. He decided there had to be more to the planning than relying on the final poll numbers to set the final switching orders that would be sent to the hacked phones.

Clearly, it was time to engage in some fevered pacing. He rose to his feet and began walking the few available spaces back and forth in his small living room.

So what else did the hacker have to work with? Well, the votes of the people with the apps, of course! As the day progressed, the hacker would have a more and more accurate idea of how people were actually voting. If they had tens or hundreds of thousands of apps in every state, that would be far more reliable than any poll. And they would also know what districts those app owners cast their votes in through the geolocation function of the game app.

He was pacing faster now, swerving out of his living room, into his tiny kitchen and down his hallway as well. The rest of the pieces fell into place fairly naturally. He had always assumed that when the owner of a phone activated her voting app, the hacked app would check in with headquarters, report its location, and be told whether or not to switch the vote, and if so, to which candidate. Now, he realized, in order to capture the predictive value of each copy of the app, the real intentions of the voter would be equally important, so the first thing that would happen when the hacked app logged into the host system would be to report how the owner of the phone was actually voting. The hacker's system would incorporate this most-current data from the field into its algorithm at the same time it was sending the vote switching message back again, thereby constantly refining its effectiveness throughout Election Day.

Well, now, wasn't that pretty slick? Frank upped his earlier estimate of the amount of computing power the hacker would need by several notches.

He sat down at his diminutive kitchen table and poured himself a cup of cold coffee. He now had an idea how the hacker would avoid shifting too many votes. But how could the hacker tell whether he had enough votes under his control? That was an interesting question, and depended on all sorts of variables, each of which would be hard to nail down.

For starters, the hacker wouldn't know whether more liberals or conservatives would get out and vote. On the other hand, the hacked app could report back whether the phone also carried a voting app. But again, the hacker couldn't know how many of the owners of those phones would actually vote, and how many of that final, smaller number of individuals would decide or remember to use their phones to vote.

He got up and started walking again. How many copies of the app would have to be out there? And were they in the right states? If not, the hacker might not have enough votes to play with to rack up enough electoral votes. If it really was a close race, then they'd have plenty of room to spare. But if one of the candidates was really far ahead, maybe the plan was already doomed to failure? Or how about this scenario – if too many of the people with hacked smartphones intended to vote for the hacker's candidate anyway, then the whole scheme would collapse, because there wouldn't be enough votes to switch. Even with 40 million downloads, it would probably have to be a pretty close race for the hacker to know for sure his candidate could win.

He stopped pacing. Okay, and so what? With the polls worthless, only the hacker knew the answers to any of the questions Frank was asking.

He looked at his watch; he'd just spent an hour analyzing something he couldn't get to the bottom of, and couldn't use anyway. He had to assume that the race was close enough to be successfully hacked, because he couldn't afford not to. It was time to get back to working on something productive.

For starters, that meant figuring out how the switch was accomplished, and there seemed to be two logical ways to do that. One was easy, the other hard.

He doubted that the hacker would have chosen the hard way, which would be for the Cavalry and Indian code to take over control of the voting app. There were multiple voting apps, and the hacker would therefore have to find a vulnerability in each one, and then exploit it. The easier way would be to find some element that was external to every version of the voting app and work with that.

The obvious one was the radio signal that all of the apps would use to send their information to the voting machine. If the hacker could intercept that signal along the way, they wouldn't have to do anything to the voting app or the voting machine. That was such an elegant and logical approach to take that Frank was sure it must be the answer.

Luckily, he was in a good position to test his theory, because at the start of the project he had been given access by Voldemort to the source code for one of the brands of voting machine. Having that was crucial, because if he only had the kind of code that was normally shipped with a computer, called "object code," all he would have would be the endless lines of gibberish that only a computer could understand. But source code was "human readable," or geek readable, anyway, so he would be able to see exactly what the software did, and how. It was time to see what would really happen on Election Day.

*   *   *

Butcher stared straight ahead as he waited for his flight to start boarding, oblivious to the other passengers milling about. His mind was more than occupied by a single, inescapable conclusion: no matter that his tormentor had said they'd be even if he delivered the secret to hacking the voting. After what the pit boss had called him, he was convinced that White Crow would never let him go. The most he could hope was that there might come a time when he no longer had anything that White Crow wanted.

What could he do? There seemed to be no way out short of killing the casino manager, and he knew he was incapable of doing such a thing, or even of hiring someone else to do it for him.

"Last call for flight 780 to Dallas-Ft. Worth."

Damn! He'd been so preoccupied he'd almost missed his plane! He was reaching for his roll-aboard when a barely audible voice at his elbow said, "I can help you."

Butcher snapped his head to his right, and found himself gazing into a newspaper.

"What did you say?" he whispered.

The soft voice from behind the newspaper repeated itself. "I can help you. I was at the casino today."

Butcher waited for more, but instead the speaker lowered his paper, folded it neatly to its original form, and then in half once more. Standing up, he placed the newspaper on his seat, with the print aligned in Butcher's direction. Then he looked at his watch, picked up his carry-on bag, and walked away.

Butcher was about to hurry after him, when he noticed that there was a telephone number written in the margin of the paper, followed by his own initials. He stared at it for a moment, and then, trying to look as if a headline had caught his eye, reached out to pick up the paper as casually as possible. Clutching it to his chest, he hurried onto the plane.

*   *   *

40

You Really Look Like You Could Use a Vacation

T HE REPUBLICAN AND Democratic conventions were anticlimactic at best. For both candidates there was the usual problem of foregone conclusions. No serious challenger to the President had arisen from within his own party, and Wellhead had piled up enough delegates to lock up the nomination before the primary season was half complete.

The big push to the finish line, however, was going to be something else again. Over a billion dollars had been raised by each of the two traditional parties. Even Yazzie had begun to pull in real money, though far less than his opponents. Now that the polls indicated the possibility of a dead heat between all three candidates on Election Day, the gloves were off as well. The President and Wellhead, as well as their PACs and Super PACS, were now buying as many attack ads targeting the CCA candidate as at each other.

As usual, Yazzie was successful in turning disadvantage into a display of virtue. The voters were sick and tired of politicians, so his lack of experience struck many as a plus. With no Super PAC money behind him and just enough grassroots economic support to keep his own name out there, he engaged in no negative campaigning at all. And with no past voting history or party affiliation to work with, the negative ads his opponents cobbled together sounded hollow and desperate. The more negative advertising the Republicans and Democrats engaged in, the better he looked.

Nor did Yazzie have to spend any time, or tarnish his own luster, by campaigning for other candidates, or defending his party's past mistakes. Every ad he ran, every statement he made, and every photo op his handlers scheduled, could be dedicated solely towards winning votes, rather than trying to avoid losing them.

Naturally, it was driving Richard Fetters crazy.

* * *

Len Butcher stared at his watch until it was exactly 10:15 AM. Then, clutching a thumb drive in his pocket, he strode out of the department store, up to the curb, and raised his hand in the air. A cab with tinted windows swerved to the curb, and he stepped in.

"Welcome aboard." The person seated behind the driver slid the window shut between the front and back seat.

Butcher's companion was unmemorable to the point of fading into the upholstery of the cab. An anonymous face, with an anonymous voice, protruded from an anonymous suit. Butcher assumed that if asked, he'd say his name was something like John Smith. Butcher felt envious.

"I assume you've been able to pull together the materials that we discussed?"

"Yes, I've got everything on a thumb drive. I can display them for you, but I can't allow you to make copies of anything. I shouldn't even have agency files on a thumb drive, let alone take them offsite."

"That's fine. We just need a bit of confirmation before we can commit to do as we've discussed."

Butcher belatedly thought to look out the window to see where they were headed.

"Where are we going? And who am I going to be meeting with?"

"We'll be there in just a few minutes. I'll tell you where to go when we get there." His escort glanced out the window. "Trees are just starting to change, aren't they?"

"Yes," Butcher said, frowning. He wondered what he was getting himself into now.

* * *

When the taxi came to a halt, Butcher stepped out, alone, under the portico of a downtown hotel. The lobby was awash in press and people of all stripes – literally. Many wore red, white and blue ties, jackets or other apparel. One contingent, wearing "Hook'em, Wellhead!" T-shirts had added red, white and blue paper top hats – with paper cattle horns, no less – to their ensembles. Perhaps the candidate himself was about to make an appearance.

But there was no time to find out. As instructed, he took an elevator to the third floor, where he found himself in an empty hallway of doors, each with a nametag outside bearing a name like, "Algonquin," "Iroquois," and "Wampanoag." Something about that seemed vaguely incongruous under the circumstances, but he was too nervous to figure out what it was. When he reached "Powhatan," he stopped abruptly and stared at the closed door. Once he passed through it, he would surely be committed. Should he turn around and leave?

Taking a deep breath, he tapped on the door. He barely heard the sound himself, so after waiting for thirty seconds, he tried again, this time more aggressively.

The door opened while his knuckles were still poised in mid-air, leaving him facing a very recognizable Vice Presidential candidate and former Cabinet member. He caught Butcher in an intense stare for a moment before turning and taking a seat at the head of a table that stretched a full thirty feet down the length of an empty and only half-lit conference room.

"Sit down," his host said, and Butcher took a chair along the side of the table, feeling like a student called to the principal's office. His chair was uncomfortably low and straight backed. He fumbled briefly but unsuccessfully to change its altitude and angle.

Giving up, he turned back to face his host, who was obviously quite comfortable in his own, better adjusted seat. Butcher guessed it was set six inches higher than his own, so that he found himself looking up, rather than down, into the unblinking eyes that were trained on his own.

He cleared his throat, but his host still said nothing. Butcher began to tremble.

"I've brought the information I was told to. If you have a laptop, I can show it to you."

Butcher glanced around the table, noticing for the first time that there was no computer to be seen.

"I'm afraid I really can't leave anything with you... I could go to jail forever if it came out I'd shared agency information with you."

"Never mind that. I'm more interested in confirming a few things in the transcript taken at your debriefing with my colleague."

"Okay, we can do that, but I need to be sure you'll keep your side of the bargain, too."

"You needn't worry about that. I can have you out of the country within two hours. You'll stay there, by the way, until after the election."

Fetters took a mobile phone out of his pocket and set it between them on the table. "If I'm satisfied with your answers, I'll make a call to my people, one of whom is sitting in a car down the block from your house right now.

"At the same time, you will call your wife, and tell her whatever you want – that there's been a family emergency, that you've secretly been the head of the CIA all these years, or whatever story you wish. My driver will arrive at your door while you are delivering your message, and you will tell your wife to go with him and pick up your children at their school."

"What if she won't go?"

"Your job is to make sure she does. The same escort will take them to the Dulles private aviation terminal where you will already have arrived. A chartered jet will be waiting to take you and your family, together with weather-appropriate wardrobes already aboard, to a very private Caribbean island. Once the election is over, you will be flown home again by the same means."

Butcher was taken aback; he hadn't expected things to move so quickly.

"But what about White Crow? Who's going to protect my family after we return?"

His host indulged himself in a crooked smile that Butcher found both disconcerting and reassuring. "I assure you that after the election your Mr. White Crow will be in no condition to threaten anyone ever again. Now tell me: how does he plan to manipulate the votes in November?"

Butcher shifted in his chair. "As far as I know, all he knows right now is that someone used a smartphone app called Angry Indians/Angry Cavalry to manipulate the primary votes."

Fetters leaned forward, "You mean he doesn't yet know how it works?"

"I don't believe so. I'd told him that much before your partner intercepted me at the airport, but that's all."

"And this person you have in the field – this Adversego person – has he figured out how the votes have been hacked since then?"

"He hasn't reported in yet to say he has, but I expect he will soon. He's figured the hardest part out already."

Butcher stared at the mobile phone that lay between them. What more did he have to say before Fetters would make his call?

"Will Adversego report to someone in your office if you are not available?"

"Well, yes. Normally he reports to someone else instead of me anyway."

"And what will they do with that information if they can't reach you?"

"There's a formal protocol for that. My second in command has clearance to receive any information that I would, and to pass it along to my superior."

"Does White Crow ever communicate with your assistant, or vice versa?"

"Oh, absolutely not."

"Might he, if you disappeared?"

"Oh God, I hope not!"

"Only fools rely on hope. Could he contact your office if he wanted to?"

Butcher recalled how White Crow had bragged about shadowing his phone calls and email – about even knowing how to contact his boss.

"Maybe. Yes."

Fetters asked no more questions. After a moment, he eased slowly back into his chair, frowning. As the silence lengthened, Butcher wondered whether his host was still aware of his presence. At last, his host reached for the phone instead of continuing the interrogation.

Butcher fumbled in his pockets to be sure he had his own phone while Fetters spoke quietly into his. "Wait five minutes and then have the wife picked up as planned. Tell the driver downstairs to watch for Mr. Butcher at the rear exit of the hotel in three minutes."

Fetters stood up and offered a cold, perfunctory handshake to Butcher. "I'm sure that you have done a great service to your country by uncovering these troubling matters. Neither you nor I will communicate with each other in the future, or acknowledge that we ever met. Do you understand?"

"Of course."

"Good. Now go spend some time in the sun with your family. I'm sure your staff will keep the trains running on time until your return."

At that moment, Butcher couldn't have cared less. He closed the conference room door quietly behind him, and feverishly entered his password into his phone.

On the other side of the conference room door, Fetters was also making a call.

"Go collect Adversego – I don't care what you had planned before – find out where he is and grab him right now."

* * *

41

Do I Know You?

I T HAD TAKEN all day, but Frank had worked out not only the concept, but also the nitty-gritty details of how the Cavalry and Indians program pulled off the voting switch.

Like the rest of the hacker's work, the approach taken was not only clean and effective, but elegantly simple. In order to take control of millions of votes, all it needed to do was take advantage of the fact that the range of the wireless signal used to transmit someone's vote was extremely short – thereby turning a security feature into a fatal security flaw.

The crucial clue came Frank's way when he realized that the voting app did not wait for the phone to be tapped against a voting machine before its radio turned on. Instead, it started searching for something to connect to immediately, just as the phone would search for an earpiece or a hands-free receiver in a car if its owner turned it on when its Bluetooth radio was in the "on" position. But instead of using Bluetooth, the app took advantage of a newer wireless technology that all phones also supported, called near field communications – "NFC" for short – the same signal Apple took advantage of with its ApplePay mobile payment app.

Unlike Bluetooth, which can connect across a distance measured in feet, an

NFC signal is so faint it can't connect to anything more than an inch or so away, making it almost impossible to be intercepted, except for another app on the same device. Although a voter might think they had to tap their phone against the wireless logo to pair the two devices, actual contact wasn't necessary at all. But it would ensure that the phone was moved close enough to the reception antenna in the voting machine for the two devices to connect, and for the voting information to transfer.

The hacker had cleverly seized on the time lag – the one between turning on a voting app and moving the phone close enough to the voting machine – to take control. All the game app had to do was wait until it detected an NFC signal. When it did, it would impersonate the voting machine, and the voting app would transfer not only the phone owner's intended vote to it, but the phone owner's secure, personalized voter registration information and location as well.

Voilà! The game app now had all the information it needed to represent the voter to the voting machine. Meanwhile, the real voting app, thinking its job was done, would shut down its radio signal.

The game app now had plenty of time to report its location and the presidential vote the phone owner had hoped to cast. And also to receive instructions to change that vote, if necessary. When the voter did tap her phone on the voting machine, the game app would identify the phone owner, and then transmit the vote the hacker had approved. The manipulation would then be complete, with no one ever the wiser.

Clattering happily away at his laptop, Frank wrote up a detailed report of his discovery. He'd revise it with a fresh eye in the morning, and then send it off to Vickie at Voldemort. Then he sat back, triumphant.

Time to share the news. He picked up his phone to call Josette, and then thought better of it. Let her wait awhile; she could be the second person to find out. He'd tell George Marchand instead.

"George! Glad I caught you. Say, I've been thinking about what you asked me do, and I've got some good news for you."

"Excellent! I'm glad you came around. Look – you caught me just walking into a meeting that's going to run into the evening. Can I call you tonight?"

"Or we could get together tomorrow."

"Better yet. What works for you?"

"Want to say Connie's again for coffee? At 10?"

"Deal. See you then."

Frank looked at his phone. He really did want to tell someone. He dialed Josette and gave her the news.

"But that is so wonderful! You are my hero!"

"Well, you helped."

"Yes, but only with the easy parts! When can you tell me all the details? I want to know everything about how they did it."

"Pretty soon. I'm almost done with a complete report for Voldemort. Things always come to me when I have to explain something complicated to others, so I'm still filling in some little gaps as I write."

There was silence at the other end of the line.

"You still there?"

"You will not really send a report to Voldemort, will you?"

"Of course I will. I know you think they're behind this, but they've given me everything I've asked for. If they didn't want me to figure out the hack, they could have put all sorts of obstacles in my way. Or just fired me and withdrawn access to the tools I needed."

"I said they were changing the polls – I think they wanted you to solve the voting hack so that they could control the election instead!"

"Look, Josette, you've got to just give that up. I can't go into the details, but I know personally that Voldemort is authorized right from the top. You might as well say that the President wants to manipulate the vote!"

"Why not? Or his people! Don't you remember your Mr. Nixon? And Watergate?"

Frank did. But all he wanted to do was to report in and then resign. He'd done and had enough.

"I'm sorry, Josette, but that's what I'm going to do. I'll give you a call tomorrow if you want. Just send me an email." He rang off before she could say anything more.

He drummed his fingers and looked at his watch. It was only 5:00. The hell with it. He'd finish the report off now.

When he looked at his watch again it was after 7:00, but he was finished. He attached the file to an email and sent it off to Vickie. He'd solved the mystery of the vote manipulation and proven to Josette that she couldn't manipulate him all at the same time.

Feeling tired but satisfied, he trotted down the stairs of his apartment building and out onto the street, figuring that he'd earned himself a fancy dinner on the town. Alright, maybe not a fancy dinner, but at least a decent plate of chicken Marsala at the Italian restaurant down the street.

After a half a block, he stuck his hands in his pockets and picked up his pace. He hadn't bothered to put on a jacket, and it had turned cold while he had been working. Maybe he'd have a half a bottle of wine with dinner.

Two men walking even more quickly overtook him. As they drew even, each took hold of one of his arms just above the elbow.

"We're going to turn around now. Keep walking, and you won't get hurt," the one on his left murmured.

Frank tried to jerk his arms loose and instantly regretted it.

"Just look straight ahead and keep walking."

"Where are we going?"

"Shut up."

What could he do? No longer cold, he was sweating profusely as they steered him back to his apartment building.

"Unlock the door."

He did as he was told. Moments later, he was unlocking the door to his apartment as well.

"Alright, where's your computer?"

"I probably left it in the living room."

They pushed him down on his couch.

"You keep notes on anything besides this laptop?"

"No, why?"

"You don't need to know."

The one that had been doing the talking began rifling the desk in the living room, looking at any tablets or loose papers he found. Frank could hear the other one opening cupboards, drawers and closet doors in the rest of this apartment. What would they do to him when they were done? He'd seen both their faces. He had to figure something out fast.

He eased his phone out of his pocket while the intruder was ransacking his desk and dropped it between his legs. He placed his thumb on the biosensor and tried not to be obvious as he looked for the phone's screen to change.

So far, so good. The man at the desk was reading some papers he'd found. Frank turned on his running app and set it to run in the background.

It was a while before Frank felt he could glance at his phone again, because the man was now moving around the room, poking through the piles of material that had accumulated on the window sills and book shelves. When he returned to the desk with a stack of junk to sort through, Frank hit a speed dial button. He gave it long enough to connect and then spoke up.

"What are you looking for?"

The man didn't look up. "For a smart guy, you're a pretty slow learner, aren't you? Now shut up."

"What if I don't?"

This time the man turned around.

"Anyone ever held your arms behind your back while another guy worked you over?"

"Okay, okay. You've made your point."

The other man reentered the room.

"You done?"

"Yeah, nothing here."

"Same. Okay, Adversego, time to go."

Damn! Frank thought. How was he going to get the phone back into his pocket? He tried to move one hand nonchalantly under his leg to reach for it.

"I said get up – now move it."

With his hand on the phone, he stood up. But no luck: the other man noticed as he moved it towards his pocket. Frank jabbed his thumb furiously around on the face of the phone, trying to disconnect the call so they wouldn't think to trace it.

"What's that in your hand?"

"Just my phone."

"You won't need that where you're going. Give it to me."

Frank was ready for that command, and willingly handed the phone over. "I may not need it, but you will."

The men looked at each other. "What are you talking about?"

"You know that laptop you're so interested in? It's just a paperweight if you can't get past the security settings."

"So? What's your password?"

"You'll have to ask my phone."

"Cut the crap, Adversego."

"All right. Hand me the phone so I can unlock it again."

His captor paused, but then did so. "I want to know everything you're going to do before you do it, understand? Otherwise you're on the floor."

"Understood. You see this icon here? I'm just going to push it. When I do, a couple of boxes are going to open. Okay?"

"Okay, go ahead."

"So there's the boxes, see? Now I'm going to enter my regular password, okay?" The man nodded.

"There – now what do you see?"

"A number. So?"

"So you need that number, as well as my password, to access any of the programs on the computer."

"Thanks, Adversego. Now that we've got the number, you can leave the phone here."

"Really? What's the number?"

The man looked down at the phone.

"Hey – it just changed."

Frank handed him the phone. "That's right. And it will keep changing every 20 seconds until the battery runs out. So that's why you need the phone."

The man looked mildly impressed.

"Okay." He dropped the phone in his pocket. "Now move it."

* * *

George turned his phone on as he walked to his car the next morning. As he unlocked the door, he heard it chirp.

Settling in to the driver's seat, he glanced at his phone to see who had left messages. One of them read, "Frank Adversego has sent you a running invitation."

A what? He'd never gone on a run with Frank before. He turned out of his driveway and on to his suburban street. Maybe the phone message would explain the text one. He called up his messages and held the phone to his ear.

A few seconds later, his car drifted to the curb and stopped.

* * *

Later the same day, Marchand was walking down the street with an understandably distraught Marla.

"Can you think of anything else that might help us figure out who would want to kidnap your father?"

"I think I've told you everything I can remember him saying that could possibly relate to this. I'll keep trying, but that's it for now."

"Well, I wouldn't say we have nothing to work with, but I wish we had more. What do you know about this Josette person?"

"Maybe not as much as there is to know, but here goes."

George frowned as he listened. Should he believe the story Josette had told Frank? If so, how much more was there to it than Marla, or even Frank, knew?

He hadn't made up his mind on either of those points by the time Marla had once again exhausted her recollections.

"Could you introduce me to her? If I contact her out of the blue she'll have no reason to trust me."

"Of course. I've only got an email address, but I'll reach out to her as soon as you want. What else will you be doing?"

"Well, there's this strange text message I got from your father – a running invitation. It's obviously supposed to be telling me something, and I've got somebody working on that now. Hopefully I'll be able to let you know soon what it means. And on that note, I'd better be going."

He gave her a hug.

"How bad do you think this is, George?"

"I'd like to say you don't have to worry. But I can't, because I just don't know."

*   *   *

42

Now Go to Your Room!

F RANK WAS SITTING in the same room he'd occupied ever since his blindfold had been removed the night before. It hadn't taken him long to conclude that no remotely feasible escape strategy was available to him. There just wasn't much to work with, and most of what the drab space did contain was problematic.

For example, there was that very large and rather thuggish looking person sitting in the chair by the door, reading a tabloid newspaper. He never left the room unless an equally evolutionarily challenged guard took his place. Each wore an impressively equipped shoulder holster.

Then there were the facts that the room had no windows, the door was locked from the outside as well as the inside, and that the only objects in the room were two chairs, the table at which he was sitting, a cot, and a small night table supporting a pile of old magazines. No, that wasn't quite accurate. He should probably include the guard in the list of inanimate objects. But at any rate, he didn't see that anything in the room could be used to help him make his escape other than the gun in the guard's holster. And he didn't seem like the kind of guy who was likely to share nicely.

So there Frank sat, with nothing to do except complete page after page in an elementary Sudoku book he'd found among the magazines. He'd tried staring at the guard with his hands folded in front of him and a goofy grin on his face, hoping to bug him, but the man never looked up. Frank thought his head would explode from boredom if he didn't get out soon.

He heard the door being unlocked from the outside, and looked at his watch; it seemed to be too early for the guard shift to change.

Two men entered the room. One was the other guard, but the taller of the two was someone Frank hadn't seen before. Judging by the body language of the guard, he was obviously the head beaver on this operation. How many more captors might he have? Frank mentally filed these two away as Boss Man and Robin.

Boss Man walked up to Frank, while Robin stood behind and to the side, holding a laptop. Frank noticed that the laptop Robin was carrying looked a lot like his own.

"Alright, Adversego. Time to get to work," Boss Man said. Robin placed the laptop on the table and then resumed his former position, with arms crossed.

"What do you mean, get to work? What do you expect me to do?"

"Not much. We're just going to answer your email so no one wonders why you suddenly went dark."

"Why would I want to help you do that?"

"You're not exactly in a position to negotiate, are you Adversego?" He gestured, and the large guard by the door now ("Guard Man," Frank decided) stepped forward to stand at Boss Man's other elbow, arms crossed. Together, the three of them looked like a bad parody of a movie poster based on comic book superheroes. Frank noticed with annoyance that Guard Man was now staring at him with a goofy smile on his face.

"Do I get to know who you are, and why you're holding me?"

"Actually, you don't. And while we're on the subject, you don't get to ask any more questions, either."

"Okay, but I'll have to call you something, so I'm going with 'Boss Man.'"

Boss Man scowled at that, but let it go.

"Whatever. Now open up your laptop and log on to your email account at the agency site."

The agency site! This was the first bit of useful information Frank had been able to glean so far. Whoever it was that had grabbed him knew about Voldemort. If these were the hackers, he wondered how they'd figured that out.

In any event, being asked to answer his email on the Voldemort site had to be good news. He didn't know how, but simply having access to his email and the agency's system had to offer some potential for sneaking a covert message through.

"Okay." He pushed the power button on his laptop and folded his hands in his lap.

"I said log on to that site!"

"How do you expect me to do that?"

Boss Man looked annoyed. "We've got Wi-Fi."

"Nice! But I can't just dial in to a super secure government network by typing 'please.' I need my security token to get through the firewall."

Boss Man turned to Robin. "Bring in everything you took from him when you brought him in."

Frank looked down at his laptop and noticed that almost all of the icons had disappeared from his desktop. He wondered whether any of the deleted programs might still be recoverable. While he waited, he casually moused over the browser box. Judging by the names of the sites that displayed in the dropdown list, whoever had deleted the programs had rather exotic tastes in pornography.

The door opened again, and this time Robin was carrying a plastic shopping bag. He held it open, but when Frank reached in and pulled out his mobile phone, Boss Man grabbed it.

"Damn it, Adversego!"

But Frank was feeling cocky now. If they wanted him to report in to the office on a daily basis, they needed to keep him alive and cooperating on a daily basis as well.

"Don't you guys talk to each other? I already explained to my chauffeur that I need my phone to log on. Or maybe you've wiped all the apps off my phone as well?"

Boss Man looked to Robin, and to Frank's relief he shook his head no.

"What does an app have to do with logging on?"

"That's where my token software is. I type in my PIN, and the app shows me a random number that gets replaced every twenty seconds with a new one. I type my password and that number into the log-on window at the agency site and it lets me in. If I get the number wrong, it doesn't. Simple."

Boss Man frowned. "Okay, but we're going to do this my way." He pointed the phone at Frank. "Just stick your thumb on your mobile phone and then stop."

Frank did, and Boss Man looked at the phone. "Okay, what does the app look like?"

Frank told him how to recognize the icon, and after squinting and poking at the touch screen for a bit, Boss Man held the phone out to him again.

"That it?"

"You're a natural." Guard Man took a half step forward at that, but Boss Man waved him away. Guard Man looked disappointed, and he wasn't smiling now. Frank decided not to push his luck, and typed in his PIN without further comment.

Moments later, he was logged on to the system after typing his user name, password and the random number on his laptop.

"Now what?"

"Now you're going to give the laptop back to me so I can answer your email."

Frank's first impulse was to let him try. Typing styles were like fingerprints or voices – everyone's was just a little bit different. The nanosecond differences between when an individual struck different key combinations could be compiled into a unique profile that was like no one else's. He knew the agency ran a keystroke recognition program all the time, and would be able to tell immediately if anyone else answered his email. But that wouldn't help him get a message through.

Now what? If he told Boss Man why he'd be smarter to let Frank reply to his own email, he'd be suspicious – why would Frank tip him off to something like that?

He handed the computer over. "Great idea! Here – make yourself comfortable and I'll show you how to log on." Boss Man gave him a strange look, but sat down.

"Okay – so what you're looking at here is my remote desktop. See that icon there? That's for my email – just tap on that."

Boss Man did.

"Good job. Now you're looking at my email client. It's a little confusing, so let me walk you through everything."

Frank nattered along, describing more than Boss Man needed to know to simply answer his email. Finally, Boss Man pushed the laptop back and stood up.

"Okay, I've heard enough. I don't know what you're up to, but you're going to sit back down and answer your email, not me. I'm not touching that computer anymore."

Frank tried to look as abashed as possible without over acting.

"Oh, alright. Suit yourself."

Boss Man smirked. "Don't worry – I'll make it easy for you. I'll tell you exactly what to type."

Frank sat down and grumbled through twenty minutes of deleting some emails, answering others, and foldering the remainder as instructed by Boss Man. When they were done and he'd logged off the Voldemort site, he started to close the laptop. But Boss Man stopped him.

"Not so fast. Now open up your personal email account."

Frank did as he was told, thankful that another potential door had just opened.

"Okay. Now open a message and address it to your daughter."

Frank's heart skipped a beat. They knew about Marla! But again, he did as he was told. Instead of dictating this time, Boss Man took a firm hold on the laptop and pulled it his way.

"Sorry, Frankie. I don't trust you with this one."

Frank surrendered the laptop and watched as Boss Man two-finger typed a brief message and then re-read it carefully.

"Do I get to know what I'm about to send my own daughter?"

"Not in so many words. Just that you need to go off-line for a while. You don't want her worrying, do you?"

*   *   *

George picked up the phone to hear a breathless Marla.

"George! I just got an email message from my father!"

"What did it say?"

"Not much – just that he needs to be out of touch while he follows up on something. I'm sure someone told him what he had to type, but at least he's alive!"

George wasn't ready to jump to that conclusion on such flimsy evidence, but there was no reason to tell Marla that.

"That's great news. And I've got some, too. We think we know where your father is."

"That's wonderful! Tell me everything!"

"It was that text message he sent me. We took a look at the app that sent it, and it turns out it's a running program that also tracks your distance, speed, and most importantly, your route and current whereabouts, using the phone's location capability. And luckily it's a cloud app, so you can share your details with your friends."

"Excuse me?"

"Sorry. It's an app that keeps all its information on a host server, not on the phone. So all we had to do was accept your father's invitation to become a running partner and we could see his running information. It looks like he 'ran' about 38 miles out of town the other day. Assuming he's where his phone is, he's inside an old office complex scheduled for demolition."

Marla felt almost faint. "That's wonderful! Will you rescue him today?"

"Well, that takes us to the harder part. I can't share all of the details with you, but suffice it to say that I'm not able to bring the police into this."

"Well, how about your CIA people?"

"No can do; they can only act abroad."

"Then the FBI!"

"I'm sorry, Marla. I know this sounds totally wrong, but I can't bring them in, either. And anyway, from the building plans I've been able to get hold of, our best guess is that your father is locked up somewhere in the middle of the building – we can't say precisely where, because GPS isn't that accurate. If we have to engage while we go hunting for him, he could be killed before we can reach him."

"But you've got to do something!"

"Of course we do, and don't worry, I've got a plan together to do just that. It may take me a couple of days to pull things together, but it should work when everything is in place. To pull it off, I'll need your help, and maybe Josette's as well."

*   *   *

It was now day three, and Frank was climbing the walls. He'd already played all of the Sudoku puzzles, and was now occupying his mind by trying to make one up himself. It was a real pain in the ass.

The locks turned in the door, and Boss Man entered. How pitiful was this? Frank realized that he had been looking forward to taking dictation from a moron just to maintain sanity. Was this what they meant by the Stockholm Syndrome?

"Morning, Frankie. Ready to get to work?"

Frank said nothing, but accepted his laptop when it was offered to him.

"No tricks. I'll be watching."

Boss Man held out Frank's phone as usual. Frank tapped in his PIN, and a six digit number, two groups of three digits, obediently materialized. The phone was a bit far away, though, so he had to lean forward and squint to make the digits out. It was a line of six zeroes! Sure, any number was as possible as any other number, but still, the odds against a perfect string of any digit were astonishing.

"What's the problem?"

"Nothing. You need to hold the phone closer. It's hard to see."

Boss Man set the phone on the table next to Frank. "Okay, there you are. Now get typing."

Frank took his time typing his log-in address in on the laptop, curious to see what number would display next. He looked up just in time to see the number refresh – and be replaced by a string of zeroes once again. Okay, the odds against that were astronomical – it couldn't just happen. Had his access been canceled?

"I'm not going to ask you again, Adversego."

Well, okay, Frank thought, and typed in a string of zeroes. To his astonishment, the log-in worked.

"Okay, I'm in."

"Good boy. Now let's get to work." Boss Man moved to Frank's elbow and turned the laptop halfway in his own direction so he could be sure Frank wouldn't ad lib. "Open your email."

Frank opened his email, but his real attention was on his phone, waiting to see what the next number would display. This time it was 123456.

He tried not to show his elation, but he was sure someone must be trying to communicate with him. But who? And how?

He opened an email and pretended to read it, closed it, and pretended to read another while Boss Man read over his shoulder. Occasionally Boss Man would dictate a short non-committal response or tell him to delete or folder it. But all the while, Frank's mind was racing. For some time now, his phone had been alternating between two new sets of six digits. It had to be a code, but which one?

He guessed it would be one the sender thought he knew, and would also be likely to guess. But there were so many possible codes to choose from – ones that matched numbers to letters of famous sayings or the first lines of a poem, or to the frequency with which letters appeared in the English language. How would he be able to tell which one it was from just twelve numbers?

He searched for a clue in what little information was available to him. Which was what?

Well, if someone was trying to contact him, they knew he was in trouble. That meant that the phone message to George had reached him and allowed him to hear enough to tell that Frank was being kidnapped. Marchand had both the skills and the access to mess around with the token software, so he would be the sender.

But George wouldn't have any idea what simple code he might know, so he'd probably contact Marla, right? And Marla could suggest a code to him. They'd used a code to communicate with each other during his last exploit, but if George was using that one now, Frank was in trouble – it was simple to use with a pencil and paper, but complicated to work out in his head in real time while simultaneously answering his email. Had he and Marla ever played with simpler codes?

Then he remembered. When Marla was very young, they had enjoyed playing number games together, so he had introduced her to a simple code or two. The first was the simplest of all – 1 meant A, 2 meant B, and so on. It was cumbersome to use, but it was a system a six-year-old could easily handle, as long as she had a cheat-sheet to work from. He could try that one out.

He looked at the phone out of the corner of his eye and watched the two numbers cycle again: 715 209/200 000, over and over again, first one pair of three digit numbers, and then the other.

Without more spaces, how could he tell whether numbers next to each other were supposed to be one letter or two? 123 could be grouped as 1,2,3 to yield ABC, or as 1,23 to give AW, or as 12,3 to mean LC. He looked again at the first number. 715 could be either 7,1,5 or 7,15, but not 71,5, since there were only 26 letters in the alphabet. Did George mean GAE or GO? Which was it?

"Pay attention, Adversego."

He jerked back to attention. "Come again?"

"I said, reply and type 'Got it' to that one."

He did, and opened the next message. If he had a piece of paper and a pen – and wasn't doing two things at once – he'd know what the message said in a matter of seconds. All he'd have to do would be to write down the letters of the alphabet in one line and the numbers 1 – 26 below them. But now he had to count them out in his head, remember them, figure out which numbers were meant to be single digits and which double, and finally pick the winning combination before he ran out of email, which wouldn't be long now. He began to sweat heavily in the stale air of the small room.

He looked at the second block of three letters again: 209. That was easier. The 2 couldn't go with the 5 before it, because that would make 52. And 0 didn't apply to any letter, so he guessed the right way to read that triplet would be "20 9." That would spell "TO," Assuming that the 0 wasn't intended to indicate a space between words.

He waited for the number to change again. It read 200000. So all he had to figure out was whether the last letter in the message was indicated by the digit 2 or the number 20. Assuming he was using the right code, the rest of the zeroes were meaningless filler.

He fervently wished Boss Man would shut up as he tried to remember and sort through all of the possible variations he now had to work with.

First he tried making as many single digit letters as possible, and got:

7,1,5,20,9,2, or GAETIB

That was clearly nonsense.

He tried the next variation, combining the 1 and the 5 to get:

7,15,20,9,2, or GOTIB.

Damn! Nonsense again.

He reverted the 15 to 1, 5 and changed the 2 to 20, and got:

7,1,5,20,9,20, or GABIT

Shit! Did he get the code wrong? He thought there was only one variation left. That was:

7,15, 20,9, 20, which was GOTIT

Did that make any sense? If so, it sounded obscene.

Of course – 'Got it' worked. But if that was it, what did it mean?

"Are you listening to me?"

Yes! That was it! It was a question! The sender wanted him to let them know when he had cracked the code.

"Yeah, yeah, I'm listening. You're just boring me to death and I was daydreaming. What did you say again?"

His elation was cut short when he noticed that only a handful of emails remained to be reviewed. Whoever was signaling him must be expecting him to use the same code to reply. But how could he manufacture a need to enter a code again?

Then he had it. He was using his right hand to click down through his email, and his left hand was lying idle on the left side of the keyboard. He'd barely need to move the little finger on that hand to reach the tiny Wi-Fi switch on the side of his laptop.

With only two emails left to open, the email screen disappeared.

"What happened?" Boss Man said. "What did you do?"

"I didn't do anything. You must have a crappy Wi-Fi modem. Or maybe one of your goons is hogging the bandwidth streaming porn again." Boss Man gave Robin a dirty look.

"Try and log on again."

Frank secretly moved the Wi-Fi switch back to the on position. Thankfully, the log-on box was set to display asterisks rather than the actual digits he was typing, so although he made a show of looking at his phone, the number he actually typed was 25,5,19,0 – which meant "YES," the last zero being filler.

Like magic, the email screen leapt back into view.

"Alright, so it works – good. Now shut it down again. I've had enough of this crap for today."

Frank was exhausted and grateful when Boss Man and Robin left the room, leaving him and Guard Man alone once again. But now he was anything but bored. He had no idea yet how he was going to escape, but at least he could communicate now with someone on the outside who must be working towards that same goal.

*   *   *

43

Surprise!

I T HAD TAKEN two days, a lot of surreptitious switching on and off of his laptop's Wi-Fi receiver and some brain-bending, real-time deciphering, but at last Frank knew how he was going to escape. Or perhaps die trying.

The plan was disarmingly simple. All he needed to do was send the agreed-upon six number code when he'd been given permission to use the bathroom. When the guards on the outside and inside had unlocked the door, Marchand and his reinforcements would make their move.

It sounded simple, but Frank had no idea what they would be up against on the other side of the door. Was there a single guard outside, or many? Was his cell in a deserted building, or in the middle of the hacker's headquarters? He had no idea how many layers of defenses lay on the other side of his prison door, and hoped that Marchand did.

George did. But with only a few six digit messages a day to work with, he hadn't been able to spare any on that type of reassurance. Frank would just have to take it on faith that George wouldn't act unless he was sure his plan would work.

But could he? Sure, George was a good friend, but the stakes were high. He knew from his last adventure that if the government thought the next best thing to freeing him would be for him to be killed in the rescue attempt, it would be full speed ahead. George might not even be in control of the operation. Frank wasn't in a position to know that, either. And here he'd always thought that nothing could be worse than a dial-up modem.

By mid-morning, he was jittery and in a foul mood. Not only had Boss Man failed to materialize at the usual time for their daily email tryst, but Frank couldn't get the last corner of his Sudoku to work. Then he heard a rap at the door, and his guard stood up.

Frank tried to look bored, but inside he was all nerves.

"Okay, Frankie. Time to play Post Office again."

Frank grew edgier as they plodded through the tedious email triage process. Where was the ready to go signal from George? If it didn't come soon, Boss Man might decide to end the email session before it did.

At last, the all but impossible string of six zeros displayed. Holding his breath, he covertly flipped the Wi-Fi switch.

"Damn!" he said, pushing the laptop away. "Can't you get this frigging Wi-Fi to stay on?"

Boss Man shrugged. "Not my department."

"Yeah, well I've had it. And I've got to use the can, too."

"So sad. Finish off those last two messages first."

Frank's fingers trembled slightly as he moved the Wi-Fi switch to the on position, typed the response into the token app that would tell Marchand that he was ready, and then finished the final email replies that Boss Man dictated.

"Okay, that's it. Now open the damn door before I piss in my pants."

"Don't tempt me." But at the same time, Boss Man gave a nod to the guard.

Frank stood up slowly; he wanted as many bodies as possible between him and the door in case there was gunfire.

Frank's guard unlocked the door from the inside, and then rapped on it to summon the guard on the other side. But nothing happened. He rapped harder. Still no response. Frank felt like he must be visibly vibrating, but luckily no one was watching him.

Boss Man pushed the guard aside and banged on the door with his fist. Again they waited, and finally Frank heard footsteps coming towards the door.

"What the hell were you up to, asshole?" Boss Man yelled at the door as the outside lock clicked open. He threw the door open, and a blinding, shattering blast of light and thunder threw him backwards into the guard.

Frank hit the floor as instructed, and rolled under the table as the lights went out. Acrid smoke filled his lungs as shouts, thuds, and flashlight beams sweeping like light sabers filled the blackness of the room. He held on to the floor for dear life, half deaf and blind and wondering whether his side was winning or losing.

Someone shone a light in his face and grabbed him by the arm.

"Got him!" a voice behind the light yelled. Frank fervently hoped that it belonged to someone on his team.

It took him a moment to realize that the room had gone quiet. Still stunned, he was surprised to see when the lights popped back on that he was alone in a smoke-filled room with what looked like a giant insect. It helped Frank stand up, and then removed a large helmet, night-vision goggles, and a gas mask. His rescuer handed the last item to Frank.

"Here – let me help you get this on. Good. Take a couple deep breaths now. Good again. You okay to walk?"

Frank peered through two circles of tinted glass and nodded yes.

The smoke had mostly cleared by the time they reached the end of the hallway. He pulled the uncomfortable gas mask off, the better to appreciate the view of Boss Man, Robin and Guard Man spread-eagled against a wall. They were being frisked by the armored men that must have fired the stun grenade and then tackled Frank's suddenly stupefied keepers. He felt like he should stop to thank the rest of the SWAT team, but his escort took his arm.

"Come with me. There's some people waiting for you outside."

When they finally stepped out into the sunlight and fresh air, he was instantly engulfed by Marla in an interminable hug. A respectful distance behind her he saw George and, to his surprise, Josette.

"Thank goodness you're alright," Marla said. "You are alright, aren't you?"

"Yes, yes, I'm fine. Other than feeding me a lot of cold take-out food they treated me okay."

He pushed her away gently and held her at arm's length, his hands on her shoulders. Her face was streaked with tears.

"But how about you? Are you okay?"

She sniffed and wiped her eyes. "Of course I am." She turned and waved George over. "Now say thanks to George. Thank God he was there to help."

"Looks like I owe you one again, George."

"How you figure? I got you into this, didn't I?"

He noticed Frank glancing at Josette. "And you should thank Josette as well. You hadn't shared that much with Marla and me. She helped fill out the picture considerably."

Josette stepped forward, smiling uncertainly.

"So good to see you free again, Frank. But where is your laptop?"

He frowned. His laptop? Why should anyone care about that right now? But he answered anyway. "I don't know. George, did one of your men pick it up?"

"I'll find out." He and Josette walked over to where the SWAT team of Secret Service agents was bundling his former captors into an unmarked van.

Frank started to follow them, but Marla intervened with another hug; she looked like she hadn't slept in days. After a moment, Marchand returned and the SWAT team drove away.

"Nope, they don't have it. You want to give us a tour of your secret hideaway?"

Frank stiffened; maybe it was just the lingering impact of the stun grenade, but he really didn't want to. But he could hardly say no.

"Sure. If your money's good, I might even let you have it."

Marla took his hand as they walked through the deserted building, talking quickly about everything and nothing now that the tension of the last few days had been released.

The smoke had cleared, but the smell of explosives grew as they approached the room where Frank had been held prisoner. They found the guard's chair in pieces, the table shoved to a corner of the room, and the floor covered with magazines. But his laptop and phone were safe, still sitting on the table.

"So here you are. All the comforts of home, as long as you don't expect a home to have any comforts. There's a whole lot more space, now that my roommate has moved out. Better air quality, too, even taking the smoke into account."

Dropping his phone in his pocket, he scooped up his laptop and turned back towards the doorway. In it he saw Josette, and in her right hand he saw a gun. Once more, it was pointed at him. But this time she wasn't smiling.

"Frank, put the laptop down. Everyone put your hands on your heads."

"Come off it, Josette. Put your toy gun away. I want to get the hell out of here."

She put a bullet through the ceiling.

Frank stared at her, his jaw dropping slowly. Then he put the laptop back on the table and put his hands on his head.

"You will now each slowly take your phones out of your pockets, one at a time. George, you first."

George frowned, and then did as he was told.

"Kneel down and slide it across the floor to me."

Once more, George did as he was told. Josette kicked the phone out the door.

"Now you," Josette said nodding at Marla, and then to Frank.

"Now Frank – the laptop. Put it in the middle of the room."

What should he do? Try and tackle her? What would she do with them after she had what she wanted?

"Just do it," George said evenly, looking at Josette rather than Frank. "Don't try and be a hero. She knows she can't shoot all of us before we're on top of her, but she can shoot you."

"Do it," Josette said, her voice quavering.

But Frank wasn't ready yet. "Why are you doing this? What do you hope to gain?"

"A world other people can live in! If you stop the hackers, your stupid people will elect another fool to the White House."

"But what's my laptop got to do with it?"

"When I know what you know, I can make sure someone does not win that may drag the world into war and economic disaster again."

"You can't possibly! We'll just stop you."

"Will you? Didn't George tell you your administration is afraid to reveal that the primaries were a fraud? Why will that change now? You know I will not allow that imbecile Wellhead to win. Once your president wins, will he launch an investigation? I think not. Now put the laptop on the floor where I told you, and do it very slowly."

Frank licked his lips. At least he had a couple of weeks before the election to think what he could do. He put the laptop on the floor.

"Good. Now all of you – turn around and put your hands against the wall. Higher!"

The next thing they heard was the sound of the outside lock turning in the door. And then the sound of footsteps quickly disappearing into silence.

They turned around and looked at each other. Then George and Marla began to examine the meager contents of the room with renewed interest.

"So," Frank said with a sigh. "Do either of you like Sudoku?"

* * *

44

Anchors Aweigh

F RANK STARED AT the ceiling of his camper as it rocked from side to side. George had provided a driver to get him out of town at night, but he couldn't sleep.

It seemed crazy; now there were two teams trying to hack the election, and for all he knew, there could be more – apparently, Butcher had disappeared the same day that Frank had, so what the hell did that mean?

Worse, George had told him that the President's Chief of Staff still intended to do nothing. He knew Marchand would expect Frank to continue working to stop the real hacker, and that Josette was going to try to make sure that Wellhead didn't win. If somehow Wellhead or Yazzie won anyway, he could always "discover" the fraud then. The upshot was that nothing had changed; Frank and Marchand were still on their own.

In the few hours between their liberation from his cell and his being packed off in his camper, Frank hadn't even bothered to ask where he was being shipped off to. Some out-of-the-way cabin or campsite or desert or who knew where; he didn't really care. As long as it was somewhere where a couple of goons weren't likely to materialize out of nowhere to grab him it was all the same to him.

He closed his eyes and rolled over. Eventually, he even went to sleep.

* * *

George had thought long and hard about how best to motivate Frank to go all out to stop the election from being stolen. If there had been less at stake, he would have felt guilty for banishing him to the quietest place he could think of.

Better get on with it, he thought. He placed the call.

"Hey, Frank! How you doing?"

A grumpy voice replied.

"You'd know better than I would."

"What do you mean by that?"

"Where the hell am I?"

George looked at his watch.

"You should be on the ferry to Moose Haven. It's an island off the coast of Maine. My family used to go there when I was a kid."

"I've never heard of it."

"That's the idea. Most people haven't. It's a pretty out of the way place."

So out of the way that the ferry made only a few runs a week in the off season. Frank didn't need to know that yet.

"You should be really safe there. Your driver left a map on the passenger seat after he drove the camper onto the boat. All you've got to do is follow the directions and you'll find a cottage we rented. The key will be under the door mat. And we've got your camper stocked with everything you'll need until after the election. You won't have to go into town if you don't want to."

"So at least there's a town?"

"Well, maybe not in so many words." George hurried on. "We also set the false location program on your camper to show that you were heading for the Great Smoky Mountains. Everything was going just fine until you tragically fell asleep behind the wheel last night and ran off a cliff. I'm afraid you didn't survive the impact. The police report has already been filed."

"But –"

"Don't worry. There won't be any publicity." He paused; now came the delicate part.

"And we've made sure that all your electronic gear is tuned up and working perfectly."

Silence.

"Frank?"

"I'm not feeling so well. This boat is rocking like hell."

George frowned. Perhaps this wasn't the best time to discuss next steps.

"Why don't you step out and get some fresh air? I'll check back in later. Bye now."

He hung up before Frank could reply.

*　*　*

Richard Fetters was wracked with indecision. His grand design was in peril. Yazzie continued to surge in the polls, and Fetters hadn't been able to come up with a shred of dirt to pin on him, or a credible plan to entrap him.

It didn't end there. Butcher had said that White Crow knew which telephone app Fetters was using to influence the voting, but not how it worked. What if Adversego had found that out, too, and communicated it before he disappeared? And even if White Crow didn't know all the details yet, he could hire his own hacker to figure the rest out. Should he try to head that off by reconnecting with White Crow and negotiating some sort of deal?

But what? It turned his stomach even to consider it, but perhaps he should offer Yazzie the Vice Presidency. Better to gain the White House first and figure out how to get rid of both Yazzie and Wellhead second.

And what about Adversego? Had he not only figured out how the app hack worked, but how to thwart it as well? Fetters had learned of the tragic "accident;" even seen pictures of a smashed camper with the right license plate. But anyone could Photoshop a picture. He wasn't prepared to believe the police report until one of his people heard it straight from the coroner who signed the death certificate.

Fetters had assigned one of his staff to supervise his team of hackers. He called him now and spent the next hour interrogating him. He wanted to know every detail of the steps they were taking to ward off any attempt to outflank them on Election Day.

*　*　*

White Crow stood at the one-way window in his office, staring at the Casino floor but oblivious to what he saw. He had been standing there for a long time.

Butcher had been his only contact at the agency, and his pawn had vanished. He cursed himself for burning his bridges with Fetters before he had all the information he needed. His arrogance was responsible for his predicament, and now it was his pride that was keeping him there. Should he contact Fetters and try to work something out?

He turned away from the window. It was likely too late for that. He'd hired an investigator to look for this Adversego person, but time was short. Whether he'd really died in his camper or evaporated as effectively as Butcher, the result was the same. Could Fetters have been behind both disappearances? What the hell was going on?

He would need to work fast. He'd seen Butcher's out of office message on the phone he'd taken from him. He would use Butcher's email account to spoof his assistant and ask for all reports from Adversego. And he would need to find and hire some hackers as quickly as possible to work with whatever information he had or could get. That would be risky; he wouldn't really know what he was doing, and he had very little time to learn. But he had no choice.

* * *

Josette, feeling rather like Liberty Leading the People in the iconic Delacroix painting, was preparing to rally a select few of the Filles de Lafayette once again to the cause of liberté, égalité and fraternité. She had made a strategic decision to be less than fully forthright with them. After all, in the primaries, the plan had been only to incentivize sensible voters to get out and vote, not to defraud them when they did.

Her call would be limited to those who were expert programmers. She would tell them that it was Wellhead who planned to steal the election, although for now that could only be a guess.

She would not tell them that someone else was already working to stop the election from being stolen, or that the information she gave them came from a laptop she had stolen from him. And she would certainly not tell them that she would use their work to turn the election herself, rather than disclosing the solution to the American authorities.

Hopefully they would believe her. But it would be fine if they did not, so long as they were content to play along as if they did. It was acceptable if they wished to preserve the ability to later claim that they were shocked to learn that she had never disclosed the solution to the authorities at all. If that was the role that destiny had assigned to her, then she would stand at the barricades alone.

* * *

45

Maine: It's the Way Life Should Be

F RANK WAS RUNNING along a muddy dirt road, condensed fog dripping thick as rain on his head from the weeping spruce limbs overhead. He'd been on this blasted island for two whole days now, and hadn't seen the sun yet.

He still hadn't set foot in the cottage. Instead, he had stayed in his familiar camper, parked at the edge of the sea, peering into thick, impenetrable mist, and foraging through his cupboards for food that appealed to him amid the goods that were someone else's idea of a normal diet.

Marchand tried to contact him twice a day, but he ignored his calls. After all, there were dozens and dozens of secret agencies out there besides Voldemort. There must be someone else who could take it from here.

He was also more wounded that he cared to admit by Josette's betrayal. Yes, he'd been well aware that first and foremost she cared about her cause. But still, it confirmed how totally she had seen him as no more than a convenient means to an end. The gun pointed squarely at his face had made that point rather convincingly.

At the end of his sodden run, he leaned against the camper to catch his breath. There must be something on this island to do, he thought. After his shower he'd go back to the ferry dock and see what the tiny town had to offer.

The answer, he found an hour later, was that it did not offer much. There was a motel, and across from it a paper store, outside of which a tall man wearing red suspenders was surreptitiously replacing the store's neat sign with a crudely lettered one that read "Carla's Cat House."

He wondered what the hell that was all about and motored slowly up the street.

Thankfully there was a more than adequate market. His spirits rose considerably as he toured its aisles and tossed easy to prepare items into his cart. Now if the damn fog would just lift.

After the market, there were a few shops, a couple of small restaurants open only a few nights a week at this time of year, and a bar and grill that was open every night. He assumed that if he showed up in any of them during the off season he'd stick out like a blue lobster.

A half-hour later, he was parking back in front of the locked up cottage after driving down every paved road on the island.

He was still staring at the ever present fog when the phone rang. With a groan, he saw that it was George – again. On the last ring before it cut over to his message service he grabbed it.

"Okay. You win. But if you gloat I'll hang up."

George gave a silent prayer of relief. "I'd never gloat, Frank. But I do need your help very badly."

Secretly, Frank felt relieved. Besides being bored, he didn't want whoever it was that was trying to steal the election to think they had gotten the better of him. And he certainly didn't want Josette to.

"Don't mention it. Is there anything new I need to know?"

"Nothing from our end. The polls are showing Yazzie ahead now, which is a bit of a surprise."

"Why's that?"

"Well, that would make you think that Yazzie's people are behind the hack. But I don't think so."

"So again, why?"

"Because for a few days, we were picking up some pretty clumsy traffic coming from one of the reservations out west. Someone was visiting dark sites trying to hire some hackers for a rush project. But they didn't look like they really knew what they were doing, or how to hide their tracks, either."

"Interesting. Could you tell whether they hooked up with anyone?"

"Inconclusive. All we know is that they stopped looking for help. And then of course there's Josette. What do you think her chances are of manipulating votes?"

Frank had spent a lot of time thinking about that.

"Well, she has my phone; she has my laptop; and I assume you told her about the security token app. If she was in the room while you and Marla were faking the token numbers, she would have seen you type my PIN number in as well.

"All she had to do was check my email before we changed my token software, and she'd immediately find the detailed report I sent to Voldemort right before I was nabbed. That's why she wanted my laptop, and she had plenty of time to hunt around while we were locked up in that damned room. Josette always thought that Butcher, or someone he was working for, was trying to hack the election, too. Since he disappeared around the same time, we have to assume that she was right, and that he also has my report. Last of all: if Butcher was using me to figure out what was going on, there's still whoever it was that hacked the game app to begin with."

George felt defeated. Three sets of hackers? "I guess it doesn't matter, as long as there's even one guy out there who can control the game app."

"Not so. The more teams there are competing for the same prize, the more strategies I need to figure out and beat. If they think I'm still out here, they'll be trying to stop me from doing that. And even if they believe I'm dead, they'll worry about the other teams. Assuming I can come up with a good blocking mechanism, one of them may very well come up with a way to control the app that keeps my strategy from working. I might think that I'm in total control, but I'd be kidding myself. This whole thing's like a game of Blind Man's Bluff, except that everyone is wearing a blindfold. We'll all be stumbling around, not really knowing where the other players are, or what they're up to. Nobody will know whether they're winning or losing until the election results are announced."

"So what's your plan to get around that?"

"Good question. I don't have an answer for that yet."

"There's less than two weeks left, Frank. That's all we've got. Let me know any time if there's anything I can do to help. Anything at all."

"Great. Call up the *New York Times* and tell them what's going on. Then I can come home."

"Other than that, Frank. Keep in touch."

*   *   *

Frank was feeling both pleased and unhappy. Pleased, because he had solved half of the problem that needed to be solved. And unhappy because he had decided he needed help on the other half. For starters, he needed George to find him a really crackerjack hacker, and it had taken some explaining to get him on board.

"Yeah, I guess I can do that," Marchand said. "But why? Don't you think you can figure this out on your own?"

"Of course I do! The problem is that I need to know how a hacker would do it. And fast!"

"Why?"

"Because I've got as many as three opponents out there who are all trying to pull off the same trick! Before I can come up with a way to beat them, I need to know what it is I've got to beat. I want someone who can not only guess what they'll do, but also go look for evidence to see if he's right. That way I can spend all my time staying ahead of them."

"Point taken."

"Great. So how quickly can you get me a top of the line black hat?"

"I hate to sound like a broken record, but since I'm on my own here, I can't use the usual CIA resources. But I do remember a guy I helped put in jail a few years ago. He ought to be up for his first parole hearing soon, and he could use a friend. I'll get back to you."

That sounded promising. In the meantime, Frank had a little programming to do at his end. He had solved the blind man's bluff problem as soon as he realized that he'd been using the wrong game metaphor. The right one was rock, paper, scissors: the children's game where each player threw their hand out making the sign of one of the three objects in the name: a rock – which could beat the scissors by breaking it; a scissors – which could defeat the paper by cutting it; or paper, which could best the rock by covering it. And so on. Any choice could be beaten by one of the remaining two options, so you could only win through luck, or by psyching out your opponent. There were only so many ways to manipulate the vote, and all of the hackers would be trying to guess the approaches the others planned to use, knowing that each of them would be doing the same thing.

Frank's big revelation had been that he didn't have to join that game. Not only was he not desperate to ensure that his candidate won a specific vote using the game app – he didn't need to care whether the game app cast a vote at all. That gave him a trump card none of his opponents could afford to use themselves.

All he needed to know was whether or not a vote was about to be cast the way the phone owner had intended. If not, he would crash the program. Then the owner of the phone would have to vote the old fashioned way. And no one could question the integrity of a vote cast that way after the election.

That left him feeling quite comfortable. How hard could it be to freeze a single app? Microsoft had been crashing entire computers for decades.

* * *

46

The Countdown

F RANK WANTED TO think that everything was under control, but he wasn't feeling that way. It was only a week until Election Day, and George's hacker, Marty, still hadn't delivered. Every additional hour Frank had to wait was one less he could use to confirm that he was on the right track with his part of the plan.

Normally, he tried to work exclusively by email. People seemed to be wired differently than he was in subtle ways. When he interacted face to face, everything he said seemed to come across as a non sequitur, even to his own ears. Email gave him time to think and the power to keep the exchange tied to questions and answers, and facts and figures.

This time, though, he needed to see how something was being said, as well as get information interactively – and fast. Plus, he had no way of knowing whether he could trust the hacker Marchand had put in jail. Maybe misleading Frank would mean more to him than getting a good word said on his behalf to the parole board. Frank needed as much data as possible to decide whether that might be the case. So he'd asked George to set up a regular Skype call for him with the hacker. The first one hadn't gone as planned.

That was because Frank realized at the last minute that he had no idea where his snap-on video camera had gotten to. So when the call came through, he saw a scrawny, squinting, twenty-something in a prison uniform, and Marty saw only a blank screen.

"So where are you, dude?"

"Hey, I'm really sorry. I thought I had a clip-on video camera for my laptop, but I can't find the damn thing."

"Ha! As if. So we're playing some games today, huh?"

"No – really. I looked for it everywhere I could think of. I'll try really hard to find it before our next call."

The reedy voice in Frank's headphones gave a snort. "Whatever. So what's with this game app anyway? Why does anybody care about breaking into it?"

One minute into the call, and already he was on the defensive. Better to tell the truth – or half of it, anyway – rather than pretend he didn't know.

"I'm sorry. I'd like to be able to tell you, but I can't."

Another snort. "Like I could give a shit anyway. All I really want is get out of this hole as soon as I can."

That sounded more promising. "I'm sure this'll help. I'll certainly speak up for you if you help me out. Anyway, what approach have you taken so far?"

"The obvious one. Why not? It was easy – they must have a bunch of newbies for security architects."

"Not that we'll complain," Frank said.

"Yeah. So anyway, all I had to do was log in as a new user, play a game, and send my score upstairs to the main server. It went straight through an open port. Can you believe that? When you log on to their server, it opens a port to receive your score, and it just stays open for as long as you're playing. What a bunch of A-Holes!"

Frank would have chosen a different word, but he couldn't disagree. With an open port to work with, a hacker could come and go as often as he wanted.

"So you'll just keep using the open port?"

"Naw, I closed it for them. I figured whatever you're up to, you don't want anyone else messing it up. So I changed their program to open a port whenever a registered user logs on, and close as soon as the log-in is complete. It'll keep opening for the same user, and no one else, whenever he has a score to enter, and that's it. Then I put in a really hard to find backdoor for us."

"Good thinking. That takes care of things going forward. But we think one or more black hats has already hacked the app. I'm assuming they've installed their own back doors, so one of the things I'd like you to do is hunt for them and let me know what you find. When one of them does use their back door, I want to monitor it."

"Cool. Cat and mouse. That works for me."

"And I also want you to check out the near field communications controls – you know, the NFC radio."

"What for? Does the game connect to something local?"

Frank was ready with a misleading but credible answer for that.

"No, but just about every phone out there has an NFC chip now. And a lot of apps are about to start using an NFC signal to do other things, like initiating the withdrawal process at ATMs."

Marty's face lit up. "Awesome! I've been waiting for this whole digital wallet thing to finally take hold!"

"Well, it is. And we think someone's going to try and use this app to intercept payment app NFC signals. It's a lot less obvious than hacking the payment app itself."

"I get it! Just like a sniffer. Wow – I could make someone do a cash transfer to my account when they thought they were making a deposit to their own! Man, I can't wait to get outta here!"

"Whoa Marty – first things first. What we want is to figure out a way to prevent people like you from doing just that. So here's what I want you to do next."

* * *

47

Rock, Paper, Scissors

I T WAS OCTOBER 31. With the election only a few days away, Frank was sitting in front of his laptop – now with the video camera attached – waiting for a Skype call with Marty. His fingers were drumming against his stomach like the legs of a dog having its stomach rubbed. Time was running out.

Finally the call came through, and Marty's smirking face lit up the screen. Frank was about to say hello, when the hacker's eyes suddenly squinted. Then his face zoomed in to the screen, eyes widening. Frank pulled back involuntarily.

"Say! You're the dude that shot down the North Korean missiles!"

"Well, not exactly."

"Somebody just gave me your book! I read the whole thing last night! Hey, man, it's really cool to be working with you!"

His book! He'd forgotten all about it. Or more accurately, he'd been ignoring it. He was still queasy about the manuscript Grover had shown him. For weeks he'd been filing every email his co-writer, his agent, and his publisher had been sending him without opening them. Suddenly he was happy to be in hiding on an island 14 miles off the coast of Maine.

"Say, would you send me a signed copy of your book?"

"Sure – absolutely. And thanks. But hey, I'm in kind of a hurry, so let's talk about the game app, okay? Are we good to go there?"

Marty was now eager to impress. "Absolutely. Here's what I did...."

He launched into a long and technical explanation, with Frank nodding and tapping away at the keys, taking notes as Marty walked him through everything he'd accomplished since their last call. From time to time Frank interrupted, asking him to fill in the details where he'd skipped past something, or testing the hacker's assumptions, or asking him if he'd considered potential weaknesses in the approach. It all seemed to hold together.

"That's cool, Marty. Really nice job."

But Marty wasn't quite done yet.

"So hey – you know how you asked me to keep my eye out for anyone else trying to hack the same program? Well you wouldn't believe it! They're going ape shit in there! Everybody's trying to plant something the other guys can't find while blocking what they find. It's wild – like some kind of hacker sitcom! You want me to join in the fun?"

"No, I think we're good if we just stick to the original plan." Frank suddenly remembered the grainy, Photoshopped picture George had sent him of his camper at the bottom of a ravine.

"In fact, it's pretty important that nobody knows that we're doing anything at all – or that you even know me. As long as we can shut down that radio when we want to, that's good enough. That, and planting the code I sent you where they'll never look for it. I want you to leave the smallest number of tracks possible."

"Works for me. They're going crazy playing their games against each other and don't even know they're doomed. What a hoot!"

"Right. So the bottom line is that I need to know that any time I want to, I can send the host site an order to tell the game apps not to send an NFC signal, and also that our command can override any directions from anywhere else to the contrary. So are we good to go with that?"

Marty smiled but said nothing.

"Uh, do you have something else to tell me, Marty?"

"Yeah. The answer to your first question is yes, except for one little detail. The command will only work for one hour."

Where could this be going? "Okay, I guess there's something to say for not having a permanent override. If it goes on too long, someone would be more likely to figure out something was going on."

Marty was starting to giggle now.

"Something else?"

"Yeah. One more little thing, dude. You can only give the command at the same time you're reporting a new high game score for the day."

"What? Why?"

"How much do you expect for just 'a good word at my parole hearing?' Go test out what I just told you, and when you see it works just like I said, we can talk again. But when we do, be ready to tell me the warden's ready to let me walk. Do that, and you'll get the full key."

"That wasn't the deal!"

"Course not! A deal takes two sides, not one. Your offer gets you one hour at a time. My offer gets you permanent control. Deal?"

Frank was speechless.

"And don't get any fancy ideas about finding the code you asked me to plant – the code that would really tell the app whether or not to block the radio. If you keep racking up the high scores, it'll keep running fine, but I hid it where you'll never find it. And if you did, and tried to change or remove it, it'll send a blast of intrusion warnings to the security admin he couldn't ignore even if he was asleep at his keyboard. Same thing if you try to install your software yourself with an override module. "

"But we don't have any control over your sentence! All we can do is speak on your behalf in a month!"

"So you keep saying. When you're ready to make a deal, you know where to find me. Meanwhile, Trick or Treat!"

* * *

"So I don't know why I even called you, but I'll ask anyway. Can you cut a deal for him?"

Silence.

Frank continued, "Okay, shall we say it together? 'Sorry Frank, but there's nothing I can do?' Am I right?"

"I'm sorry Frank, but nothing's changed. Do you have an idea?"

"Not one I'm very wild about."

"What's the one you're not?"

"Get real good at Cavalry and Indians before Tuesday."

"Are you serious? Is that the best you can do?"

"It's not as harebrained as it sounds. The whole game has to do with trajectories. In the real world of three dimensions and wind, that's super complicated, but here it's just a matter of figuring out what two-dimensional elevation works best at each cycle of the game. And the target window is always really small. I've started writing a program that just keeps playing the game, firing incrementally higher at each cycle until it nails it, and then goes on to the next cycle till it's got that one, and so on. Nothing fancy like a real artificial intelligence program, because I don't have time to write one. Just repetitious trial and error, like a password cracking program. Unless you get access for me on a super computer I can't speed up the game, but there should still be time if I get started soon."

"Really."

"Well, that's all I've – we've – got. Anyway, once I've got all the data I need, all I have to do is reverse the process, and feed the same data back into the game controller. That part's a little tricky, but it's still just programming, and I can do that piece while it's cranking away on trajectories."

"So you're telling me that the election of the next leader of the free world is going to depend on whether you can build a better fourteen year old?"

"Something like that. Got any better ideas?"

"You don't want to hear me say it again, do you?"

"Right."

"Then I guess I'd better let you get to work."

"Right again."

"Then good luck, Frank. Here's hoping you can do it."

* * *

Someone walking up the long dirt driveway to Frank's unoccupied cottage over the next few days would have heard a constant stream of war whoops, bugle calls and bellowing ruminants emanating from the camper parked by the ocean. It wouldn't matter whether it was night or day; the only difference would be that at night the camper glowed with flashing colors.

Anywhere else, such a person might have been surprised. But not here. Everyone on the island knew that people from Away were strange.

* * *

Election Day was rapidly approaching, and Frank was getting nervous. There was so much riding on him, and he had so little to work with – including any way to know for sure what the opposition would do on Election Day. He was also fretting over his lack of a back-up plan. What if one of the other teams found out what he was up to, or just came up with a more clever plan than he had?

What indeed? Marty continued to assure him that everything was fine. But he also refused to budge on telling Frank how to get past the one-hour refresh requirement, and it was too late for Frank to figure out a way around it on his own. Anyway, he had no reason to doubt Marty's claim that his code was booby-trapped – it would be too easy to do.

With nothing else to distract him, Frank had started playing Angry Indians/

Angry Cavalry as soon as he arrived on the island. He'd never been a gamer, so at first he only fooled around with it to kill time. But it wasn't long before his anxiety over Election Day made him compulsive. By his third day there, he was playing it almost non-stop whenever he wasn't working. Now he was trying (unsuccessfully) to beat his robot program. He was rationally relieved but irrationally pissed off that so far he hadn't.

That ambivalence evaporated by the second to last day before the election, because his robot program was starting to bog down. The problem was that every time the robot made it to a new level, it was confronted with a more complex situation, with more target elements, more randomness, and more defenses. That meant the program had to test at least an order of magnitude more alternatives each time it graduated to a new level, and now it seemed to be making no discernible progress at all. What if it didn't make it far enough to maintain control all day when it really mattered?

With no time left to switch strategies, all he could do was try to get better at the game than his program did.

Like the program, he'd made good progress and then leveled off. After most of a sleepless night spent wracking his brains for some way to accelerate his progress, he invested a couple of hours adapting his game controller to interact with a virtual reality helmet he had lying around. His hope was that immersing himself more completely in the game space would give him an added edge over anyone else playing on what he had begun to think of as VE Day dawned. Assuming he didn't throw up first.

Happily, his guess proved to be true; his skills began improving again. He had made it to the eighth level several times, which was one tier above where the robot was still laboring away.

He was taking a break to let his reeling head return to its normal configuration when there was a tap on the camper door. Who in the world could that be? No one was supposed to know where to find him.

To his delight, it was Marla.

"How did you know where to find me?"

"From George, of course."

"I'm surprised he told you. Wasn't he afraid someone might follow you?"

"It's possible I might have promised him I wouldn't come here. But don't worry. I was more than careful leaving Washington. And when I got to Maine, I spent the morning window shopping and then ran on the ferry at the last possible second. Nobody got on after me, and there won't be another boat till the day after the election."

He bet there were lobstermen who'd take a passenger across for the right price. But there was nothing to be done about it now, and he was starting to get anxious again.

"It's great to see you and I'd love to catch up, but I've got to put this helmet back on and practice as much as possible before Election Day."

"Of course you do. But might I ask what, and why?"

"Oh. Right. So…" He brought her up to date. "Anyway, I can't stand more than a couple more hours inside this helmet. There are a couple of restaurants in town, so let's talk then. Meanwhile, there should be a key under the doormat of the cottage, so why don't you make yourself comfortable there."

Marla would have asked another question, but he had already disappeared into the helmet, and now resembled a futuristic storm trooper. One glance around the rat's nest of the camper's interior persuaded her to take his advice.

*   *   *

It wasn't far to town and the ever-present fog had finally lifted, so a somewhat wobbly Frank suggested they walk to dinner. Except for his morning run, he hadn't left his camper since his first trip into town. Now he was startled to see how beautiful his surroundings were. The weathered shingles of the fish houses perched at the ends of stone and timber wharves gleamed a pearly gray in the last light of the setting sun, and the fleet of lobster boats swinging in the wind at their moorings like synchronized swimmers completed the classic picture of a Down East fishing community.

Main Street was mostly quiet when they arrived; the handful of stores and the post office were already closed, but the bar and grill was jumping. One of the two restaurants was open, and only half full. They took a quiet table there.

"How's the food here?" Marla asked.

"No clue. But I'm expecting it to be cooked and not right out of a can. I can't wait.

"So what's happening with the election?" he continued. "I haven't been keeping in touch."

"Not much new since you left, really. Nobody knows what to make of a real three-way race. The pundits keep saying nowhere near as many people will vote for Yazzie on Election Day as the polls indicate. But a lot of people aren't so sure."

"Maybe the pundits are right. After all, you and I know you can chuck the polls if the hacker is still in control."

Marla shook her head. "But if that's so, I don't understand why he's keeping the three front runners so close together? Why doesn't he show his candidate pulling ahead?"

"Good question. Maybe the poll hacker's candidate is actually pretty far behind. There are only so many votes the game app can control, so maybe pulling off anything more than a squeaker of a victory is beyond their power."

"I guess that would make sense," Marla acknowledged. "Anyway, we don't have long to wait to find out."

When their dinner arrived, Frank wolfed his down, and fidgeted until Marla was done. Then he insisted they head back to the camper so he could disappear once more into his virtual race with parabolic destiny.

* * *

Meanwhile, Randall Wellhead was puddle-jumping around the country in his private campaign jet, making last minute stops wherever Fetters thought it might make the biggest difference. Ironically, Fetters was now desperate to garner as many legitimate votes for his candidate as possible. Wellhead was still blissfully ignorant of how the election would actually be decided, as he was about most matters of importance. He was having a great time, smiling, hand-shaking, and, as much as possible, keeping his mouth shut.

Fetters, on the other hand, was busy doing what he had been ever since he learned from Butcher that White Crow was falsifying the poll numbers: scanning endlessly through multiple sets of numbers – downloads of the game app, downloads of voting apps, and projections of voter turnouts by Congressional district and party affiliation. Would they all align well enough to allow his candidate to win?

And was it all just a fool's errand, anyway? He'd been hounding his hackers unmercifully to watch out for other black hats. But he had no way to tell what was really going on, since he was communicating through the same layers of intermediaries he had maintained from the beginning in order to cover his tracks. Certainly his hackers were gouging him unmercifully on their fees. Whether they were really fending off multiple opponents or simply fabricating that story to extract ever higher payments was just one more thing he had no way of confirming.

If they were being straight with him, there were *two* other teams of hackers going at the game app. Could that really be true? If so, and if Adversego really had been killed in an accident, who could the third team be? Was the President of the United States hacking elections now? What was the world coming to?

* * *

White Crow was on a rare trip away from the reservation, taking up temporary residence in the same hotel the Yazzie campaign had chosen for its election night activities. He had rented two adjacent rooms, one for himself, and the second as a war room he had filled with tables, computers and a large wall monitor that would provide a live video link to the crew of Uzbeki hackers he was relying on to outfox the competition and bring his own candidate across the finish line in first place. His assistants had moved all of the original furniture from the war room into his sleeping room, where he could now barely move.

The report he had spoofed out of Voldemort had been very helpful, but he would have liked to feel more confident than he did. Amazingly enough, the real poll numbers – the ones only he had access to —showed that Yazzie's message was connecting ever more powerfully with the voters as their disgust with business as usual politics continued to build.

Nor was that all. Despite the best efforts of his handlers to contain him, Wellhead had made enough new gaffes to leave many conservatives privately aghast. Turnout predictions in hundreds of red state districts were waning as a result. At the same time, the Republicans had succeeded in convincing the voters that most of the blame for the country's numerous woes should be placed on the President, causing the slide in his popularity to continue unchecked.

Truly, the nation seemed to be poised on the edge of a defining moment in the grand narrative of the American experience, with the presidency of the United States tantalizingly within reach of a Native American.

But only if the Cavalry didn't wipe out the Indians. Some things never seemed to change.

* * *

Josette and her fellow *filles* were hunkered down in their respective apartments, in constant communication online. The last two weeks had been exhausting as each hacker team played hide and seek – and seek and destroy – with its opponents. Each was forced to continually update its strategy as it discovered, and was discovered in turn. And what about Frank? He must be plotting to foil them all.

Lately it had taken on the dynamic of an eBay auction, with each team plotting its last and final bid in secret. What would the other teams do on Election Day? There would be no way to tell until tomorrow arrived.

* * *

48

Frank Hits the Beach

F RANK OPENED THE scoring page of the Cavalry and Indians game site and stared at the tiny numbers in the bottom corner of his laptop screen. In just a few minutes, it would be 7:00 AM, Eastern Standard Time, and the big game would be on. Had he thought of everything? Had he left anything to chance? What if he had?

Marla had made his bed for him; the smooth surface of the blanket floated calmly amid the chaotic mess inside the camper like an ice floe riding serenely on a stormy sea. Frank had set his computer to display four separate news feeds on his muted, flat panel TV. Its surface resembled the side of an ant farm, bustling with the activity of tiny, silent figures going about their daily tasks.

With only seconds before the top of the hour, Frank was relieved to see that the current high score was still low. The game vendor broke the day into multiple contest periods: midnight to noon, Eastern Standard Time, noon to 6:00 PM, and then two game periods for the busy after school and evening hours: 6:00 PM to 8:00 PM and 8:00 PM to midnight. Each time a period ended, the top three scorers were awarded points that counted towards their over-all game ranking. Then the scoreboard was reset to zero, and the process began again.

The first few hours of the morning would be the first important test of the day as people voted on their way to work. Frank had considered letting these hours go by without interference, worried that early reports of phones failing to register votes would start hitting the news. That might tip his hand to one or more of his opponents, giving them an opportunity to figure out how to respond. But it would also mean that enough invalid votes would be registered to taint – and maybe even lose – the election. In the end, he decided he couldn't take the chance.

A few days before, he had contacted Marty to say that he could finally reveal, in great confidence, additional information regarding what the project was all about. He told him that months before, the CIA had picked up terrorist chatter indicating that rival terrorist groups were competing to launch a major assault against ATMs on Election Day. These were the groups Marty had been observing as they fought for the glory of causing confusion and disrupting the election – and also for the millions of dollars that would be diverted to the winner's coffers when it succeeded in controlling the game app. He also informed the hacker that he'd arranged with the warden to make Marty available all day and into the evening via a live video link to keep Frank informed about what the opposition might be up to.

It was still one minute to 7:00 AM. To stay in control, he needed to be totally engrossed for several minutes at the top of each hour until the polls closed. But in between, he would have nothing to do but fidget, run the same tests on the robot he'd run a hundred times before, and pray: pray that the scores of innocent gamers would never exceed the robot's capabilities before the last voting stations closed; pray that none of the other teams would discover what he was up to; pray that none of them simply got lucky and made a change in their own interest that inadvertently screwed up his own hack; and pray that his brain didn't explode.

At last the alarm on his computer went off, as it would every hour for the rest of the day. Time to go into action. He ordered the robot to begin playing, and in less than a minute its score was high enough to win. He instructed it to fire the next hapless cow into the ground, thereby avoiding driving the score up for no reason. Then he immediately commanded it to report its score, as well as fire the phone control message in the split second after its score was paired to its player ID on the game site. He looked at the clock on the screen: 7:01. Success, he hoped.

Now what would he do with himself for the next hour? He'd already drunk a pot of coffee, but he started to make another. While he did, Marla turned up the sound on the TV. The ten civically minded adults of Dixville Notch, New Hampshire had as always cast the first votes of the election – using paper ballots – just after midnight. And as usual, they announced the results: Yazzie had edged the competition by one vote each. That gave the talking heads something to talk about for the first few minutes of their broadcasts. Because exit polling was no longer permitted, this would be the last reliable data anyone would get until the first state closed its voting stations at 8:00 East Coast time that night.

Of course, that didn't stop any of the pundits from nattering on endlessly. He clicked through the various stations, each of which was rehashing the run-up to Election Day from its own particular point of view. For the liberal channel, that meant recapping the amazing rise of Henry Yazzie. A panel of self-appointed experts who had never heard of the Native American candidate ten months before were opining authoritatively on what a Yazzie administration would be like, despite the fact that they had no more insight on that topic than a pack of Labrador retrievers.

Over on the network channel, the smiling cabal of morning news people was working the crowd on the street, shoving microphones across a barricade and asking anyone that wasn't too busy yelling "Hi Mom!" who they thought would win. Some even knew the names of all three candidates.

Over on POX News, the anchors were running archival footage of the truly incredible number of ways the President had already doomed this once-great nation to the ash heap of history. It was clear that if he were to win a second term life as we know it would cease to exist at the precise moment when the last polling station closed.

Frank put on his virtual screen helmet, as much to escape the nonsense of the real world as to practice his game. It was going to be a long, long day.

*   *   *

He had just ordered the robot program to send in the 10:00 AM signal when he got a call from George.

"We're getting the first reports of voters having trouble with their voting apps."

"Hmmm – that didn't take long. I was hoping we'd get a few more hours before the news people caught wind of it."

"News people? Haven't you ever heard of social media?"

"Oh. Right. Anyway, that's fantastic news. It means our strategy is working."

"What do you think the opposition is doing about it right now?"

"I'm hoping nothing, yet. I'm hoping they'll be too busy to pay attention to the news. But if they have heard, I think first they'll want to try and make sense of what should be pretty conflicting and vague reports. Remember that the voting app will work fine if a vote isn't changed, so that ought to confuse them. If we're lucky, the next thing they'll think is that it's a glitch in the voting apps themselves. After all, this is the first election where they've been used at a national level, and they didn't have any way to put their servers under this much stress until people actually started voting."

"Makes sense. Then what?"

"After that, I'm banking on them thinking they somehow screwed up the voting app themselves, with all the unanticipated messing around they've been doing trying to edge each other out. It would be great if they just started madly searching through the game app to check their own work to make sure they didn't leave a pair of forceps in the patient."

"Here's hoping. I'll let you know when I hear anything new."

Frank checked the time. It was only ten past the hour. Why not check in with Marty?

The hacker looked worried when his face popped up on the screen.

"What are you seeing?" Frank asked.

"Nothing – I think they're stunned. I don't see any changes being made at all, but I bet they're going nuts trying to figure out what's happening. Say – I've got a special, one day only offer for you! For five years off my sentence, I'll fix it so you don't have to grab control every hour!"

Frank would have dearly loved to take him up on the offer, but he knew he couldn't deliver. "Sorry – no can do."

"C'mon! You can't blame a guy for trying to work with what he's got. How about four? Four years off! That's my final offer!"

"Sorry, Marty. And I gotta go now."

Marty had just time enough to yell, "Think about it!" as Frank disconnected.

Marla laughed. "He must think you're a lot better poker player than you really are."

"Yeah, I'm sure he expected us to fold yesterday. Tough luck for us both I couldn't."

Finally, it was a minute to eleven. He looked at the current high game score; it was still in the low level seven range.

* * *

Richard Fetters was as close to raising his voice as he had ever been since he entered the political world. At the other end of the phone, his hacker supervisor was wishing that for once his boss would start screaming, because the intensity of the animosity in his voice was frightening. He couldn't help imagining himself as some sort of hapless creature in an animated movie, cowering in horror while the evil villain morphed into a cobra that towered and grew to enormous size until at last it struck and annihilated him.

"Look, I just don't know what's happening. We did lose control to somebody – I'm guessing White Crow's people – for a while, but then we figured out what they were up to and got the phones back again. But we've got no idea why some voting apps aren't working. We're trying to figure out what's up, but we've never had any reason to try to get inside them before. It's really hard to do that all of a sudden."

"Do you think I care if 'it's hard?' We may be losing tens of thousands of votes every minute and you're telling me 'it's hard?'"

"I know, but it is! And there's only so far I can push these guys. We've already paid them a ton of money, and if they want to just walk away from their terminals, what are we going to do? Report them to the voting commission? Or worse yet, how about if they report us?"

"If we win the election we can worry about that later. Now go make that happen or I guarantee you'll have something much worse to worry about."

* * *

White Crow gazed intently at the screen on the wall of his hotel war room. In the dim background several people were hunched over laptops, while the foreground was filled with the face of someone with Asian features and a week's worth of sparse, black stubble on his chin. Anyone walking in would think they had just entered the bridge of the Starship Enterprise, where Captain James T. Kirk was staring down the captain of a Romulan warship.

"I need to know more than you are telling me."

"So? I'm needing to know before I can tell you. What can I say?"

"You can tell me a number of things: how many phones are failing to work, and why? Have you or our opponents crippled them? Are any signals getting through, and if so, which ones?"

"And I tell you, I don't know. So, you want me to make up answers?"

White Crow was barely able to control his temper. There was nothing to gain and everything to lose if he antagonized the man. "No – I want you to get answers and get back to me."

"So! You let me get back to work then!" The screen went dark, and Captain Kirk bowed his head in frustration.

* * *

Josette was feeling isolated and helpless. The Daughters of Lafayette had done what they could to help the incumbent President survive the election, but their opponents overwhelmed each ploy that lay within their technical skills. Now it seemed that some voters' phones were malfunctioning. Could they have bungled what they had done, again making matters worse?

This was not what she had hoped Election Day would be like. Someone – her team said probably two different "someones" – was trying to steal the election. And a few days before, she had learned of Frank's death from a terse email from Marla. Josette was startled by how shocked she had been, nearly fainting when she read the news. She told herself it was because it made her fear for her own safety, since someone certainly must have had him killed. Everything was in ruins, and she was afraid to answer her own door.

She remembered how she and her friends had so recently congratulated each other for being courageous revolutionaries, challenging the complacency of Europe and the arrogance of the United States. But as she watched the streams of social media scrolling down her screen and thought of what might lie behind what they were reporting, she felt overwhelmed and very alone.

*   *   *

With the scoreboard once more swept clean, Frank's robot made short work of its first log-on of the afternoon. One, two and three o'clock also passed without serious challenge. But a half-hour later, a glance at his computer nearly took his breath away. Somebody logged on as "Zomboy" had just entered a level seven score. And it was only 3:30! He'd never seen a level seven score before late in the evening.

He checked the second copy of the robot he'd left chugging away after he dedicated the first one to hourly use: it was just barely into the eighth level. Not much farther along than the version he'd been using all day.

He returned to the game site. Days ago he had skimmed through the last several weeks of top scores to see what he might be up against, and couldn't recall seeing that name. He went back and checked another month of high scores – still nothing. Was this an old player returning to the site, or had one of the other teams caught on?

He looked around for Marla, and then remembered she'd gone out for a walk. He wanted someone to watch the scoreboard while he went back to practicing. Damn.

Pulling his helmet on, he plunged into the game, without logging his scores in. The last thing he wanted to do was make Zomboy feel like he was being challenged. Maybe the guy would get bored and log off.

Just before 4:00 he took his helmet off and looked at the scoreboard. Thank goodness – either Zomboy had moved on, or he'd just had a single lucky game. Or maybe it was another team waiting for Frank's next move?

He logged the robot on and let it play until it topped Zomboy's score by 100 points. Relieved, he triggered the score and phone signals, and then disconnected as Marla came in.

"How goes the battle?" she said.

"Not good. Someone named 'Zomboy' popped up a half hour ago with a really high score. I'm worried."

"Don't you think the robot can beat him?"

"Dunno. It's getting close to the top of its range. I've been watching the scores all week, and I was thinking it would never come to this. I was hoping all we'd really have to worry about would be the geek community deciding to figure out what was going on with the voting apps. If one of them did, they'd be sure to brag about it."

He glanced at the scoreboard.

"Shit!"

Marla jumped. "What! What is it?"

"Zomboy just came back and topped my score! He must be on to me!"

"How can you tell? How would he know you were different than any other player?"

"The robot uses our back door to send the phone signal. The other teams must be going nuts trying to figure out what's going on. Maybe they noticed Marty nosing around and followed him to it. Damn it! I should have told him to stay away today instead of lurking!"

Then he had an awful thought. "Maybe one of them even found the back door and closed it! Maybe my scores aren't doing anything at all!"

She put a hand on his shoulder. "Take it easy – don't get so wound up. You're jumping to conclusions with no reason to think they're true! If someone really was on to you, wouldn't he lie low? If he attracts your attention, wouldn't he be worried you might be able to adapt somehow?"

"Okay, good. So that makes me feel a little better – thanks. But what is he up to then? Maybe he figured out I may be up to something, but doesn't know what it is."

"Well, that's good then, right?"

"As long as it lasts, yes, but what happens when the robot taps out? And what if he notices that I always log on precisely on the hour? If he figures that out, all he has to do is run the score up out of my range right before the hour and the game's over."

"The scoreboard clears at 6:00, right? So you get a clean start then, and it clears again at 8:00."

"Yes, but what do I do if he turns in an incredible score each time right after the board clears?"

She leaned down next to him and peered at his screen. "It looks like he only beat you by 100 points. Maybe he's already at the edge of his ability."

"But maybe not! Remember, if this is the original hacker, he's been playing around with the game for a long time. Or it may even be the game developer that's hacking the election. If that's the case, he can probably just plug in any score he wants! I bet he's trying to learn as much as he can by watching me. He might even think that whatever it is I'm doing, he's reversing it by topping my score by the same margin."

"So that would be great, right?"

But Frank wasn't listening any longer. He looked at the screen for the time: it was 4:20.

"I've got to start playing again so he never guesses what the top of the hour means. I've got to start blowing some smoke."

He started scribbling on a piece of paper.

"What are you doing?"

"I'm writing down a random sequence of log-on times that won't be predictable. That way there'll be less of a chance he'll notice that one of my games is always at the top of the hour."

He logged on and upped the score by 100 points. Two minutes later, Zomboy out-scored him by 100 points as well.

He pointed at the screen. Marla peered over his shoulder again and shrugged.

"So what? That means he doesn't know what's going on, or he would have run the score up, right? Or maybe he's just a gamer yanking your chain."

"Maybe. But it still means that every time we both play, it'll push the score up by another 200 points. And it gives his team another chance to monitor the action and figure out what's happening."

She couldn't think of anything else that might be soothing. Frank returned to staring at the screen and drumming his fingers on the desk. At 4:49 he triggered another sequence, and the game threshold crept up another 100 points towards the robot's rapidly approaching upward limit. Zomboy immediately topped him by the same amount.

Precisely at 5:00, Frank logged in and successfully claimed the next hour of control. The scoreboard would clear at 6:00, but he planned to play twice more before then to keep the opposition guessing. The robot only had 350 points of skill left, so that meant he was in danger of losing control as soon as the board cleared if Zomboy wanted to show off.

But what else could he do? The answer seemed to be nothing, and the tension was beginning to wear on him. He checked in with George before playing his next camouflage round (no new news) and with Marty after he did to tell him to stay out of the game site ("Two years! But that's it! That's absolutely my last and final offer! Two years!")

He had saved the last game within the robot's capability for 5:55, leaving the shortest interval so far between two rounds. He watched with grim attention as Zomboy topped his score by 100 – and the robot's upward limit by 50.

He felt numb. The election was on his shoulders alone now. Too late, far too late, he mourned his wasted youth. He should have spent it playing video games.

* * *

49

Now is the Time for All Good Gamers to Come to the Aid of Their Country

F RANK WAS ONCE again staring at the clock in the corner of his computer screen, one finger poised above the start key on the robot program. His heart was pounding, because he had decided to wait a minute after the top of the hour to keep the opposition in the dark. But what if the hacker had already guessed and intended to pick up the score where he had left off?

After fifty seconds his anxiety got the best of him and he stabbed the key. He let the score run up into the fourth level and then, holding his breath, terminated the game and sent the signal. With an enormous feeling of relief, he saw the robot register a top score on the screen. Then he waited.

And waited. But this time Zomboy failed to appear. At 6:30 Zomboy still hadn't posted a score. Had his low score puzzled whoever was toying with him? He decided to take no chances, and continued to nudge his score up at random times and point intervals.

He turned to Marla. "This is driving me crazy."

"You mean, everything going fine?"

"Okay, you're right. But the suspense is still driving me crazy."

"Let's watch the news then. It'll keep your mind occupied." She flipped the TV to the liberal cable news station, where one of the evening political show hosts was speaking to a reporter in the field.

> *So it sounds like this new technology we were all talking about isn't doing so well, is that right?*
>
> *That's right, Leah. There seems to be some sort of bug affecting all of the voting apps out there. And it doesn't seem to matter what phone someone's using, either.*
>
> *Does that mean everyone is voting the old fashioned way again this election?*
>
> *No, and that's the funny thing. Some people step up to a voting station and everything works fine, but others tap away and nothing seems to happen.*

But Frank was hardly listening, keeping an eye on his laptop instead. With a sudden spasm, he cried, "He's back!"

He looked at the time: it was 6:55, and Zomboy had just logged in with a score 1,000 points above the robot's range! Either Zomboy was on to Frank, or he'd simply tired of playing cat and mouse.

Frank started sweating. "This is it, Marla. If I don't beat that score, it's all over. Dammit, why didn't I write an artificial intelligence program that would learn the game faster!"

"You told me you didn't have near enough time to do that!"

"Yes, but I could have tried!" He logged on using the robot's player ID and settled the virtual reality helmet on his head.

Sitting now in total silence, he settled back in his chair and tried to clear his mind of everything except the perfect trajectory attainable by a virtual Holstein. He had to loosen up. Become unaware of every sensation outside the helmet.

He focused on the rippling, red lights of the game's welcome screen trembling before him. Gradually, they gave way to the opening image of a herd of cattle. He imagined himself pacing warily forward, swinging one foot deliberately ahead of the other, arms akimbo, hands poised above imaginary, holstered Colt 45s. Like Wyatt Earp, approaching the OK Corral.

Outside the infinite black depths of the virtual reality helmet, Marla watched her father anxiously: at first he seemed stiff, and raised his elbows out to a peculiar angle on each side. But then his shoulders eased, his arms dropped to his sides, and his hands began opening and closing, forming fists and then stretching each finger out as far as possible. Was he okay? Was he trying to loosen up, or having some sort of seizure?

She watched the clock anxiously. Did he know what time it was? She didn't want to disturb him, but the clock on his laptop said that it was only thirty seconds before 7:00.

Just then, his arms began to rise slowly from his sides, until they were almost vertical. Entranced, she watched as the fingers bent forward until they were at right angles to his hands, extending like the talons of an eagle. Then she watched as they descended slowly to the game controller in his lap, like the expressive hands of E. Power Biggs majestically approaching the keys of a mighty cathedral's pipe organ.

When they reached his lap, his hands enveloped the game controller, fingers precisely positioned on the controls. Exactly at 7:00, his index finger touched the start button, and the game was on.

Instantly, Frank was engulfed in a swirl of sight and sound. From the left, the Indians entered the field of battle. From the right, the heads of the Cavalry rose above the palisade walls of the fort, jeering like silly French persons in a Monty Python vignette. Yelling and screaming, the Indians stampeded the cattle amid a cacophonous storm of sights and sounds.

In the world Frank now inhabited, the tiny, blocky game figures visible on a mobile phone had been transformed into enormous Lego-like creatures with unworldly, pixelated faces that stared blindly toward him, mouths gaping and shutting like zombies.

Some had what looked like stakes jutting up behind their heads, only barely recognizable at this scale as feathers identifying the Native Americans. When several grabbed one of the hapless cows, its struggling legs rotated like pinwheels of pulsing squares of light. As it was catapulted towards the fort, his helmet magnified the tiny moo! designed for mobile phone use into the sort of reverberating, existential cry of despair that Edvard Munch must have imagined as he created The Scream.

But Frank was ready. He had become One with The Machine.

Marla watched in fascination as her father's fingers cradled the game controller in his lap, alternately caressing or stabbing the buttons and joy stick as the moment required. Unbeknownst to her, he was imagining he was floating invisibly above the prairie scene as the battle unfolded. No longer Wyatt Earp, he had become a mighty Manitou, helping his people achieve justice and avenge themselves for the White Man's unforgiveable crimes.

He pressed the attack mercilessly, through round after round of play, gleeful each time the fort disintegrated before his assault. Poor fools! The Cavalry always tried desperately to restore their defenses, but no matter! As quickly as they rebuilt a wall, he destroyed it again. He felt the rising joy of his people, saw them raise their Lincoln Log-like arms, heard them whoop with joy. His strength and theirs was as the strength of thousands, because their cause was just.

And then, a cow sailed just over the fort. What had happened? Horrified, he watched the scene before him shimmer and then disappear. Suddenly, all was silent and dark.

With a jolt, he returned to the real world.

Trembling, he took off the helmet and pressed the button that would report his score. He had edged Zomboy's last score, but only barely.

"Here," Marla said at his side, concern evident in her voice. "Drink some water."

He did as he was told, but his eyes remained fixed on the screen of his laptop.

"You did it Dad! You beat him!"

"No, Marla," he said, his voice exhausted and quavering.

"What do you mean! You just bought another hour! And the voting on the East Coast will be over when the game scores clear!"

"But that leaves all the voting districts in all the other states still open. I gave that game everything I had. I've got nothing left. I can't possibly score any higher than I just did."

He leaned back, shaking.

"It's all over."

She put her arms around his shoulders. "You can't know that! So many people have already voted! Maybe you've already won! Maybe it doesn't matter how many more votes are switched!"

He shook his head.

"No. There are just too many votes left. California has over 10% of the electoral votes all by itself. Most people there probably haven't even voted yet."

She felt terrible for her father; his life had revolved around this contest for the past year. Everything now seemed to be dissolving in front of him.

"Is there anything I can do? Can I get you anything? The first election returns should be coming in soon – we can watch them together."

"I can't do that. I couldn't bear to see the numbers come up on the screen, knowing they were manipulated. *Look!!*"

She jumped as his arm shot out, index finger extended and trembling. "Look! Look! He just hit the ninth level! He annihilated me! He's telling me he knows exactly what I was doing, and that the game's over. Now there's nothing to stop him from stealing the election!"

Marla tried to hug him, but he pushed her arms away and stood up. "I need to get some air."

"Can I come with you?"

"No, I need some time alone. I'll probably be awhile, and anyway, it's getting cold outside."

"What about the election?"

"What about it?"

"Dad!"

He picked up his coat. "Well, okay. If you want to go through the motions, push this button exactly at 8:00 when the scoreboard resets. Let the robot run through five levels and then push this button, and then that one. Maybe he hasn't figured the timing part out yet. But after that, it's no use – I won't be able to beat him at 9:00, and that still leaves an hour of Mountain Time, and two hours of Pacific Time. Like I said, it's over."

He pulled his coat on, and stepped outside. Overhead, a crescent moon flickered through the black branches thrashing in the wind. He shoved his hands in his pockets and trudged up the long dirt track that ran from the cottage to the main road. Behind him, waves crashed on the granite ledges that ran up to the bayberry and tamarack edging the yard of the cottage, sending wind-borne spray splattering on his back like rain.

From the window of the camper, Marla watched as his silhouette glided across the lawn, and then disappeared from the knees down as he crossed the meadow beyond. Finally, his outline dissolved into nothingness as it entered the shadows of the forest.

* * *

Hundreds of miles away, Zomboy was exultant. It had been cruel fun toying with his adversary before putting him away for good. What a fool – this was Zomboy's game, and nobody was going to beat him when he was ready to make his move.

He savored the moment when he ran out his score. His recent setback had been galling, but it hadn't held him back forever. He'd waited for months for this day to come, and victory was just as sweet as he had hoped. By tomorrow everybody in the world who knew of this battle of wits would know who had won.

He heard a rap on the door behind him.

"Zack?"

He ignored the sound, but the rap came again.

"Zack?"

Damn it all, he knew they wouldn't give up. He gave a grudging "Yeah?"

"Zack, are you doing your homework?"

He crossed his arms and said nothing.

"Zack, you've only had your gaming privileges back for one day. If you don't want to lose them for another three months, you'd better open this door right now!"

His mother stared at the door, but still there was silence. She rapped again.

The lock clicked and the door opened.

"Give it to me."

"Do I have to?"

"You know you have to! Now hand it over."

Slumping from the weight of all the burdens of the world descending upon his thin, adolescent shoulders, he took his time walking over to his bed, unplugged the game controller from his laptop, and handed it to his mother.

"Good boy! Now you come work at the kitchen table where I can see you."

With a single, decisive exercise of parental determination, the presidential election had been saved.

*   *   *

Marla was watching the first returns from the last states to finish voting when she heard the door open behind her.

"I'm sorry I left you alone so long. But I couldn't help it. I had to get out of here until the polls closed."

He took his coat off and was about to throw it on the bed when he caught himself. He hung it up in the small closet instead, and then moved into the kitchen area. He didn't often drink anything stronger than beer or wine, but he recalled seeing an unopened bottle of scotch among the random provisions included in his Care package.

"Can I pour you a scotch?"

"No thanks, Dad."

He shuffled in, sat down in his desk chair and took a sip. "So I guess now we find out. We may not know who the hacker is, but at least we'll know who they were working for. Have they called the winner yet?"

"I thought you said it didn't matter?"

He sighed. "Of course it matters. It just matters in a different way now."

"Don't you want to know Zomboy's highest score for the evening first?"

"Not really. If you want to tell me, go ahead."

She gave him the score, and he took another, deeper sip of his scotch. He looked up at the screen, where the first numbers were starting to flash on the screen. Yazzie was leading, but only 8% of the precincts in California had reported in so far. Most of the other western states hadn't returned any results at all yet.

Then he put his glass carefully down on his desk, fingers trembling.

"Wait a minute, that was his high score before 8:00. What was his last score?" She gave the same number again.

He picked up his glass and emptied it in one gulp before grabbing her shoulders. "You mean that was his last game?"

"That was his last game. He never came back."

His face turned white as he stared wide-eyed into her face, still clutching her shoulders. "Please God tell me you triggered the robot every hour after I left!"

"Of course I did," she said softly, as she drew him in and gave him a hug. "You see? Everything turned out all right."

*   *   *

50

Many Happy Returns

B ACK IN WASHINGTON, Frank had some explaining to do. When he finally got around to listening to his voicemail, he found a series of unrequited messages that escalated rapidly from chiding through anxiety to barely suppressed rage before, thankfully, his voicemail box was full. Authors, he learned, were not expected to disappear the day before their books were released.

There was no avoiding his publicity duties now, so the day after his return to Washington he dropped by his co-author's apartment, where he received a warm greeting.

"Hey man! Great to see you! And how about those book sales, huh? We got ourselves a best seller! Just like I said we would! High five!"

"Well, you get all the credit. Other than providing the facts, I didn't add much."

"Ah, don't sell yourself short. Without a story, you got no book, right?"

"I guess. But still."

"Whatever. The important thing is that we got ourselves a hit. And hey, I'm really glad you were okay with my final edits. I think they made a really big difference."

"What final edits?"

"You know, the ones I sent you a few weeks before the launch date. The ones the publisher insisted on. I sent them off to you and never heard back, so I figured you were okay with them."

Frank had paid no more attention to Dan's email than his publisher's after the first draft of the manuscript was in the can.

"Yeah, I'm sure I got them. But I got really busy on other things. How many changes were there?"

"Oh, not all that many I guess." Grover swiveled around in his chair and started shuffling papers from one pile to another and then back again on his desk.

"How many?"

Grover rolled his eyes up to look at the ceiling and shuffled harder. "So... let me think. Five, six, you know, a few... or maybe thirty?"

"Yow!"

Grover swiveled back. To his relief, he saw that Frank's reaction had been triggered by Molly taking a giant leap from the top of his bookshelves to the back of Frank's chair.

"Bad Molly! That's no way to treat a guest!"

Grover plucked the cat off the chair as Frank, rubbing the back of his neck, cautiously sat down again.

"There, there. You'll have the whole office back soon." He was planning to hold the cat in his lap to prevent further mischief, and then thought better of it. He placed it back on top of the bookshelves.

Frank turned sideways in his chair so he could keep an eye on the cat. "Well, I guess that's okay if all you're talking about is minor changes. They were minor changes, right?"

"So... I guess that depends on what you mean by 'minor.'"

"Well, what did you mean when you said 'minor'?"

"Well, you know, maybe adding a new scene here and there."

"A whole new scene? Like what? Did you just make them up?"

"Uh, not always. Maybe most of the time. So okay, I might have made up all of them up. But they were all true to what was going on at that place and time."

"I can't believe you did that! Give me an example."

Grover perked up. "Well, here's a really good one. So you were all alone out in Nevada, right? Up in the clearing on that mountain pass a million miles from anyone else? Well, you killed this rabid wolverine that was attacking you at your campsite with one shot – right between the eyes! That one came off really well!"

Frank was appalled. "I don't think they have wolverines in Nevada!"

"Oh they must. Publishers use fact checkers, and he would have flagged that right away. At least they usually do. I think."

"I'm going to be a laughing stock!"

"Look, maybe I did take a little bit of license, but I did email them to you. And here – take a look at the sales figures – maybe that'll make you feel better."

He handed a spreadsheet to Frank who ignored it while he continued to rant at Grover. When he did finally glance at it, he stopped speaking, and his eyes grew very wide.

*　*　*

Throughout the campaign, Henry Yazzie had told himself not to fall into the trap of thinking his chances might be real. Even when his standing in the polls started going up and up, as if drawn along by an invisible hand.

Still, when the money started flowing in from individual voters, and not just the CCA, it had been hard not to think something historic might be happening. Day after day, he was whisked by faceless teams of handlers from one stump speech to the next, and the crowds just kept getting larger. But he had been adamant with himself. He'd gone into this campaign knowing it was impossible, and he was not going to allow himself to be taken in by all the hoopla and attention. Still, he had thrown himself into the effort with everything he had to give, day after exhausting day. He didn't want anyone – especially himself – to ever have any doubt on that score.

When at last the voting began and the news media entered into its final frenzy, he could control his enthusiasm no longer. Finally, he was convinced that a dramatic change in his life was about to occur...

But alas, it was not to be.

He sighed. Good God, he was tired. It had been such a long, long race. What he really wanted to do was just go back home; sleep in his own house, see no one and do nothing until he felt physically and spiritually restored.

But then, as he had every morning since Election Day, he surrendered to an enormous grin. Sure, nothing had changed. He was still being whisked around the country by nameless teams of handlers. But now they called him "Mr. President!"

*　*　*

Richard Fetters looked out the window of his study, where driving sheets of sleet were encasing the neglected bushes in coffins of ice. It was early afternoon, but already it felt like it had been a very long day. His phone was always silent now, his email reduced to a trickle of insignificant chaff. The smell of failure lay upon him, and in politics, no stench was more retchingly absolute than that of defeat.

He turned to the pictures over his desk and studied them: the victorious young man in the first; the calculating professional on the rise in the second; the powerful Cabinet Secretary in the third, ready to make his mark on the nation and the world; the cocky CEO making his fortune in the last. He was in his mid-sixties now, and had staked everything on this election; exploited every connection he had, cashed in every chit he had banked during a long career. He doubted there would be another celebratory picture to add to the tableau.

He sat down at his desk. What next? Maybe it was time to get away; go back to Colorado, where he'd spent his youth. Take stock. He couldn't go fly fishing at this time of year, but he could ski. He hadn't done either in decades. Something in his life would come along next.

He turned on his computer to see where he might want to stay, automatically checking his email first. The only message he found was an email informing him that he would shortly receive a summons from the Federal Election Commission, and instructing him to restrict his travel pending its receipt.

* * *

Otto Barbash was feeling out of sorts. It wasn't the loss of the election as such; failure had been a guest at his table in the past, though rarely. One moves on.

But he was not used to being talked about in other than an admiring way. Lately he had begun to suspect that some in his social circle – and especially those he had persuaded to become major contributors – were holding more than the loss against him. Even at his club, he had noticed the occasional gesture in his direction, followed by side-long looks and laughter.

Perhaps he should not be surprised. With the election over, the gentlemen and women of the press were readjusting, as they always did, to the eternal turn of the news cycle. The end of the election left a void that needed to be filled with new political content. It also left those who had been on the campaign trail scrambling for something else to put under their bylines. Thankfully, there was Randall Wellhead.

Now that Wellhead was no longer protected by his handlers, journalists could walk right up to him on the street, or at the coffee shop where he went every Monday to look accessible to the people. And God bless him, he would say the most outrageous things, offering them up like a department store Santa Claus rewarding a line of children. Reporters delighted over each new present they received, and rushed to share their good luck with anyone who would read about them. Which was everybody.

* * *

George Marchand was accompanying Frank as he walked to his first book signing, something Frank had been dreading since he'd signed his publishing contract a year before. He had barely known what to say to his own co-workers after fifteen years of inhabiting the same grid of cubes. What would he say to a room full of strangers – or worse yet, three random bookshop visitors who happened to notice the sign? He'd been counting on Grover to do most of the talking at these events – and he had, while Frank was off gallivanting. But that afternoon a hairball had taken a wrong turn in Molly's gut and he was still with her at the vet's. Frank was grateful for the distraction of George's company, and also anxious to hear what George had learned since Election Day.

"So at this point, the President can't do anything but keep everything hushed up. I bet he's kicking himself now for not blowing the lid off when he could. Whatever his handlers might have thought before, now that he's lost a fraud-free national vote no one is going to want to hear anything from him about the primaries."

"Amazing. So how about the hackers? Have you caught any of them?"

"With all the hysteria on Election Day, the hackers – or I should say the people who were paying the hackers – got sloppy with their communications. Once we found the hackers overseas, it was easy to follow the breadcrumbs back to the people pulling the strings. We've got evidence that would hold up in court to convict all three groups that were out to fix the election."

He saw that Frank looked concerned. "Don't worry about Josette and her friends. We can't prosecute any of the hackers in the open without risking everything coming out, including how little the government did to stop them. In the case of Josette, it would also embarrass the French government. Right now that wouldn't be helpful to our foreign policy. We will let them know privately about some 'cybersecurity persons of interest' they should keep an eye on, so Josette had better be on her best behavior for a good long while. If I were her, I wouldn't be in any hurry to go home."

"Does she know that?"

"Yes. I paid her a visit to let her know where things stand – for now. Let's just say that her Green Card will self-destruct if so much as a single text or email strikes the NSA the wrong way, and that anything they see will be passed along to their friends in France."

"I guess she can't hope for more than that," Frank said, wondering how that message was sitting with her. "So who were the other two?"

"I'm relieved to say that neither was the President or his party."

Frank stopped short, forcing a pedestrian to jump sideways to avoid a collision.

"Are you kidding? You thought the President might have been one of them?"

Marchand smiled and pointed up the street. "C'mon. You don't want to be late for your first book signing."

"But really – you thought the President might try to hack an election?"

"Yes, really. Or at least his campaign manager. Either way, no one would ever be able to trace it back to the President. People play for keeps in this town, if you haven't noticed. Anyway, as we always assumed, the other two groups had something to do with Wellhead and Yazzie. But it looks like both candidates were in the dark, thank goodness. Otherwise, we'd really be in a bind about what to do."

"So who were they?"

"One was Richard Fetters – Wellhead's politico running mate. He was planning on being the power behind the throne. According to some intel we picked up, he might have been planning on being even more. But we're not exactly sure how he intended to pull that off. He was the one that had you yanked off the street, by the way."

"He was? And you're going to let him walk, too?"

"Oh, now, I didn't say that. He was shipping a whole lot of campaign cash overseas to his hackers, and he couldn't put that down in the finance reports candidates are required by law to file. Before we're through, we'll have documented a long list of money laundering, currency trading and campaign finance laws violations. I doubt it'll take him long to decide that accepting a quick, quiet plea deal would be a smart move. He should be Uncle Sam's guest at a minimum security federal prison for a good long time. And he'll have to agree to never be involved in an election again."

"Well, the longer the stay the better. And the last one?"

"Oh, the last one! Now, he turned out to be pretty interesting – a casino manager on a reservation out west who was Yazzie's campaign finance director. Guy named Ohanzee White Crow. Quite an impressive guy in his own way, but ruthless. We've got more than we need on him already, so we grabbed him quick. We had White Crow tell Yazzie that 'sudden medical issues' will prevent him from playing any role in the new administration. That's got to be a pretty bitter punishment for White Crow right there, but he'll be off the street for quite a while as well."

"Speaking of off the street, what about Marty? Has he had his parole hearing yet?"

"Matter of fact, yes. I was able to tell the parole board that I had a job waiting for him as a cybersecurity consultant, and that impressed them. He's working for me now, and I think we'll all feel more financially secure knowing I'll be able to keep an eye on him."

They had reached the book store.

George looked at his watch. "Looks like we're here just in time. I'm afraid we can't let you get a book out of this adventure, but you can plan on a nice termination bonus from your no-name agency. Oh – I forgot about Butcher.

"Turns out Butcher has a gambling problem. White Crow had him in his pocket. We also learned that White Crow was in cahoots with Fetters – until he double-crossed him. Then Butcher double-crossed White Crow. Ratted him out to Fetters, not knowing that Fetters was hacking the election, too! Yeah, it is pretty complicated. There's more to it, but we'll have to cover that later. You've got some books to sign!"

With that, Marchand shook Frank's hand and abandoned him on the threshold of his debut as a celebrity author.

*   *   *

Frank scanned the busy store for the marketing intern he'd been told would be waiting for him. He wasn't sure what someone from a publishing house should look like, but his general expectation ran towards thick glasses and mousy hair tied back in a bun. No one in view seemed to meet those criteria, but while he was waiting a very attractive young woman in her late twenties caught his eye as she hurried into the store. Now she was approaching him and reaching out to shake his hand.

"Mr. Adversego! My name is Lila Carberry. I'm so pleased to meet you! I loved your book! I read it almost all in one sitting, and I can't tell you what an honor it is to meet you! I'm not quite sure what you say to someone who saved the world from nuclear destruction, so I guess I'll just say 'thank you so very much!'"

Normally he would go to great lengths to avoid calling attention to himself. But as her lovely face continued to radiate unabashed admiration he felt a sudden inclination not to disabuse her of her opinion. He settled for ignoring her last statement.

"That's extremely kind of you – I'm glad you enjoyed it. I really can't claim much credit for the book, though. Mostly I just talked and Grover wrote. Of course, I... I revised and approved everything he wrote."

"Oh, but still! All of the insight and ingenuity you used to foil the plot! And the chances that you took! I'm sure I wouldn't know what to do if I was attacked by a rabid wolverine!"

"Almost everything. Look –," he pointed at his watch. "Shouldn't we get started?"

"Of course you're right. Let me check in with the store manager and see where they want us to set up."

He watched as she walked to the front desk and spoke to someone at a register; he pointed her towards someone else. As Frank waited, he found himself comparing her to Josette; a bit taller, with quite an appealing figure. Blond hair, carefully cut and styled, and a strikingly attractive face. Judging by her clothes, her parents must be helping her out financially. Not much money to be made as an intern.

The manager was speaking with her now, looking down occasionally at a computer screen. Now the manager was shaking her head. Lila walked back to him, her face burning.

"I don't know what to say. There's been some sort of mix-up. The store manager thinks you're supposed to be here on Thursday night, not tonight. I really don't know what to say," she repeated, her voice quavering.

"Please – don't worry about it. To tell the truth, this isn't the kind of thing I look forward to." She still looked crestfallen, so he added, "And I didn't turn down any other plans for this evening anyway."

"That's really very kind of you, but still, I really do feel terrible. Look – I was supposed to offer to take you to dinner after the book signing. You, know, to discuss how it went and go over your schedule. Why don't we still do that – well, most of that – tonight? Since you're free?"

"Uh, so, sure. I guess that makes sense. Did you have any place in mind? We could get a sandwich right here at the book store cafe. How about that?"

She laughed. "No way! Your book is flying off the shelves! As your publisher, we want to treat you like the author of a book we're very proud to have brought to market! I made reservations already at a restaurant nearby. I'll call to see if they can take us earlier."

What could he say? Nothing, of course, so he allowed her to lead him out the door while she called ahead.

"They aren't quite ready for us, but they should be soon," she reported. A few minutes later they were approaching the entrance to an obviously expensive restaurant.

"Have you been here before? It's only been open a few months, but it's been a big hit. I like it a lot."

"No, I guess I've missed this one." He tried to say it as if missing a trendy new restaurant was a rare event in his life. "It looks nice."

He followed as she entered and walked up to a hostess standing between the dining room and the bar. It was hard to hear her over the sound of the after-work crowd in bar.

"It won't be too long. We can wait in here," Lila said. She led him to a couch along the wall, attracting the appreciative notice of several men standing at the bar. One gave Frank a quizzical look, likely doing the math to guess whether Frank was a lucky guy or just her father. Being neither, he continued his poodle-like pursuit of Lila with his ears burning.

A waiter materialized at her elbow almost immediately.

"Nice to see you back. It's a Mojito, right?"

"Yes!" She favored him with the kind of smile any man would happily receive in lieu of a sizable tip.

"And for you?"

For once Frank had thought ahead; he had decided that famous authors didn't drink beer.

"Scotch on the rocks, thanks."

"Do you have a preference?"

Okay, he wasn't that ready. His mind went blank. "Surprise me," he said finally, his ears burning more brightly than ever.

But Lila didn't seem to notice. She leaned towards him to be heard, and put a hand on his arm.

"I hope you don't mind me saying this again, Mr. Adversego, but this really is quite an honor for me."

"Frank, please, Miss Carberry – call me Frank."

She laughed. "Miss Carberry and Frank?"

He had to smile at that. "Okay, Lila. Please call me Frank."

To his relief, Lila was happy to do all the talking. He learned that she had been with the publisher for only a few months, and that he was the first author she was assisting on her own. It was easy to tell she was excited to be involved in the world of publishing, but also nervous; he tried to help by making appreciative noises at appropriate intervals. By the time the hostess came for them, her glass was empty, while Frank left most of his behind.

When they were seated, she drew a few sheets of paper from her hand bag. "Time for a little business, I guess. Is that all right with you?"

"Of course."

She started with his book tour, but had trouble remembering what some of the abbreviations on his schedule meant. Soon she was looking distressed, concerned that she was not coming across as the professional she yearned to be.

Frank tried to help again. "You know what? I really don't feel like thinking about schedules right now. Would that be okay?"

She brightened, but still seemed off balance. When the waiter arrived to ask if they cared for a drink, she waited for Frank to speak first. "I think I'll just be having wine," he said.

She put her hand on his arm again. "Has anyone toasted you yet on the success of your new book?"

"Why no – I guess not. But I've been on the road until just a few days ago," he offered, as if it would have made any difference.

"Well! In that case, as your publisher's representative, I think we should order a bottle of champagne. What do you say to that?"

"Why not?"

She became more confident as she launched into a description of what she called the "current perilous state of the publishing world." Now that he had a book, Frank's curiosity was piqued. Lila was pleased with his close attention.

By the time their wine arrived, Frank was asking questions and nodding at her answers. He found that she had a sharp mind, and an original way of thinking. To his surprise, he found himself in an unusual state: enjoying himself in a social situation.

He ordered the first thing his eye noticed on the menu, and they continued their conversation without interruption. The smoked glass dividers that hung from the ceiling throughout the dining room were interspersed with flocks of clear incandescent light bulbs dangling from wires, their filaments burning with an orange glow that contributed substantially more atmosphere than useful light. The combination provided the illusion of dining alone while surrounded by holograms of other couples, dimly visible and doubtless many dimensions away.

By the time their entrees arrived, Frank had become less talkative, happy to just appreciate the rare experience of having dinner with someone who was not only intelligent and attractive but pleasant and engaging as well. So very different from spending time with Josette, who usually kept him off balance and uncomfortable. Lila even appeared to be genuinely interested in him.

He began to lose the drift of what she saying, more intent on watching her as she spoke. It had been a very long time since he had spent an evening like this. He was under no illusions why; over the years he had increasingly chosen the safety of solitude over the risks and effort of interacting socially in a world where everyone seemed to be so much better at it than he was. He didn't often allow himself to realize what he couldn't ignore this evening: that he had been lonelier for quite a while longer than he cared to admit. Perhaps that was why he had been missing his brief interactions with Josette, unsatisfactory as they were.

Lila had stopped talking. He tried to pull her last words out of the ether. "I'm sorry?"

She laughed. "I asked if you'd always wanted to write a book?"

He was about to say 'no, not at all,' when he paused. "I guess I can't really say no, at least not completely. I loved to read when I was young. Almost as soon as I could read, I started devouring everything I could get my hands on. So being an author seemed like something that must be wonderful."

She nodded. "Me too. What did you like to read?"

"Gee, I guess just about anything. But by the time I was in middle school, I decided that if I was going to be reading a lot, I might as well tackle real literature. So I tried a bit of everything. Sometimes I got stubborn for no good reason and kept reading an author I didn't really like all that much. For example, I read just about everything Nabokov wrote, even though I found some of his devices irritating."

"I always wanted to read Nabokov, but never got around to him. What bothered you?"

"It seems kind of funny to say now. Little things, like how many of his main characters were always fiddling with a little piece of meat stuck in a hollow tooth."

She laughed. "Did you find everything he wrote annoying?"

"No, actually. Some of his books I really liked. 'Speak, Memory,' was semiautobiographical, and started with his family leaving Russia. It was a lot less affected than some of his other books. And he wrote a little book about an elderly professor called 'Pnin' that I found really charming."

He went on to critique other authors he'd read, moving through Faulkner and Hemingway, Waugh and Maugham, Tolstoy and Solzhenitsyn, as Lila listened avidly, her eyes glistening a little in the flickering light.

He realized that he had been talking for quite a while and finished a little abruptly, saying, "So reading all those great authors, I thought being a writer must be one of the greatest things in the world to be. But I never let myself think that I could ever write a book." And for good reason. It was time to change the subject. The waiter poured the last of the champagne into Lila's glass, and Frank noticed that he had yet to finish his second glass.

"How about you? Did you ever want to be an author?"

"Oh, I don't think I have that in me. I took a creative writing course once, and I think I just embarrassed myself. But I adore books, and that's why I wanted to try and have a career in publishing."

"Is that hard to do?"

She laughed a little too loudly. But at the same time, he marveled at how lushly lovely she looked.

"Yes, I'm afraid it is. I worked very hard in college and graduated summa cum laude from an Ivy League school – as an English major, naturally. I might as well have gone to a community college. You have no idea how degrading it is to go back and live at home, endlessly sending your resumé off to apply for entry-level jobs and never even getting an interview."

"Really? With that kind of résumé? That seems really unfair."

She shrugged her shoulders and looked down at her hands. "Yeah. Life sucks sometimes, doesn't it?" She stopped and rotated her champagne glass slowly between her fingers.

"So what did you do?"

"Oh, what everyone else does. I went back to grad school and got another degree. This time in marketing. Marketing! How's that for sad?"

"Well, not if it worked. And it sounds like it did."

Half of her mouth smiled. "Ask me how long it took to get this unpaid internship after I got my second degree."

He didn't know what to say. "Six months?"

"Closer to a year."

"That's terrible." Maybe he could think of a happier topic. "Did you grow up in Washington?"

"I don't live in Washington. We have a small office in D.C., and I'm rotating through it for a couple of months. I grew up in California, but if you want to get a job in publishing, you pretty much have to move to New York. That's where all the big publishers have their headquarters, and there aren't many small ones left."

"New York must be exciting, though."

"I guess it would be for a lot of people, but not so much for me. I'm a pretty private person, and I don't know anyone in the city. Plus, everyone at the office is all caught up in their own lives. And now I'm here."

She was silent again. He was touched by her reference to herself as a very private person and to the sense of isolation that could accompany that character trait. He wondered how someone with so much going for her hadn't found more success.

"I'm sorry," she said, her voice a little quavery. "I'm afraid I haven't been very professional this evening."

"You've been lovely," he blurted out, and meant it.

"Really? You're very sweet." Then she paused and said, "Do you think it's kind of hot in here?"

He didn't, but there was no reason to say so. He realized for the first time that she was a bit tipsy. Maybe some fresh air would help. "Why don't I ask for the check?"

"Thanks. I guess it's getting late."

As he helped her on with her coat, he felt a pang of loneliness. The evening had been an unexpected, but too brief, pleasure. All he had to look forward to now was another solitary evening in his messy, rundown apartment.

He was no longer following her when they left the restaurant. Instead, she walked by his side.

"Nice night, isn't it?" she offered.

"I guess it is, now that you mention it." It was unseasonably warm, and the sidewalk was full of chatting couples and groups of friends entering and leaving the busy restaurants and bars that lined the avenue. He didn't know what to say next, so he said what seemed like the right thing to say under the circumstances. "Can I get you a cab?"

Her face fell. "Oh, I usually just take the Metro. But it's such a nice night I think I'll walk home. And you?" It seemed obvious what she wanted him to say, but he was unsure whether he should say it. But then he did.

"I guess it would be nice to walk for a while. Mind if I keep you company?"

She gifted him with the same smile she'd given the waiter, and he couldn't help melting a bit. He gave a lopsided smile in return, and she slid her arm through his.

For a little while, he felt on top of the world. He was walking through a busy city with a lovely young woman on his arm who thought his life was interesting and might even find his company enjoyable. He didn't know what would happen next, and didn't particularly care. For the moment, he was simply happy to feel like he was back in the land of the living.

But too soon that pleasant feeling passed as the cool air, the walking, and the bottle of champagne began to take their toll on Lila. Her speech became less clear and her laughter more loud. Gradually, he became simply a hermetic middle-aged man once again, one who had somehow found himself escorting a much younger woman who had had too much to drink.

Lila stopped, and wavered back and forth.

"Are you alright?"

"All of a sudden I don't feel very good."

"I'll bet it was something we ate. I'm feeling a little queasy myself," he lied. "I think I better get you a cab."

He walked her to the curb and held her steady as he watched for a taxi.

"I'm so sorry," she said. "I've been having such a lovely evening."

A cab changed lanes and began to slow down.

"Me too – but don't worry; here's a cab now."

She looked up at him expectantly, but he spoke before she had a chance to say whatever it was she had in mind.

"You'll be home in no time. I can't tell you how much I enjoyed this evening. It was very kind of you to spend it with me." She frowned and wobbled a bit as she tried to pull herself together.

He opened the door, and helped her in. "Good night, Frank," she said softly and, he thought, a little gratefully. "I'll meet you at the bookstore on Thursday." She gave a little smile. "I really am sure it's Thursday this time."

He smiled and closed the door, and the cab pulled away. He watched as it merged into the river of red and silver taillights weaving and flowing away into the distance. Then he turned and began the long walk home.

* * *

51

Au Revoir

F RANK MANAGED TO survive all three weeks of his whirlwind book tour, if only barely. Now he was back in Washington, and suddenly he had absolutely nothing to do.

It shouldn't have been such a shock, but it was. With all of the frantic activity of the past year, he hadn't had the time or the inclination to think about what he would do when the election and his book were behind him. Now he realized he didn't know what to do the next morning, let alone for the next year.

He had already sorted through the small pile of impersonal mail that had piled up while he was away, and paid all the bills. He'd even straightened up his apartment, sort of, and thrown out everything he'd found in his refrigerator and freezer. Now he really and truly had nothing else to do.

He pulled on a coat and stood on the pavement outside, looking one way and then the other up the street. Both directions looked about the same. He'd neglected his running while on the book tour and felt out of shape, so he set off walking at a brisk pace in the direction of nowhere in particular that was slightly uphill.

Later he found himself on the bridge to Georgetown, and stopped to look out over the park below and the river beyond. He recalled stopping there with Josette once, pointing out the points of interest, enjoying the enthusiasm she showed as she recognized monuments that until then had only been names to her.

He leaned on the side of the bridge and mused a while on the banal, but nonetheless unsettling, tumult of his personal life over the last year. So this is what it felt like to be sadder but wiser. All those silly thoughts he'd had about Josette. His evening with Lila had finally sorted that out for him. It hadn't so much been Josette, really, that had him in a twist. It was really all about her youth, or more properly, the way her company forced him to be aware of the likelihood that his own youth, and with it all the possibilities and pursuits that life offered to the young, were in the past. When he was with her, he could flirt with the illusion that the door on that period of his own life might still be ajar.

But of course it was not. Those days, and everything he had then taken for granted, and – worse – those things he had not taken advantage of, were behind him. Even if he were capable of reintegrating socially with the world around him, that particular time was past.

That was the clear, if bittersweet, realization he was now examining. He knew objectively that everyone grew older, and that when they did, their lives changed. He prided himself on being objective, and hoped that if at times he might act like a fool, at least he'd notice.

He wasn't going to deny that he had reached out to Josette for companionship, but he was disoriented by how much he found himself mourning the failure of that effort. And all the more, because his instinctive shrinking away from human contact seemed to relegate the possibility of female companionship of any sort to the past as well.

So good-bye to that view and to the memories it brought back. He turned and headed back towards his apartment, hands in his pockets. And then he heard a voice behind him with a French accent.

"Frank? Is that you?"

The voice belonged to Simone Falconet.

"Simone! How nice to see you. I thought you would be back in Paris by now."

She gave a wry smile. "I am afraid not. It seems that there is no room for me in my old department, at least for now."

"But that's terrible! How did that happen?"

"Ah, but that is a long story; office politics can be so awful, you know? But now I am a visiting professor at George Washington University, and I am enjoying your city very much."

"Well, I'm glad for that," he said.

"Are you busy? I am just out for a walk, and I want to tell you how much I enjoyed your book!"

Please God, he thought. Don't start with the wolverine scene. But what could he say? Clearly he was already out for a walk.

"No, not busy. But let's leave the book behind; I'm just back from a promotional tour, and I'm all 'booked' out."

She gave him a warm smile. "Of course. I understand completely – I have sometimes felt the same way. And please – let me take you to lunch. I have so much to thank you for."

"Really? I can't think what."

"For helping Josette stay out of trouble, or I should say from getting in worse trouble. Come! Do not look so surprised, and no, we need speak of it no more. But I know how much she is in your debt."

He frowned but said nothing. How much might Josette have shared with her about the election? But as they walked towards Georgetown, Simone was true to her word. The subject did not come up again.

He was surprised how easily they fell into a conversation. Perhaps she gave him the benefit of the doubt in the way he spoke. Maybe a non-native English speaker was less likely to recognize a non sequitur if she heard one. Whatever the cause, she seemed to be enjoying their interaction.

When they sat down to lunch, Simone told him that she must teach him how to eat like the French. She ordered for both of them, asked whether there was any decent cheese to be had, and then instructed the waiter to bring the salads after the entrees, followed by a selection of the cheeses she specified and some grapes. Rather than feeling embarrassed, he found himself laughing when she poked gentle fun at his lack of sophistication regarding food.

Somehow it was more than an hour and a half before they finished the last of their cheese and wine and left the restaurant. She saw him look at his watch, and told him he was still too American – a good meal took time to enjoy. And then she said that he must allow her to continue to help him become more Continental.

He told her that he'd like that very much. She smiled, and kissed him on both cheeks. Then she walked away, turning to give him another smile and a wave of her hand. He waved back, and stood there in the bright sunshine with a silly smile on his face, not giving a damn who might see him.

Across the street, a solitary figure noticed the two of them saying their good-byes. Had he glanced her way, he might at first have thought it was a young man, because she was thin, and her dark hair was short. But really it was a young woman, looking a bit forlorn and alone before she turned and walked away.

* * *

Did you enjoy The Lafayette Campaign? Please consider recommending it to others and posting a brief review at your favorite online book site.

You can read the first chapters of the first Frank Adversego thriller in the pages that follow.
The Alexandria Project,
a Tale of Treacher and Technology,
is available at Andrew-Updegrove.com

The complete Frank Adversego Thriller series is available as eBooks and in paperback at your favorite online book site as well as at http://andrew-updegrove.com/books/

They can also be ordered in paperback through your favorite local book store.

The Alexandria Project, The Lafayette Campaign and *The Doodlebug War* are available as audiobooks published by Tantor Media. You can find them wherever else audiobooks are sold.

Follow the further adventures of Frank at my author site, Tales of Adversego <Andrew-Updegrove.com>, and on Twitter @Adversego.

Acknowledgements

I'd like to express my gratitude to a number of individuals who generously assisted me in completing this book. First off, my thanks to cybersecurity expert Ralph Rodriguez, who reviewed the text at the technical level to confirm that everything described in the book could actually happen, and made a number of helpful suggestions to make the plot more interesting. I'd also like to thank Andrew Oliver, Robert Minchin, Rob van Son, my brother Steve, and my daughter Nora, each of whom volunteered to read, error-spot, and comment on a near-final draft of this book. The suggestions of all of these individuals made this a better book than it otherwise would have been.

I'm also grateful for the constant encouragement of Nora, as well as for the patience and support of my wife Kathy, who had to put up with having Frank around the house (again) through the several years it took to get him packaged up and back out the door.

And finally, thanks to Frank. You've been good company along the way. I know you've had some other interesting adventures that deserve to be shared, so I'll be back in touch soon.

THE ALEXANDRIA PROJECT

Prologue

LATE IN THE afternoon of a gray day in December, a panel truck pulled up to the gate of a warehouse complex in a run-down section of Richmond, Virginia. Rolling down his window, Jack Davis punched a code into the control box, and the gate clanked slowly out of the way. Once inside, he wheeled the truck around and backed it up against a loading dock as the gate closed behind him.

After unlocking and raising the loading dock door, Davis threw a light switch, revealing long rows of pallets, each stacked eight feet high with boxes of paper plates, cups and towels. He closed and locked the door, and stamped on the brake release pedal of a hydraulic lifter parked against the wall. Counting to himself, he pushed the lifter along the wall of pallets. When he reached row nineteen, he turned the lifter and maneuvered its long tines under the pallet. Raising it a few inches, he backed up until he could swing the pallet through 180 degrees. Then he pulled it behind him until it was back exactly where it had been before.

Davis had plenty of room to work, because where the pallet in the second row should have been, there was only a large metal plate set in the floor. Near the edge was a small hinged panel, which he unlocked with a key to expose a biometric security pad.

When Davis pressed his thumb against it, he heard a familiar click. Stepping back, he watched as the plate swung slowly upwards, followed by the telescoping ends of a ladder extending up from a deep shaft barely illuminated in red light. Grasping the ladder firmly, Davis descended through twenty feet of reinforced concrete while the door overhead swung silently closed above him. At the bottom, he remembered to don a pair of sunglasses before opening an unlocked door.

As usual, even with this precaution the bright lights in the enormous room beyond nearly blinded him. But soon he could clearly see the endless rows of floor to ceiling metal racks crammed with identical gray boxes. Each box displayed a row of rhythmically blinking lights, and sprouted a bundle of brightly colored wires that ran down into conduits embedded in the floor.

The room hummed purposefully with the sound of thousands of cooling fans, one to a box. Davis felt more than heard the other vibrations that filled the room, generated by the pulse of the thousands of gallons of cooling water that every minute coursed through the collectors lining the walls of the room, absorbing the waste heat that the racks of computer servers threw off. No heat signature would give this facility away from above; once warm, the coolant was directed to the water intake of a nearby power plant, happy to take the pre-heated water from wherever it was that it came from, no questions asked.

Walking along the perimeter of the room, Davis could look down through the open metal grid of the floor at the first of many additional tiers of computer servers. But that always made him a little dizzy, so instead he looked out for the guard he was relieving. No surprise – there he was, heading Davis's way, more than happy to call it a day. When they met, the guard stopped to slip on the coveralls he carried over one arm. Like the semi-automatic pistol the guard wore in a shoulder holster, they were identical to those that Davis also wore.

"What's the weather like?"

"Sucks. Sleet and more of the same predicted till morning."

"Figures. Tomorrow's my day off."

With that, the other man was on his way. In a few minutes he would drive off in the truck Davis had parked outside.

Well, the weather won't be bothering me in here, Davis thought. The room was climate controlled to within a tenth of a degree of a chilly 54 degrees Fahrenheit, and well-insulated by the bomb-proof walls and roof installed above. It had taken two years for a fleet of delivery vans to carry all the dirt and rock away that had been excavated from beneath the warehouse. The same vans had returned with cement, steel, and, eventually, those thousands of servers, accompanied by technicians to set them up. The process had been tedious, yes, but not a single satellite picture had ever shown a trace of the ambitious construction project proceeding underground.

Of course, the effect worked in both directions. With no links to the outside world other than a voice line to his supervisor, the whole bloody world could come to an end and Davis would be none the wiser until after his shift was over.

Davis walked up a flight of steel stairs to the bullet proof, glass-walled security booth attached to the wall overlooking the room. His major challenge for the next twelve hours would be to stand watch in that booth without falling asleep. There'd be hell to pay if he did, because another guard, in another security room far away, would be watching him on a video screen.

The row of displays in front of Davis allowed him to see every inch of the outside of the warehouse complex. Racked on the wall behind him were a high powered rifle and a shotgun, but it wasn't likely he'd ever need to use them. One flip of the large red switch in front of Davis would flood the server room with enough Halon gas to not only put out a fire, but asphyxiate any intruder careless enough to leave a gas mask at home. Not for the first time, Davis wished that the house where he lived with his wife and their two small children could be as well protected.

But the government didn't put as high a priority on protecting suburban starter homes as it did on safeguarding its most critical computer network facilities. Some storage facilities, like those serving the needs of the Pentagon and the National Security Administration, were located not far away at Fort Meade. Others, like this one, were scattered far and wide, hidden in plain sight but highly secure nonetheless. No way was anyone going to crack this nut. He was dead certain of that.

If Davis had been able to electronically monitor what was happening on server A-VI/147 on Level Three, though, his confidence might have taken a hit. True, concrete and steel walls, surveillance cameras and Halon gas were more than adequate to protect the physical wellbeing of his facility against anything short of a direct hit by a "bunker busting" nuclear weapon. But the data on the facility's servers had to rely on virtual defenses – firewalls, security routines and intrusion scanners.

And those defenses hadn't been enough. Someone had gotten inside.

*　*　*

1

Meet Frank

T HE NEXT MORNING, a morbidly obese Corgi named Lily was sniffing a tree on 16th Street, in the Columbia Heights neighborhood of Washington, D.C. A cold, insistent drizzle fell on her, but Lily didn't care, because Lily was sniffing at her favorite tree. Indeed, the meager processing power of Lily's brain was wholly consumed by sampling the mysterious scents wafting up from the damp earth, for this was also the favorite tree of every other dog in the neighborhood.

Something was nagging at the edge of her senses, though.

"C'mon, Lily! Hurry up!"

Lily turned her head. The annoying distraction was coming from the person at the other end of her leash, someone with sockless feet jammed into worn, black loafers. Above bare ankles, a pair of pajama-clad legs disappeared into a rumpled raincoat. She saw there was an arm holding an umbrella, too, and under the umbrella, a stubbly, forty-something face topped by thinning black hair. Lily decided that the face did not look happy.

"Ah!" she thought. "That would be Frank." Relieved that the distraction could be ignored, Lily returned to the important work at hand.

"*C'mon*, Lily!" the voice said again.

The fact that Frank's face was unhappy was unremarkable. Even in pleasant weather, Frank tended to dwell pointlessly on the minor miseries of his life. Not long ago, those miseries had become much less minor when his mother Doreen entered a retirement home. After helping her move in, Frank took a deep breath and prepared to leave. No use dragging things out, he thought. Transitions are difficult and best dealt with quickly.

Still, it was sad. His mother was standing by the doorway of her new apartment, lower lip a-tremble and Lily held tightly in her arms. It was clear that she was rapidly nearing her emotional limits. Better hurry up.

"Well, Mom," he said, "I guess I'll be leaving now."

Then it happened. With a lunge, Doreen thrust Lily into Frank's arms. He stepped back with surprise into the hallway, too horrified to allow himself to grasp the obvious, while struggling to maintain his grip on the suddenly manic animal.

"The home doesn't allow pets," his mother blurted. "I could never have signed the lease if I hadn't known that Lily would be safe with you. Now don't you worry; I've made you her legal guardian, so it's all set. Now go! Get out of here, before I change my mind."

Frank desperately wanted her to change her mind. But his mother had already shut the door in his astonished face. He stared blankly at it as the enormity of his plight sank in. Now what? Lily was just three years old, and acknowledged his existence only by barking. He heard his mother sobbing piteously on the other side of the door. He felt like crying, too.

That had been two long, loud months ago. Only recently had he progressed from the denial stage to active mourning.

"*Come on!*" Frank hissed. At last, Lily turned away from her tree. She looked up at him reproachfully, and barked.

"Okay, okay," Frank said, fumbling in his pocket. He held a dog treat up for Lily to see. "*Okay?*"

Satisfied that her efforts would not go unrewarded, Lily began looking for just the right place to do what finally needed to be done. At last, she squatted, looking blankly ahead. Frank sighed with relief.

A blue plastic bag inverted over his free hand, Frank scooped up Lily's grudging gift. He handed over the treat, jerking back with his fingers barely intact.

Isn't that just the story of my life? he thought bleakly as Lily happily consumed her treat. Every day I give her a cookie, and every day she gives me a bag of shit.

Trudging home through the rain, Frank reflected that his day generally went downhill from here.

* * *

Lily shook herself mightily inside the foyer of Frank's dingy apartment house, wetting what little of Frank that was still dry. Satisfied, she planted her substantial hindquarters firmly on the floor, looked up at Frank, and barked. Frank sighed, picked up the still-wet dog, and labored his way up the stairs to his second floor flat.

As he climbed to the top, Frank's rising eyes met a pair of fuzzy pink slippers, a floral house dress, and then a pair of folded arms draped with a bath towel. Just above them, he knew, would be the perpetually hostile face of his across-the-hall neighbor. As that scowling visage hove into view, Frank once again noted the uncanny resemblance his neighbor bore to North Korean president Jong Kim-Lo. Only with hair curlers.

"Morning, Mrs. Foomjoy," Frank offered as Lily twisted wildly in his arms. He deposited the dog at her feet.

"Shame on you!" Mrs. Foomjoy barked as she knelt to massage Lily with the bath towel. "Poor, dear wet baby!" she crooned.

"It's raining, Mrs. Foomjoy," Frank observed. "Lily hasn't learned how to use the indoor facilities yet."

"Then why she not wear the lovely rain jacket I give her?" she snorted. "What is *wrong* with you? You don't deserve dog like this!"

Frank couldn't have agreed more. Lily groveled at Mrs. Foomjoy's feet, and then leaned to one side until gravity obligingly rolled her onto her back. The dog gazed up with adoring, goggle eyes as Mrs. Foomjoy rubbed her stomach.

His neighbor grabbed the leash from Frank's hand when she stood up. "I see to welfare of this dog!" she snapped, shutting her door loudly behind her. Frank stood suddenly alone in the poorly lit hallway, a warm, blue plastic pendulum swinging slowly from side to side in his hand. Relieved, he entered his own apartment and quietly shut the door.

Frank hung his dripping raincoat on a hook in the linoleum floored hallway inside. At one time, his apartment's décor might have charitably been described as "Late-Twentieth-Century Divorced Middle Aged Male." Now the most obvious theme was random clutter. He poured a cup of coffee and sat at the small table in the small kitchen. Before him the large screen of his laptop stared blankly back at him. With resignation, he turned the computer on.

Normally, the sound of a computer booting up would have struck him as cheerful; the imperceptibly soft whir of the cooling fan spinning up to speed; the blinking, blue light that assured him that the device was powering up; the screen phosphorescing into life with a pearly glow. After all, information technology – IT – was not only his profession, but the primary foundation of his existence.

Email was Frank's preferred link to the outside world, providing a social firewall between him and the random messiness of direct human contact. Frank was convinced that digital relations were far safer than their in-person analogue. Electronic communications brought him as close to his fellow man as he usually wished to be. Any more intimate than that, and things were apt to become at best unpredictable, and at worst, well, he'd been *there* all too often before. You never got enough time to think before things started spiraling out of control.

Which brought him back to the night before. Be honest, he mused ruefully. You got what you deserved. Or didn't get what you didn't deserve, to be more precise.

He stared at the keyboard. Should he check his email or shouldn't he? The rational side of his brain said, yes, what's there is there. Deal with it.

But the other side of his brain had a different opinion: "Go back to bed," it whispered urgently, "It's Sunday. You don't have to deal with anything today."

That was true. And who knows what might happen by Monday? There could be a typhoon tonight. Or maybe giant pterodactyls would erupt from a wormhole next to the Lincoln Memorial, scattering screaming tourists towards the safety of nearby Metro stations. That side of his brain was lobbying strongly to take two aspirin, pull the covers back over his head, and let reality take care of itself for another twenty-four hours.

He sighed and made up his mind. Might as well see sooner rather than later what people from his office had posted on line about the night before. A few clicks later and he was at the Facebook page of Mary, the sullen receptionist. Yes, there were pictures from the party. Lots of them. Later would do just fine after all, he decided. He snapped the laptop shut without turning it off.

The sad thing was, for once he had actually been looking forward to the Library of Congress IT Department Holiday party, even bringing his daughter Marla with him, a Georgetown University grad student. He appreciated the great impression she always made on his co-workers. Unlike her dad, Marla was self-assured and sociable. She worked the crowd like a pro, chatting and shaking hands, poised and laughing. How could he feel anything but proud? It was hard not to drink a bit more than usual as he watched her from the security of the bar in the rear of the function room.

More to the point, Frank had been looking forward to making Marla feel proud of her old man as well. Everyone knew that George Marchand, the Director of IT at the LoC, was going to announce his choice to head an important security initiative mandated by the Cybersecurity Subcommittee of the House Committee on Science and Technology. Frank figured he had the spot all sewn up. After all, he was – or at least at one time had been – a recognized cybersecurity innovator; a McArthur Foundation "Genius" Award recipient, no less, in recognition of his widely acclaimed creative work in the early days of computer networking.

So when George stood up and tapped on his glass, Frank sat up straighter. He listened impatiently as his boss welcomed the spouses, thanked the staff for their work that year, and told a joke at his own expense. At last, he began to make the announcement that Frank was waiting for.

And then it happened. One moment Frank was looking sideways to see the reaction on his daughter's face when his name was called, and the next he was hearing someone else's name ring out instead. And not just any name, but Rick Wellesley's – "only out for himself" Rick, a self-satisfied slug of a middle-manager who had never had a creative thought in his life. Someone who had even briefly reported to Frank when he first came to work at the LoC. *Rick Wellesley?* How could this be happening?

But it was. There was Rick, standing and basking in the applause, glancing briefly and triumphantly in Frank's direction. Frank was stunned, his face burning. And then he was angry. Without a word to his daughter, he stood up and marched to the bar, turning his back on the party as George finished his remarks. Knocking back another drink, Frank now felt foolish as well as angry. Everyone was probably looking at him, but he was afraid to turn around and find out. He sulked at the bar until Marla came looking for him.

Sitting now in his kitchen, Frank felt his face grow flush again. After all, everyone had expected the job to go to him. Then, with a wrenching feeling, he had a worse thought – what if no one had expected him to get the job? Maybe he was the only one in the whole damn department who hadn't seen it coming. Maybe everyone had been laughing up their sleeves as they watched him bask in his expected glory, just waiting for his jaw to drop when he realized that he had been skunked by Rick.

Of course that had been the case, he thought wretchedly. He was sure of it.

* * *

And why not? What had he really done in the last twenty years? Sure, he'd become a star at the Massachusetts Institute of Technology – "MIT" to anyone in the know. He'd enrolled at the age of sixteen after skipping two years of middle school. Not that skipping a few grades was unusual at MIT. As an undergraduate, he'd become part of Project Athena, an ambitious effort to create a distributed computing system for the whole university. Of course, the goal for the project's corporate sponsors was to use MIT as a testbed. Later, they hoped to productize the design and make a ton of money.

For some reason, Frank had intuitively locked onto the security challenges that such a system would present. He already had privileges to use MIT's gateway to the government-funded Advanced Research Projects Agency Network – the now-famous "ARPANET" that was the precursor to the Internet. Only select institutions had access to it then, but Frank immediately grasped where Project Athena and the ARPANET together could eventually lead. It hit him between the eyes that this was the start of something big. Linking terminals together around a campus was today's goal, but the next step would be to connect those networks together, using ARPANET technology.

That sounded awesome, but how would you restrict access to any particular data to one person, and not let it be seen by everyone else? MIT was already a hotbed of hackers. If students were going to great lengths now to break into restricted sections of university computers just for fun, what would criminals, or enemy countries, not do to break into classified computers, once someone had linked them all together? Frank tackled that issue with gusto, if not discipline. He was a big picture guy, and what a big and exciting picture it was! The idea of wide area networks was brand new, and big ideas were needed to make sense of it all; the details could come later. When Frank graduated, he stayed on at MIT, nominally in a PhD program, but for all practical purposes he lived at a terminal in the Project Athena lab, surviving on coffee and code like so many other young computer engineering students back in the day.

Luckily for Frank, he found a mentor – an engineer on loan from one of the sponsoring companies. Surprisingly, the two hit it off, and the older man reined in the younger one enough to keep Frank's ideas from flying off into too many directions at once. He also insisted that Frank get his best ideas recorded in some sort of coherent order. Often they talked until all hours, the older man channeling Frank's enthusiasm and helping him follow his insights down the most productive paths.

Frank never completed his doctorate, but he did finish his Masters thesis – and by anyone's account, it was brilliant. He anticipated just about every security challenge that would arise over the next twenty years as the Internet took off. He also suggested most of the solutions that were later refined and implemented to deal with a massively networked world. Even today, his thesis remained an obligatory foundational reference in just about every new network and Internet security paper that was written.

Frank's thesis also brought him to the notice of the mysterious keepers of the MacArthur Fellows Program – the unknown judges that every year contact a select group of exceptional individuals they have decided, "show exceptional merit and promise for continued and enhanced creative work."

Receiving a MacArthur Fellowship had been the high point of Frank's professional career. But as a practical matter, it also brought an end to it, because the payments of $25,000 every three months for five years gave him the freedom to do whatever he wanted to without ever having to acquire the discipline of making his way in the world. It also allowed him to get married.

It was not helpful that what Frank wanted to do usually changed every other week. It wasn't long before his work at Project Athena suffered. He no longer listened to his mentor, and his assigned tasks no longer got done. Instead, he plunged from one question that intrigued him to another, never getting very far along with any of them.

Like many people whose intellectual abilities matured before their social skills, Frank developed an abrupt and assertive manner that helped mask his discomfort around others. That was unfortunate, because his new–found fame encouraged him to become even more obnoxious than ever. Soon, the other guys in the lab were annoyed with his failure to meet his commitments, and also sick of hearing his latest revelations about security – or about any other topic on which he had decided he was now an expert.

Eventually, it was his mentor who took Frank aside and told him that if he didn't shape up, his days in the lab were numbered. Frank didn't take that well. What right did some middle aged, middle-management type with a degree from a state school in the Midwest have to tell a certified Genius anything about anything?

Quite a lot, Frank now reflected, gazing at his closed laptop. Like the immature idiot he was then, he had cleared his things out of the Project Athena lab the same day his mentor had called him out and never returned. Eventually, the MacArthur Fellowship money ran dry, and with a wife and young daughter, Frank had to get more serious about working. Or at least he should have. For a while, his thesis and MacArthur reputation carried him from job to job. But when the bottom fell out of the economy, employers received a flood of great résumés for every job they posted.

By then, of course, Frank's résumé was also getting pretty long in the tooth. He had no "continued and enhanced creative work" to show for his five years of subsidized, random behavior. He'd never published another paper, and it was others, and not Frank, who turned his thesis ideas into real protocols and products. As the jobs got scarce, reference checks counted a whole lot more, and the feedback about Frank always came back the same: brilliant, arrogant, unfocused, unreliable. That was more charitable than what his soon-to-be ex-wife had to say. But he hadn't listened to her, either.

Frank usually tried not to think much about the years that followed: the start-up that had signed him up as Chief Technical Officer and the VCs that fired him; the time spent without a job at all; the rut he fell into for years after his wife moved out with their daughter, when he said the hell with everything and everybody. That time was a blur of punching the clock in whatever high school, small business or municipal IT department would take him on until he got fired again, then waiting until his unemployment ran out before finding something else he could do in his sleep, until even that became too much to bother with.

Through all that time, though, industry insiders still sought Frank out, so he maintained a low-key consulting business on the side to make sure he could always cover his child support payments. Among the elite in the world of security, Frank still had the reputation of a wizard, able to come up with the kind of insights that would make the most impenetrable problems suddenly transparent. An emailed plea for help describing something dense and dark that had already defied all of the usual solutions would reliably generate a response from Frank an hour or two later, usually beginning, "It strikes me that…" and ending with, "I suggest you try…." Invariably, what Frank suggested worked. But requests for his ongoing assistance went unanswered.

It was his daughter Marla that finally set Frank back on his feet. One Friday when he was once again out of work, he picked her up for their weekend together. But something was wrong; his normally chatty preteen wasn't saying a word. As they walked, she looked down at her feet. Then she looked up as if to ask him a question, only to look down again. After a while, Frank got irritated. "Marla, if there's something you want to ask me, just ask it already!"

But Marla still paused. Finally she said, "Dad, you know I'm in a computer class now, don't you? It's something you have to take in seventh grade."

"Yes," he said, surprised. "So?"

"Well," she said, and stopped. He waited, now curious.

"Well," she started again, "today we went on a field trip to the computer department of a big company, and we all had to sign in and wear these name tag things. One of the people that worked there gave us a tour, and when she saw my name, she asked if I had a father named Frank, so of course I said yes."

"Uh huh," said Frank, not liking where this was going.

"Well…" Marla paused again, and then the words came rushing out. "She said that she went to school with you and you were the most brilliant person she had ever known and that you'd gotten a big award for being a genius and she wanted to know what you were doing now." Marla stopped abruptly for a long moment. "And I didn't know what to say."

Frank wished this could be all over, and quickly.

But, Marla, of course, needed an answer. "Dad, the guide said you used to be somebody really important."

Frank felt like he was dangling at the end of a rope, turning slowly in the breeze. He looked away, and tried to think what to say. What *could* he say? And then, with all of the disarming innocence of a child, Marla finished for him.

"Dad, she wasn't telling the truth, was she?"

Frank couldn't breathe. His daughter thought so little of him that she had to believe that the guide was thinking of someone else? Or was it that she would be too ashamed of what he had become to be able to deal with the truth? He felt sick.

By then, they were standing in front of the door of his cheap apartment building. The traffic rushed past the garbage cans and trash piled up on the curb, and Frank took it all in. The sights, the smells, his life – they all fit together perfectly, didn't they? Still, he couldn't think of a word to say.

Finally, Marla put her hand on his arm. "It's okay, Dad," she said softly. "Let's go upstairs."

That had been ten years ago. The following Monday he sucked it up and called his old mentor, George Marchand, and asked for a job. George was the head of the IT department at the Library of Congress now, and Frank called him out of the blue to ask if they could get together for coffee.

George had been as gracious as Frank had been uncomfortable. Frank had sent his résumé along by email, for what it was worth, and George cut straight to the chase after the opening pleasantries.

"You know I'll need to bring you in at the bottom, Frank. Can you deal with that?"

Frank was prepared. "Sure, sure, George. I'll be fine with that." George nodded, brows furrowed. Then he changed the topic.

"How's that cute goddaughter of mine these days? I can't even remember the last time I saw Marla."

"She's great," said Frank, suddenly determined; it helped to remember why he was sitting there. "Just great. We get together every weekend. She's in seventh grade now. She's smart as a whip and gets straight As."

They chatted about family for a few more minutes, and then George looked at his watch. They both stood up, and shook hands.

"I won't let you down," Frank said as he looked George in the eye for the first time.

"I know you won't," his new boss said. But Frank could tell he was only being polite.

* * *

Sitting in his kitchen, Frank reflected that he'd been as good as his word. But not much better, he made himself admit. Yes, he'd rarely missed a day of work, and no one could say he hadn't earned his paycheck. And yes, he'd earned every promotion he'd been given.

But the promotions had been few, and the last one had been awarded seven years ago. Frank still had tremendous insights into IT architecture, and he remained as interested as ever in new developments in security. His cubicle at the LoC was stacked high with articles covered in scribbled notes, and he read voraciously online as well. For anyone in the office with a thorny problem, Frank was the go-to guy who could always solve it, provided he was allowed to tackle it alone. Sitting at a keyboard, Frank was still The Man – the tougher the problem the better, just bring it on.

Three hours, eight hours or twenty hours later, he'd still be turning it over in his mind until suddenly an elegant and creative solution would spring to mind.

Management level work, though, was something else again. Every time George gave him a shot at a long term project with a couple of others to supervise, Frank could never pull it all together.

Half the time, he'd be up in the clouds thinking big thoughts that went beyond the task at hand, and the rest of the time he'd be down in the weeds, diving down rat holes to solve problems that could easily be ignored. The folks he was supposed to be supervising never knew what they would be doing from one day to the next, or what, if anything, Frank did with the work they submitted. Inevitably, George would have to take the project back. It didn't take long before the big projects stopped coming, and Frank settled into the solitary niche where he had stayed ever since.

He wasn't done beating himself up, though. Admit it, he demanded, you were relieved when the projects stopped coming. You've been marking time for years now, and that's all you'll ever do. What right did you have to think George would throw this project your way?

But this had been a *security* project, damn it. That (and the drinks he'd had last night) were what had led him to corner George later on in the cloakroom.

"I'm sorry, Frank," George had said, wrapping his scarf around his neck. "I thought about letting you know ahead of time, and then I didn't. I guess I should have."

"That's not the point, George! Rick can't find his own ass with both hands in a well-lit room. What were you thinking?"

George buttoned his overcoat, and reached for his hat. "Of course Rick can't hold a candle to you when it comes to security, Frank. There's nobody I've ever worked with who has the insight and ideas that you do. And everybody knows nobody covers his butt like Rick."

Frank let his breath out with a rush of exasperation as George settled his hat on his head. "So then why did you pick him?"

George squared off to Frank as he pulled on his gloves, looking him straight in the eye.

"Frank, you may know security, but when it comes to understanding people and how to manage them, you haven't got a clue. Yes, Rick is one hell of a weasel. But you can always rely on a weasel to watch out for himself. That means that if you give him a job to do and tell him his job is on the line, well, by hook or by crook, he'll get it done. And I can't say that about you."

Well, what could Frank say to that? He'd asked George for an explanation and now he'd have to listen to it.

"How many chances have I given you over the years, Frank? I can't remember, can you?" Frank looked away.

"You're twice as smart as I am," George continued. "You should have had my job by now! But that's never going to happen unless you grow up and learn how to perform. If you thought I'd stick my neck out for you with Chairman Steele grandstanding in the House, looking for the next poor bastard to eviscerate in front of the cameras during a public committee meeting, well, you're just delusional. Good night, Frank."

There hadn't been anything Frank could say to that, of course, so he was relieved when George turned and walked away. Furious at himself, Rick and George, in that order, he stalked back to the bar.

Frank decided that was as much of the night before as he was up to reliving; he'd leave the scene with Rick for his next exercise in psychological self-flagellation. It had all escalated so stereotypically anyway; Rick's approach and his smarmy condescension, Frank's insult in response. Okay, enough.

He felt the anger well up again, and with it, a sudden sense of purpose. Screw the jerk; just because Rick got the project didn't mean that Frank couldn't still show him up. After all, Frank had been so sure he had the spot in the bag that he'd already started writing up a proposal with his plan of attack outlined. No way was Rick going to be able to pull this job off; George would realize that soon enough, and then there'd be no one to turn to but Frank.

He snapped open his laptop and punched the keys with fury, rushing through the complicated log-in sequence that would take him into the heart of the LoC's system, where his proposal was archived. Highlighting the file name, he hit the Enter key, leaned back, and waited for the proposal to display.

Except it didn't. Frank leaned forward and poked the Enter key again. Still nothing. Perhaps his laptop was frozen. But no – he could still move his cursor.

Then Frank noticed that something on the screen was changing: the background color was warming up, turning reddish, orange and yellow, as if the sun was rising behind it. Now that was different! Frank watched with growing astonishment as the colors began to shimmer, and then coalesced into shapes that might be flames.

Yes, flames indeed – but not like a holiday screen-saver image of a log fire – this was a real barn-burner of a conflagration!

Frank wondered what kind of weird virus he'd picked up, and how. After all, he was an IT security specialist, and if any laptop was protected six ways to Sunday, it was his. So much for whatever he had planned for today; he'd have to wipe his disk and rebuild his system from the ground up.

He was about to shut the laptop down when he saw that the flames were dying away. Now what? An image seemed to be emerging from behind the flames as they subsided. Frank leaned forward; the image became a tall building – maybe some sort of lighthouse? Underneath, there was a line of text, but in characters he couldn't read. Truly, this was like no virus he'd ever seen or even heard of before. He reached for his cellphone and took a picture of the screen just before it suddenly went blank.

Frank was impressed. Whoever had come up with this hack certainly had a sense of style. A weird one, but hey, graphic art of any type wasn't the long suit of most hackers.

Frank got a pad of paper and a pen from his desk and punched up the file directory again, highlighted his proposal, and pressed the Enter key again. This time, he would watch more closely and take notes.

But all that displayed was a three word message: "File not found."

Frank tried again – no luck. He did a search of the entire directory using the title. Nothing. His proposal was gone.

Now he was alarmed. After all, the directory he was staring at was in the innermost sanctum of the Library of Congress computer system, and the LoC was the greatest library in the world. Within its vast holdings were books that could be found almost nowhere else on earth. Recently, the Library had begun digitizing materials, and then destroying the physical copies. If someone had been able to delete files in the most protected part of the Library's computer system, what else might be missing?

Frank raced through a random sampling of sensitive directories, and then let out a sigh of relief; it was hard to tell for sure, but everything seemed intact. He checked the server logs for the Library's indices, holdings and various other resources; everything appeared to be undisturbed, with no unusual reductions in the amount of data stored.

Frank drummed his fingers on the table in the cramped dinette. How to go about figuring this one out? Then he remembered his cellphone, and sent the picture of the screenshot to his laptop. The picture wasn't great, but once he enlarged it he could tell that the characters were Greek. He cropped the image until just the text remained, then ran it through a multi-script OCR program to turn the picture of the Greek characters into text. Finally, he pasted the text into a translator window. No luck – all he got was a "cannot translate" message.

Frank's fingers started drumming again. He reopened the drop down menu of languages in the translator screen and noticed that another language option was "Ancient Greek." He highlighted that choice and hit Enter. This time, the screen blinked.

Frank looked, and then he blinked, too. But the translation still read the same:

THANK YOU FOR YOUR
CONTRIBUTION
TO THE ALEXANDRIA PROJECT

---

* * *

Order **The Alexandria Project** at Andrew-Updegrove.com

www.ingramcontent.com/pod-product-compliance
Lightning Source LLC
Chambersburg PA
CBHW030015180626
46810CB00001B/51